MW00527812

AND SO
WE
DREAM

A NOVEL

LINDA MAHKOVEC

ISBN: 978-1-64704-499-2 (paperback)
ISBN: 978-1-64704-498-5 (eBook)

PROLOGUE

Stage lights, glittering chandeliers, ornate balconies. Crimson brocade curtains and period costumes, a deafening applause. All the stuff of magic and dreams she had so loved.

Joseph's eyes burned with pride as he watched his old friend and mentor, Vita Vitale, standing center stage bathed in adulation from the audience. Luminous. That was the word that kept coming to his mind. Tall and graceful, the stage lights casting a golden halo around her long auburn hair. She was as beautiful as ever. No. More so. She owned it now. When he knew her, she didn't know who she was, what she had. She was just a bundle of adolescent yearnings with vague visions of her future.

"Vita!" "Brava!" "Vita!"

All around him the audience cheered her—Vita, Vicky, Victoria, Vi. The girl with all the names. Joseph rose to his feet with the others and continued to applaud. He smiled down at his wife, happy that she was finally encountering one of those three magical sisters he had told her about— Anne, Vita, and Beth. His work had taken him to the far-flung parts of the world, and he had lost touch with the family that had helped to shape him.

Now the gap of almost twenty years had, in an instant, closed on this New York City Broadway stage. And he saw that Vita had kept her promise.

There had been updates from his mother over the years, news that Vita had met with some success. But it wasn't until recently, now that he was back in the States, that he understood just how successful Vita had become. An unexpected trip to New York City had him reaching out to all his contacts to help get tickets for the final night of her performance.

And now, there she was, the star of a play that had been written for her. He realized with a jolt how appropriate this role was, a play that reminded him of *The Tempest*. From high above—cliff tops, a tower, a balcony—she wielded her power. Vita—the girl who had been afraid of heights. The brave girl who had sought out the high places in her small, flat Midwestern town in order to conquer her fears.

The curtain briefly closed, and then reopened for another round of applause. The cast linked hands and took another bow. Calls of "Brava!" and "Vita!" continued from the crowd, flowers falling about her feet. Vita took a step forward, gathered up a large bouquet into her arms, and graciously swept a low bow. She placed one hand on her heart and let her eyes travel over the audience, as if thanking each person individually.

Joseph looked about him. They loved her. Wanted more of her. She had made them feel the weight of sorrow, the desperate longing for love, and the ultimate transformation—triumph after despair. They were grateful that she had confirmed hope and love, after loss and hopelessness. She had made them believe in themselves and in the magnificent beauty of life. They didn't want this moment to end and clapped harder in hopes of prolonging the affirmation.

The crimson curtains slowly closed, and the brightness of the house lights increased. The audience became aware of themselves now, self-conscious of their clapping, of the awkward smiles that passed between people, of the desire to linger in the afterglow of the performance.

After several minutes, the applause lessened, and eyes left the stage. The closed curtains in the bright lights no longer held the universal and the wondrous. The show was over, the magic dispelled. The lights revealed the disarray of people gathering their coats and playbills, exiting the rows, commenting amongst themselves.

Joseph put his arm around his wife's shoulder and kissed her hair. He saw other couples with arms linked, friends placing a gentle hand on an arm or shoulder, "after you" gestures allowing others to exit the rows—he laughed at himself. Was there really such kindness and gentleness? Or was he once again seeing her world vision?

"We must hurry if we want to catch her," his wife said, pulling Joseph into the aisle.

They wove their way through the lobby and, once outside, fell in with the line of eager fans. As they waited, the crowd grew larger.

They stood close together in the crisp autumn night, trying to maintain their position by the police barricade that separated the star-struck crowd from the path Vita would take to sign playbills and smile for photographs. Across the street, Joseph saw a similar crowd burst into cheers as the star of that show greeted his fans.

Joseph's eyes filled with worry. Perhaps she wouldn't come. She should have been outside by now. When would he have another chance to see her—

His wife drew a sharp breath. "Here she comes! Oh, look at her." She pulled Joseph a step closer. "Stand here. You haven't seen her since she was fifteen and you were— what, ten, eleven?"

"I was twelve." Joseph realized he sounded like a boy again.

"I wonder if she'll recognize you."

He shook his head. Of course she wouldn't.

He could see her clearly now. Though close to twenty years had passed, he recognized the charm and beauty, the smile and determination—and, behind the gaze, the yearning. An unanswered hunger in her eyes. The quest always in the distance.

Joseph had his playbill ready. He overheard the comments from the crowd:

"Don't worry, she'll sign."

"She always makes time for her fans."

"She's even more beautiful up close!"

Joseph inched forward. He felt like an overgrown groupie, but he wanted to see Vita face to face, to see if she might remember him.

She made her way down the line. Though she was tall, the crowd diminished her size. Outside, she was an ordinary mortal at the end of her workday.

Yet, there was also that element that made her different from everyone he had ever known. Something that set her apart. Something solitary, otherworldly. Both proud and vulnerable. A contrast that pulled you in.

She had access to the world of magic and beauty, and like an alchemist, could transmute the ordinary into the extraordinary. But it came at a price. He saw the world weariness behind the smile and imagined that she desperately needed to be alone now—or was he projecting again? They were alike, after all.

Playbills were thrust forward as Vita's name was called out. Her manager-husband shielded her from the pressing line of admirers and kept a protective hand on her shoulder, his eyes scanning the adoring crowd.

She was close now and Joseph's heart beat faster at her nearness. Would she recognize him?

The woman next to him extended her playbill. "To Debbie, please."

As Vita signed, the woman bounced on her toes in excitement. "Oh, thank you! You were just wonderful! Can I take a picture with you? My sister won't believe me otherwise." Vita nodded as the woman twisted sideways so her friend could snap a photograph. "Thank you!"

Joseph leaned forward and offered his playbill.

Vita took it. "How shall I sign?" Her face lifted in a quick smile at him.

His heart sank. Of course, she wouldn't recognize him, after so many years. She posed for a few cameras, poised her pen, and asked again. "To . . .?"

Joseph swallowed. "To—D'Artagnan."

Vita's head snapped up and her eyes flashed. "Joey!" She threw her arms around his neck and squeezed him.

"Oh, Joey!" Her embrace tightened. "Let me look at you!"

Tears shot to his eyes as she said his name. There she was, his old small-town, ordinary friend. Smiling her familiar smile.

"Hello, Vita. You were brilliant!" He took his wife's hand. "My wife—Souad."

"Your wife!" Vita embraced her as well. "So pleased to—"

Vita's husband leaned forward to shake Joseph's hand. "So this is D'Artagnan! How nice to finally meet you. I wasn't sure you really existed."

Joseph flooded with happiness. She had talked about him? His head turned from Vita to her husband to Souad as they all talked over one another.

"Oh, how I wish we could visit—" said Vita.

"But we leave for London in a few hours," finished her husband. "The show opens in the West End next week."

Vita clasped Joey's hands. "Mom sent us photographs from your Moroccan series. They were magnificent!" Her eyes locked on Joseph's in pride.

"They hang in our London apartment," said Vita's husband. "National Geographic!" "That's—"

"Please sign," a young woman said, snapping a photo and handing Vita a playbill.

Vita's husband shrugged in amusement at the demanding fans. "We must get together. Soon."

Vita looked up from signing and placed a hand on her husband's arm. "Give him—"

But he was already handing his business card to Joseph.

Vita squeezed their hands in goodbye as she was pushed and pulled down the line. "Call us! We simply have to—" Her words were lost but she kept turning her head back, seeking Joseph, as if convincing herself that he was really there.

In a flash, he remembered her old word. "You were *wondrous!*" he called after her, and was rewarded by a sweet smile—the shy smile he knew so well, not the professional smile of the actor.

As she signed and posed, her eyes kept searching for him in the crowd.

"She's just as you said, Joseph!" Souad linked her arm with his and craned her neck to keep Vita in sight.

He followed Vita with his eyes. He was filled, once again, with visions of the world as beguiling and beckoning, and the wild desire to set off on a quest.

He wrapped his arm around his wife. "I knew she'd make it."

Souad reached up to kiss his cheek. "Just as she knew you would."

Vita stood tall, scanned the crowd, and found him one last time. Their eyes locked and she gave the old nod of collusion—and waited, just a moment, to see if he would remember.

He broke into a smile at their old "handshake," their unspoken pact that nothing would get in their way. Their "I will, if you will" bond. He nodded back.

He filled with all the things he wanted to say. That it was she who planted the seeds of hope in him. She who believed in the part of him that was bold and brave and adventurous. She who convinced him that nothing was more important than playing an active role in this wild and wonderful world.

Joseph watched the crowd as it closed around her and her magic. The glittering lights of the theater marquees doubled in brightness for the Night Queen. Or perhaps it was tears of joy that blurred his vision.

Seeing her again had conjured up the past, and he remembered—as if it were just yesterday—that summer.

The summer he learned to dream.

CHAPTER 1

1970

This was why he didn't like Chicago. The train station so crowded you couldn't see anything. Just a swirl of people, brushing and bumping against him as he stood next to his parents. His dad reluctant to hand over the small suitcase.

His mother leaned over one more time to kiss his cheek, smooth his hair, and straighten his collar. "You be good. And call us the moment you arrive." She handed him the sack lunch she had made.

Joey wished she hadn't stayed up late baking cookies for him. Her face looked strained, as if she hadn't slept.

They moved closer to the train.

"You brought your books?" his father asked.

Joey patted his jacket.

"You have a good time," his mom said. "Play with the neighborhood kids. Remember, the girls are older now and have jobs and boyfriends."

Joey nodded. "I won't bother them."

"And remember, Victoria—as she'll always be to me—now goes by Vita."

Joey added that to his list of things to remember.

His father gave a smile that didn't reach his eyes. "Everything will be all right, son. We just need a little time to work some things out. That's all. And in the meantime, you'll be with your friends, having all kinds of adventures. And the girls . . . What did you used to call them? The *Petticoat Junction* sisters?"

Joey shrugged. "I don't know." He reached for the suitcase.

"Take care, son." His father's voice broke.

Joey's eyes darted around his dad's face, looking for an answer. Inside, he said, *Please don't cry, please don't cry*, not sure if he meant him or his dad.

"ALL ABOARD!" came the conductor's long up-reaching cry.

The people in line began to make their way onto the train, waving goodbye, giving a few final embraces. Joey turned around and hugged his mother. "Sorry, Mom."

"Nonsense. This will be good for you. A little break is all you need. We'll—we'll . . ."

"Call when you get there, son." His father lurched forward in an awkward embrace.

"I will. Bye, Dad." His eyes began to burn and he squeezed them shut. For one safe moment, he let himself sink into the comfort of his dad's chest. Then he broke apart and boarded the train.

Joey turned to the left and walked down the aisle behind the other passengers. Midway, he found an empty row. He stashed his suitcase on the overhead rack and sat at the window.

There was his dad, standing marooned, his shoulders pulled down by heavy rock hands. A pasted-on smile that matched his mom's.

She touched a hankie to her nose, raised her hand, lifted her head.

Joey waved back. *Please don't cry.*

Then, in a gesture Joey would always remember—because it was so unfamiliar—his dad draped his arm around his mom's shoulder. They stood smiling with worried eyes, looking like cardboard-cutout parents that he didn't recognize.

He became aware of the shuffling all around him as people took their seats. A quick reassuring glance out at his parents. He waved again. And again. They hadn't budged.

Joey's hand tightened on the armrest when the train began to move, leaving his parents behind. A final wave, in case they were still looking, in case they could still see him.

He leaned back and released his clutch on the sack lunch, keeping his eyes fixed on the back of the seat ahead of him. Like gazing into a deep black pool that had no reflection. It grew deeper and darker.

He rubbed away the vision and raised his head above the seats, looking in front of him and then behind.

He didn't see any other kids on the train—none by themselves anyway. He had never traveled alone before. He felt a little older. Like he was already thirteen and had been for a long time.

People were settling in, putting bags and suitcases on the overhead rack, then deciding that they needed a jacket or book that was packed, and getting settled again.

Across from him, two older ladies arranged their knitting projects on their laps. One had a ball of pale pink yarn. The other had shades of blue.

Behind them, two men with Afros were talking about 'Nam. Twisting in their seats, spitting mad. Saying it wasn't *their* war. Joey's next-door neighbor in Chicago, Tony, also had to go to Vietnam. He gave Joey his football pennant when he left. It had felt like a goodbye gift. Maybe it was.

One of the men shot his eyes to Joey and raised his chin.

Joey leaned back in his seat, realizing that he had been staring.

He wanted to tell them that he hoped they would come back. That they wouldn't get hurt. That's what he had told Tony. But once the words were out of his mouth, he wished he had thought of something better to say.

Joey looked at the seat back again. In six years or so, it would be his turn to go to war. And who knew if he would come back.

People from the train car behind his were pushing the doors open, hoping to find seating together. He was beginning to think that maybe, just maybe, he would have the whole seat to himself.

No such luck. He moved his jacket to his lap as a large man claimed the seat beside him. Joey looked up at him, ready to give a smile, but the man wasn't interested in being friendly.

Joey leaned his head back. They were outside the station now. A fine drizzle on the window obscured his view.

The conductor made his way from seat to seat, waddling with the rhythm of the train. Joey lifted his ticket and tried another smile, but the conductor didn't feel like being friendly either. He punched Joey's ticket and continued down the aisle.

Joey wondered if his parents were out of the station by now. Were they seated in their car yet? Were they talking on their way back home? Or sitting quietly, deep in their faraway worlds.

After chugging along, the train picked up speed. The drizzle blew sideways in little streaks and cleared the window somewhat, revealing the wide railyard and the world outside. The pale morning air looked sooty. Like some kid had chosen a gray crayon and colored the world blah. His stomach tightened as he gazed out at the rails and tracks converging and splitting off to countless destinations. If the train broke down and he had to get out, he would be lost for sure. This time, without any idea of how to get back home.

Broken bottles and papers littered the tracks. Farther away, industrial warehouses and sad-looking buildings leaned against the gray sky. Not a speck of color anywhere. He shut his eyes against the dizzying pull of so many different directions, glad he was going to one place. One very specific place where it would be hard to get lost once he was there.

He rubbed his eyes. They felt grainy from barely sleeping last night. "Don't bother the girls," his mother had said as she packed his suitcase. "They're four years older since the last time you saw them. Teenagers now. Play with the neighborhood boys. And help Sal with his garden."

"I will." He would try not to get in anybody's way. His parents had talked late into the night, this time in soft voices. The one time he wanted to hear them, he couldn't make out what they were saying.

They were sending him away for the remainder of summer. Alone for the first time in his life. Shipping him off. Dumping their problem on someone else. Joey folded his arms. For the rest of July and all of August, he would be far away from home.

And he was glad.

Anything was better than the arguments. Sitting in his room. Waiting for it to be over. Trying to read. Sometimes covering his ears. Pretending to be asleep at night. His dad sitting with his head in his hands. His mom staring out the window while tears rolled down her cheeks. Was it really so hard to get along? Sometimes he wished they would get a divorce. Just to make it end. But then—he didn't want to be without either one of them. It was at such times that he wished he had a brother. Or sister. A big family.

He twisted angrily in his seat and stared at the passing world. Shoving him off to his mom's old friend so he wouldn't be in the way while they probably got divorced. Then what? Or more likely, they would move somewhere. Again. They had moved many times—three towns or cities that he could remember. Four different houses. It always seemed to help for a little. He bounced back and forth between anger and sadness and just plain old feeling lost in it all.

He looked out the rain-streaked window again. The same sad buildings were still there—as if they had moved along with the train. Making their escape. Or maybe they just went on forever.

The train was speeding along now. The wooden ties and rails ran on and on, a low heartbeat throbbing beneath the wheels. Now and then the long, sad wail of the train whistle sounded above the heartbeat. It was comforting, somehow. Like it was on his side. It was comforting to be moving. Going somewhere. Anywhere.

He pulled up the collar to his jacket, tucked his head between the seat and wall, and closed his eyes. His body rocked with the rhythmic rumble of the train. The fatigue of the past few days took over, and he gave into a deep, welcoming sleep.

CHAPTER 2

S unlight on Joey's face woke him. He opened his eyes
and saw blue sky. Lots of it. And green. The train was
chugging through the outskirts of a small town. He
knuckled his eyes, almost ready to exclaim, "Look! Color!"
But no one else seemed to notice.

The seat next to him was empty. He stared out the
window again, arched his back, and rubbed the kink in his
neck. He looked up and down the aisle and saw that many
people had gotten off.

He must have been asleep for a long time. The last station call he remembered hearing was for Joliet. But by the
change in the landscape, that must have been hours ago.

The porter was making his way down the aisle, checking the tickets of a few new passengers. Joey waited for him.

"Excuse me, sir. Where are we?"

The porter lifted Joey's ticket stub and held it at arm's
length, squinting. "'Bout an hour and a half."

Joey's face broke into a smile. "Thanks!"

He was getting closer to Greenberry. Closer to the Vitale family.

Outside the window the scenery had dramatically changed. There was no sign of a city anywhere. Just green fields and green trees and blue sky. Farmhouses and fields. Cattle grazing.

An Oz-like world of emerald and sunlight and the unmistakable sense of hope. Excitement. No train lines anywhere except for the one he was on. Pastures. A red tractor driving along the road by a man in overalls and a straw hat. An occasional pickup truck, a car here and there.

There was more space, more sky, open fields. Just the way he remembered. He was suddenly happy that he would be spending the rest of the summer here. Nothing else mattered.

This was a land just ready for adventure. This was boyland—trees to climb, lakes for fishing and swimming, long country roads for bike riding. A land where you could go barefoot! All summer long if you liked. His friends hadn't believed him when he told them this.

"Don't you step on broken glass?"

"Isn't the concrete too hot to walk on?"

"Nah," he had explained. "There's grass everywhere. The road feels warm under your feet. And you can pop little tar bubbles with your toes. If it gets too hot, you just step off onto the grass."

They also hadn't believed him about the *Petticoat Junction* sisters.

"Three teenagers? All pretty?"

"Seventeen, fifteen, and fourteen. Anne's going to be a senior. Vicky—I mean Vita—will be a junior. And Beth will be a freshman."

"And do they really all have different hair color like on that show? I don't watch it, but my sisters do."

"Yep. Except it's the middle one who has the red hair. Vita. The oldest has blonde hair and blue eyes."

"And the youngest one?"

"Beth. She has black hair and dark-brown eyes. She used to tell me she was part Indian. Navaho, or maybe it was Sioux."

"Is she?"

Joey screwed up his mouth in thought. "She looks like her dad. He's Italian. Anne and Vita look more like their mom. Irish. Anne has her own car now. She's going to take me riding around."

They had stared in quiet astonishment.

"And there's a county fair with rides and animals and hotdogs and cotton candy. And a whole bunch of neighborhood boys. And there are lemonade stands, and penny carnivals all over the place selling old comic books and games and stuff.

"The Vitales have a big grass yard with apple and plum and pear trees. And a really good climbing tree in the front. And Uncle Sal—he's not really my uncle but that's what I call him—has a huge garden. Full of every kind of vegetable you can imagine. Peppers, green beans, lettuce, tomatoes." Joey had told them everything he could remember about his trips to Greenberry.

He smiled as he thought of Sal's vegetable garden. It sat in the corner of the yard with a tall hedge on two sides of it.

It felt like a separate little world. Joey remembered the secret path between the garden and the hedge where the girls had picked violets, and where he had sometimes seen rabbits.

He had loved to help gather vegetables, crawling between the tomato plants where Sal couldn't reach. It was like a treasure hunt. He remembered an enormous rhubarb plant next to the clothesline pole and a three-layered strawberry mound next to the garden that had the smallest, sweetest strawberries Joey had ever tasted—warm from the sun. Not as big as their neighbors Fran and Abel's strawberry patch, but every bit as sweet.

And a tall trellis of grapes that ran parallel with the hedge of Abel's yard, forming a wall of sunny green. One summer he and Beth had mashed a bunch of grapes to make juice, using a baseball bat and bucket. They had delivered it to all the neighbors, who were kind enough to accept it. Now at almost thirteen years old, Joey laughed at the memory, sure that no one had dared to taste it.

Joey's neck was getting stiff from staring out at the farmland. He became aware of his growling stomach and opened his sack lunch. A bologna sandwich with mustard, a bag of potato chips, homemade chocolate chip cookies, and an apple.

He took a big bite of his sandwich and spread open one of his comic books—*The Three Musketeers*—and smiled the whole time he flipped through it. Chewing, looking out the window, and remembering the last time he visited the Vitales. Four years ago. It was in the fall and the sisters had taken him trick-or-treating with them. They had gone as the Three Musketeers with homemade costumes of capes and hats, and drawn-on mustaches and goatees. They had outfitted him as D'Artagnan.

He gave a laugh as he remembered how he had to hold up his makeshift pantaloons all night with one hand, and how he kept tripping over the plastic sword that was roped to a belt loop.

Vita—back then she had been Vicky—had been Porthos and the old pillow she used to add some girth to her slender frame was ripped and kept leaking out feathers. She finally had enough. She climbed the three-railed fence alongside a yard, and cried out dramatically, "I should have been Aramis!" and hurled the pillow away from her. It landed in a soft explosion of white feathers, causing the girls to roll over with laughter. Until a door opened and they heard the sharp voice of the retired science teacher Mrs. Kennick.

"Who's there? Who's there! Pick up that mess! I'm going to report you to the police."

When she realized her threats did not have the effect she expected, she stepped outside, her hair in curlers, and shouted. "I demand to know who you are!"

"Porthos! That's who!" Vita had hollered. Anne and Beth managed to cry out a defiant "Aramis!" and "Athos!" Joey held up his plastic sword. "D'Artagnan!"

"Give me your names, you young hooligans!"

"Never!" cried Vita. She held out her hand, palm down. "All for one," and the others, layering their hands over hers, had finished, "And one for all!" They took off running and laughing. They had stayed up late eating candy from their paper bags, trading pieces.

They had also let him play the Daring Game with them. After their parents were in bed, the sisters gave dares to each other and tried not to get caught.

"Go out into the kitchen and dial five zeros on the telephone."

"Climb out the bedroom window and come in the front door." This was risky because it was close to their parents' bedroom.

"Get a bowl of ice cream with four spoons and bring it back."

It usually ended when one of them got caught—their laughter often giving them away.

Then Uncle Sal would turn on the hall light and yell and threaten to ground them all. Those girls were never scared—they just buried their faces in their pillows and laughed all the harder.

Joey had gotten caught the last time, and when he heard his uncle's booming voice, he had shoved the bowl of ice cream under the couch and waited in the dark.

"Where's Joey!" he shouted. "He better not be outside."

All three sisters said he was probably sleepwalking again. "Joey, oh Joey," they called out, their voices dripping with concern.

He had mustered up his courage and staggered slowly down the hall, his arms stretched out in front of him, eyes wide open.

"Shhh. Don't wake him," Anne whispered and led him back to his room.

His uncle had muttered vague threats and gone back to his room. They heard him relating the incident to Aunt

Millie as he crawled back into bed—followed by her burst of laughter.

Joey remembered them as the easiest girls in the world to pal around with—yet mysterious, being girls. Whisperings and giggling he could only imagine at.

Anne was the oldest and in charge but was sweet and gentle. Vicky—Vita, was a puzzle to him. Part of her was always somewhere else. Beth was kind of a tomboy. They were all fun.

Joey looked out at the passing green fields. When he thought about it, his visits to Greenberry were some of his best memories. He remembered how they all rode bikes, climbed trees, hiked through the woods outside of town, and played flashlight tag at night with the neighborhood kids. The freedom and sense of exploration could not compare with apartment living in Chicago, with no sisters or brothers.

The train made its way through the wide green and blue openness of central Illinois. White puffy clouds sat high over the fields and he remembered how they used to find pictures in them. A herd of stampeding buffalo, an angel with wings, a puppy.

He observed the pastures and farms. Cows and horses peacefully grazed. Small towns began and ended as the train passed by—houses with porches and big grassy lawns and gardens. And trees everywhere. With tire swings, some of them.

He sat up quickly on seeing a deer but then felt foolish when he realized it was just a statue of a deer in a yard. Maybe he would see a real one outside of town.

The last stretch was all flat corn and soybean fields. You could see the whole world, stretching away into the horizon. Two towns away. Then one.

There it was! Joey sat up taller as he recognized the town's features rising up from the flatness of the fields, growing larger as the train got closer—the courthouse dome, several pointed steeples, the grain elevator. The train rounded a curve, and the water tower came into view, silver against those puffy white clouds.

He was entering the land of Greenberry with the *Petticoat Junction* sisters. His problems were far away. He was entering the fanciful world of small-town magic.

The train whistle blew, announcing their arrival. Joey wanted to stand up and holler, "Hey everybody—I'm here!" like he had four years ago with his parents.

He reminded himself that he wasn't that little boy anymore. He was older, like the sisters. And didn't yell and act goofy.

He lifted down his suitcase and walked to the open doorway and waited next to a few other people who were getting off at Greenberry. He felt brave as he stood near the open door, the wind blowing his hair.

The train slowed and he could see the streets, the cars, people out walking, some boys riding bikes. The train squealed to a stop. He wanted to push ahead of everyone, but he waited his turn.

He smiled a goodbye at the porter—this one smiled back—and stepped off the train. People came up to greet the few arriving passengers. A handful of people boarded the train.

He shielded his eyes from the sun, looking for his Aunt Milly and Uncle Sal. Or the sisters. Or all of them.

Maybe the train had arrived a little early. He walked towards the station. Maybe they were waiting inside for him?

The train tooted a few times and was soon pulling away. With a surge of panic, he feared he had gotten off at the wrong stop.

He turned to a man next to him in overalls who watched the train depart. Joey noticed that he had a hook for an arm and tried not to stare.

"Excuse me, sir. What town is this?"

The farmer pushed his cap back, rearranged the wad of chew in his mouth, and pointed to the sign in front of them. *Greenberry*.

"Oh."

Joey walked inside the station. It was mostly empty. It was cooler in here. An overhead fan spun slowly over the waiting area. A man leaned against the counter, talking to the ticket master. Another man, dressed in green coveralls, pushed a broom over the floor. A little old lady, her hands folded on top of her purse, sat on the bench in the corner. Every time Joey looked her way, she smiled at him. Otherwise, the station was empty.

A clock hung above the ticket counter.

Joey placed his suitcase on a bench and stood next to it.

He suddenly remembered the last time he arrived at the Vitale's house. He had run into the family room, waiting for a warm welcome, and stood wondering where they all were. After a moment of silence, the girls had burst out of the coat closet, tumbling over each other in laughter and hugging him.

Were they hiding? A smile came to Joey's mouth as he turned in a circle, looking for them, waiting for the joke.

Had he arrived on the wrong day? At the wrong time? Should he start walking? He could walk in the direction of the water tower and ask people were the Vitales lived. But what if they came and he wasn't there?

He sat on the wooden bench, polished with years of waiting. He would just have to wait.

CHAPTER 3

Joey kept his eyes on the station door that was propped open with a rubber wedge. He grew hopeful every time a car or truck drove by. Then, disappointed, he leaned back on the bench and looked at the clock. Five minutes had passed. He noticed that the clock had a second hand and watched it move for ten seconds.

The entrance darkened as a man passed by—and then came back and planted himself in the doorway. He stared hard at Joey. A tall, gaunt figure in a long brown coat. Joey froze. Things were going from bad to worse.

Rufus Sharp.

Joey was afraid to look away. He swallowed. Did Rufus recognize him? Surely now that four years had passed he looked like a different boy?

Rufus's tall body jerked and spasmed, but he kept his eyes fixed on Joey.

Was he remembering the name Joey had called him the last time he was here? Was it payback time?

Rufus muttered sounds while his hand snapped up and down, as if firing a gun or shaking something off his fingers. Now and then his other hand smacked the side of his head. His words were unclear because of the rag that was stuffed in his mouth to muffle his uncontrollable cursing. It looked like the same rag as last time.

The man at the counter heard the mumbling and waved Rufus away. "Go on. Get along, now, Rufus. On your way." He then addressed the little old lady. "Ready, Aunt Betsy? Best get you home."

Rufus twisted around and staggered away.

Joey let out his breath and pulled his suitcase closer. He watched the man link his arm with that of the little old lady. Joey was surprised when she turned around and gave a little wave to him. Joey smiled back, grateful for the small gesture.

Just as he looked up at the clock again, he heard car doors slamming, excited voices, and footsteps. His Aunt Millie, Anne, and Beth rushed in and threw their arms around him and all talked at the same time. Joey found himself in a sudden swarm of arms and hair and laughter and hugs and he didn't know where to look or who to listen to.

"Joey! Thank heavens you're here!"

"I told you he would be."

"Hello, Joey! Oh, look how tall you've grown!" A big hug from Anne.

A punch in the arm from Beth. "Hey, Joey. Bet you thought we weren't coming."

"Hi, Mrs. Vitale. Mom said—"

Millie threw her hands up. "Mrs. Vitale? I'm Aunt Millie to you!"

Joey let himself be squeezed by her.

"I'm so sorry we're late." Millie kissed him, took the suitcase, and set it back down as she hugged him again and marveled at how much he had grown. "My goodness, look at you! What a commotion. Anne's car was parked behind mine and she couldn't find the keys—we searched everywhere!"

"Anne's been driving for a while," said Beth, "but she just got her car. She always forgets where she puts the keys." She moved to his other side. "So I said, 'Are you sure they're not in the car, Anne?' And I ran out and found them."

"I should have remembered from last time. They were in the ignition!" Anne threw her arms out and laughed.

Joey stared from Anne to Beth, unable to believe how beautiful they were. And cool. Hippie girls, with long hair and—"

"In the ignition!" Millie pressed Anne's arm. "I guess there's some logic in that. I'm sorry we're late. But here we are. Oh, how you've grown! Are you hungry?"

He had forgotten how pretty and lively his Aunt Millie was. And happy. She lifted his suitcase again, only to have it snatched away by Beth. Millie looped her arm around his shoulder.

Joey looked around. "Where's Vicky—I mean Vita?"

"That's my fault," said Beth. "I told Vi the train arrived at 6:00. She was still at her friend's house when we left, practicing their lines. They're going to be in a play."

Anne tucked a long strand of blonde hair behind her ear. "I got my car just two weeks ago. Dad bought it for me. Nothing fancy, but it—"

"She's teaching me and Vita how to drive out on the country roads."

"Anne, I told you not to let Beth drive. She's too young. Next summer will be time enough." Millie turned to Joey. "Vita turns sixteen in the fall. She can't wait to get her license."

"She's already saving for gas money," said Anne.

"She only lets me if there's not a soul in sight. And what can happen? The country roads are pencil straight."

They led him to an old green Rambler and Anne got in the driver's seat.

"Joey, why don't you sit in front so you can see the town better?" His Aunt Milly opened the car door, but Joey shook his head.

"I'll sit here." He darted into the back seat with Beth. His mom would have his hide if he took the front seat while his aunt sat in back.

The ten-minute drive to their house was filled with fragmented sentences and a thousand questions and bursts of laughter. Joey turned his head left and right and leaned forward facing one way and then the other to answer Beth and Anne and Millie. He was almost dizzy with happiness.

"Did you even recognize me?" Another punch on the arm from Beth. "Do we look different? You do!"

"You're so much taller!" said Anne, glancing in the rearview mirror.

"You must be starving. Blinker, Anne. Supper's all ready. I just have to boil water for—"

"I know, I know," said Anne, turning on the blinker. "We remembered how much you liked Mom's spaghetti and meatballs."

"Oh, thank—"

"Whew! It's hot." Beth leaned over Joey and rolled down his window all the way. "Hey, the county fair's on this week, did you know? You've never been here during fair week, have you?"

Joey again opened his mouth to respond.

"And the neighborhood boys have been asking for you," said Millie. "We told them you were coming."

"You can ride Dad's bike. He never rides it, but if it's too big you—"

Millie gasped and pressed her foot to the floor. "Anne! Stop sign!"

"I see it!"

"Too bad you weren't here for the Fourth of July," said Beth. "There were fireworks at the lake and—"

"Girls! Give him a chance to breathe. Goodness, you'd think we never have visitors."

"We don't!" both girls said at once.

"Unless you count that guy Dad brought home from the bar."

"The one who looked like Santa Claus?" asked Anne.

"No, that cowboy guy, or whatever he was supposed to be."

"That was your father's friend from the war. The co-pilot."

"Oh my gosh, remember that salesman who came to dinner?" Beth gave an impression of a long airy guffaw that lasted fifteen seconds and they all burst into laughter.

"Here we are."

Anne pulled into the driveway and the car lurched forward.

"Park! Put it in park."

"I was trying to but—"

The doors popped open, and the whirlwind continued.

"I'll get your suitcase."

"Do you have anything else? Is that it?"

Beth nudged Joey. "Anne made a carrot salad. You have to say how delicious it is."

"Better than your tuna salad. The keys!" Anne opened the car door and took the keys from the ignition.

Beth made a gagging face. "That was terrible! Too much mustard or horseradish or something."

"You put *horseradish* in it?"

Joey found himself laughing at everything they said. Anne led the way and Millie followed with his suitcase.

A small mongrel dog ran out to the driveway and tentatively approached Joey with a wagging tail.

"Princess!" Joey dropped to his knees and hugged the dog. "Remember me? Sure you do! There's a good girl. I'm back!" When he stood, the dog kept putting her paws on Joey's leg, eager to play.

Millie put her hand on her hip. "Okay, Princess, that's enough." The dog wagged its body back and forth as his aunt bent over and petted her. "Silly dog. There will be plenty of time for playing, Princess. If you're good, we'll bring you a banana Popsicle." She winked at Joey. "That's her favorite."

Joey smiled. He had forgotten how his aunt fed the dog odd treats now and then. He wondered how she knew that Princess liked banana flavor instead of orange or—

"We fixed up the den for you. I think you'll be comfortable there."

"Come on in," said Beth, holding open the screen door.

When he stepped into the house, Joey had a sense of coming home. There was the coat closet the girls had poured out of on his last visit. There was the television where they had watched *Petticoat Junction* and *Gun Smoke* and *Bonanza*.

"Make yourself comfortable, Joey. Are you thirsty?"

He took off his shoes, eager to be barefoot.

"Like the new couch?" Beth asked. "We had to get rid of the old one. Princess chewed a hole in it and all the stuffing went flying."

"What a mess that was!" said his aunt, already in the kitchen. "Anne, show Joey to his room. There's Vita's notebook. She must be home. Vita! Beth, go tell her we're home."

"Joey knows where the den is, don't you Joey?" Anne lifted his suitcase. "I'll take this for you."

"She's not here," came Beth's voice from the back bedroom.

Millie turned to Joey. "Do you want to check outside? I bet she's out in the flower garden."

"Sure." He ran outside while Beth called for her down the hallway.

He patted Princess on the head as she followed him. His heart swelled on seeing the back yard. Lush green grass, cool to his bare feet. A tall leafy hedge surrounding the whole yard. Uncle Sal's vegetable garden in one corner, the flower garden with a stone bench in front of it in the opposite corner.

A quick glance showed him that Vita was not in the garden, or anywhere in the back yard. She must be inside. He took a minute to let his eyes fill with the densely growing gardens, the fruit trees, the sense of openness. He walked barefoot in the grass, enjoying the cool softness.

A voice floated down to him. "D'Artaaaagnan!"

Vita! He looked around, to one side and the other. He didn't see her. He spun around.

This time there was a laugh in her voice. "D'Artagnan—up here!"

It sounded like she was up in the oak tree. He craned his neck. There was no way she could climb up that high without—

"No, up here—on the roof!"

He took a few steps back and shielded his eyes from the lowering sun. There sat Vita—on the roof! Knees bent, a wide smile, the sunlight illuminating her long coppery hair. She didn't look real.

"Come on up!"

Joey looked around for a ladder but didn't see one. How did she—

"The antenna. Shinny up the antenna pole!"

He eyed the silver pole that led to a TV antenna at the top. It was only a one-story house, but the pole was anchored to the peaked roof over the garage. He squinted, thinking it was kind of high up.

"Cuff your pants so you don't slide."

The adventures were already beginning. Joey walked over to the antenna pole and rolled up his pants to his calves. He grabbed the pole, and then spit on his hands to get a better grip. He used his hands and feet to hug the pole and pull and push himself up—like a caterpillar, he thought. He soon reached the roof. This was a little trickier. He had to use his legs to climb onto the roof, only then letting go of the pole.

Vita stood, waiting for him. "You did it! First time. It took me so many tries. Hello, Joey. Welcome back!"

He walked over to her, trying not to stare. She was beautiful, the kind where you wanted to keep staring to figure out exactly why. Her startling green eyes? The wavy hair down her back? The excitement in her face? He averted his eyes.

Vita sat down. "Have a seat."

"This is great!" Joey looked out beyond the hedge to the houses, the school, the courthouse dome off to the right, and, straight ahead, the water tower in the park.

He sat down next to Vita, who gave him a warm smile. "I knew you'd like it." She nudged him with her shoulder, causing him to grin.

"I thought—" he began, then changed his mind and looked back over the yard.

"You thought what?"

He gave a shrug. "Does Anne come up here—and Beth?"

"No. Just me. Beth prefers the trees. Anne likes the ground. I come up here to clear my mind. And to make plans."

"Plans for what?"

"Wait till I tell you all the plans I have. And I want to hear all about yours."

"I don't really have any."

Vita turned an astonished face to him. "How is that even possible?"

Joey felt like he had already failed a test. "I mean, Mom wants me to be a doctor. Dad thinks I should be an engineer. So I can get a good job." He hated conversations about his *career path*. The future was not something he was looking forward to.

"What do *you* want?"

Joey didn't want to talk about home and jobs. "I don't really care."

"I seem to remember you were going to be an explorer."

He focused his eyes on the treetops. "I think everyplace has already been discovered."

Vita leaned to one side and studied Joey. "Where's my wild D'Artagnan?"

"I don't know. I guess he grew up." Joey thought it was a good answer and that he sounded mature.

Vita peered out at the trees and water tower. "Hmm. It's a good thing you came. We need to work on that."

Joey grew uncomfortable with the attention on him. "I know you're going to be in a play. They already told me."

"That's part of my bigger plan."

"Vita, Joey, come inside!" Beth's voice came from one of the open kitchen windows. "Joey, your mom's on the phone!"

Joey stood. "I forgot. I was supposed to call her as soon as I got here."

They carefully walked over to the gently rising slope to the high point. Joey moved aside for Vita to go down first.

That's when he saw it—the fear in her eyes. So she *was* still afraid of heights.

She stared at the pole. "You go first. I'll follow."

Joey swung his legs over the side, holding on tight to the pole, and slid down. Just like a fireman! He raised his head and saw Vita more gingerly moving as she gripped the pole and eased her legs onto the pole.

She slid down and rubbed her hands together. "I'm getting callouses."

"Coming!" she answered to another call from Beth, and they ran inside the house.

CHAPTER 4

Millie waved Joey over to the phone. "Here he is. And don't worry, we'll take good care of him and make sure he has a wonderful time. Hello to Walter." She handed the phone to Joey.

After the climb to the roof and the view among the treetops and the exhilarating slide down the pole, everything came to a halt.

Joey became self-conscious as he spoke. "Hi, Mom." Millie and the three girls kept glancing over at him as they set the table.

"It was fine. I think I fell asleep for a while." He twisted the phone cord around his finger while he listened. "I ate them all. They were good."

For the most part he let her talk, nodding and giving an occasional yes or no. His father came on briefly and told him they would speak later, after he had settled in. Then his mom asked for Millie again. "I will. No, I won't. Bye, Mom."

Millie took the phone and put her arm around Joey. "We couldn't be more delighted. He's brought a breath of fresh air with him and he'll be sure to make this summer a memorable one for us."

Me? Joey thought and raised his head to her in surprise.

With Millie's arm locking him in place as she chatted with his mom, Joey observed the sisters. They moved about the kitchen and arranged the food on the table, saying soft things amongst themselves. His friends back home would pester him about what they looked like so he wanted to have details to give them.

Anne took a small vase of blue flowers from the counter and set it in the middle of the table. "I just love cornflowers," she said. "They're a happy flower. Like daisies." She hummed to herself as she took out paper napkins from a side cupboard.

Most people would probably say she was the most beautiful. He watched her as she folded and placed napkins around the table. She didn't look like a kid at all. She was completely grown up. Her shimmery blonde hair fell to her waist, and there was a tiny braid on each side. She had on a long blue skirt and a blue-and-white flowered top that showed her stomach, and big silver hoop earrings, paper thin. Her blue eyes were the same color as the flowers.

Or was Beth the prettiest? With her big brown eyes and dark eyelashes. Black hair that went past her waist. Perfectly straight and thick and shiny. She had changed the most. There was nothing of the tomboy in her anymore—except for the punches. In four years, she had really shot up and, to his disappointment, she was now a good head taller than him. Maybe it was the cut-offs she was wearing, but her legs looked really long. And tanned. Her yellow t-shirt had embroidered butterflies on it, and she wore little gold peace-sign earrings. There was something brisk and energetic about her—like she was in a hurry and couldn't wait to get where she was going. And that it was going to be fun, wherever it was.

He tipped his head to study Vita as she poured iced tea into the glasses. She was different. Harder to describe. It was like there was something else going on behind her prettiness. She was wearing blue jeans and a green fringed shirt that made her eyes appear even greener. Beaded earrings hung from her ears, and her hair was long and full. Something about her made him think that she was from another time. A long ago time. Her eyes were kind of dreamy, but with a fight in them.

Was she worried about something? Or just thinking about those plans she mentioned? He remembered his mom describing some film star who was said to "have beauty." Some quality that went deeper than prettiness. He had a feeling that was what Vita had. Something hard to pin down, something that made you want to watch to see what would happen, what she would do next or—

Millie's sudden squeeze to his shoulder interrupted his thoughts. He would ask her to take pictures so he could show his friends back home and they could decide for themselves. He couldn't say who was the prettiest. He decided it was whichever one he was looking at and was glad to have decided the matter.

He could hear his mom laughing on the other side and he wished he had paid attention to what they had been talking about. He rarely heard her laugh like that. He smiled at Millie, grateful that she was able to make his mom happy.

Millie looked exactly as he remembered. Wavy reddish-blonde hair that brushed her shoulders, greenish eyes, lipstick. His mom said Millie had always been beautiful and could have had any man she wanted but she had chosen Sal.

She squeezed him again and said goodbye to his mom. "We'll take good care of him. Don't you worry about anything, Dorothy."

Joey gave another glance at the *Petticoat Junction* sisters. They kept smiling at him and seemed happy that he was there.

"You still have the map," Joey said, walking over to the large world map behind the kitchen table.

"With a few new islands in the South Pacific, thanks to a shaken soda." Millie raised her eyebrows at Beth.

"I didn't know it was going to explode. I think Anne shook it."

"I did no such thing." Anne placed a hand on Joey's shoulder as he looked at the map. "I remember how you spent hours studying all the countries. You and Vita made a list of all the places you wanted to visit."

"I remember that list," said Vita. "We picked places that sounded exotic. Ulaanbaatar. Kuala Lumpur."

"Addis Ababa," Joey added. "The Kalahari Desert."

"Dad's home!" cried Beth.

Millie clapped her hands together. "Perfect timing. Now we can eat."

Joey went out to the family room. It led to the garage where his Uncle Sal parked his pickup truck.

When Sal walked in, he embraced Joey in a bear hug. "Hey, hey! There he is. Let me take a look—No! This can't be the same Joey who helped me in the garden." He ruffled Joey's hair. "You look all grown up!"

Joey indulged in the sense of ease he always felt with Sal.

"So you rode the train all by yourself, did you?"

Joey nodded. "I'm almost thirteen." He stood a little taller.

Sal gave a low chuckle. "So you are." He compared their heights with his hand. "Why, you're almost as tall as me." He wrapped an arm around Joey, and they walked into the kitchen.

Sal inhaled the air and went to Millie by the stove. "Smells good."

Millie held out her cheek to be kissed. Joey remembered the signs of affection they always showed to each other. He was embarrassed by it, yet it also made him happy. Like he was a part of a big, loving family. Like this was how it was supposed to be.

"I'll just go and wash up," said Sal. "Go ahead and sit."

"Me too," said Joey. He washed his hands at the bathroom sink. His palms were still red from the antenna pole.

Millie was filling a basket with garlic bread when he returned to the kitchen. "Joey, you can sit next to Beth by the window."

"Here," said Beth, pulling out a chair. She gave a mischievous glance to Anne and Vita and took her seat.

Joey felt their eyes on him and he tried to behave like a thirteen-year-old boy, cool, at ease with hippie girls. He pulled his chair out and began to sit, wishing his friends could see him. Suddenly, the world tipped and he let out a cry, his arms windmilling in frantic circles to keep him from falling backwards. Amid the girls' laughter. He caught his balance and put his hands on the table for stability.

"Oh, you girls!" said Millie, setting the garlic bread on the table. "Put that crazy chair away. They think it's the funniest thing in the world to give the broken chair to their friends. I told them they're too old for that kind of thing." Then she too began to laugh, seeing how hard the girls were all laughing.

"I wish I had a camera!" cried Beth, wiping tears from her cheeks. "Your face!" She did a quick imitation of Joey and burst into fresh peals of laughter.

Joey also began to laugh, realizing how silly he must have looked—all panicked and scared over nothing.

"I did put it away," said Anne, "but Beth insisted it would be funny."

"And it was!" said Beth. "You wouldn't have got hurt. It's just the back that gives way and makes you feel like you're falling."

"Vita, put that chair away and bring him another." Millie shook her head. "Honestly."

Sal walked into the kitchen. "My girls already torment-ing you? Fresh meat. Better be on your toes." He pulled out his chair and checked the back, which made the girls laugh again.

"That's our only trick, we promise," said Anne. "You're perfectly safe with us."

Joey looked around at all of them, still laughing at himself. Nothing like making a fool of yourself to break the ice.

Beth gave him a light punch in the arm. "We have the whole summer all planned out for you. Starting with the fair tomorrow."

"I've been working at the Corner Café on the square," said Anne. "Do you remember it, with all the good desserts?"

"Then there's swimming at the pool," continued Beth. "Bike rides, and oh! You can help with our photoshoots. Do you like photography?"

"We're working on some projects, Joey," said Vita. "You remember David? He's working on a photo assignment for when he goes back to college. He gave me the idea to put together a portfolio of the different roles I've done. He'll use some of them for his assignment."

Sal dished spaghetti onto his plate. "I guess you've heard the big news." He pointed his head to Vita. "Got a movie star in the family. All you'll hear about is the audition. The audition."

"Dad, I'm going to be an actress. That's different."

"Don't tease her, Sal. She's serious about drama." Millie turned to Joey. "She's been studying all year."

"Shakespeare, no less," Sal added with a wobble of his head and his version of a haughty accent.

Vita winced at the jab. "Always study the best. That's what Aunt Nellie says."

"Do you remember my sister, Nellie?" asked Millie. "I think she came to visit while you were here last time.

Joey started to reply, but the others talked excitedly over him.

"Every summer there's a huge audition over in Hawthorn," said Beth, "for the fall festival. They do a Shakespeare play. Hawthorn's a lot smaller than Foreston, but they have a really good theater. And Vita's going to audition for the role of Titania in *A Midsummer's Night Dream*. And of course, she'll get it."

Vita's face sparkled with excitement. "I don't know."

Anne served herself some salad. "She's just being modest. The directors who run it—a husband and wife team—came up after the school play at the end of the year and gushed over her. Vita played Viola in *Twelfth Night*."

"Dressed as the twin boy for most of the play," added Beth.

"They didn't gush," said Vita. "But at least they know I've done Shakespeare. The main thing is that whoever makes the play gets to be in their drama workshop, juniors and seniors only. It's the best thing around here. Until I can get to New York. So I hope I get a part."

"New York, Shakespeare, auditions . . ." Sal muttered, taking a piece of garlic bread.

You will," said Beth. "She's a natural, that's what everyone says."

Anne nodded. "She got every part she ever auditioned for. She's going to be famous."

Vita laughed in embarrassment. "Not every part. Besides, there have only been a few roles."

"But we only have one play a year," said Anne, "beginning with the seventh grade. She got a big role each year."

"You're giving Joey the wrong idea. I've only been in three or four plays, depending how you count. And my eighth-grade role hardly counts." Vita turned to Joey. "I had a small part as one of the witches in *Macbeth*."

"Because of her red hair," Beth explained.

38

"That wasn't the reason." Vita took a helping of salad. "I was a really good witch. That's why. Even though I only had twenty-eight words." Her voice crackled with evil glee. "*Fair is fowl, and fowl is fair.*" Her mouth pressed into a line. "Besides, it's not red."

"I keep forgetting," Beth said to Joey. "It's auburn, or copper, or chestnut—depending on her mood."

Anne gave an admiring glance at Vita's hair. "Red was fine until Mr. Horton's comment. He's the English teacher and runs the high school productions, along with Mrs. Simon. He said all the witches and nasty characters in medieval plays had long noses and humps on their backs—"

Anne and Beth looked at each other and said at the same time, "And red hair!" They burst into laughter.

"Who cares what they call it," said Vita.

"You have gorgeous red hair, Vita, just like your Aunt Nellie."

"And there was your latest performance, in your French class," said Anne. "That counts."

"Hardly. I was a clown." Vita pushed the salad around her plate.

Millie set her glass down. "Oh, Vita, how can you say that? She was Pierrot! A wonderful, dreamy Pierrot. Her friend Priscilla was the dancer Columbine, and Vita's boyfriend was Harlequin."

"Ex-boyfriend," Vita said.

"We all loved it! Short, sweet, and magical! You were superb, Vita."

"Anne," Vita said, "can you pass the carrot salad? It looks good."

Sal took the bowl from Anne and handed it to Vita. He peered at it skeptically. "Marshmallows?"

"They make it at the restaurant, and everyone loves it," said Anne, somewhat defensively.

"I'll be glad when she gets the part," said Sal. "Walking around, reciting Shakespeare . . ."

"Ha!" said Millie. "Don't let him fool you, Joey. He's always the one who wants to get there early for a front row seat."

"Well, it's not every day you get to see your daughter brandishing a sword, or cackling by a cauldron."

Vita laughed. "Oh, Dad. You were the one who helped me come up with that cackle. Don't you remember? You did it better than I did!"

Sal waved his hand. "Enough of witches and plays. Joey didn't come here to do girly things all summer, did you?"

Vita paused mid-sip. "Drama is not a girly thing."

"At any rate . . . Joey, how about you and me do some fishing? Would you like that?"

Joey sat up. "I sure would!"

"We'll pack a lunch and go out to the lake. We can fish off the dock or take the john boat out."

"Me too!" said Beth. "Can I come?" She looked back and forth between her dad and Joey.

Sal winked at Joey. "What do you think?"

Joey had just taken a bite of garlic bread. He bobbed his head up and down and took a sip of iced tea. "Sure!"

Sal gestured to Beth. "She's the only one who likes fishing around here. The rest will have nothing to do with it."

"I don't mind holding the pole," began Anne, "but the worms . . ." She gave a shudder.

Millie raised her eyebrows at Sal. "What are you talking about? I used to fish with you when we went camping. And I loved it. Pitching a tent, fishing along the river. Building a fire at night and cooking our catch. I even helped clean them! Do you girls remember?"

All three nodded.

"That was back when we took a camping vacation every summer," Millie explained to Joey. "Sleeping on the hard ground began to bother Sal's back so we had to stop. Anne, this carrot salad is delicious! I want another helping."

Anne's cornflower eyes sparkled with pleasure.

"Did you know Dad was hit by shrapnel in the war?" Beth asked. "Flak. Pieces of metal that pierced his B17 and went right into his hip and lower back. He still has a piece of it, don't you, Dad? In a drawer with his medals."

Sal reached for another piece of garlic bread and wiped up the last of the sauce on his plate. "No talk of war—any war—at the dinner table."

Joey saw Millie give a little shake of her head to Beth.

"Your garden looks extra big this year, Uncle Sal. Are you getting a lot of tomatoes?"

"Bumper crop. We'll be doing a lot of canning." The easy smile returned to his face. "Can I count on you to help me weed and water? And hunt for tomatoes like you used to?"

"You bet."

Beth continued with her list of all the things they would do over the summer.

"And we'll have lots of cookouts," said Millie. "Hamburgers and hot dogs, barbequed chicken."

"Corn on the cob, and watermelon." Vita smiled. "Summertime food."

Sal pushed his chair back from the table and the girls began to clear the dishes. "Now. What are we going to give our guest for dessert?"

"We made homemade ice cream. With peaches." Millie's print skirt swirled as she went from the table to the sink with dishes. "We'll have it outside. On the picnic table. How does that sound, Joey?"

"Sounds really good," he answered with a big smile.

Anne brought the dishes to the sink and Vita began to put them in the dishwasher. Millie lifted down several bowls from the cupboard and took out spoons and napkins.

"Beth, bring these out to the table."

The phone rang and Anne ran to get it. She covered the receiver with her hand. "Can he come for ice cream?"

"Her boyfriend," Beth mouthed to Joey.

"Of course!" answered Millie. "The more the merrier." She leaned towards the open window, listening. "Vita, leave the dishes. I'll do them later. Go ask Abel to join us. I hear the harmonica."

"Come with me, Joey," said Vita. "You remember Abel from next door, don't you?"

"With all the parakeets? Sure I do."

Vita spoke in a softer voice as they went outside. "He gave away most of them—except for a pair of lovebirds he keeps in his living room. His wife died. Two years ago. Remember Fran? He misses her so much. He often just wanders around the yard, tending to her roses. Sometimes he talks to her."

In his back yard, Abel sat on a porch swing that was placed under a big sycamore tree. He was playing a song that sounded familiar to Joey. *Clementine*? Was that it?

"Hi, Abel. Look who's here! Remember Joey?"

Abel tapped the harmonica on his sleeve, pocketed it, and stood up to greet them.

"Hello, Joey! I heard you were coming to visit." He extended his hand.

Joey was surprised to see him looking so much older. Grayer and more bent. And thin.

"Hi, Abel." He took his bony hand.

"Been a number of years, hasn't it? You used to help me and Fran find strawberries in the patch over there. Remember that?" He chuckled. "You ate half of them," he added, laughing even more. Then his face grew serious. "You know she's gone. Did Vita tell you?"

"Yeah. Sorry." He searched his mind for something kind to say. "She used to make sugar and cinnamon crisp for me."

Abel chuckled again. "She knew how much you loved it." He hitched up his gray trousers.

"And she gave me strawberry jam to take home with me. To Chicago. It was good."

"That sounds like her." Abel motioned to the swing. "Have a seat, have a seat."

Joey and Vita sat on either side of the old man.

"We came to invite you for homemade ice cream," Vita said. "Peach."

The lines on Abel's weathered face deepened as he smiled. "Well, can't pass up peach ice cream."

Joey heard a pretty warbling and looked around from tree to tree. He was surprised at how clear and piercing it was. "What is that?"

Abel found the bird at the top of one of the sycamores. "A robin redbreast. Happiest sound of the summer. Can't be sad with them around."

Vita lightly pushed off with her feet, sending the swing rocking. "I just love it here in your yard. It's so peaceful. All your rose bushes. The birdbath." She leaned her head back and gazed at the trees. "Just look at all those birdhouses."

"Fran loved to watch the birds. I still put out feed. The squirrels get most of it." He pointed to a red birdhouse. "That's a new one."

Joey nodded at it with interest and saw several others dotting the yard with color—a few blue ones along the fence, some white and yellow ones hanging from low tree branches, and a green one mounted to the clothesline pole. "Your yard looks real nice, Abel."

"I try to keep it up for her. Best I can." He pointed to the little flower garden on the other side of the sidewalk. "Fran had a real green thumb. Her roses . . ." He shook his head in memory. "People would stop by, just to see and smell her rose bushes. She'd always cut some blooms for them to take home."

Vita smiled at the old man. "She gave us roses all summer long. We have two rose bushes in our flower garden but nothing like these."

Abel pushed himself to his feet and took some clippers from a small table. "I'll cut a few for you girls. Want to give me a hand, Joey?"

"Sure."

They walked to the different colored rose bushes. "These pink ones, I think." Abel carefully inspected the blooms before snipping a few stems and handing them to Joey. "You know how girls are. They like pretty things. Watch out for the thorns."

Abel went into his garage and came out with an old glass jar. He brushed at it, held it up to check for cracks, and handed it to Joey. "This'll do. You can fill it at the spigot there."

Joey put the stems in and filled the jar halfway with water, and then handed it to Vita.

She buried her face in the roses, her hair forming a curtain around them. "They smell heavenly. Gosh, they're beautiful, aren't they?"

Abel raised his head and peered at them through his bifocals. "Yep. Well, let's go taste that peach ice cream."

Millie was just setting the ice cream container on the picnic table, and under the pin oak, Sal positioned the metal chair that Abel favored. "Have a seat, Abel."

Beth brought two more lawn chairs from the patio and opened them.

"Look what Abel cut for us," Vita said, placing the jar of roses in the middle of the table.

Millie admired the burst of pink. "What gorgeous blooms! Thank you, Abel."

Anne caught their fragrance and exhaled a soft, "Ahh!" She began to dish out the ice cream, handing the bowls to Beth and Vita to pass around.

Beth sat at the picnic table next to Anne and savored a spoonful. "This is what I love about summer! Homemade ice cream."

Abel took another taste. "I have to agree with you there, Beth. Pretty tasty."

Joey sat across from them and nodded in agreement. It tasted different from store-bought ice cream. Princess came out and sat at his feet, perfectly content.

The sound of a car in the driveway caused Anne to run to the garage. Her long blue skirt floated behind her, and her hair swayed around her shoulders. She came back with a young man with longish hair. He looked at Anne the same way she looked at him.

"Joey, come meet Mark."

Joey walked up to him and smiled.

"Hello, Joey! So you're here for the summer?"

"Uh huh. Almost two whole months."

Before they reached the table, Joey heard Anne say softly to Mark. "Remember, don't bring up—"

"I know, I know. Evening, Mr. Vitale. Mrs. Vitale." He gave a nod to Vita and Beth. He noticed Abel and reached over to shake his hand. "Abel. How're you doing?"

"Fair to middlin'. Can't complain."

Anne dished out a bowl of ice cream for Mark.

Sal and Abel were soon discussing their gardens, and what the farmers were saying about the crops in the fields. Mark sat close to Anne at the picnic table, and Joey saw him rest his hand on her leg. Beth was already scraping her bowl.

While everyone was talking, Joey looked around and felt like he was in a different world. The sky through the yards to the west was getting orangey. It was all so different from Chicago. He couldn't even see the setting sun from his home. There was homemade ice cream and visiting neighbors, and a big grassy yard, and gardens. Birds chirping. And Princess at his feet.

Eventually the light began to fade, and a few glows near the grass began to rise.

"Lighting bugs!" Joey cried. "I remember those. We used to put them in jars, and then let them go."

Beth jumped up. "Let's see who can catch the first one."

He and Beth chased a few bugs, caught and released them. Then Beth demonstrated her cartwheels. "Three in a row! Bet you can't do that."

The daylight slowly faded and the earlier sound of vibrant birdsong gave way to evening quiet. A few crickets could now be heard.

Abel rose to his feet. "Well, better be getting' home. Need to tend to the birds."

"We'll see you home, Abel," said Vita.

Later that night in bed, with a light quilt over him, Joey realized that he was smiling up at the ceiling. Chicago and the land of trouble were far away. He was in a new land, and the rest of summer lay before him. With a hint of a smile still on his lips, he rolled over and fell into a sweet slumber.

CHAPTER 5

Joey pedaled hard and then coasted down the street, his arms out to the side—no hands! He grabbed the handlebars and pedaled some more. The wind ran over his face and ruffled his shirt. He had forgotten how much fun it was to ride a bike where there was so much room.

He remembered the basic layout of Greenberry and how Uncle Sal had described it. For the most part, the town was flat, but to the south and west the land became more rolling as it got closer to the Mississippi River Valley. Joey would save the hills on the outskirts of town for another day.

For now, he rode around the neighborhood and then ventured down the street that led to the small college. It was mostly empty over the summer, which allowed him to ride on the sidewalks that crisscrossed the campus and over the wooden bridge. At the edge of the campus he came to a road that led out to the country. He would save that for another day too.

The plan for today was to later meet Vita at her job and then they would have lunch at the café where Anne worked. Afterwards, he would stop by Sal's shop. And in the evening—the fair!

He rode more slowly back through town, looking at the houses and yards. There were girls jumping rope, boys playing pitch and catch, and little kids riding around the driveways on tricycles or Big Wheels.

Joey crossed the train tracks, reached the other side of town, and then circled back. It was easy to orient himself by keeping his eye on the courthouse dome and the water tower in the Lone Tower Park. He headed to the park now to see if any of his old friends were there.

Just as he turned onto the street by the park, he saw the figure of Rufus Sharp. Coming straight at him. Joey skidded to a stop. Should he make a quick U-turn? Would he have time? And was it safe to turn his back?

He soon realized that Rufus didn't see him. Didn't even look his way. He was in some kind of animated conversation with himself that Joey couldn't make out because of the rag stuffed in his mouth.

Rufus walked alongside the street, his head jerking, his hand pointing and shaking downwards. He seemed angry, but Joey knew that Rufus couldn't control his hands or head or speech. Did he walk all the time because he wasn't able to sit still? Maybe. And yet there was something scary about him—like he could snap at any moment. Do something crazy.

Joey stood immobile and watched Rufus pass by, in that brisk, stiff stagger of his. In a hurry to nowhere. Joey followed him with his eyes as Rufus walked alongside the park. Once he was safe enough away, Joey walked his bike to the park and over to the small playground.

Most of the park was a grassy field dominated by the tall silver water tower. Joey remembered how he had been in awe of it when he was little. When he had stood next to it and gazed up, it seemed to reach all the way up to the clouds. Like in "Jack and the Beanstalk." Now it just looked like a water tower, all boarded up at the bottom.

At the other end of the park was the playground with a few baby swings and a row of bigger swings for older kids. Wooden slabs attached to chains. There was the same old sandbox—still mostly empty of sand—and the teeter-totter that always sent some kid bawling as it landed with a thud when the other kid hopped off.

Across from the swings sat a scattering of colorful animals on enormous coils for little kids. He looked for the blue pony that had been his favorite. It had a few rust spots and the blue had faded, but a boy was riding it for all it was worth, rocking back and forth as far as it would go.

A group of boys waved to him. "Hi, Joey!"

"We heard you were coming!"

Joey recognized Eddie, Greg, and Wiley, some of the boys from the neighborhood.

"Hey, guys! Just got here yesterday. Rode the train from Chicago." He smiled at two younger boys he didn't know.

Wiley used his right thumb to introduce one boy. "Matt," he said, and his left thumb to introduce the other one, "Mutt."

The smaller boy rolled his eyes at the name Wiley always called him. "My name's Felix."

"Matt and Felix moved to town last year," explained Greg.

Wiley was older and taller than the other boys and Joey
had never liked him much. He was always picking on someone. Joey scanned the playground, hoping to see his old pal.

"Where's Jonno?"

"Don't you know? He moved. To Indiana. Just last
month."

"Oh." Joey tried not to show his disappointment. He
turned to Eddie. "What about Timmy and Jimmy?"

"Grand Canyon. Not to live. On vacation with their
family."

"Wow. I always wanted to see that." He rubbed his shoe
on the dirt. "You guys got a team this year?"

"We did," answered Wiley, scrounging around for small
rocks. "Until everybody left. We still hit balls sometimes
and practice. Interested?"

"Sure."

"We use the ball diamond at the Jack and Jill Park," said
Eddie. "Unless someone else has it. Then we come here."

"In the meantime," Wiley said, bouncing the pebbles
in his hand, "we're working on target shooting." He aimed
a few rocks at the legs of the water tower. Joey heard a
small ping.

"A moving target!" Wiley watched Rufus Sharp cut
through the park. He squinted, took aim, and fired a rock
at Rufus. It bounced off his coat, unnoticed.

Joey's eyes popped open. "What'd you do that for?"

Wiley sneered. "I told you. Target practice. He doesn't
know the difference, anyway."

"You could set him off!" cried Matt, his eyes wide
with fear.

Greg shook his head. "Sometimes you're a real a-hole, Wiley."

Joey turned his bike around. "Well, I gotta go."

"You just got here," said Wiley.

"I have to do something before lunch."

"So do we." Matt and Felix got on their bikes and rode off in one direction, Joey in the other. When Joey glanced back, he saw that Eddie and Greg had jumped on two of the painted animals—a yellow duck and a zebra. They were way too big for them but were laughing all the same. Wiley was scrabbling for more rocks.

Joey pedaled slowly back to the center of town, not wanting to get to Vita's job too early. He remembered what his mom told him about not bothering the girls. He rode alongside the courthouse street, and circled the town square, checking the time on the bank clock. Then he turned onto Maple Street where Vita worked at a little plant and gift store.

He found the shop, just down from the library. It was the kind of place his mom would like. There were all sorts of potted flowers outside, and a window box overflowing with red, pink, and blue flowers. On either side of the door, baskets hung with trailing yellow and white flowers. A painted blue bench nestled beneath the window box, with a white cat curled up on it, licking her paws.

Joey leaned the bike against a tree and bent over the cat.

"Hello there." He bent over and stroked the cat. "Got yourself a nice little spot." When Joey stood, the cat shook her head, causing her collar bell to ring, and jumped off the bench. She rubbed against Joey's leg, and then lapped at a bowl of water under the bench.

Joey opened the door, causing more jingling. He saw that a string of bells hung from the inside doorknob. He closed the door behind him and saw green plants and flowers crowded in the front room. Vita and a little old lady were huddled over a selection of plants in the larger room to the side.

"Hi, Joey!" Vita wore a green apron over her clothes. Her hair was pulled back in a loose ponytail, tied with a white ribbon. She wore bell bottoms and sandals and a white top with flowers on it, the sleeves rolled up. She didn't seem to know how pretty she looked.

"Why, hello, young man!" The older woman clasped her hands together. "I saw you at the train station."

Joey recognized the lady who had waved to him while he waited. He remembered how her kindly smile had put him at ease. Her long dress and black-tie shoes made her look old-fashioned. A black straw hat sat atop her gray hair, and a purse was looped over her arm.

"Hello. I remember you." Should he say, *Pleased to meet you*? What would his mom want him to do?

"This is Joey. A friend of ours who's staying the summer with us. He's from Chicago."

"Chicago!" the old lady exclaimed with wide eyes. "The big city. What an exciting place to live."

"This is Mrs. Higgins. She has a green thumb like no one else. She can make anything grow."

A pleased chuckle escaped the older woman, along with a dismissive wave. "I love them, that's all. All plants. But I do have a soft spot for flowers. Say, why don't you bring Joey by one afternoon and I'll show him my garden."

"That would be real nice," Vita answered. "We'd be happy to."

Joey smiled politely. "Thanks."

"She has the most amazing garden. A brick sidewalk goes all through her back yard, with tall trees, and flowers everywhere."

"Oh, it's nothing special. Rather small. But I do love it out there. Mostly perennials now. The older I get the harder I find it to dig in the earth." She gave another little chuckle.

"I can help you, Mrs. Higgins," said Vita. "Anytime you want. I'd be happy to dig around in the dirt."

"Me too," offered Joey. "I'll be here for the summer."

"Well, thank you, both. I'll give that some thought. I'd best be on my way. I'll take the little ferns for now." She and Vita carried two small potted ferns to the counter.

While Vita rang her up and placed the ferns in a paper bag, Mrs. Higgins pointed to two small ceramic planters. "I'll have to come to a decision about those." She dipped her head to one side. "What do you think, Joey? I just can't make up my mind. I love the arrangements of greenery in the swan planter, but this little cottage planter speaks to my heart. See its lovely thatched roof and rounded blue door? Oh, to live in such a place."

Joey showed his interest in the details. "Yeah, it's real nice." He winced. His mom told him to say *yes*, not *yeah*, especially to older people. But Mrs. Higgins didn't seem to notice.

"Why don't I switch them for you?" said Vita.

Mrs. Higgins put her hand to her chest. "Oh, would you? That would solve all my problems."

"Sure. I'll work on it today."

"Thank you, Victoria." She winked at Joey. "I call her Victoria. Such a dignified name, isn't it? Queenly. It suits her. Her hair is like a golden crown." She opened a small coin purse, took out a dollar bill and a few coins, and placed them on the counter. Then she opened the paper bag and addressed the tiny ferns. "I must get you planted. I think you'll like your new home."

"They'll be in heaven," said Vita, walking with her to the entrance. Joey ran to open the door for her.

"What a gentleman! So nice to see these days." She held her hand out to Joey. "It was a real pleasure meeting you." She patted Vita's arm. "As always, thank you, my dear."

She exited the store and gave a final wave through the glass door. Joey saw that she also said goodbye to the white cat that had resumed its position on the bench.

"She's one of the nicest people in town. I just love her. I think kindness is what matters most, don't you?"

Joey agreed and looked out the window at Mrs. Higgins.

"She walks everywhere. Always in a dress down to her calves and those sturdy black shoes." In a lower voice, she added: "Mom said her husband died a long time ago, in the war. She said they never had a chance to have a family."

"Oh." Joey wasn't sure how to respond. "What war?"

"I'm not sure. I guess the first World War." Vita watched Mrs. Higgins until she rounded the corner. "So!" she said. "How did you spend your first morning in Greenberry?"

Joey told her about who he saw at the park and how he might play baseball with the guys, but that most of the friends his age were gone. So he wasn't sure what he was going to do.

"Good! That means you can help with the photoshoots. David and his girlfriend Darlene do all the setup and organizing. They go to the same college. And Abby helps, David's little sister. Remember her?"

"Sort of." Joey remembered Abby as the little girl who always wanted to race him, and always won. A real pest. Beth's friend.

"David was president of the high school photography club and he's really good. He loves photography the way I love acting. There's a bunch of us who work on staging the scenes. You can help with that if you want."

"What would I do?"

"Help Beth and Abby with painting backdrops, help us find props for scenes, maybe help David with the lighting. I'm sure he can use you. He's working on a lot of different things, but together we're working on shooting scenes from Shakespeare. We started with *Macbeth*, since I already had a costume and knew the role."

"More Shakespeare?"

Vita caught the boredom in Joey's voice. "You'd be surprised. There's a lot of fighting and intrigue in his plays. Besides," she said, standing up straight, "Aunt Nellie says to start with the best. So I am. She's a university professor, you know."

"I remember her. She played the map game with us last time I was here."

"She's a great traveler. And can speak five languages. She's in Europe for the summer, teaching a college course in Paris. What a dream! And traveling all over whenever she gets a chance. She sent me a postcard from Venice. It looks so beautiful. I want to see it someday. And Paris, of course. And—"

The little bells jingled again, and Vita stepped into the front room. Joey saw her face change.

A teenaged boy stood in the doorway, shoved his hands in his pockets, and stared at Vita.

Vita took a step towards him. "I asked you not to come here, Vic. Mrs. Cole doesn't like it. Besides, I told you. It's over." She folded her arms and waited for him to leave.

"Vita—" he began.

"It's over. *Your* choice." She whipped around and went to fill a watering can at the basin in the back room.

Vic waited a moment, and left the shop.

Joey wondered if Vita was going to say anything about him, but she busied herself watering the large potted plants near the front window.

She stopped and stared out at the floor. Then she asked abruptly, "Would you help me with my lines while I water? That's all that matters. I *have* to get this part, Joey. I have to make things happen."

"I'll help." He was happy to be of some use.

Vita went to the counter and reached for the script underneath. He noticed some writing on the inside of her arm and tried to read it.

She pushed up the rolled sleeve a little higher. "My freshman English teacher, Mrs. Simon, had posters all over the wall with quotes. Sometimes I write them on my arm. To remind me." She showed him the words: *If you can Dream it, you can Become it*, and tugged her sleeve back down to cover it. "Do you believe that?"

"I don't know." Joey's mouth twisted up on one side. "It sounds too easy."

"Not easy, but it's a beginning. You have to start with something, some idea, in order to have something to work with. Mrs. Simon explained it better, but it makes a lot of sense to me. She's my all-time favorite teacher. She was the first one to encourage me about acting. She said I had a knack for it. Did you ever have a teacher who helped you to know what you want?"

Joey made a sound of disbelief. "No."

"Hmm. Well, maybe you will one day." She handed the battered script to Joey. "We'll work on this scene. Just the marked passages."

"*A Midsummer Night's Dream*," Joey read.

"The part I want is Titania. She's queen of the fairies. But I'll read for the other female parts as well. Just in case. The H parts. That's what Beth calls them—Helena, Hermia, Hippolyta."

Joey followed along with the passages. Vita recited the lines as she watered the hanging baskets and potted plants that filled the store. She paused now and then to gaze up at the imagined moon, or down at the little fairies, or, with a flash of anger in her eye, to address her husband, Oberon. Joey thought that she believed every word, and that she really did see the moon and fairies and the forest at night.

"Carla—she's one of my friends in the photo club and is auditioning too—says I should be more dramatic. She said that's how she got some of her commercial acting jobs over in Foreston. She's gotten a few small parts, mostly background stuff, and she was a teller once in a local bank commercial."

"Do you try for those parts?"

She shook her head. "No. To me, it's so far from what's in here." She held up the script. "Almost like its opposite. And yet, I think most actors try for commercial roles because they pay. So I might have to when I get to New York."

She filled a small water container with a long narrow spout. "For the tiny plants on this table. Do you mind listening one more time? A quick go through. With more drama, like Carla says."

This time she read the lines differently—with a head toss, bigger gestures, a louder voice, more everything.

"Better?" She waited for Joey to respond.

He leaned his head. "I'm not sure."

"Well, pretend you're a critic. What would you say?"

Joey blinked in thought. "I would say . . ." He looked up at the ceiling. "That the second time I noticed you more. Your hair and arms and stuff."

"Huh. And the first time?"

"I don't know. Maybe I noticed what you were saying more. Or what you were feeling."

When two customers entered the store, Vita helped them find a gift and rang them up.

She returned to the side room and flipped the pages to a different section. "Let's do this scene. Will you read the lines of the other characters?"

Joey gave a little laugh. "Okay."

Every now and then she coached him: "Deeper voice. Sound like you really mean it."

Vita swept around the room, getting into the role. She was just throwing her arms wide open when she became aware of the owner standing in the doorway to the room.

Vita dropped her arms. "Oh, hi, Mrs. Cole."

"Vita?" Mrs. Cole looked at her disapprovingly. "There's a customer in the front room."

"There is? I didn't hear the bells."

"That's because the door was left open. Letting all the cool air out."

"Sorry!" Vita hurried to the front room, introducing Joey on her way. "This is Joey. He's staying with us for the summer."

Joey smiled at her. "Hi."

"Nice to meet you." Mrs. Cole glanced at him and went to the front counter.

While Vita updated her on the morning's sales, Joey made a show of inspecting several tiny plants. He reached into his pocket and counted his change. He chose a small palm plant, about the size of two fingers, and placed it on the counter.

Vita rang it up for him. "I'll bring it home for you when I leave."

Mrs. Cole chatted with the customers and thanked them for stopping by, though they didn't buy anything.

"You can go to lunch now. Don't be late."

"I won't," Vita said cheerfully. "We're going to the Corner Café on the square. Want me to bring you a piece of pie? They're all homemade, you know."

"No. Thank you. Just don't be late. I have some errands to run. Including a dentist appointment that I'm not looking forward to."

Vita gave a soft sound of commiseration. She slipped off the green apron and tucked it behind the counter. "I won't be late. Promise. Bye!"

CHAPTER 6

Joey and Vita walked to the end of the block. Before turning onto the square, Joey looked behind him at the shop, half expecting Mrs. Cole to be watching them with her fists on her hips.

"I hope you're not in trouble. She seemed kind of mad."

"No. She just sounds like that sometimes. She's really nice."

They walked to a restaurant tucked in the corner of the square. Vita pulled open the door to the café. "Here we are. There's Anne."

Anne pointed them to an empty table near the window as she jotted down an order from an elderly man.

They took their seats and Joey eyed the glass cabinet, filled with pies, cakes, and cookies. "Wow."

"Mrs. Finlay is an amazing baker. Her husband cooks the food, and she makes the desserts." She looked back at Anne. "Why is she all smiley and blushing?" Vita scanned the restaurant. "Oh. That explains it."

Joey followed her gaze. "There's Mark!" He waved at him.

Vita also waved. "Here with his mom and grandma."

Vita took out the menu tucked between the condiments. "Soup and sandwiches, for the most part. Chicken noodle soup today. She makes her own noodles. You should try it."

Joey skimmed over the menu. When Anne came to take their order, he decided on a small soup and a grilled cheese. Vita ordered the same. "And pie, of course."

"We have lemon meringue, cherry, and chocolate."

"Cherry," said Joey.

"For me too."

"You two think alike," Anne said, writing down their order. She leaned closer. "Mark's here."

"I know. We saw him."

"They went to Foreston and he bought me this." Her hand went to the silver pendant at her neck. "Entwined leaves. Like Galadriel's 'leaves of Lorien.' I just love it."

Vita looked at the necklace. "Beautiful."

Anne turned to Joey. "We've been reading *The Lord of the Rings*." She smiled and left to place their order.

Even Joey noticed the blush in her cheeks and the happiness in her voice. But he also noticed Vita's frown.

"You don't like Mark?"

"Everybody likes him. Basketball star, straight-A student. He's working at his dad's store, saving up for college."

"So?"

"I don't want Anne getting any ideas. We have plans to move to New York City. We can go to college there. We'll get jobs and I can audition. Anne wants to study costume design. But lately, all she talks about is Mark."

Anne soon brought their soup and a basket of bread and butter.

"Still," said Vita, "we're all afraid he'll have to go to Vietnam. His number was called at the last draft. Anne's a nervous wreck about it."

"I guess nobody wants to go." Joey thought about the two men on the train and his neighbor Tony in Chicago.

"Mark used to think it was the right thing to do, but now he isn't so sure. Especially after Kent State. He and Dad had a few bad arguments about it."

Joey tasted the soup.

"Good, isn't it?"

"Sure is. I didn't know I was so hungry."

The café began filling up.

"This is my favorite restaurant in town," Vita said, tasting her soup. She looked up at the high hammered tin ceiling, the wood and glass desert case, the lace curtains in the windows. "Mrs. Higgins is right. You're lucky to live in a big city. There must be hundreds of beautiful restaurants there."

"I guess."

"Do you remember when we visited you there? It was in your old apartment. You were pretty little."

"Kind of. I remember we slept on the living room floor. Except Anne. She slept on the couch."

"I remember it so well, like it just happened. I loved everything. How busy it was, and that train that ran above the streets. All the lights. Your mom took us to the museum and out to lunch and shopping. She bought us three little white purses with flowers on them. 'For Anne, Victoria, and Elizabeth—the three little queens.' She used to call us that."

65

Joey tilted the bowl and scooped out the rest of his soup. "You were named after queens?"

"No. They're family names. Anne was named after Mom's mother. Dad's grandmother was Vittoria, and he had an aunt Elisabetta."

"Here you go." Anne brought their sandwiches and cleared away their soup bowls.

Joey lifted the grilled cheese. "My dad's middle name is Joseph. I guess that's where I got my name." He bit into the sandwich.

Vita was just about to do the same when a memory surfaced from their last night in Chicago. She and Anne and Beth had crowded around Aunt Dorothy on the couch. She wrapped her arms around them and said, "I just love you girls!" Then she jumped up and left the room, wiping her eyes. Uncle Walter looked worried and brought them all cake and soda, even though it was late at night.

"Your mom and dad were so nice to us." She smiled at Joey's enjoyment of the grilled cheese. "Tell me about the city, Joey."

"What about it?"

"What do you like best about it? What does it sound like at night? Can you hear the trains? Do you walk along the lake? Do you ever go to performances or plays?"

"Mostly it just sounds noisy. Once in a while we see a show or something. Mom likes to go. We all went to a Christmas show this year. That ballet."

"You're so lucky."

"I'd rather be here. Fishing, climbing trees, bike riding."

Vita gave it some thought. "I guess it depends on what you like."

"The houses are big here with big yards and trees. There's so much to do." He bit into one of the dill pickles on his plate.

"Well, I'm determined to get to a big city. Dad wants me to go to college here in town. He says it's cheaper. But I don't want to. As soon as I'm out of high school I want to go to New York to study."

"Do you know anyone in New York?"

"No one."

They watched Anne gracefully sweep around the next table and smile in greeting.

"Do you know, all Anne has to do is *walk* and everyone falls in love with her. Look." She pointed her chin at the table Anne stopped to check on. The elderly couple smiled admiringly at her. Behind them Mark had his dewy eyes glued on Anne, while agreeing with something his grandmother was saying. Anne went through the double doors into the kitchen. Her long blonde braid shone against her white top, her silver jewelry shimmered. "She's like a princess in a fairytale."

Vita finished her sandwich and brushed the crumbs off her fingers. "But where does that get you? Nowhere! We're going to make our dreams come true in New York City. Hopefully Beth will join us when she graduates. Though you never know with her. Right now, she's obsessed with the Southwest."

Anne placed two slices of cherry pie in front of them with a small scoop of vanilla ice cream. "There you go, Joey. I'm so glad you came."

"Me too." Joey noticed a few people waiting in the front, sitting on a bench just inside the door.

"Good thing we got here early," said Vita. "They always fill up."

They finished their dessert and Vita placed some bills on the table. "Mom's treat. She was sorry she couldn't join us, but Dad got an order in and she and Beth have to help him unpack."

Vita glanced at the clock. "Better go."

They waved goodbye to Anne who was seating a table of four, clerks from the county courthouse, and then she began to clear a table. Her eyes kept darting to Mark who was also starting to leave.

Vita opened the door for Joey. "She can juggle about ten things at once. It's harder than it looks. Especially when it gets busy."

Vita and Joey cut through the square and went back to Cole's Plant and Gift Shop.

"See you later, Joey."

Joey took his bike and waved goodbye. He rode down Oak Street, deciding to stop at Sal's shop. Say hi and see if he could be of any help.

He passed a house that looked familiar and slowed down. Then he placed it. It was the house of their friend Hogie. He was about five years older than Anne. He used to live next door to the Vitales and was like an older brother to the girls.

Joey remembered how Hogie had taught them to play badminton and baseball. And how he had come to their defense against the Halloween charges of feathers. Hogie had covered for them, saying they were with him all evening, which had been partly true. Joey remembered him as a big, strong guy who played touch football with his friends in the empty lot next to the school and worked at a construction company in town.

Now there he was, working in his garage, seated at a worktable with a big table saw and a bunch of tools. He was hammering away at a piece of wood.

Joey hopped off his bike and walked up the driveway. The air smelled like fresh cut wood. Low shelves and pieces of lumber lined the garage walls, and sawdust covered the floor.

Joey stood near the entrance. "Hey, Hogie! Remember me?"

When Hogie raised his face, Joey saw a different person from the one he remembered. This face was not friendly and smiling. It was angry. Then Hogie jerked his head back and broke into a smile.

"Joey! Joey Roland. Vita said you were coming this summer. But I didn't expect to see you so grown. How you doing?"

Joey walked towards him—but then halted, his eyes wide. His smile dropped when he saw that Hogie was in a wheelchair. He looked down at the legs. They were thin and wasted and looked lost in the blue jeans. Joey's eyes scrunched up and his mouth opened and stayed open, pouring out unspoken questions.

Hogie slapped his legs. "Yeah. They don't work anymore. But check out these arms, huh?" He flexed his biceps. The top of his body was huge. Behind him stood a rack of barbells.

Joey stayed silent, shocked. He forced himself not to stare at those bony knees.

Hogie spoke in a matter-of-fact tone. "Signed up to do my duty—came back like this. Now I'm a bad guy for going in the first place. Can't win." He took a swig from the beer bottle on the table and wheeled his chair to the other side of the garage to get a piece of wood. He eyed it for straightness, then came back and threw it on the table. "Following the war?"

Joey lifted and dropped his shoulders. "Not really."

"Good. Don't. It'll just screw up your head." Hogie started to sand the piece of wood. He reached for the bottle again, drained it, and tossed it into a garbage can by the door. It made a loud crash when it landed on other bottles. "You drink?"

Joey glanced at the brown bottles. "Not really."

Hogie gave a low chuckle. "How long you here for?"

"The summer." Joey couldn't think of anything to say. All he could think about were those thin legs and how Hogie used to be so big and strong. He shifted from one foot to another and watched Hogie reach into a small refrigerator and take out another bottle.

"Well, I got some work to do. I make birdhouses now. Benches and footstools. Sell them at the hardware store uptown. Gonna be rich one day, Joey." He laughed and took another swig.

Joey gave a tentative smile.

"All summer, huh? Stop by if you dare. You might catch me in a good mood. If not, just keep moving on. Deal?"

Joey nodded. "Well, see you." He walked his bike to the street. He didn't feel like riding anymore.

He arrived at the shop and left his bike by the front door. Sal sat at a wooden desk opening envelopes. Millie and Beth asked Joey how lunch was and said how dusty and dirty it was restocking the shelves.

"Even though I clean the shop every Saturday," said Beth.

Millie stopped brushing at her slacks and stared at Joey, wondering why he was so quiet.

"I—I just saw Hogie." Joey saw Beth look quickly at her dad and mom. "I didn't know."

Sal muttered words under his breath that Joey didn't catch.

Millie shook her head. "This terrible war. He came back injured." She rested a hand on Sal's shoulder as she reached for her handbag from the counter. "Oh, there's dust all over me. You too, Beth. I can't wait to wash this grime off me." She brushed at her sleeve and then gave a big smile. "Come on, kids. Let's go home. Clean up before the fair. We can have fish sandwiches at the Elks beer tent. Or corndogs. Doesn't that sound good?"

"Sure does," said Beth. "You go ahead, Mom. I'll walk with Joey." She turned at the door. "Hurry home, Dad!"

"I'll be home in an hour or so. Need to get through these bills."

Joey walked alongside Beth in silence.

Beth looked up at the sky. "Dad hates talk about the war. He's mad. Mad that it's lasting so long. Mad at the boys who don't want to go. Even madder when he hears about boys dying or getting hurt. Like Hogie. So we don't talk about it."

Joey pushed the bike along. "My dad doesn't like to talk about it either. He was in the Korean War. Mom said he was different when he came back."

Beth picked up the pace and changed the tone. "Abby's going to stop by for some brushes for the next shoot, even though she has plenty. I think she just wants to see you again. Do you remember her?"

"Yeah. She's a fast runner." He couldn't think of anything else to say.

Beth explained that she and Abby did a lot of the scene building and painting. "Abby's a whiz with spray paint; she paints the most amazing skies. And she helps David with developing the film. They have their own darkroom."

As they walked up the alley and into the back yard, a girl waved from the street and rode her bike into the yard.

"Hey, Beth!"

A pretty girl in cut-offs and a pink and white embroidered peasant top rode over to them. She stayed seated on her bike, and raised her eyebrows at Joey, waiting for him to speak.

Joey stood rooted to the ground. He couldn't stop staring.

Beth punched him in the arm. "Don't you remember Abby? Aren't you going to say hi?"

"Yeah. Hi. You look different. I mean, of course I remember you. Hi."

"So, you're back in town!" Abby got off her bike and used the kickstand. "The fair's on. Are you going tonight?"

"We wouldn't miss it," said Beth. "In all the times Joey visited here, it was never during the fair week. He can't wait to see it."

"We have to get there early. David has to work. But we could meet later." She turned to Joey. "Remember my brother? He's going to photograph the 4-H exhibits. For the newspaper."

Joey looked from Beth to Abby. "Yeah. We can meet you there."

Abby shoved her hands in her back pockets. "So you're going to be here all summer?"

"Until the end of August," Beth answered for him.

"Nice timing. The best part of summer. Starting with the fair and ending with the carnival." She waited for him to answer.

Joey couldn't think of a good response. He nodded and rubbed his foot at the grass.

"Except he missed the Fourth," said Beth.

"That's so much fun. Out at the lake. But you probably have better celebrations in Chicago."

"No," Joey answered quickly. "I mean, they're bigger I guess, but—"

"Hey! Want to race? To the hedge and back?"

All Joey's awkwardness disappeared. He gauged the distance to the hedge. "That's not very far."

"Okay, two times."

"You're on."

They used the sidewalk as their starting point and faced the hedge on the far side of the yard.

Beth positioned herself as referee. "You have to touch the hedge—grab a leaf so I can be sure. On your mark!"

They placed their feet at the edge of the sidewalk and leaned forward. Joey glanced down sideways, noticing that Abby was barefoot and had a little silver bracelet around her ankle. Her toenails were painted pink, and her legs and feet were tanned as if she'd been outside all—

"Get set, go!"

Abby darted out ahead of him. They raced to the hedge, almost even. Joey grabbed a leaf and dashed back. On the second lap, Joey took the lead and held it. He grabbed more leaves, turned, and smiled as he passed Abby going in the other direction. He won by several yards.

He flopped down on the grass and laughed as Abby crossed the sidewalk.

She stood with her hands on her hips, panting, her cheeks flushed. "I can't believe it! That's the first time you ever beat me. The first time!"

"I wasn't even trying that hard," teased Joey.

Abby plopped down next to him, pulled a bunch of grass, and threw it at him. He rolled away, laughing.

"It's only because your legs are so long. You have an unfair advantage."

Beth sat down, cross-legged. "I think your days of winning races with Joey are over, Abby. He's a lot taller now."

"How old are you, Joey?"

"Almost thirteen."

Abby leaned back on her elbows. "I'm fourteen."

Joey's face filled with disappointment.

Abby narrowed her eyes in thought. "You look a lot older. I guess because you're tall."

His expression shifted back to happiness.

Abby leaned her head to one side and then the other, studying Joey. "Do you always wear your hair so short?"

Joey ran his hand through his hair. "I guess. I never really thought about it."

"You should grow it long for the summer. That would look cool."

No more haircuts, Joey decided.

Beth picked up a whirligig from the ash tree and placed it between her fingers, making a short whistle.

Abby picked one up and gave it a try. She laughed and handed it to Joey. "I never could do that."

Joey tried but couldn't get a sound out of it.

Beth blew again and made a long clear whistle, her eyes brightening at her success. "I told Joey he should come to our photoshoots."

Abby sat up. "Yeah, come! We have so much fun. The guys from the photography club are really great. You'll like them. Dylan and Rob. Becca and Carla and Darlene. There's about ten of them. David and Darlene and Rob are in college. The rest are in high school."

"Vita told me all about it and asked me to help. I'll definitely be there."

Abby sat on her legs. "Vita's the actress. Carla too, but she's not really serious about it. Me? No thank you. Who wants to memorize all those lines? I don't mind being a background character, but what I really love is painting the scenery. You should have seen the stage set Beth and I helped with for our seventh-grade play—*Alice in Wonderland*."

Beth sighed. "I loved that set. I wanted to keep it. But there was no place to put it." She jumped to her feet. "Let me get the brushes for you. They're in the garage."

Joey didn't know what to say, now that they were alone.

Abby laughed and threw more grass at him. "You caught me off guard this time. We'll have a rematch."

Joey also laughed. "Sure. Anytime you want."

Beth ran back with two paint brushes. "Here you go. Let's meet at the Ferris wheel at 7:00."

"Okay." Abby took the paint brushes and splayed the bristles. "If I'm not there, wait for me."

Beth waved and hurried back to the house. "I still have to take a shower!"

"See you soon." Abby went to her bike and released the kickstand. "Bye, Joey." She slipped onto the seat and gave him a wide smile before riding away.

Joey stood and brushed the grass blades off his clothes.

"See you later!" He watched her pedal off. "Abby."

Chapter 7

Joey leaned in the doorway to the girls' bedroom, wondering why it was taking them so long to get ready. He had put on a clean blue shirt and was ready to go. He wanted to spend as much time at the fair as possible. And see Abby again.

He watched in curiosity at the commotion. All three girls were doing things to their hair, asking each other questions about their clothes, and leaning forward to the dresser mirror to put on lip gloss and mascara and other stuff. He glanced in the mirror and ran a hand through his hair. It *was* kind of short.

Anne had unbraided her hair and it now filled out like Vita's. Twice the size. She wore wide-legged gray-and-white striped pants—almost like a skirt. And a white top that showed her tanned stomach and shoulders.

"I love that eyelet tube top," said Vita. She watched Anne slide a silver snake bracelet onto her upper arm. Vita smiled at the effect. "Like Cleopatra."

Beth brought out two tops from the walk-in closet. "Your hair looks like spun gold, Anne. Should I wear mine down or in braids?"

"Braids, if you're going on the rides," Vita said.

"Of course, I'm going on the rides." She held up the tops. "Which one?"

Anne leaned her head while Beth held up one, then the other. "The red one."

Beth changed in the bathroom and came back wearing a red-and-white plaid top that tied at the waist. "Cut-offs for me. You can do more. Long dresses and flowy pants just get in the way."

Vita frowned at her reflection in the mirror. "I wish I could tan like you guys."

"Vita's like Mom," Beth explained to Joey. "She doesn't tan at all, just burns. Just the opposite of me and Dad. Anne is somewhere in the middle; she tans."

"But it takes me a while." Anne put on long silvery earrings and adjusted the necklace from Mark.

"I don't even bother trying anymore." Vita wore a long gauzy sundress, pale purple shot with gold thread. It went down to her ankles and was gathered at the waist.

"A tan is overrated," said Beth. "It's not like it changes your life or anything. Anyway, you look beautiful, Vi. That color really suits you. I would feel ridiculous in those dangly earrings, but with your hair, they're perfect." She turned to Joey. "Anne always wears silver, and Vita gold. I wear everything."

He saw that Beth was wearing a long piece of rawhide with a blue rock at the bottom.

She saw him looking at it. "Turquoise. From Arizona. I bought it a few years ago at the fair. There used to be a real Indian who came every year. He wore a feathered headdress and sold jewelry and belts. Chief Gray Hawk. The year I bought this he performed a rain dance at the grandstand."

Joey waited to hear more. "Did it rain?"

"Of course," said Beth. "Two days later. I don't think he comes anymore. He was pretty old."

Anne checked her reflection in the mirror, lifted a small bottle, and dabbed some of its contents on her wrists and neck.

Joey was used to his mom's spray perfume. He leaned forward to get a better look at the little vials clustered on the dresser.

Anne handed him the tiny bottle. "Perfumed oil. We get them over in Foreston. I like the floral scents. That's rose gardenia, my favorite." She lifted another one for Joey to smell. "Beth likes patchouli."

"And I love amber." Vita reached for her oil, rubbed some on her wrists and neck, and waved the bottle under Joey's nose.

Even though he was fascinated by their rituals, his mind was on Abby. She had light wavy brown hair, soft brown eyes, and was just plain old pretty. Really pretty. Plus, she seemed to like him. That was something. He wished he was older. She was already a teenager. He stood a little taller.

After more adjustments and selecting handbags and sandals, the girls were ready and walked into the kitchen where Sal and Millie were waiting for them.

Vita gave her mom a hug. "You look nice, Mom. I love that dress."

Millie wore a brighter shade of lipstick and a coral-and-pink sundress that set off her strawberry blond hair. A pair of sunglasses hung from her neckline. "Ready, kids? I'm famished!"

Anne had been looking out the family room window. "There's Mark! See you out at the fair." She ran outside and got into his car. Joey saw that they leaned together for a kiss.

Sal threw an arm around Joey as they went into the family room. "Best fish sandwiches in the county. Sound good to you, Joey?"

"Sure does."

They went out to the garage and piled into the car. Joey leaned down to pet Princess before getting in the back seat with Beth and Vita. Beth explained that they were going to meet Abby at 7:00 and that Joey would help out with Vita's next photoshoot.

Millie twisted around to smile at Vita. "Titania?"

Vita nodded. "I thought it would help me to get into the spirit of the role."

"We're using the woods behind Abby's house for the scenes," said Beth. "Dylan said he would come. He's Rob's brother. Dylan said he can arrange to get us a horse if we ever need it."

"A horse?" asked Vita.

"Or a cow or chicken. His friend Ernie lives on a farm."

When they turned onto the road that led to the fairgrounds, Joey saw Rufus Sharp walking along the highway, coming towards the town.

"Gosh! Does he walk out into the country too?"

"We saw him over in Hawthorn a few months ago," said Beth. "That's far for a walk. He always wears that long coat. You think he'd be hot."

"We once offered him a ride," said Vita, "but he just kept walking. Like he didn't even see us."

Joey looked back at the figure. "The guys at the park say he's dangerous. That he could snap at any moment."

Sal's eyes shot to Joey in the rearview mirror. "Rufus? Nah. He wouldn't hurt a fly. Keeps to himself, is all."

"What happened to him?"

"I think he was born that way," Millie said, putting on her sunglasses.

"The guys say he was injured in the war. Shellshock."

Sal gave a low grunt. "Rufus Sharp, in combat?"

Joey remembered the taunt he had hollered at Rufus the last time he was in Greenberry. The boys had dared him to yell, "Hey Otis! Where're you going?" and they ran away as if their lives depended on it. "They said his best friend died next to him in the war. Otis. And if you call him that name, he goes crazy."

Beth's head snapped over to Joey. "He's already crazy. But he's not mean. And he can talk normal when he wants to."

Millie turned around. "How do you know that?"

"It's true," said Vita. "I once asked him for directions."

"Directions! In town?"

Beth burst out laughing. "Like you could get lost. All you have to do is look around and you can see where to go."

"I wanted to talk to him. I asked him how to get to the square. And he told me. Perfectly clear. Then I said something about the weather or temperature, but he put the rag back in his mouth and kept walking." Vita turned to Joey. "I think he just lives in his own world."

Joey's old vision of Rufus had been as a sort of monster all the kids were afraid of. Now, he thought it was kind of sad. Rufus seemed all alone. But he was still scared of him.

Beth pointed her finger. "Oh look! There's the Ferris wheel. See it, Joey? And the grandstand?"

Joey leaned forward, his eyes bright with excitement.

"Look at the lines!" said Millie. "I think the whole county is here."

Up ahead to the right, Joey saw the fairgrounds and tents and rides. He could hear music and voices calling out through a loudspeaker.

They pulled up to one of the admission booths, paid, and were directed where to park in the large grassy lot. It was already filled with cars parked in long neat rows.

Joey noticed that Sal and Millie held hands as they all headed towards the fair. Up ahead lay a fun-filled land of lights and sounds, music and movement, rides, and food.

They made their way to the Elks tent and found seats at the end of one of the tables. Millie and Sal went to the counter and were greeted by some of Sal's fellow Elks. They placed their order and were soon walking back with drinks and fish sandwiches.

While they ate, several people stopped by to say hello, and Joey was introduced to everyone.

A girl in bell bottoms and a lacy halter top stopped by and tentatively approached Vita.

Beth waved at her. "Hi, Priscilla! We just got here. This is our friend, Joey. He's staying the summer with us."

"Nice to meet you, Joey. Hey, Vita."

"Hi, Priscilla."

Joey noticed that Vita didn't smile.

"I hear that you're going to try out for the play. For Titania?"

Vita gave an almost imperceptible lift of her shoulders.

"I'm sure you'll get whatever part you audition for."

"You never know what will happen." Vita took a sip of her soda.

"I'm here with Karen and Tina. Want to walk with us?"

"Thanks, but I'm going to meet Carla."

Priscilla watched Vita for a moment. "Well, see you around. Good luck with the audition."

Vita pressed her lips together in a smile as the girl left.

"You weren't very friendly." Beth leaned over to Joey. "They were best friends for a while. Priscilla moved to town last year. She's really popular. Everybody likes her." She looked at Joey's sandwich. "Are you about finished? It must be almost 7:00."

"Vita!" Carla called from a few tables over and snaked her way through the chairs and tables. She pulled up a chair next to Vita. "I've been here since the afternoon." She touched her face. "I think I got sunburned." Carla drummed her fingers on the table. "Hope you don't mind, but I decided against auditioning for the play."

Vita couldn't hide her disappointment. "Why? I thought you really wanted the role of Helena."

"It all takes up too much time. I don't have your discipline. I want my summer to be open."

"I feel the same way," said Beth. "Summer is too short as it is." She cranked her head to check her mom's watch.

83

"Ready, Joey?" They dumped their paper plates and cups into a trash can. "We're going to meet Abby."

Millie smiled and called after them. "Have fun! Back here at 10:00, okay, kids?"

Vita cleared a few more plates to make room for some neighbors who were just sitting down next to her parents. She noticed Vic watching her from one of the tables. She hoped he wouldn't say anything.

Carla nudged Vita. "Feel like walking around?"

"Sure. I want to see the exhibits."

"That's where David and Darlene are." Carla pulled Vita's arm and whispered. "Oh my gosh. There's Easton Smith."

"So?"

"So, he's staring at you! And no wonder. You look gorgeous in that dress. It really hugs your figure."

"I thought you said he was stuck on himself."

"He is, but who cares? He's so cute. Oh my gosh, he's coming this way."

Easton walked up with two of his friends. "Hey, Carla. Hello, Vita."

Vita glanced over at Vic and saw that he was watching her. She smiled at Easton and tossed her hair to one side.

Easton responded to her charms and was soon talking to her while his friends and Carla chatted. Vita laughed and smiled, and her gauzy purple dress came alive with her movements. Her hair and earrings and the gold threads in the fabric glinted in the lowering sun.

Easton said something that made her laugh, and she leaned her head back. He touched her arm. "Well, maybe another night." He walked backwards, with his eyes on Vita. "See you around."

Carla waved at the group of boys, while saying in a low voice to Vita, "Dang, you can turn it on when you want to. You do that at the audition and the role is yours."

They began walking in the other direction, towards the exhibits. "Did Easton ask you out?"

"Kind of."

Carla pulled Vita's arm. "You *didn't* turn him down, did you? I thought you said you and Vic broke up."

"We did."

"So what's stopping you?"

"Guys like Easton are only interested in themselves. He wants someone on his arm. Nothing more."

"Most girls would be only too happy to be on his arm. Let's get a lemonade. I'm parched."

❦

Joey, Beth, and Abby left the funhouse and were still laughing at how funny they looked in the mirrors. They walked around the entire fairgrounds and were now trying their luck at the ring toss and throwing darts at the balloons. Joey won two prizes and let Abby and Beth choose them.

Beth chose an Indian-style beaded bracelet and slipped it on her wrist. "Look. It matches my necklace."

Abby decided on a stuffed animal. "Oh, thank you, Joey!" She kissed the velvet puppy on the nose.

"That's the grandstand I told you about. That's where all the big stuff happens."

"Something different every night," said Abby. "The demolition derby, musical performances, pig wrestling, the horse show. And the beauty pageant, of course."

Joey almost asked, "Pigs wrestle?" but caught himself. He didn't want to sound like some city kid who didn't know anything. He had already made Abby laugh by asking her what 4-H meant, and again by admitting that he had never eaten a corndog.

He wished his friends back home could see him, walking around with two cool girls, in the middle of a county fair with carousel music, and laughter, and screams from the scary rides. The sun had set and now the fair was filled with little lights everywhere, turning it into a wonderland.

Joey saw a few of his friends from the park—some were walking with their families, some were with each other. Joey surprised himself by thinking that he was having more fun with girls. They had gone on all the rides for big kids—the Rockets and Octopus, the Scrambler, and the Ferris wheel. He had a moment of fear when Beth began to rock their carriage at the top and was glad when they began to descend.

"Let's get cotton candy!" cried Beth, running up to the booth and getting in line. "This is what I love about summer—cotton candy at the county fair."

Joey inhaled the sweet air surrounding the stand and smiled at the little kids in line. Their eyes grew big as the vendor made big cottony puffs as if by magic.

"My treat," said Beth. "I have money from working at the shop."

"Thanks, Beth." Abby saw the customer in front of them leaving with a large pink cotton candy. "I want pink."

"How about two pinks and a blue?" Beth said to the older man in an apron and cap. She dug in her pockets for cash.

Joey had money that his dad had given him, but he was going through it fast. Maybe he could get a job while he was here. So far, they had paid for their own tickets and food, but it would be nice to be able to say, "I'll treat."

Joey watched as the man took a white paper cone and rolled it around the metal pan, gathering the pale-colored wisps that formed along the sides. Then he handed Beth the airy creations.

Beth gave a pink cotton candy to Abby and the blue one to Joey. They stepped aside as she paid.

Abby tipped her head sideways to take a bite. "Mmm. Did you know my mom is three years older than my dad?"

"No. I didn't." He thought parents were usually the same age, or maybe the father would be a few years older.

"Uh huh. Mom says it's good for the woman to be a little older than the man. That way he can't boss her around." She pulled off a piece of pink cotton candy and offered it to Joey.

He opened his mouth and took in the sweetness, marveling at its immediate disappearance when it hit his tongue.

"Let me try yours," Abby said.

Joey pulled off some of the blue cotton candy and tucked it in her mouth. She leaned her head, savoring it. "I can't really taste a difference. It all tastes like summertime sweetness."

"Mine is like eating a pink cloud," said Beth. "Come on. Let's go look at the animals."

On their way, they passed Sal and Millie. Millie wore strands of shiny beads that Sal must have won for her at the ring toss. Joey noticed that they were still holding hands and smiling as they talked.

Beth led the way to the far side of the fairgrounds where the farm machinery and animals were located, along with demonstrations by the 4-H Club, the Boy Scouts and Girl Scouts' stands, and the exhibits for quilts, canning, and baked goods.

After wandering through different buildings and tents, they ended up at the art exhibit. They strolled through the photography shows. "Here's David's collection," Abby said with pride.

Joey stood before the pictures of the town, some photos in black and white, others in color. Something about these images captivated Joey. One photo showed the town square at dusk, with the streetlights making it feel kind of lonely. The library was shot from the bottom step, changing the way it would usually look. The county courthouse was taken in the rain, again changing it from all the other pictures he had seen of it, always with a cloudless blue sky. Everything was a little different, making you think about the places in a new way. He leaned his head and studied a photo of the train station.

"So, what do you think?"

An older girl stood next to Joey, watching him as he examined the photographs.

Joey's brow creased as he tried to give his impression. "These are different from the others. I like them. They're . . . interesting."

Abby walked up with a tall boy. "You remember David? I see you've already met Darlene."

Darlene looped her arm through David's. "He likes your work."

David smiled. "Hey, Joey. I think I met you a couple of years ago. Abby said you want to help with our shoots."

"Yeah. If I'm not in the way."

"We can use the help." David listed several ways Joey might be able to assist.

They all left the building and strolled over to one of the animal tents. David looked through his camera and took a few shots.

Beth and Abby talked with Darlene about the animals and petted the lambs. But Joey watched David, fascinated, as he focused the lens and tried different angles.

David saw that he was intrigued. "You ever take pictures?"

"With my mom's camera." Joey admired the one around David's neck. "That looks a lot more complicated. Is it hard to use?"

"Not once you get the hang of it. First you find something interesting. Then you frame it." He held up his hands and made a square. "See what you have." He raised the camera, studied the subject, adjusted the lens, and clicked. "Course you can't see the results until the darkroom. But sometimes you just know when you get something good. You get a feeling."

David lifted the camera from around his neck and handed it to Joey. "Go ahead, take a look."

Joey took the camera, surprised by its weight, and held it up to his eye. He panned it around.

"Now, find something specific. Focus on the cow."

Joey slowly found the image. He pointed the lens at the cow and saw big soft eyes blinking back at him. He lowered the camera, tilted his head at the cow, seeing it anew, and focused the lens again. The cow was looking right at him, saying something even, unspoken. Joey smiled up at David, amazed that he was seeing something different when the camera was focused on it.

David laughed. "I know that look. Go ahead, take a shot."

Joey shook his head. "I don't want to waste your film. I don't really know what I'm doing."

"Go ahead. Let's see what you find."

Joey hesitated. He lifted the camera, found the image again, and clicked. "I think I moved."

"That's okay. That's how you learn."

Darlene walked over. "Is David talking your ear off about taking pictures? He can't help himself."

"He was teaching me how to look."

David grinned at the explanation. "I think we got a budding photographer here."

They exited the tent and Beth asked if anyone knew what time it was.

David glanced at his watch. "It's 10:15."

"Oh my gosh!" cried Beth. "We have to go." Before running off, they made quick plans about going to the fair the next day.

"Bye, Joey!" Abby called after them. "See you tomorrow."

They hurried back to the beer tent and found the others. Sal and Millie were laughing with friends and didn't notice that they were late. Vita rested her chin in her hand, listening to Anne and Mark.

Anne waved them over. "Look what Mark won for me! She held up a small teddy bear with a red heart on its chest."

"Oh, that's so cute!" cried Beth. "Joey won a stuffed puppy for Abby. And this bracelet for me. Nice, huh?" She sat down next to her parents and rested her head on her mom's shoulder. Millie reached up with one hand and held her, while laughing at Sal's story.

Now that Joey was sitting, he was aware of how tired he was. He gazed at Sal and Millie, leaning into each other, relaxed and happy. Sal had his arm around her waist, kind of loose, like that's where he always kept it. With Beth on her other side, Millie looked surrounded by love.

Joey couldn't help but compare them to his parents. What was missing in them was affection and happiness. He used to tell himself that the problem with his parents was that the war came between them. That's what his mom once said. But Uncle Sal had also been in a war. Joey looked around. Probably every man in the beer tent had been in a war. So why weren't his parents happy?

He knew the truth. It was his fault. But it was easier to say it was a war or something else, than to blame a kid.

Vita had been watching Joey and placed her hand on his arm. "What are you thinking about?"

"Nothing."

"Are you happy you're here?"

Joey nodded and smiled. "Real happy."

"Good," she said, squeezing his arm. "Me too."

CHAPTER 8

There were several parks in town and Joey knew them all. The closest one to the Vitale's house was the Jack and Jill, four blocks away. Joey and Beth rode their bikes there in the morning and Joey found it exactly as he remembered.

They climbed the monkey bars and competed on the overhead bars pulling themselves one hand over the other, and then got on the swings to see how high they could go. Across from them, five or six kids were going up and down the tall slide and there was a smaller slide where a mother helped her little girl to go down.

Joey and Beth strolled around the picnic tables and looked at the crafts that were being made. A few teens, employed by the park department, were there to give instructions. Several kids were making potholders, selecting colorful loops of stretchy fabric from a large plastic bag and then weaving them on small metal looms.

Others were making mosaic coasters in thin metal discs, arranging tiny oval tiles inside and then smearing plaster of Paris over them and wiping it off. Joey decided that before he left at the end of summer, he would come back and make a set of coasters for his mom and dad.

Older kids were braiding long lariats with a clip at the end for keys, and some of the real little kids were making items out of Popsicle sticks and pipe cleaners. Almost everything cost a nickel or a dime and most kids had that.

Joey and Beth bought snow-cones at the concession stand and sat on the top seat of the wooden bleachers behind the wire batting fence. A Little League baseball team was practicing hitting balls and catching them. They cheered the kids on whenever any of them got a hit or made a good catch. When one ball was popped over the wire fence, Joey ran to get it and threw it back over.

Joey looked all around him while he ate the snow-cone. Kids at the concession stand were getting candy bars, hots dogs, sodas, and bags of popcorn. He could hear the squeak of the swings, the laughter and shouts of kids playing on the merry-go-round, the rustle of tree leaves high above him blowing in the summer breeze. It was a hot day, but the shade of the trees and the snow-cone made it feel just right. This was exactly how summer should be.

"I wish I could live here," he said, looking up at the sunlight flickering through the green leaves. "I love this town."

"Grass is always greener, Joey," Beth said with a nudge. "But it is nice here."

When the town's noontime whistle sounded, they headed for home. Sal had just arrived and was seated at the table, sampling the vegetables and dip while he related his morning.

Anne helped Millie arrange lunchmeat sandwiches on a plate and Vita poured tomato soup into bowls. Joey was hungry as usual. Playing hard and eating good food were a big part of summer in Greenberry.

Beth talked to Joey about the fair, and Vita and Anne discussed the Titania costume.

"Are you all going to the fair tonight?" asked Millie.

Anne shook her head. "I picked up the dinner shift, since Mark has to work."

"We can catch a ride with David and Darlene," said Beth. "He's not working tonight so it won't get too late."

"I want you home by 10:00," said Millie.

"Are you coming with us, Vita?" Beth asked.

"Not tonight. I have to work on my costume."

When they finished their meal, Sal scooted his chair back. "Okay, Joey, let's you and me go see what needs picking in the garden."

Joey downed the last of his milk, wiped his mouth with the back of his hand, and jumped up to help Sal.

"I could use a few things for a dinner salad," said Millie, bringing dishes to the sink. She gave Sal the blue enamel colander and a pair of scissors for the leaf lettuce.

Joey followed Sal in between the rows of vegetables as he inspected the various plants. Grass clippings from a recent mowing covered the soil, preventing weeds and making each step soft and silent.

Sal bent over and picked a few weeds among the lettuce. "Go ahead—you know what to do. A couple of tomatoes, firm and red. Two or three cucumbers."

Joey began searching for ripe tomatoes and found two perfect ones. He held out his shirt and placed them there.

Sal was on his knees cutting bright green lettuce leaves and setting them in the colander. "Hey, Joey! You hear the radishes growing?" He cocked his ear and held up a finger.

Joey had expected to be teased about that and grinned.

Sal gave a long laugh at the memory. "You got down on your belly and put your ear by the radishes. Your eyes got as big as saucers!"

"I really thought I heard them. Making whispering sounds as they grew. I thought the whole garden was magical."

"Well, there you were right." Sal pulled a few slender carrots from the earth, rubbed the dirt off, and set them next to the lettuce. "It *is* magical."

Joey was on guard against another setup, but he saw that Sal was serious. "That's what my old man taught me. He grew up in Italy, you know. Lots of sun. Said everything grew in abundance there." Sal picked a few weeds and tossed them behind him on the grass. "Taught me how to plant seeds and nourish them, water the plants as needed." He looked out over the garden. "To give thanks when you harvested the ripened crop.

"And he told me to listen to the radishes growing. He got *me* on that one, too." Sal laughed silently at the memory and added three green onions to the pile of vegetables. "Had a strong accent. Sometimes I didn't know what he meant and he'd get mad. One time he hollered at me. 'Fetch me the rock.' I looked all over the place for a rock. 'The rock, the rock!' he said, pointing harder. Then he went and got the rake himself."

Joey smiled at the story and wondered if Sal still missed his dad. He knew that he had died when Sal was just a boy. It felt good to be with Sal. He reminded Joey of his own dad. Kind of quiet. Gentle. Joey knelt down by the cucumbers, chose three, and added them to the tomatoes.

Sal inspected a pepper, and decided against it. "Needs another day." He added Joey's tomatoes and cucumbers to the colander. "That's more than enough for dinner. Let's go inside."

He draped his arm around Joey's shoulder as they walked up the sidewalk. Joey wondered if his dad would be happier if they had a garden. Something they could all do together. But they lived in an apartment in Chicago. Maybe someday.

Sal handed the colander to Millie and kissed her goodbye before returning to work.

"Lovely!" she said, setting it in the sink. She began rinsing the vegetables. "Thank you, Joey. You always did have a knack for picking perfect vegetables." She placed them on a dish towel to dry.

Joey looked over at the girls. They were now grouped around the table with fabric, a sewing basket, scissors, and rolls of trimming. When they were all together like that, he thought of them as magic princesses or fairies out of a storybook. Vita wore a long white dress, Anne a navy skirt and a pale blue top. Beth had on cut-offs and an orangey t-shirt.

Anne was cutting a shimmery olive-green piece of fabric, checking it against the length of a skirt next to her. Beth was searching for matching green thread in the basket, and Vita was sewing a thin garland of leaves and flowers to a piece of the green fabric.

Joey poured himself a glass of iced tea and sat at the table to watch them work. He suddenly sat up. "Am I in the way?"

All three sisters looked up and laughed. "Of course not!" said Anne.

"What are you talking about?" asked Beth. "You're one of us now."

Vita smiled over at him. "All for one . . ."

"And one for all," he finished.

Vita held up the item she was sewing. "So, this is 'the bodice,' as we call it. And this," she said, lifting the skirt draped over the chair, is 'the skirt.' My core pieces. Anne made them." Vita bunched up the pale gold fabric of the skirt. "We call this color *moonbeam*. I use them for different roles, adding fabric and trim to make them look different. We're going to add this mossy green fabric for the *Midsummer Night*'s shoot."

Joey smiled at the mention of photography. "David let me take a few pictures at the fair. He showed me how to get different results with the same image. He said he could use my help with the photoshoots."

"Sounds like you'll be an official member of the club." Vita spread the bodice in front of her and inspected it.

"Sometimes it's a lot of waiting," said Beth, "getting the lighting just right, reshooting over and over. David's a perfectionist."

"But the results are amazing," said Vita.

Millie dried her hands. "Let's show Joey your portfolio, Vita." She went to the living room and came back with an album. She sat next to Joey and opened it.

"There's not much to see, yet," Vita said.

"Yes, there is. Everything you've ever done." Anne leaned over to see the album.

Joey studied the various photographs. Some were kind of grainy, but others were clear. There were group shots, others were close-ups of Vita.

Beth glanced over every time Joey turned a page. "The good ones were taken by David. That one was taken by Darlene. She's pretty good, too."

"I wish I had more," said Vita. "These don't show much range. David thinks we can get in several more shoots before he has to leave for school."

Beth placed her hand on her chest, in mock self-importance. "*I'm* the location scout, Joey. I have a couple of places in mind that I want you guys to check out today."

Joey was engrossed in the photographs. Some of them didn't even look like Vita, like the witch picture. Some of them were exceptionally beautiful. He looked over at her, as if reconciling the girl with the images.

Millie leaned back in the chair. "Too bad there aren't better pictures of the French class skit. Just these two, taken from a distance and kind of fuzzy. Perhaps you could restage the scene."

Vita tied a knot and cut the thread. "I didn't have very many lines. It wouldn't be worth the effort."

"She was magnificent," Anne said. She mimed holding her heart and gazing up at the moon, then wiping a tear. "It was so real. I swear I saw an actual tear. That's why Vita will be successful. She makes you feel what the character is feeling." She turned to Vita. "I bet Vic and Priscilla would love to recreate the scene! Why don't you ask—"

"I told you, Vic and I split up."

Anne waved away the words. "Lovers' quarrel. You should ask them, anyway." She held up the pieces of green fabric. "All ready to be attached."

Vita stood and held up the bodice. "What do you think? More leaves and flowers?"

Anne tipped her head one way and then the other. "I think it's just right." She lifted the spool of floral garland. "You could use some of this for your hair. To suggest— woodland romance, right?"

"Yes. Titania's bower of mismatched, disastrous love. A comedy."

Joey thought Vita sounded sarcastic. He watched her fold up the bodice, and return the sewing supplies to the basket.

"I'll finish the skirt tonight." Vita glanced at the clock. "Let's go look at those sites, Beth."

"What are they for?" Anne asked, adding her supplies to the basket.

"David wants to do a Victorian ghost shot—you know, with the transparent figures," explained Beth. "I thought the Ashgrove mansion would be perfect. And I might have found a balcony for the Juliet scene." She jumped to her feet. "Come on, Joey. Now that you're part of the club, we'll need your opinion. Coming with us, Anne?"

"Sure. I don't have to be at work until 5:00." She looped her arms around her mom. "Need help with anything before we leave?"

Millie closed the album. "No, no. I have a few errands to run. You kids show Joey the mansion. Well, it's really just an old Victorian home. But it is lovely. In a run-down sort of way."

The girls and Joey went to the back yard to get their bicycles.

"Did we ever take you there, Joey?" asked Anne.

He searched his memory. "I don't think so."

"It's all boarded up now," said Vita. "Kind of haunted looking. But you can still see how beautiful it once was."

Joey felt a surge of happiness. It was a hot, sunny afternoon, with a big blue sky and cottony white clouds high up in the sky. And he was riding bikes with the three *Petticoat Junction* sisters. They needed his help. Kind of like being on a quest or adventure.

The perfection of that day rooted in his mind. Like a scene moving in slow motion, all of them riding bikes, their long hair flying, blue and white skirts fluttering. Beth putting her feet up on the handlebars and coasting. There was no place else he'd rather be.

"The Three Musketeers and D'Artagnan," Vita cried out. "All together again!"

Anne laughed as she struggled to overtake them. Beth, her long black hair whipping around her face, was determined not to let her.

They rode over the train tracks and turned onto a road at the edge of town. They slowed as they neared the old Victorian mansion. It was set among a grove of trees, and behind it stretched fields of green corn. There were two other houses down the road.

They hopped off their bikes and walked along the side of the house. It was an elegant, but weathered, two-story house with a square tower at the top and a porch that wrapped around two sides. The windows on the first floor had boards nailed over them, and up close, Joey could see the thinning white paint. Tall trees stood all around it, rustling in the summer breeze.

"Isn't it beautiful?" asked Vita.

Anne shielded her eyes and gazed at it. "Dad said it was built in the 1880s by a banking family."

"We came here a long time ago with Dad," said Beth. "He had to inspect a broken pipe and he told us what he knew about the house."

"It's been empty for a long time." Vita walked her bike to the side of the house and leaned it against the porch. Joey did the same. He was eager to explore.

"The last person lived here about twenty years ago," said Beth. "An old lady. After she moved out some robbers broke in and stole things. So they boarded it up." She and Anne parked their bikes beneath the trees.

They walked around to the back of the house. Vita strolled around, assessing the house and grounds for the ghost shoot setting. "It's perfect, Beth. We'll tell David that the side and back will give him a lot of options."

"Oh, no," said Anne. She pointed to a sign: NO TRESSPASSING. "I think that's new."

"No one will mind," said Beth. "As long as we stay away from the house. We'll just use it as a backdrop."

"Kind of sad," said Vita. "Something so beautiful, now left forgotten. I can imagine how they would have strolled around the grounds, sitting under the shade trees in summer."

"Hot as blazes in all those Victorian clothes they had to wear," added Beth.

"I love it out here." Vita took a deep breath. "It smells like dried grasses and wild roses." She bent over a cluster of small pink roses growing alongside an old water pump. "I bet they used to pick them and make posies for their dresses." She plucked a single rose and held it against her white eyelet dress, then tucked it behind her ear. She chose two more for Anne and Beth and they did the same.

Anne pointed out a separate small wooden structure to Joey. "That's the smokehouse. I think they did some of the heavy cooking there." She turned around and faced the back porch. "And over there, where Beth is now snooping around, is the kitchen. You can see where the ice was delivered."

Beth was checking the windows. "You guys! Look!"

"What is it?" asked Anne, walking to the porch.

"The window's been opened. I think someone got inside." She raised the sash higher and peeked under the crisscrossed boards. "It's wide enough to get through." Her eyes smiled with the invitation to adventure.

"I don't know, Beth," said Vita, climbing the porch steps.

"What if it's against the law?" asked Anne. "That's probably why they put that sign up." But she too, was trying to peek through the window.

Joey thought of Rufus Sharp. "What if whoever broke in is still in there?"

"Nah," said Beth, putting one leg through the window. "Probably just kids on a dare." She disappeared into the kitchen.

"Beth!" Anne cried and turned to Vita.

They looked around, making sure no one was watching them. Then, one by one, they followed Beth inside.

It took a moment for their eyes to adjust to the dimness. They stood still and carefully listened for any sounds. Then they walked through the kitchen and into the large hallway. It was musty and dark, with light filtering in through the upper part of the tall windows and through the stained-glass windows at the landing of the staircase.

"This is so cool!" said Beth. "It's like stepping back in time. Look how high the ceilings are."

They tentatively walked from room to room, looking at the dust-covered interior.

"I remember this parlor from when Dad took us," said Anne. "It looks the same."

Vita touched the carved arched doorway to the foyer. "It's all so beautiful. Wondrous! Isn't it?"

"Wondrous," Beth said mockingly. "Let's go upstairs. She was already climbing the first flight of wide carpeted steps that led to the landing.

Joey and Vita followed. Anne had walked into the parlor and cried out, "Wait for me!"

They inspected all the upstairs rooms, commenting on the old furniture, the carpeting and drapes, the tiled fireplaces, and the carved panels in the wainscoting.

"It's all so elegant," said Anne.

Joey was thrilled at the adventure. It was like being in a haunted house. He would never do something like this in Chicago. Wait until he told the guys back home.

"It's completely abandoned," said Beth. "Just a bunch of old furniture and dust everywhere." She walked over to another flight of steps leading to the attic rooms. "I think up there is where the servants stayed."

Feeling more at ease now, they followed her up the narrower flight of stairs. The ceilings of the rooms sloped under the eaves.

"Such small bedrooms," said Vita. "And a nursery—look. A little cradle. How sweet."

Joey walked over and lightly rocked it.

"Whew, it's hot!" said Beth, fanning her face. "How could they have stood it in the summer?"

"They probably stayed outdoors a lot," suggested Anne. "I would have."

Beth pushed open a narrow door that revealed steep twisting stairs. "I bet this leads to the tower." She craned her neck. "It does!"

"We never came to this floor with Dad." Anne looked up as Beth climbed the stairs. "They're so steep."

They climbed the creaking steps, wiping the sweat from their faces.

"It's so hot up here," said Vita, lifting her hair off her neck.

They took turns peering out the small windows.

"But worth the climb. Look how far you can see!" said Anne. "I can imagine being up here to watch my husband coming home from the fields. It's so romantic, isn't it?" She moved aside for Vita to see.

Vita nodded, gazing out the back window. "Having dinner, then strolling through the grove at dusk. Everyone dressed in summer white. I can almost see it. And the sun setting over the fields."

Joey stood near the front window. "Wow! You can see so far!" He could see part of the town, the steeples and water tower. He framed his hands around the view. He moved to a different window and made another frame of the treetops and fields, amazed once again at how a focused view changed what he was seeing.

Beth wound her hair and knotted it on the top of her head. "Too hot. I'm going back down." She stopped suddenly and listened. "What was that?" Her eyes grew wide, and she moved quickly down the steep stairs.

Joey imagined Rufus Sharp trudging up the main stairs.

"What?" cried Anne, grabbing Vita's arm. "I'm getting out of here." She and Vita hurried behind Beth.

Joey peered above him, listening to the scratching sound. A squirrel poked its head through a small hole. "It's just—"

Anne let out a scream when she heard the noise and bumped into Beth who also screamed, startling Vita. Terrified, but laughing all the same, they took off down the stairs.

"Joey! Run! This is creepy!"

Joey ran behind them, laughing, trying to tell them about the squirrel. "It's just a—"

"Hurry! Go!"

They ran down the main stairs and piled into the kitchen. They kept looking behind them as they crowded around the window.

Beth bumped her head in her hurry to get out. "Ow! Don't push!"

They poured out of the window, scrambled for their bikes, and rode away.

They looked back at the boarded-up house, laughing. "What *was* that?"

"Do you think someone was in there? A tramp? A ghost?"

"Maybe the old lady still lives there."

"It was just a squirrel!" Joey said, pedaling fast to keep up with them.

"No squirrel could make that much noise."

"It was . . . I saw it! There was a hole in the roof."

Anne glanced back. "I think that place is haunted."

They looked at each other and burst out laughing anew at how afraid they were. Soon they were howling.

"I was terrified! My heart's still pounding," said Anne, and gave a loud laugh.

"What a bunch of scaredy cats we are!" Beth threw her head back in laughter.

"Squirrel or not," said Vita, "I'm glad you were with us, Joey."

"Me too!" said Anne.

"Me three," added Beth, and she let out a whoop as she took the lead.

Joey smiled widely. He might be good at quests and adventures after all.

They coasted back down the street by the train tracks. Joey held his arms out, thinking he was having the most fun he'd ever had. He was laughing just to be laughing.

"Come on, we still have one more site to check out," said Beth.

"You guys go ahead," said Anne. "I have to get ready for work."

They parted ways at the corner near the house and hollered goodbye to Anne.

"So where's this balcony, Beth?" asked Vita. "I can't think of a single one in town."

"Well, it's not exactly a balcony. It's height we need. I'll show you."

She rode her bike into the schoolyard. Joey remembered the old brick schoolhouse with its arched front door and peaked turrets. But he didn't remember any balconies.

"Around the back," Beth called over her shoulder.

They followed her to where she had stopped. She looked up at the back of the schoolhouse. "Well?"

"The fire escape?" asked Vita, disappointed. "Juliet? On a fire escape?"

Beth hopped off her bike. "Use your imagination! We can use a cloth as a backdrop. And make something to cover the railings. But the angle is right." She started to climb the stairs.

Vita remained skeptical, trying to envision the shoot. "I don't know." She looked at the brick background and frowned. "It would have to be a real tight shot. But then why be here at all?"

"Come on, Joey," cried Beth. "Nice view at the top. And it's not as hot as the mansion." She ran up the fire escape, sending a slight vibration through the slender structure. She passed the first and second floor landings, not stopping until she reached the top—a small platform outside the third-floor classroom. She put her hands on her hips as if she had just climbed a high mountain.

Joey followed her up. He looked back at Vita and saw that she hesitated.

"Come on!" cried Beth.

"Two high places in one day? Thanks, Beth." Vita carefully mounted the slatted metal stairs.

"You climb to the roof all the time. This is higher but at least there's something to hold on to."

Joey went back down and met Vita on the first landing. "Want to take my hand?"

Vita laughed away his suggestion. "No. Thanks, Joey. It's just . . . I can see the ground through the stairs. That's what does it. When I'm on the roof I'm looking out. Until it's time to get down. That's the part that always bothers me."

"So maybe look up."

Vita raised her head and smiled. "Yes. That's better."

She slowly followed Joey up the thin silver slats of the stairs.

When they reached the top, Joey was surprised to see that Vita was pale. Sweat glistened above her lips and on her forehead, but she was trying to be brave.

"It *is* exhilarating at the top." Vita filled her eyes with the sky, the clouds, the summer day. "I love being so high up." She took a deep breath and looked out over the treetops.

Joey noticed that she gripped the rail with both hands.

"And it's perfectly safe." Beth jumped up and down to demonstrate the soundness of the structure. The entire fire escape shuddered.

"Stop it, Beth!" Vita looked down and saw the ground shift through the slats. Overcome with dizziness, she dropped to the top step and squeezed her eyes shut.

"Sorry, Vita. I didn't think it would bother you. I thought you had gotten over it, climbing to the roof all summer."

"So did I," Vita said in a whisper.

Joey sat down next to her. "Are you all right?"

Vita nodded, but the color was gone from her face.

Beth climbed over between them so that she was a few steps below. "Okay. This was a dumb idea. Forget about it. Maybe you don't even need a balcony scene."

"Maybe not." Vita's chest rose and fell. She tried to take slow breaths to calm her breathing. She looked straight ahead.

"Let's get back down on the ground," said Beth. "You'll feel better."

"Just . . . just give me a minute."

Joey saw that she was terrified. Not like the fun scared at the mansion.

Beth stroked Vita's hair. "Come on, we'll do it like we did the escalator in St. Louis. Joey and I will walk in front of you, and you'll look at our heads. Not down."

Vita shakily got to her feet. "Okay." She placed one hand on Joey's shoulder and the other on the railing.

They went down one step at a time, pausing now and then while Vita took a deep breath, until they reached the bottom.

When she finally stepped on solid ground, Vita sat on the raised concrete slab at the base. "I don't know why that happened."

"It *is* kind of an airy fire escape. I was a little scared too," said Joey.

Vita smiled at him. "You're just trying to make me feel better." Her eyes showed bewilderment and she took a few more calming breaths before standing. "Let's go."

They got their bikes and walked them through the schoolyard.

"I'm really sorry, Vi."

"It's not your fault, Beth." Vita's pale brow was creased in worry. "Can you image if I ever got the role of Juliet and panicked on the balcony? I *have* to get over this!"

"That would never happen," said Beth. "This just took you by surprise. Especially with me jumping on it like a nutcase."

"I don't know why I'm so afraid of heights. I have dreams where I'm on a rocky mountain climbing higher and higher. And then I look down and freeze with fear, wondering how I'll ever get back down."

Joey saw that a little color had come back to her cheeks. "Were you always scared of high places?"

"Yes. But not like this."

"It was that damned high dive," said Beth. "That's what did it. Ever since, she's been terrified of heights. Before, it was just normal scared."

Joey couldn't remember a high dive in the town. "Where?"

Vita shut her eyes. "I still hate to think about it. I was never more afraid in my entire life."

"Over in Hawthorn," Beth explained. "There's a big lake there. A few summers ago, Mom drove us over to go swimming and everyone was jumping off the newly added high dive. So Vita lined up with us and climbed the ladder to the top. It was so crowded. Like a trail of ants going up the ladder. Everyone wanted to jump off—some even dove!"

"I thought it would be wonderful to be so high up," said Vita. "To see the world spread before me. I was fine climbing the ladder. I was excited to reach the top."

Vita halted and stared straight ahead, seeing it again. "But when I stood at the top, all alone, I froze. I saw how high up I was, and I . . . I couldn't move. I wanted to climb back down, but everyone was yelling at me to go. And the more they yelled, the more afraid I got."

"That bully Todd Taylor was next in line, right behind her, yelling, 'Go on, chicken, jump! You're holding us up!' I wanted to smack him. I remember how you inched your way out there, gripping the side rails." Beth turned to Joey. "But for the last part, there is no railing. Just the diving board."

Vita's face filled with dread as she remembered. "I made myself go out to the end. Baby steps. I lowered my eyes and saw the black water below. And then I just . . . stepped off. I really thought I was falling to my death."

"Mom was so mad about it when we told her. Remember? She wanted to beat the living daylights out of Todd and the lifeguard and everybody. She never let us go there again."

Joey looked at Vita. "I would have been scared too."

They left the schoolyard and walked down Oak Street."

"What a day!" Vita said, determined to change the tone. "I'll be happy to be back working on my costume. Sitting in a chair."

"And we'll be happy to be at the fair tonight, right Joey? Rides, corndogs, maybe the funhouse again? Hey, there's Hogie. Want to stop?"

Hogie was out in his garage with loud music blaring. His back was to them as he sorted pieces of wood.

Vita squinted and watched his movements. "No. I know his moods. Today is not a good one."

"I want to cool off with a shower anyway," said Beth. "Before the fair!" She got on her bike and rode off.

"You can go ahead, Joey. I feel like walking."

"So do I." Joey continued to walk alongside her. "Hogie said sometimes he's not up for visitors."

"That's true. Especially me."

"I thought you guys were good friends."

"We still are." Vita glanced back at Hogie's house. "We used to get along better. I mean, before he went away. We used to go to his house all the time. That was back when his mom lived there. After his dad died, she moved to a nearby town and left the house to Hogie. Mom said it was because he was going to marry Laura. But then he came back, and . . . changed his mind."

She turned to Joey. "Did you ever meet Laura?"

He tilted his head, trying to remember his past visits. "I don't think so."

"She kind of reminds me of Aunt Nellie . . . a hippie version. She's smart and confident and knows everything about music. She can play the piano and the flute. And she's beautiful.

"But most of all, she's kind. To everybody. She volunteers at the summer camp teaching kids about music. She helps her neighbors and does the grocery shopping for one of them. She takes in stray cats and finds homes for them. She brought one to Hogie not long ago. Laura lives in an old Victorian house she fixed up. The front porch is like a magical garden."

"You mean . . . they're not getting married?"

"Laura still wants to, but Hogie says no. They fight about it. He's angry a lot of the time. Can't blame him.

Laura comes into the plant shop now and then. I think mostly to ask about him."

Joey looked over to Vita. "Why don't you get along with him?"

"I do, but he's still mad at me right now. He says I stick my nose in where it's not wanted."

"Do you?"

"No! Well, sometimes. Last week, I saw Laura outside his door. He wouldn't let her in. I had never seen her cry before. After she left, I went and pounded on his door. When he finally opened it, I said, 'Why do you have to be so mean?' He was furious. He said, 'You don't know what mean is, little girl! Stay out of my life!' And he slammed the door. So I've been keeping my distance lately."

"He told me to stop by sometimes."

"That's good, Joey. Maybe he'll get along better with you. Just don't mention Laura. And whatever you do, don't feel sorry for him. That really sets him off. His friend Al told me pity is the one thing that will take him down."

"I'll be careful."

Vita was silent for a while. "Hogie and I will always be friends. No matter what. He says we're fellow misfits." She remembered their conversation on Memorial Day, not long after she broke up with Vic. She had been out walking and saw Hogie working. She went into the garage and folded her arms, watching him work.

"What are you doing here?" Hogie had asked her. "Why aren't you at the parade?"

"I don't like parades," she answered, unable to shake her sullen frame of mind.

"Why not?"

She had shrugged and looked away.

"A misfit, that's what you are. Welcome to the club." He was painting a birdhouse and set his brush down. "How you going to make it in this world?"

"I already told you—I'm going to be an actress. That's how."

"A damn good plan," he said, chuckling.

"I am!"

"I don't doubt it for a moment."

Was he mocking her? Had he picked up on the shift in her? She tried to ignore it, but she felt different, less confident. Was it because of the breakup with Vic? Or was she starting to doubt herself?

Vita let out a deep sigh. "I miss the way things used to be with Hogie. He always encouraged us when we were little. He would never let me give up on anything—riding a bike or roller skating. 'Don't cry. Get up and try again,' he'd say."

"Yeah, that's how I remember him. One time when I was here, he showed me how to hammer a nail. I felt really important. He was building a doghouse."

"I remember that doghouse," Vita said with a smile. "He built it for his mom, and he let us paint it. He gave us each paint brushes and showed us how to avoid drips. Beth set her brush down on the grass and got grass clippings in the paint."

"Did he get mad?"

"Not at all. He said it added a nice touch."

Joey laughed at the idea.

"Hogie was always there, part of our growing up. Like a big brother."

Vita turned to Joey and smiled. "And you're like my little brother. With a sister on either side? I'd say I'm pretty lucky."

CHAPTER 9

Joey rode his bike around the neighborhood in the afternoon, stopping at the Lone Tower Park to see if any of the guys were playing ball. Only Eddie and Wiley were there, sitting on swings. Joey sat with them, and Eddie talked about the fair and how he was going again that night with his family.

Out on the street they saw Rufus Sharp walking. He cut into the park and began to cross the grassy lot.

Eddie watched him and shook his head. "Never stops walking. Goes from one end of town to the other. Over and over."

"Crazy as a loon," Wiley said. "That's what my dad says. The war really did a number on him."

Joey was skeptical but couldn't be sure. "What war was he in?"

"He was in a couple, I think. But it's the one where his friend Otis was killed that made him like this. A grenade exploded right by them and . . . well, it wasn't pretty."

Eddie began circling in his swing, twisting the chains. "My mom said he was in a car accident. A long time ago. Some of the guys say he keeps a knife strapped to his leg." He stopped twisting and spun around.

Joey considered this explanation. "Mrs. Vitale said he was probably born that way. And Mr. Vitale said Rufus wouldn't hurt a fly."

Wiley scoffed. "That's because they don't know. They weren't there when that kid from Hawthorn or some-where called him Otis, and Rufus attacked him. Grabbed him around the neck. It took ten grown men to pull him off." Wiley wagged his head. "Superhuman strength when he snaps."

"What kid was that?" asked Eddie.

"I think his name was Pete. He's never come back to our town. He knows Rufus is just waiting to get him again."

Joey wondered if Rufus remembered that four years ago, he had called him Otis. Was he waiting to get his hands around *his* neck? What if there weren't ten grown men around if he attacked him? Or was Wiley full of it? Rufus appeared to be locked in his own world, but it could be a pretense.

Eddie pushed off and began to pump his legs, leaning back in the swing to gain momentum. When he got as high as he could go, he yelled out, "Weee-hee! I can touch the sky with my feet!"

Joey stood up to go. Eddie was a nice kid, but he was only ten. And Wiley? He never had a single good thing to say about anything.

"See you guys later," Joey said, riding off.

He kept thinking about the fair last night and how grown up he had felt with Beth and Abby and later with David and Darlene. Especially when David let him take several photographs. As soon as the roll was finished, David was going to develop it and show him the results. Joey thought it was probably the most grownup thing he had ever done. That, and riding the train by himself.

He rode around the town square and decided to stop by the library. It was Millie's day to volunteer there. He picked up speed and coasted up to the library. He parked his bike under a shade tree.

Millie was at the front desk, taking an armload of books that a woman had just dropped off. She stacked them on a cart and smiled when she saw Joey.

"Well, hello, Joey! What a nice surprise. Vita's here, too."

"She is?" He glanced around for her.

"She just got off work. She's in the drama section, of course."

An idea popped into Joey's mind. "Do you think there are any books on photography for kids? How to take good pictures?"

"I'm sure there's something. Let's go see what we can find. That would be in the arts aisle, where Vita is."

Vita held two books in the crook of her arm. "Joey! What are you doing here?"

"He's come to learn about photography." Millie pointed to three low shelves opposite where Vita stood.

"That's a great idea, Joey." Vita smiled to see him so eager.

Milly ran her finger over a few books. "Take a look at this section. I think you'll find something. Do you know the work of Ansel Adams and Alfred Stieglitz? You might as well check out one or two of these larger books. They're full of amazing photographs. You can learn a lot just by looking."

Joey kneeled down to the lower shelves and began to browse through several books.

Millie pulled out another one on the basics of photography and showed it to Joey. "Why don't you practice with my camera? You could try out some of these ideas."

Joey's eyes grew wide. "Could I? Thanks!"

"I dropped it off at the camera store over in Hawthorn. The film jams now and then. I'll call them today to see when I can pick it up." Millie took the books in Vita's arms. "I'll put those on the counter for you."

Joey carried several books to a nearby table to browse through while Vita selected her plays. He soon became engrossed in the images. Mountains and streams, people and animals, sometimes just clouds or water. He paid attention to light and shadow and distance. He saw that some photographs seemed to be telling a story, and he tried to figure out what—

"Joey!" said Vita with a laugh. "I called your name three times."

Joey looked up. "You did?"

"You're hooked, aren't you? Why don't you choose three or four for now? We can always come back for more."

Vita and Joey checked out the books and placed them in Vita's bicycle basket. They walked their bikes, talking all the way home about the upcoming scenes they were going to shoot.

Vita told Joey how David always talked about the center of the photograph, and contrasts, and horizontal and vertical lines versus perpendicular. Things Joey had never thought about.

"David will be happy to teach you stuff. And you can start taking some pictures on your own. You can practice on us."

"I can't wait to start." Joey already had several shots in mind that he wanted to capture. Certain trees that had caught his attention, an old fence outside of town. The swings at the playground when they were empty. It kind of felt like exploring.

They cut through the alleyway and rode into the back yard. They saw Anne and Mark stretched out on a blanket under the ash tree near the flower garden. They brought their books inside and went back out to join the others.

Beth was watering the flowers with the hose, making an arc of glittering water in the sun. "Where were you guys?" she hollered.

Mark lay on his side, listening to Anne read. She lay on her front, propped up on her elbows with her legs bent, feet skyward lightly rubbing one another. Her pale skirt fell about her like a small blue lake. Mark absentmindedly twisted her long blonde hair in his hand, seeing the images in the story as she read.

When Joey and Vita joined them, Mark sat up. Anne rolled on her side and showed them the Tolkien cover. "We're almost through this volume. It's hard to stop once we get into it."

Beth set the hose down in a cluster of bright zinnias and plopped down on the blanket.

Mark had taken the book and was searching for a passage. "Listen to this part, about *The Mistress of Magic who dwells in the Golden Woods.*" He held the book out in front of him and stroked Anne's hair. "'*Beautiful she is, sir! Lovely! Sometimes like a great tree in flower, sometimes like a white daffodowndilly, small and slender like.*'"

"Oh, Mark," Anne said in soft protest, and playfully reached for the book.

He held it higher. "Wait. Here's the part I like: '*Hard as di'monds, soft as moonlight. Warm as sunlight, cold as frost in the stars.*' Remind you of anyone?"

"That's Anne exactly!" cried Beth. "Sweet but tough. Hard as nails when she wants to be."

Anne brushed at her skirt and threw Mark a sharp look.

He raised his finger and continued. "*Perilously fair . . . because she's so strong in herself.*" He laughed to see her annoyance shift to pleasure. "My golden-haired Galadriel. Tall and fair." He closed the book and took her hand.

"Vita's taller than I am. And Beth is going to be the tallest of us all."

"I think they're all part Elvin, Joey. What do you think?"

Joey gave a laugh. He liked Mark. So it wasn't just him who thought the sisters were magical.

"Enough about us," said Vita. "Joey's going to learn about photography. And we're all going to help by sitting for him."

Anne's eyes brightened and she squeezed Mark's hand. "We'd love to have some pictures of us, wouldn't we?"

Mark raised his eyebrows. "I don't know about posing. Going to the fair tonight, Joey? Anne said you've been twice already."

"I think so. I hope so."

"Of course, we're going," said Beth. "Aren't you guys?"

"Vita and I promised to help Diane tonight with favors for the shower." Anne gave Mark a smile full of secrets, and then turned to Joey. "My friend's hosting a wedding shower for her cousin. We can take you to the fairgrounds and pick you up later."

"Just pick us up," said Beth. "We'll ride out with David and Abby. They have to shoot the demolition derby tonight, so they'll be late."

Beth went back to the hose and kinked it to stop the flow of water. "I'm going to water the vegetable garden—want to help?"

Joey jumped to his feet. "I'll do it."

Beth handed him the hose, letting it unkink right before handing it to him, and getting everyone sprayed. She laughed and ran as Joey picked up the hose and tried to get her with the water.

"That actually felt good," said Vita.

Anne lightly touched Vita's arm. "Looks like you got a little pink."

Vita glanced at her shoulder and frowned. "Probably. I spent most of the afternoon tending to the flowers outside, while Mrs. Cole worked on the books."

Mark rose to his feet, holding Anne's outstretched hands and lifting her. "Better go. I'll see you later." He walked around to the front of the house, turning back to look at Anne.

Anne shook out the blanket and Vita helped her to fold it. Anne pressed the blanket to her chest as she watched Mark drive away. She glanced at Vita, as if both pleased and shy. "I'm his Galadriel."

Vita smiled. "You look pretty happy together. Right out of a fairytale."

"We are happy." Anne gave a sidelong glance to Vita as they walked towards the house. "I wish you would give Vic another chance. I saw him fixated on you at the fair the other night. He seemed sad." When she got no response, she pressed a little further. "True love is not so easy to come by, Vita."

"It wasn't true love. Besides, he would pull me down. Keep me from doing what I want."

"You don't know that. He's a nice guy. Why don't you—"

"I told Mom I'd get dinner started."

"Okay, I won't push it." Anne's face filled with worry. "I hope he doesn't get called."

Vita turned to her. "Who?"

"Mark! I'm so afraid he'll have to go. It's like there's this thing always looming over us."

"You said his number was high. So it probably won't come to that."

"Sometimes I think we should run away to Canada. I'd go with him in a heartbeat."

Vita stopped to see if Anne was serious. "Canada! You would? Does Mark want to go there?"

"No. He doesn't know what he wants. He's against the war. More and more. But he feels bad for all the guys who are over there and says it wouldn't be fair to them not to go."

"Gosh, Anne. What a terrible thing to have to think about."

"I know. So I try not to. I try to pretend that everything will be all right and that he won't have to go. And that the war will be over soon."

Anne looked over at Beth and Joey. She gave a laugh at their attempts to make rainbows with the hose and getting soaked in the process. "Joey seems so happy. Happier than when he first came, don't you think? He seemed a little sad when he got here."

Vita nodded. "I thought so too. I think he's having a good time."

Vita and Anne went inside, heated up the casserole, and chopped vegetables for a salad. By the time the table was set, Millie walked in the door.

"Smells good. I was hoping you'd remember to put the casserole in. Thank you, girls."

"How'd it go, Mom?"

Millie set her sunglasses on the counter, opened the oven to check on the casserole, and poured herself a glass of iced tea, talking all the while. "I love my day at the library. I might even start volunteering two days a week. It's so interesting to talk to people about the books they've read. You learn so much." She heard laughter from outside and looked out the window. "Those two!" she said, laughing at Joey and Beth. "And there's Sal!"

Sal shut off the water from the spigot on the patio and called out to Beth. "You got more on you than on the plants."

Beth laughed and wrung out her t-shirt. "Hi, Dad! We were making rainbows. And mine was the best, whatever Joey says." She ran ahead into the house to change her clothes.

Sal and Joey walked inside together. Joey ran his hand through his hair. It was almost dry.

"No fair!" cried Beth, coming into the kitchen. "Your hair dries faster." She was blotting her long hair dry with a towel.

"But my shirt doesn't." He went to put on a dry shirt. When he came out Beth was relaying their plans for the night.

"Out again?" asked Sal. "You girls are out late every night."

"It's fair week," cried Beth, as if no other explanation was needed.

Anne brought the salad to the table. "And Vita and I are going to help with Diane's shower. We can't miss that, Dad. Anyway, we'll pick up Beth and Joey from the fair."

"We'll catch a ride out there with Abby, okay Mom?"

"All right," said Millie. "But I want them home by 10:00, Anne. No later."

Over dinner, Sal told them about the job he was bidding over in Hawthorn. "As soon as the bid is in, how about you and me do some fishing, Joey?"

"That'd be great."

"Out at the lake. Maybe we'll ask Abel to come. Pack a lunch. Fish off the dock."

Joey dug into the casserole and saw that Beth was trying to catch his eye. She pointed to her chest and mouthed, *me too.*

He grinned and nodded.

Vita had been lost in her thoughts. Now she looked up. "Dad, I was thinking a bench would be nice outside your shop.

Sal's head jerked up. "A bench! What do I need a bench for?"

126

"It would look welcoming. Especially in nice weather when the door is open."

Anne picked up on the idea. "We could put a potted plant next to it. Something flowering."

"Flowers? In front of a plumbing shop?" Sal looked at Millie and then at the girls.

Vita gave a light wave, as if it was just a passing thought. "It would add a nice touch."

Sal took a bite of the casserole. "Sounds like girl stuff. What do you think, Joey?"

"About benches? You mean like the kind Hogie makes?"

"Oh, so that's it, is it?" said Sal. "Why didn't you just say so, instead of dancing all around it?"

Vita didn't want it to look like they were doing Hogie a favor. "Just a thought. Beth, can you pass the bread?"

"Course I'll buy one from him."

"Maybe one on either side," Millie added with a glimmer in her eye. "Joey, how about I take you to the swimming pool this week. I seem to remember you like to swim."

Joey's face lit up. "I love swimming."

"Especially once the fair is over," said Beth. "We can go in the evening, when it's not so hot." She was soon asking Joey if he remembered the pool at night and how the lights came on under water.

After dinner, Joey noticed that Vita had gone outside. He saw her under the oak tree, looking up at the roof. When she went to the antenna pole, he followed her.

"Maybe you should wait." He could still see her hands gripping the fire escape railing, her face drained of color.

"How else will I ever get over my fear?"

"But so soon afterwards?"

"Because of that. I'm not as sure about myself as I thought I was, and I can't let that show at the audition. People can tell when you're afraid."

She took a deep breath and shinnied up the pole.

Joey watched her reach the top, hesitate just a moment, and climb onto the roof. He followed her up and sat next to her.

"See?" she said, smiling. "That wasn't so bad. It's better to face your fears. That's what Hogie says. Besides, it's part of my grand plan for the summer. Something I have to accomplish. I told myself if I could climb up here ten times, my fear would be gone. Then I decided it had to be twenty times."

"Is it working?"

"I thought it was."

Joey looked out at the birds flying from tree to tree and singing once they landed. Then he gazed out at the town.

"I'll tell you a secret, Joey. The real reason I come up here is to stare down my nemesis." She made a slight gesture with her head.

Joey followed her gaze. He didn't know what she meant. "Nemesis?"

"Something I learned in Mrs. Simon's class. Your foe. The thing that challenges or threatens you."

Joey now saw that she was staring at the silver water tower in the distance.

"That? But—it's just a water tower."

"Yes and no. When I sit here, I pretend I can see into the future. To all the places I want to go, all the things I want to be. And I can almost see it all." She narrowed her eyes. "But *that* is always blocking my vision. Taunting me with its height. Reminding me of my stupid, paralyzing fear. My nemesis."

She leaned back on the roof and stared up at the clouds.

Joey did the same, crossing his arms behind his head. "It's nice up here. It's like being in the treetops, closer to the sky."

"It is. That's why I come up here to dream. And I decided that the only way to dream, is to dream big."

He glanced over at her to see if she was going to say more.

"Sometimes, Joey, I'm so sure of it. My dream path. I know exactly what I want and what I have to do."

"That must be a good feeling. Like having a map."

"Well, I don't know exactly, but I can imagine it." She gave a side glance at him. "Because I had a taste of it."

"When? What happened?" Joey knew that getting just a taste of photography was enough to fill his head with all sorts of plans.

Vita's eyes grew bright. "It was on my last birthday. Oh Joey, it was the most exciting time I ever had! I went to St. Louis alone and stayed with my Aunt Nellie for three nights. I'd been there before, but never by myself. And not since I decided wholeheartedly that I want to be an actor. That I'm *going* to be an actor.

"She met me at the train station, and we did so many things. We went to two plays, *A Doll's House* one night and *The Tempest* the next. I was mesmerized. The acting was unbelievable! So inspiring." Vita lightly shook her head at the memory. "And so humbling, of course.

"And we went to the most amazing restaurants, and one afternoon I went to a café all by myself. For my birthday, she took me to a place that served desserts. Only desserts!

It was so beautiful, Joey. There was lute music, the first time I'd ever heard it. Gosh, it was pretty." She used her hands to help describe her memory. "There were pastoral pictures on the walls, and flickering candles, and velvet fabric on the seat cushions. The desserts were like works of art. I loved it."

She continued to stare up at the clouds.

"I knew then that I just *have* to live in a city. And pursue the path of acting." She turned to Joey, as if to convince him. "I know I can do it. If I just keep trying. If I can just keep moving along that path, I'll eventually get there."

Joey gave it some thought. "Makes sense." He wondered if he could also find a dream path. Something fun.

"Even if I don't get to the end, at least my life will be lived on that beautiful path. That's all I really want. Just to try."

She looked over at Joey. "Does that sound crazy?"

"No. It sounds like a plan. You can do it. Why not?"

She sat up and frowned at the water tower. "Because of *that*." She tilted her head. "In a strange way, I think it actually helps me. I need a thing to fight, to conquer, not just an idea. It's the dragon blocking my path. All my hopes and fears are tangled up with it."

Joey sat up and looked at the water tower, seeing it in a new light. He framed it with his hands.

"Everything about that tower scares me." Vita gave a light shudder. "Teenagers used to climb up there and spray paint their initials. So stupid and dangerous! That's why they boarded up the bottom."

Joey eyed the tower with skepticism. "Maybe you're giving it too much power. It's just a simple old water tower. All these towns have one. I saw them from the train."

Vita considered his words. "That makes it both better and worse. It *is* ordinary. Like me. Do you realize how ordinary I am? Middle, middle, middle. Middle sister in a middle-class family in a middle-sized town in the middle of the United States. There must be thousands and thousands like me."

For a brief moment, Joey saw her as just another teenager, an average girl like all the rest. But she wasn't. There was something different about her. Maybe because she wanted there to be.

Joey thrust his chin at the water tower. "I bet you could climb that old thing if you ever wanted to."

Fear flashed in Vita's eyes, and she pressed her hands to the roof on either side of her. "Don't even *say* that. Especially when I'm up here, with nothing to hold on to!"

"Sorry Vita. I just meant that—that I think you could do whatever you wanted to. That's all I meant." He saw how afraid she was and realized what a stupid thing he had said.

"I don't really mean to climb the tower—that would be crazy."

Vita placed her hands on her stomach.

"Sorry! I mean—you could be a successful actress. Easily. I know it. Look. I'll be part of your plan. I'll be here the whole summer. I can help you with your audition and lines and photoshoots." He almost added that he would climb the roof with her anytime she wanted but thought it best not to mention any heights.

Vita let out a deep breath and put her hand over Joey's. "My D'Artagnan. So we'll work together. Partners."

Joey nodded vigorously. Another quest.

"On one condition. You have to pursue your dreams, too."

"Me? But I don't really have any dreams."

"I know. And that makes me sad. It's so much better to have a dream to move towards. I'm a hundred percent sure of that."

Joey stared out at the treetops, a thought slowly taking shape. "Maybe . . ." Joey wasn't even sure what he wanted to say.

"Maybe what?"

"I guess photography could be part of my dream. I like it. At least what I know about it. I can practice with Aunt Millie's camera."

"That's a good place to start. We'll help each other with our quests. Our pact. Deal?"

"Deal."

Vita gave a short nod, and he did the same. He wasn't sure what he was agreeing to, but he felt excited. Like he had something—an idea, a glimpse of a fun future—that he didn't have before he climbed up on the roof. His chest was a little fuller, like a tiny *maybe* inside of him just burst into being.

"There you are!" cried Beth from down below. "Abby's going to stop by in ten minutes."

Joey and Vita stood and moved to the antenna pole.

"How about you go down first?" Joey asked.

Vita accepted the challenge and went down the pole with a little less hesitation than when she went up. Joey slid down after her.

❧

Joey would always remember that night as a sort of beginning. Vita's talk had shifted the way he thought about the future, his future. And the fair just added to the sense of possibility and wider realities.

While David photographed the exhibits, he patiently taught Joey about shutter speed, and depth of field, and going with your instincts. Joey was beginning to see the world in pictures, everywhere he looked. He found himself discovering little compositions all over the place. Little stories.

David had also let Joey take several pictures again with his camera: of the fruit pie and preserves show, the Miss Pork Queen booth, the tractors and combines exhibit, and a few of whatever Joey wanted to take. He chose an old carny taking a cigarette break behind a ride, a little boy on his dad's shoulders holding a green balloon, the edge of a red-and-white striped tent with a sunset field behind it.

Joey had a good feeling about these. At least he didn't think that he had moved, and there was a composition to them this time. He also took pictures of Beth and Abby acting goofy, blowing chewing gum bubbles and laughing as they posed.

They had two hours before the demolition derby began, so while David and Darlene met up with some friends, Joey walked around the grounds with Beth and Abby.

After eating popcorn and roasted peanuts, and riding several rides, they ended up back at the Ferris wheel. Abby's friend Dylan had joined them, so it was just Joey and Abby in one carriage, and Beth and Dylan in another.

As the wheel slowed to let new people on, Joey had a good chance to look out over the fairgrounds. One by one, the carriage rose higher and higher over the crowds and the red-and-white striped tents. He looked over at Abby; she was pointing out the activity below.

The sun had set and the sky in the distance kept a barely-there pink tint under the aquamarine. All the colored lights from the rides and booths shone brightly and the strings of clear lights glittered in the evening. Joey knew a magical moment was just about to happen, when he would be at the very top and the Ferris wheel would pause for just a few moments.

He filled his eyes with Abby and the backdrop of lights and music and the cornfields in the distance. And then it happened—their carriage stopped at the very top. It rocked ever so gently back and forth. He was at the top of the world in a magical place with that pretty, pretty girl. At just that moment, she turned to him and smiled. Vita's word came to his mind—at that moment, the world was wondrous!

Even without a camera, he knew that image was forever imprinted on his mind. Then the Ferris wheel began to move, and they went round and round and Joey wished that it would never stop.

Abby leaned forward, trying to see Beth, who was calling out to them.

"Hello, Joey! Hello, Abby!"

Then Abby let out a burst of laughter and Joey laughed too, though he didn't even know why he felt so happy. It was in a new and hopeful way, like the future might be a pretty good place after all. Like he caught a glimpse of that dream path that Vita described, and he wanted to get started on his. Take that first exhilarating step forward. Why not?

By the time the ride was finished, the sky was dark blue with a sliver of moon. They knew that they would soon have to leave. Dylan left with his friend Ernie to get seats for the demolition derby. Beth, Abby, and Joey wandered around the main area one last time.

Joey stopped by the balloon man. "Pick a balloon. I'll buy one for you."

"That big yellow one for me," said Beth. "It looks like the sun."

Abby walked around the collection of balloons choosing carefully. "I want the swirly pink-and-white one. Pink is my favorite color."

When Joey handed the balloon to Abby he felt a surge of happiness. He was starting to feel like he could make things happen.

They walked with Abby back to the exhibits and left her with David and Darlene. Then they hurried to the entrance to wait for Vita and Anne.

It was a good twenty minutes before they heard Anne tooting the horn. They ran to her car and jumped in.

"Where were you?" asked Beth. "It's almost 10:30. Now we're going to get in trouble."

"No you won't," said Anne. "We called Mom and told her we were going to be a little late."

They turned onto the road back into town. Beth noticed their wet hair. "Did you guys go swimming—and not tell me?"

"We didn't plan it," said Anne. "After Diane's we went out to the lake and . . ."

"In the dark?"

"Under the stars and a crescent moon," said Vita. "A Pierrot moon, full of dreams. It was wondrous! Absolutely magical."

Beth looked around the back seat to see if she was sitting on anything wet, then checked the floor. "Where are your swimsuits?" After a moment's silence, she gasped. "You went *skinny* dipping?"

Anne shot Beth a warning glance in the rearview mirror. "Don't you dare say anything about it at home."

"I won't. But I can't believe it. Were there any boys there?" After no answer, she said, "You guys! Weren't you embarrassed?"

"It was dark," said Anne.

"Except for the glimmer on the water. It was like swimming through a thousand tiny stars." Vita turned around to face them. "It was so beautiful. And the water was just right. Like swimming in a fairy world."

"Well, next time *I'm* going," said Beth.

Joey sat silently, amazed at the boldness of these girls. He smiled out at the passing fields, the farmhouses, and the lights outside the shops at the edge of town. Riding around with three cool hippie girls, like it was something he did all the time.

CHAPTER 10

Joey rode his bike past the college and coasted down the hill holding his arms out. The wind whipped through his hair. He liked the houses on this side of town. Some of them looked like they were once old farmhouses. One of them sat at the top of a low hill and had a pasture with sheep and goats.

Now and then he stopped and pointed Millie's camera at an image. She had just given it to him and showed him how to use it. It was loaded with a fresh roll of film. He attached a strap to it—like David's—and it now hung around his neck. He was afraid of wasting film and so far had only taken a few pictures.

He passed a house with a couple of kids manning a lemonade stand. One of them was Eddie.

"Hey, Joey!"

"Hi, Eddie. I'll have a cup." Joey gave him a nickel and took a sip of the cool lemonade Eddie poured. "Pretty good. How's business?"

"Not bad. You're our third customer since we set up at lunch." He looked up at the sky. "But Mom says it's going to rain. If you see anyone, send them this way."

"I will." He finished the lemonade and Eddie pointed to a box under the table. Joey tossed his cup in. "See you around."

Joey hopped on his bike and headed towards home. When he passed Hogie's house he saw him out in the garage, working at his table. Another guy sat in a chair, drinking a beer. Hogie looked up and smiled.

It was safe to stop. "Hi, Hogie!" Joey pulled his bike into the driveway and leaned it against the garage entrance.

Hogie gestured to the guy in the chair. "My buddy, Al. This is Joey."

Al jumped up and slapped Joey on the back. "Hey, Joey. I heard about you. Here for the summer, huh?"

"Yeah. Until school starts."

Al finished his beer and set the bottle in the trash. "Just stopped by to shoot the breeze. Better get home before the rain. See ya around, Joey. See ya, Hoge."

Joey noticed that Al walked with a limp. He turned to Hogie. "Was he in the war too?"

Hogie simply nodded.

Joey looked at the worktable. "What are you working on?"

"Checking my supplies, sorting pieces." Hogie lifted a piece of scrap wood from an old five-gallon paint bucket and eyed it for straightness. "What about you?"

"Just bike riding." Joey held up the camera. "And practicing with Aunt Millie's camera. We have a photoshoot later today. My first one. I'm going to help."

Hogie glanced out at the darkening clouds. "Outdoors?" He set the piece of wood to one side and reached for another. "So where's the pain in the ass?"

Joey raised his eyebrows. "You mean Vita? I thought you liked her. She said you're like her older brother."

"Yeah, well, siblings argue, don't they? You got any? Brothers or sisters?"

Joey shook his head. "Vita says I'm like her little brother. I'm glad she thinks that."

Hogie gave a silent laugh. "You're loyal. Best quality there is. But wait till she starts butting into your life. Telling you what to do. Still, I miss her when she's not around. All that talk about plans and dreams."

He set three pieces of wood together and compared them for length. "You be careful, or she'll be filling your head with ideas. She has a way of rubbing off on you."

Joey realized that she had already filled his head with ideas. And he liked it. "Maybe that's not so bad."

"Until it all falls apart." Hogie rejected two of the pieces and threw them into a pile behind him. "Don't know why I bother with all this," he muttered. He lifted another scrap of wood that had a shorter piece nailed to it and tried to pull it off.

"Vita says you have to at least try. I mean—people, everybody."

"Oh, she does, does she?"

"Yeah. She says not to try is the only sure way to fail."

"Yeah, well, Miss Vicky-Victoria-Vita is full of shit." He reached for the hammer and swung it hard, knocking off the shorter piece. He then pried the nails off with the claw end of the hammer.

Joey hesitated. "It kind of makes sense, though."

Hogie's mouth tightened. "Hand me that piece."

Joey reached for the scrap of wood at his feet.

"The other one."

Joey gave him the larger piece. He knew the conversation was over.

Hogie darted his eyes to the sky again. "It's going to come down soon."

"Yeah. I better go. See you around, Hogie."

Joey pedaled down the street, turned onto the alleyway, and rode up the back sidewalk. He parked the bike in the garage. He gave Princess a quick pet and reached for a dog biscuit from a box on the tool shelf.

"There you go, girl."

Joey ran inside the kitchen and handed Millie the camera. "I was afraid it might get rained on."

Millie was at the counter looking through her recipe box. "You keep it. Use it whenever you want. I think you came home just in time, Joey. That sky's going to open any minute."

The kitchen windows were open, letting in a breeze that ruffled the curtains.

Anne and Beth were huddled over a catalog at the table. Vita stood near the window with her arms crossed, her face tense with worry.

"Where were you?" asked Beth.

Joey washed his hands at the bathroom sink and then told her about Eddie and the lemonade stand and stopping by Hogie's.

"Gosh," said Anne, turning on the kitchen light. "It's getting so dark."

A low rumble sounded in the distance and the trees outside began to sway. A gust of cooler air blew through the windows.

Joey went to the world map on the wall. Still thinking about Hogie, he studied the countries around North and South Vietnam and traced his finger over rivers.

Vita let out a soft groan. "It can't rain. I switched my workdays and I'm all ready for the Titania shoot. I thought it would bring me luck."

"I don't think professional actors rely on luck, Vita," said Millie.

"I know. But if we don't do it today, it won't be until after the audition. David's got jobs lined up for the next few days."

Millie prepared the percolator for coffee and took a card from her recipe box. "Keep things in perspective. The main thing is that you're moving ahead: studying, auditioning, putting together your portfolio. Even if you don't get this part, there will be plenty of others."

Vita faced her mom with surprise. "What do you mean?"

"I'm saying that you can't control auditions any more than you can control the weather. You have to learn to be realistic if you really want to pursue this career."

"I know. I was just ready, is all."

Beth looked up from the catalog. "If it rains too hard, the fair will be all muddy." The phone rang and she jumped up to answer it. She chatted for a few minutes, hung up the phone, and announced, "Yep. The shoot's been canceled. David will let us know when it's going to be."

Vita dropped into a chair and let out a sigh of disappointment.

Anne turned the page of the catalog. "Oh, come on, Vita, you love the rain."

"Not when I have a photoshoot scheduled that will help me with a major audition."

Beth looked over at Millie. "What are you going to make, Mom?"

"I thought a batch of cookies would be nice. Oatmeal. How does that sound?" Millie turned on the oven and began mixing ingredients.

"I'll help." Beth went to the counter and read the recipe card. She went to the refrigerator, measured out the butter, and began heating it in a pan. She glanced over her shoulder at Joey studying the map. "Making travel plans, Joey?"

"No. Just wondering where I'll have to go."

Vita turned to Joey. "What do you mean?"

"Where the war will be when I'm older." He pointed to Korea. "My dad was here." He ran his finger down to Vietnam. "Hogie here." He moved to the middle of the map. "And Uncle Sal, over here in Europe."

Anne lifted her head. "Hopefully there will be no war by then."

Millie overheard them and shifted the subject. "Remember the map game, Joey? You were always so good at it."

"Yeah, and I bet I can still find . . ." He moved back to the Pacific Ocean and scanned the expanse of blue. He moved his finger down among the tiny islands. "There it is! Yap."

They all laughed. "Joey the world explorer, that's what we used to call you," said Vita.

Joey smiled at the memory. "I guess there are no new lands to discover. But *if* I was going to travel, I think I would go to Africa first. Or maybe some of these islands. I wonder what they look like."

"I would go to Mexico," said Beth. "Practice my Spanish. Or maybe Spain or Chile. Peru! Climb to Machu Picchu. That's why I took Spanish. So many places speak it."

"I took French," said Vita, "because I want to live in Paris one day. Or at least visit it. But if you go to Machu Picchu, I'm going with you."

"Where would you go, Anne?" Joey asked.

She looked up from the clothing catalog. "I want to see the United States. All of it. All the National Parks. Then come back here."

Vita turned from the map to Anne. "You mean after we live in New York City. You might love it so much you'll want to stay there."

Anne flipped the page of the catalog, remaining silent.

"I think I'll end up in the Southwest," said Beth. "Desert. Sun. Mountains to hike. Georgia O'Keeffe. Artists all over the place. I could learn how to make pottery."

"You might like New York, too, Beth. I'd love for us all to live there together, at least for a few years. Then you could go to the Southwest."

A sudden crack of lightning made them all jump.

"Look at that rain coming down!" cried Millie. She went to the window above the sink and inhaled deeply. "Ah, that storm smell. Sharp and fresh." She lowered the sash and returned to her baking. "These cookies are just the thing for such a day." She spooned out dough onto the cookie sheet, put it in the oven, and checked the time. Then she glanced out at the rain again. "I love a good storm. So dramatic!"

"So do I," said Beth. She rinsed the pan and utensils and placed them in the dishwasher.

For a few deafening minutes the sky crackled with lightning followed by booming thunder. They looked out the windows at the white sheets of rain, blurring everything. Wind and rain gusted in, blowing the curtains by the table. Raindrops splattered the windowsills through the screens. Vita lowered the windows, and sat down, resigned.

The sounds lessened as the storm swept to the east, but the rain continued to fall heavily. The scent of fresh coffee and baked cookies filled the kitchen with coziness, contrasting with the drama of the storm. Joey went back to studying the map.

Anne saw the disappointment in Vita's face. She slid the catalog over to her. "Look at this smock top. I bet I could make it."

Vita leaned over the image. "It's pretty, tied at the waist like that. The pattern's like old-fashioned wallpaper."

"And I like the square neckline. What pretty hair she has, so shiny. I bet she washes it in rainwater." Her eyes shot to Vita, and she raised her eyebrows.

Vita's eyes brightened. "Good idea, Anne. We haven't done it in a while."

Joey glanced over his shoulder, wondering what they were talking about.

Beth called from the counter. "Count me in. Joey, want to help?"

Joey kept his finger on the Solomon Islands and turned around. "Sure. With what?"

"We're going to wash our hair in rainwater," said Vita. "Nothing makes it softer."

Joey's face scrunched in confusion. "You want me to help wash your hair?"

They all burst out laughing. "No!"

"Mom!" Beth cried, "Did you hear what Joey said?" The idea of him washing three heads of hair sent her into peals of laughter. "Like a hair salon! Can you imagine? No, Joey. You can help gather the rainwater."

"Only if he wants to," said Millie. She used a spatula to lift the cookies from the baking sheet and set them on a plate. "And no one is going out in the rain while it's lightning."

"The lightning's already passed, Mom," said Beth, looking out the window.

"We collect the rainwater," Vita explained to Joey, "heat it on the stove, and then wash our hair. And we add flowers or scents to the rinse."

"It makes it so shiny," Anne said. "I'll clean the sink."

Millie put the second tray of cookies in the oven. "Wait until I get this batch out. I know how this works—you girls will take over the whole kitchen."

"We will," said Beth, laughing in agreement. "Don't worry. It takes us a while to set up." She bent over the bottom cupboards and searched for the largest pans.

"What a storm that was!" Sal said, coming into the family room.

"Sal! You're home?"

He came into the kitchen. "Just to pick up a few tools. Forgot I left them in the garage after I helped Abel."

"I just made a pot of coffee. You have time for that, don't you?"

"Something smells good." Sal came over to her by the counter and looked around. "What's all the commotion?"

"I'm baking cookies, and the girls are going to wash their hair in rainwater. And poor Joey doesn't know what to make of it all." Millie inhaled the percolating coffee with a sigh of pleasure and took out the cream from the refrigerator. She poured Sal a cup and added sugar and a splash of cream.

Sal frowned at all the noise Beth was making in the cupboard. "Don't let them rope you into doing anything you don't want, Joey." He brought his coffee to the kitchen table. "We should be talking about gathering the worms that come out in the rain. For fishing."

Joey smiled, thinking that both things sounded like fun. Both meant that he would be outside in the rain.

Millie set a plate of cookies next to Sal and he wrapped his arm around her waist. "No coffee for you?" He lifted a cookie and dunked it into his coffee.

"I'll wait a bit," she said. "And finish up the baking before the girls take over. Try a cookie, Joey. They're still warm."

Joey sat next to Sal and took a cookie. He watched with curiosity as Anne and Vita made several trips to the bedroom and linen closet, coming back with towels, jars, shampoo, and brushes and combs. They set some items near the stove and sink, others at the table, like an elaborate ritual. He almost asked, *All that just to wash your hair?* He bit into his cookie.

"Uncle Sal, I have a question. Where could a boy find work around here?"

"You? You need some cash?"

"Mom and Dad gave me pocket money, but I thought maybe I could find a part-time job while I'm here to earn some extra."

"But this is your vacation," said Millie. "You're supposed to be playing and enjoying yourself."

"Work is good for kids," said Sal. "I had a paper route when I was your age."

The girls exchanged glances at the oft-told story and hid their smiles.

"Shoveled snow in winter," said Sal. "Not just me. Most of the kids were always scrambling for odd jobs. Times were tough back then." He rubbed his chin. "I could use you at the shop now and then. Mostly sweeping and dusting. It gets dirty in the back."

"I'll help you anytime you need, but I can't take money. I mean like a real job."

"Hmm. Let me think." He took another cookie. "Guess you're too young for the soda shop."

"Far too young," said Millie, taking out the second batch.

Sal dipped the second cookie into his coffee. "Abel's taking on another cemetery while Rusty Cooper's away. He mentioned he might need some help. Mowing, trimming. I could ask him about it."

"Could you?" Joey brightened at the possibility of working with Abel. Surely he could figure out how to do that kind of work.

"*There* it is!" cried Beth, with another bang. She pulled out the black speckled roasting pan from the back of the

147

cupboard. "Come on, Joey. I'll show you how we gather the water."

"And on that note," said Sal, finishing his coffee, "I'll head back to work. Don't want to get tangled up in all this . . . this . . ." He waved his hand at the kitchen, not quite sure what to call it.

"Bye, Dad!" the girls called out to him. He exchanged a look of amusement with Millie before leaving.

Millie fixed herself a cup of coffee and added two cookies to the saucer. "I'll leave you girls to it. I'm going to curl up with my novel. The book club meets in a few days and I'm only halfway through."

"Ready?" Beth asked Joey. "Hope you don't mind getting wet."

Barefoot, she and Joey went into the garage and waited a moment at the door that led to the back yard. The thunder and lightning had passed, but the rain was still coming down hard, pounding the patio in little stars and puddling in the low parts of the yard.

With a yell, Beth ran out into the back yard. "Come on!"

Joey followed her out into the rain and over to the gushing downspout. Beth placed the pan underneath it, watched it fill. She turned her face up to the rain. "Don't you just love this?"

Joey lifted his face too, exhilarated, and laughed along with Beth. Water was splashing into the pan and overflowing the sides.

"I'll get it," said Joey. He lifted the pan while Beth whooped again and ran for the garage. He could barely see through the rain.

When Beth opened the door to the family room, Vita was waiting with a towel. "I'll take it from here."

"We're drenched!" cried Beth, mopping at her face.

Vita emptied the water and returned the roasting pan to Beth.

"We need lots more," said Beth.

"I can do it," said Joey.

"You sure?"

"Yeah. I like it." He took the pan from Beth.

"Okay. I'll help Vita and Anne in the kitchen."

Joey smiled as he ran out into the rain. He placed the pan under the downspout and watched it fill. The grass around the spout was long and the water made it all soft and wavy. He loved being barefoot. He splashed his feet around in the long grass and raised his face again to the summer rain.

He brought the second pan to the door, where Beth was waiting for him. She soon had it emptied, and returned to the doorway.

"Beth?" Anne called from the kitchen. "Rose water? Lavender?"

"Lemon!" Beth hollered back. She gave the pan to Joey. "For the rinse. Anne likes rose scent, Vita lavender. I like that squeaky clean feel from lemons."

Joey dashed out again. Making travel plans at the map and now running through the rain made him feel like an adventurer. He felt bold, part of something fun and exciting.

Princess poked her head out of the garage door. Joey patted his leg. "Come on, girl. Let's run!"

The dog hesitantly walked over to him. Joey ran around the back yard, from the vegetable garden to the flower garden, followed by Princess. She gave a few barks, and then ducked back into the garage, shaking off the water.

Beth wasn't at the door for the next pan, and he had to rest it on his leg to open the screen door. He stood at the entrance to the kitchen, dripping water onto the linoleum floor of the family room.

All three girls stood at the stove, good witches concocting magical potions for their hair. Long blonde, really long black, and long wavy gold. He felt like he was in a fairytale.

Beth saw him and came for the pan. "Thanks, Joey. Look at you, you're soaked!" She poured the rainwater into waiting containers in one side of the sink.

Anne dipped her finger into one of the pans on the stove. "I think we can start." She placed the pan of warm water on the counter. Then she leaned over and let her long hair spill into the sink.

Vita dipped a large measuring cup into the water and poured it over Anne's hair. "Too hot?"

"Just right."

After a few more pours, Anne began to lather up her hair, while Beth filled the pans on the stove.

"Two or three more should do it," said Beth, returning the empty roasting pan to Joey.

He went back outside and walked more slowly now. The rain was letting up, but he didn't want the adventure to end. He put his fists at his sides and raised his face. He was at the prow of a ship, or a mountain top, or on horseback journeying into new territory. Maybe Vita was right. It has to start with a dream. Faraway lands, new adventures. Why not? Why not try? Just for the fun of it!

He ran to the roasting pan, lifted it from the down-spout, and brought it inside. Standing on the towel Beth had placed for him on the linoleum, he once more handed the pan to her.

"You're soaking wet," she said, laughing with him. "Hold on. Let me empty this."

He slicked his hair off his forehead and waited for the pan.

Anne was still bent over the sink. Vita poured water from the pan with a cup, again and again, as Anne turned her head, getting all the shampoo out.

"Now for the rinse." Vita lifted a smaller pan and slowly poured rose-scented water over Anne's hair.

"Can I go next?" asked Beth. "My hair always takes the longest to dry."

Anne leaned over the sink twisting her long hair and squeezing out the water. Vita handed her a blue towel. Anne draped it over her head, made a few twists and tucks, and when she straightened, the towel was in place. Like a crown or headpiece.

"One more should do it," said Beth, returning the pan to Joey. "Then you can dry off."

He filled one more pan, and when he came in, Beth was all lathered up. Anne sat at the table, combing through her hair, and using the towel to blot it dry. She jumped up to take the pan from Joey and brought it to the counter.

"Ready," said Beth.

Vita once again became the water bearer, pouring, pouring. When all the suds were out, she slowly added the lemon rinse over Beth's hair. Beth wrung the water from her hair and twisted a towel around her head. "This is what I love about summer—washing our hair in rainwater."

Anne brought Joey a towel to dry himself with. "We have plenty now. Go put on some dry clothes and come sit with us. Unless you want to wash your hair in rainwater?"

"That's okay. I'll just go change."

By the time he came out, Anne was pouring water over Vita's hair. A hint of lavender scented the kitchen. Soon they all sat at the table combing their hair, and toweling it dry now and then.

"Thank you, Joey," said Anne. "Our hair will look beautiful, thanks to you." She stood and looped her hair on her head. "I'm going to work on my blouse while my hair dries."

"Can you bring mine too?" Vita called after her.

"And mine!" hollered Beth, reaching for a cookie and pushing the plate over to Joey. "We bought matching peasant blouses the last time we were in Foreston with Mom. We're embroidering them."

Anne came back with the sewing basket and three gauzy blouses in soft shades of blue, green, and yellow. Joey guessed that the blue one would be Anne's, the yellow Beth's, and the pale green would be Vita's. He felt a small sense of satisfaction when his guess was confirmed.

Joey ate a cookie and watched them for a while. With towels around their shoulders, they threaded needles and embroidered birds, vines, and flowers around the necklines, down the front, or on the sleeves. He leaned closer and saw that some of the flowers had been made with tiny beads. Sometimes the sisters seemed so different from one another, and other times, like now, they seemed exactly the same. He had a feeling they would always be somewhat mysterious to him.

152

Joey went to get one of the photography books so he would have something to do too. He really liked photography, but it had just kind of happened. Did that count as a dream?

He reached for another cookie. "Do you know what you want to be, Anne?"

She looked up from her embroidery. "I can't decide. I really like the idea of being a costume designer. But I also like the idea of being a teacher. Grade school, I think. Maybe I could do both."

"What about you, Beth?"

"No idea. I think I'll try a lot of things and see what sticks. My latest thought is having a gallery somewhere in the Southwest. How about you, Joey?"

"I'm not sure. But I don't think I want to be a doctor." He turned a page and looked up at Vita. She was the surest of her direction.

"How did you know you wanted to be an actress?"

Vita pulled the needle through the green gauze and gave it some thought. "Mom always took us to performances when we were little. She's from St. Louis, you know, so we always went there for shopping and shows with Aunt Nellie. And there were plays in Foreston. I always loved the stage."

Anne nodded. "That's how I got the idea to be a costume designer."

"And there are plays out at the college we go to," added Beth. "Twice a year. And the high school."

"We used to put on shows for Mom and Dad when we were little," said Anne. "Vita would make up the stories and I was in charge of the costumes."

"And don't forget the skits in grade school," said Beth. "In one show, all three of us were trees, remember that?"

"Vita was a good tree," said Anne, "swaying lightly in the breeze. Beth sat down, right in the middle of the stage."

Beth held up her blouse and assessed the red embroidered sunrays. "I was tired of standing. I was a better snowflake the next year. I could whirl around the stage."

"And off the stage," added Anne. "I loved the costumes for that show." She looked through the different spools of thread in the basket, chose a deep rose, and threaded the needle.

Vita worked on a flowering vine along the neckline—dark green with roses and coppery beads.

"It was the *Macbeth* production that decided me. The whole thing. I loved the words, connecting with the cast and the audience. Being a part of another time. Being a part of the night realm. That's how I began to think of it. I was lucky to have Mrs. Simon as my teacher. She really helped me to understand the language of Shakespeare. It was so hard at first. It still is."

"I always thought I didn't like Shakespeare," said Anne. "But last summer Mom took us to the drive-in to see *Romeo and Juliet*. It changed my mind. We all fell in love with Juliet and wanted to be her."

"*I* fell in love with Romeo," said Beth. "He was so cute!"

A dreamy softness suffused Vita's face. "That was such a beautiful movie. So romantic, and sad. I've only seen four Shakespeare plays and a few movies. But I love them and wish I understood them better."

"Vita keeps a list," Beth said.

"I do. Of all the plays I've seen and read. Not just Shakespeare."

"Acting makes me nervous," said Anne. "What if you forget your lines? But Vita's at home on stage."

"Makes me dizzy," said Beth. "All that memorizing." She scooted down in her chair so that her hair draped over the back. "I'd rather be riding a horse, or making something, or camping."

Vita held out her hand to an imagined character and recited: "'*Thou art as wise as thou art beautiful! . . . Therefore, go with me. I'll give thee fairies to attend on thee, and they shall fetch thee jewels from the deep, and sing whilst thou on pressed flowers dost sleep.*' Isn't that just so beautiful?"

Beth made a scoffing sound. "Uhh . . . she says that to a donkey, doesn't she?"

"Yes, but that's because . . . oh, you know the play."

"I should. I've been helping you with it for over a month now."

Anne laughed. "We know the lines almost as well as Vita."

"All true. I couldn't do it without my sisters. They've helped me every step of the way."

Joey briefly wondered what it would be like to have some brothers to help him with his plans, or some sisters.

"Oh my gosh—two days before the audition!" said Vita. "Then . . ." She pressed both hands to her heart as if to still it. '*Two days will quickly steep themselves in night.*'"

"I thought it said four days," said Beth. "Don't go changing the lines."

Vita ignored her and continued. "'*Two nights will quickly dream away the time. And then the moon, like a silver bow*"

new-bent in heaven shall behold the night of our solemnities.'"
She faced Joey. "That's Hippolyta. She's a queen and that
would be a nice role too—but I *really* want Titania. Queen
of the fairies. Two more days!"

Anne smiled at her. "Don't worry, Titania. You know
your lines inside out. You'll be the most beautiful and talented one there."

Beth felt her hair and jumped up. "This is taking
too long."

They soon heard the hair dryer in the bathroom.

"That defeats the whole purpose!" said Anne. "Letting it
air dry afterwards is part of the secret. Beth is so impatient."

"Two days," said Vita, pulling the dark green thread
through a vine.

Joey saw how much Vita wanted the part of Titania and
he hoped so badly that she would get it.

CHAPTER 11

Joey sat at a table with Millie, Vita, and Beth at the Corner Café. Their desserts had just been placed before them. Anne was working the lunch shift and moved gracefully around in a blue-and-white floral midi. The braid down her back had a blue ribbon that Beth had woven into it.

Beth was taking credit for the hair style and told Vita she could do the same for her for tomorrow's audition.

"I think simple will be best," said Vita. "I won't want to look like I'm trying too hard."

Vita wore a shimmery green top over a long coppery paisley skirt. Her eyes glittered with excitement about the audition. That's all she could talk about or think about.

Joey noticed that other people in the café kept glancing at their table and smiling, as if in admiration. Beth wore a short coral-colored sundress and her long black hair hung loose down her back. And Millie looked as beautiful as any of them, in her rose print dress and lovely smile.

"I'm glad you took the day off, Vita," said Millie.

"And tomorrow. I don't think Mrs. Cole likes me being off so much, even though she knows how important the audition is. She's been so upset lately."

"And we all know why," said Beth. She leaned over to Joey. "Her husband is having an affair and the whole town knows about it. I'd be mad too. I'd dump him."

"Beth!" Millie said in a sharp whisper.

"Oh, look!" Vita spotted her old English teacher sitting with a friend at a four top, as if expecting two others. "There's Mrs. Simon! The teacher I was telling you about, Joey. I want to say hello." She left the table and walked over to them.

"Why hello, Vita." Mrs. Simon introduced her friend. "Do you know Mrs. Carlisle? She teaches out at the college. I assume you'll be auditioning tomorrow?"

Vita answered that she was going to read for Titania.

"I'm sure you'll shine," said Mrs. Simon. "And what a coincidence. Harold and Daphne are going to join us for lunch."

Vita blushed to hear that the director and his wife were coming to the restaurant. She didn't want to bump into them.

"Well, I just wanted to say hello. Nice to meet you, ma'am."

Mrs. Simon squeezed Vita's hand. "I wish you all the best."

Vita slid back into her seat. "The Radcliffs are going to join them. The directors for the play," she whispered to Joey. "I'm so nervous." She pushed aside her piece of pie. "I can't possibly eat this."

Beth took the plate. "Well, I can. Joey?" She sliced the pie down the middle and put half on Joey's plate.

Vita glanced sideways when she saw the directors come in and join Mrs. Simon. She saw that they were soon looking her way and she was sure they were talking about the audition.

"Don't look so nervous," said Beth. "They're just eating lunch."

"I didn't expect them to be here." Vita twisted the napkin on her lap.

Millie placed her hand on Vita's arm. "Don't make more of it than it is. There will be many auditions up ahead. Think of this as practice."

Vita gave a small laugh. "You're right."

Millie soon paid the bill, and they said goodbye to Anne. Vita smiled at her old teacher and nodded to the others at the table. Just as they reached the door, she heard one of them say, "She'd make a *stunning* Titania!" and Mr. Radcliff answered, "Indeed, she would."

Beth pushed Vita as soon as the door closed behind them. "Did you hear *that*?"

Vita kept walking, wanting to get past the café.

"Did you?"

"Yes." Vita couldn't help but smile.

They caught up with Joey and Millie.

"Mom, did you hear what they said?" Vita asked in a whisper.

"Don't count your chickens. But it does sound promising."

"You're a shoo-in, Vita!" Beth said with a wide smile.

LINDA MAHKOVEC

Vita bit her lip. "It's hard not to be hopeful. I mean, they've seen my work. They know what I can do. Mrs. Simon must have told them that's the role I'll be trying out for."

"What else could it mean?" Beth asked. "Stunning!" she added dramatically.

"This is all very exciting," said Millie. She looped her arm around Vita's shoulders. "I have to pick up a few things at the dry cleaners. Do you want to come with me?"

"I need to walk. I can't possibly sit still right now."

Beth took Millie's arm. "I'll go with you, Mom. Joey?"

"I'll walk too."

"See you at home!" Beth waved as they crossed the street.

"Oh my gosh, Joey, that just goes to show you, you really *can* make things happen, if you just keep trying and work hard and believe that it really will happen."

Joey caught her enthusiasm. "It's happening just like you said. According to your plan."

"I'm actually looking forward to the audition. I'm not a bit nervous." She popped open her hands in the air. "It's like all that anxiety just vanished!"

They walked down Oak Street and when they passed Hogie's house, they saw him talking to his friend Al.

"Let's go say hello," said Vita. "It's been a while for me."

Al sat on the hood of his car, drinking a beer. "Hey, Joey! Vita."

"Joey!" said Hogie.

Joey was happy to see that Hogie was in a good mood.

"Hi, Al." Vita walked into the garage. "What have you been working on, Hogie?"

"The usual."

160

While Al chatted with Joey, Vita looked over Hogie's work. She noticed a small two-leveled birdhouse sitting on the worktable. "That's so pretty." She turned it around and inspected the design. "By the way, Dad said he wants a bench for outside his shop."

When she didn't get a response, she turned around.

Hogie glared at her. "Thought you knew better."

Vita made a soft sound of protest. "Everything doesn't always have to be bad! He wants one, that's what he said. Joey was there."

Hogie turned to Joey.

Joey nodded, as cheerfully as he thought Hogie could tolerate.

"The truth. Whose idea was it—Sal's?" He jerked his head towards Vita. "Or this one's?"

Joey stiffened and blinked as he considered how to answer. Hogie would spot a lie in a second.

Hogie shook his head at Vita. "You can take your charity and shove it." He wheeled over to the fridge and took out two more beers. "Ready for another?" He tossed one to Al who threw back the empty. Joey waited for a crash, but Hogie caught the bottle.

Vita tried to laugh it away. "Hogie's always mad at me, Al. I'm always butting in or saying the wrong thing." She looked back at the worktable. "It really is a nice birdhouse. If I was a bird, I would want to live there."

Hogie gave a short laugh. "You're full of shit. So when's the big audition?"

Vita put her hand on her stomach. "Tomorrow! Wish me luck."

"I wish you luck."

Vita put her hand on her hip.

"Nah, I mean it. Let me know how it goes."

"I will. Did you know Joey is learning photography?"

"I knew he was taking pictures. So, you're learning all about it, huh?"

Joey shoved his hands in his pockets. "Kind of. David is teaching me. You know, Abby's brother. If I get good, maybe I can take a picture of you."

"I don't think I'm the right material." Hogie took a long guzzle from the bottle.

Joey leaned his head to the side and studied Hogie. Under the scruffiness, he saw a good-looking man, kind of hiding behind stuff—the beer bottle, the shaggy hair, the troubled eyes . . ."

"What?"

Joey averted his eyes from Hogie's questioning stare. "Nothing."

"Well, we have to go," said Vita. "Just wanted to say hi."

"Hey!" said Al. "How about you let Joey party with us. He's good company."

Vita grabbed Joey's arm and walked away. "*Not for thy fairy kingdom!* Come on, Joey."

"Bye, Al. See you later, Hogie!" Joey hollered.

"She's a piece of work." Hogie smiled and raised his head in goodbye.

࿔

By 6:30, the house was buzzing with activity, with everyone moving to and from the bedrooms and kitchen. Millie and Sal were getting dressed to go to the Elks dance uptown, and the three girls were deciding what Vita should wear for the audition.

Joey was on the phone with his parents, part listening, part watching all the commotion, and part telling them the latest news.

"Uncle Sal and Aunt Millie are going to a dance tonight, so we're going to order a pizza from a place on the square, and Vita is getting ready for the audition tomorrow and Anne and Beth are helping her. She'll get it for sure. And then the next day is that photoshoot I was telling you about and I'm going to be a part of it and take some pictures. Millie's letting me use her camera." He paused to listen and nodded. "Yeah, I'm learning a lot. I got some books on it from the library." He listened again. "She's right here."

Millie had come into the kitchen dressed in a pale aquamarine dress and was clipping on matching earrings. She kept one in her hand and stood behind Joey, taking the phone. He smiled as he heard his mom talking with the sound of happiness in her voice.

Millie laughed. "He is! I think he's having a really good time. Oh, he loves the fair. And he's been such a big help with everything." She nodded and listened. "I'll let you say goodbye to him. Bye, Dorothy."

Joey took the phone and said goodbye to his mom and dad. He saw Sal come into the kitchen wearing a sports jacket, slacks, and a shirt and tie. Joey was surprised at how different he looked. Kind of like a movie star. He hadn't realized how handsome Sal was.

The girls came out and said goodbye to their parents. "You look beautiful, Mom. You too, Dad."

Sal pulled out some money from his wallet and gave it to Anne. "For the pizza."

"We better be off," said Millie. "The dinner starts at 7:00. Make sure you take out the salad, Anne. It's in the fridge, all ready to go. We have to make sure Joey eats enough." She hugged them goodbye.

Half an hour later, Joey was riding in the front seat with Anne to pick up the pizza. He even went inside alone to pay for it, while Anne waited outside in the car.

Vita and Beth had the table set and they were soon eating pizza and salad. They talked about the audition and the directors, how his wife seemed really nice, but Mr. Radcliff was a little stern, but that it didn't matter because Vita had mastered the lines and was as ready as she could be.

Anne was at the kitchen counter putting together a plate of cookies and brownies. "And now, we're going to have a little pre-celebration for Vita. Outside. Beth, get the floral tablecloth, we'll spread it under the ash tree."

"No, no celebration yet," said Vita. "I don't want to jinx it."

"Okay. We'll just celebrate . . . summer. Bring this plate out, and Joey, can you bring the lemonade? I'll get the paper cups."

They sat on the tablecloth and placed the cookies in the middle. Then Anne came out with a paper bag.

"What?" asked Beth. "What's in the bag?"

"A surprise. For later."

Joey held up Millie's camera. "Can I take some?"

"Of course, you can."

Joey took a few pictures of them individually and then of them all leaning together.

While they munched on the treats, Joey thought how he was beginning to feel like a part of the family. They were always nice to him and included him in most things. And he never felt in the way at all. Millie even told his mom he was helping them.

Vita still wore her long skirt and green top, but Anne had changed into a navy tank top and a long rose-colored skirt. Beth had put on cut-offs and a white t-shirt. While she talked, she untied the piece of rawhide to her ponytail and divided her hair in two sections. She began braiding it, pausing to eat a brownie after one side was done, then braiding the other side.

"I'm thinking of changing my name," Beth said. "Just a little."

Anne was setting out the cups. "Now you sound like Vita."

"There were too many Vickys in my class. What do you mean, a little?"

"I'm thinking of going by 'Bette'. It's shorter. Crisper. What do you think, Joey?"

He spoke both names. "Beth. Bette. Beth. Bette." One sounded as short as the other.

"There's not much difference," said Anne. "They both have one syllable."

Beth leaned her head in thought. "But Bette sounds shorter. Shorter is better." She tied the piece of rawhide around her forehead.

"But Bette has an extra letter," Vita pointed out.

"Shoot. I didn't think about that. There goes that idea."

Joey took a picture of Beth. She sat cross-legged with two long unbound braids hanging down the front of her shirt. And with the rawhide around her forehead . . .

"You *do* kind of look like an Indian."

Beth's eyes lit up. "Thank you, Joey!"

"Don't encourage her," said Anne. "She's already set on the Southwest."

"Speaking of . . ." said Beth. "Secrets and Dreams! Tonight is the perfect night for it."

"What is it?" Joey asked.

"I forgot all about that," said Vita. "It's a game we used to play."

"Basically, we just ramble on about what we want." Beth looked at Joey and whispered. "And tell our secrets."

Anne opened the bag. "In that case, *this* will be perfect to sip on while we talk about our dreams." She lifted out a bottle of pink wine.

"Anne!" cried Beth. "Where'd you get that?"

"Diane let me have it. It's only half full, but it's enough for me and Vita to have a small glass. Don't get this in any pictures, Joey."

Vita lifted her cup for some wine. "Thank you, Anne. I can imagine we're on a Paris balcony, overlooking the rooftops at night."

"What's wrong with here?" asked Anne, filling her paper cup.

Beth held out her cup. "If we're going to tell secrets then I'm old enough for my own glass. Joey?"

"Nah. I'll have lemonade."

"Mom and Dad would kill us if we gave wine to Joey."
Anne poured out a tiny splash. "Just a taste for you, Beth.
You're only fourteen."

"Kids in Italy drink wine all the time. They grow up
with it. Dad said so."

"Oh, so now you're Italian?"

"If Vita can be queen of the fairies, I can be whatever
I want."

Vita broke a twig into three pieces and held them up
to Anne and Beth. "Draw. Don't worry, Joey. You don't
have to play."

They all drew a stick and measured them. "Beth
goes first."

Beth took a deep breath. "I usually do secrets first. And
end with a dream. So . . ." She looked up at the sky as if
deciding between her many secrets. "Well, I kind of posed
sort of nude for a photograph."

"Beth!" cried Anne, choking on the wine. "You better
not have!"

"What do you mean *kind of sort of*?" asked Vita.

"Relax, Anne! I had my cutoffs on. But you couldn't
really tell. I was sitting on a horse and the saddle kind of
covered me, but it looks like I'm nude."

"Horse?" asked Vita. "What horse?"

"Dylan arranged it with Ernie. He lives on a farm and—"

"And on top?" Anne demanded.

"That's the sort of nude part. But my hair was down
and completely covered me."

Anne exploded again. "Beth! What were you thinking?
Who took the picture?"

"I was posing as an Indian." She smiled at Joey. "I did look a bit like Zitkala-Sa, if I do say so myself. I read about her in a book from the library. She was the most amazing—"

"Beth! Who took the picture?"

"I told you. Dylan. My *friend*. Nothing romantic."

"I see the way he looks at you."

"The way Mark looks at you? Besides, my hair covered more than your midriffs do."

"Those show my stomach! Who cares about that?"

"Anyway, it turned out nice." Beth took a sip of her wine.

Anne huffed. "Mom always tells me to keep an eye on you and this is why." She put a hand to her head. "And here I am, giving you wine."

Vita laughed at their sparring. "I'd like to see it, Beth. And your dream?"

Beth leaned back and put her hands behind her head. "I think after I graduate from high school, I'll go to New Mexico. Find my people."

"You're *not* an Indian, Beth," said Anne.

Beth sat up and rolled her eyes. "I'm talking about artists! Sculpture, pottery, paint big canvases like Georgia O'Keeffe. Live in an adobe house in Taos. Doesn't that sound like fun? Get a potter's wheel—I'd love it. Maybe I'll fall in love with the desert and settle out there."

Anne shifted to being dismayed. "So far from us?"

"You and Vi are going to New York. Think how much fun it will be to visit each other all over the place. Joey, you'd visit us, right?"

"Yeah. Sure."

Beth tossed her stick away. "Your turn, Anne."

Anne smiled and spread her skirt around her. "Well, it's no surprise, but—I really love being with Mark. We talk about how it will be later. When we're a little older."

Beth let out a bored sigh. "Is this a secret or a dream?"

"Okay, okay. I dream that one day Mark and I will live in a beautiful house with flowers all around it, and a little stream with a foot bridge over it. And in the winter, we'll make fires in the fireplace and—well, you get the idea." She sipped her wine and smiled.

"It's a lovely dream," said Vita, "but I hope it's in the distant future, because we have a lot do before that happens."

"I know."

Beth made a show of yawning. "And your secret?"

Anne looked at them and bit her lip. "You have to *promise* not to tell anyone."

Beth leaned forward. "This is more like it."

"You have to swear. I mean it. I could lose my job. And my reputation."

"I swear, I swear." Beth crossed her heart.

Anne looked at Vita and Joey.

"We won't tell anyone," said Vita.

"I won't," said Joey. "I promise."

Anne blew out a deep breath. "Okay. So. Tuesday was really busy at lunch, busier than usual. There was a table from the courthouse. The judge was there at a table of four. You know how he loves Mrs. Finlay's apple pie."

Beth nudged Joey. "Brace yourself. This is going to be a real shocker."

Anne grew flustered at the memory. "I was trying to do ten things at once, and they all ordered coffee and dessert at the same time. I brought out two and went back to get the judge his pie. And . . . and it slid right off the plate."

She waited for their reaction. "Onto the floor."

Vita waited a moment. "And?"

"It was the last piece. What could I do?"

Beth's eyes widened. "You served it? You served the *judge* a piece of pie from the floor?" She rolled onto her back, laughing.

Anne closed her eyes. "I know. I looked at it carefully and kind of molded it back into shape, and blew on it, even though I didn't see anything on it."

"Blew your germs all over it?" This made Beth howl even more.

Anne covered her face with her hands. "See? I could ruin their business!"

By now Vita and Joey were also laughing, mostly because Beth was laughing so hard.

"I'm sure it tasted as good as ever," Anne said. "The ice cream helped to cover it." And then she burst out laughing and could barely get out the words, "You can never tell anyone! I can't believe I did that! I can't even tell Mark!" She pressed her hand to her side.

Beth lifted her shirt to her eyes, and when the laughter finally died down, Anne refilled their cups.

"Remember, not a word!" Anne took a sip and leaned her head on Vita's shoulder. "Your turn."

Vita cast her eyes down. "I wasn't ready to talk about it. Like Anne's dream, mine is nothing you don't already know." She hesitated a moment and brought the cup to her lips.

"Let me guess, you're going to be an actress."

Anne gave Beth a light shove. "Let her speak."

"It's more than just wanting to be an actor, Beth. This is the most important summer of my life. This will be my first professional production. And it means acceptance to their fall workshop. That would give me two years in their workshop, two Shakespeare plays. Don't you see? That could help me to get into a good college. Next summer will be too late. So this play *has* to happen. It has to. Even if I don't get Titania."

"You'll get Titania," said Beth, finishing her wine. She hesitated a moment, then added, "But what if you don't?"

"I can't think that way. I have to *make* it happen. This summer marks my first real step on the path. I'm working on my portfolio, and saving money for college, and—"

"And you've been studying so hard," said Anne. "You know so much."

"So what's your secret?" asked Beth.

They all stared at Vita when she didn't speak.

"Well, what is it?"

Vita's shoulders dropped. "I'm scared to death."

Now Beth took notice. "You? Afraid? You're not afraid of anything. Except heights. And even that you don't let get in your way. Look how you've been climbing the roof all summer."

"You sure seem really brave," Joey added.

"I'm not. I pretend to be, but really I'm terrified."

"Of what?" asked Anne.

"Of failing. Of misreading the lines. Of trying too hard and messing up. This audition is *everything*. The Radcliffs don't have callbacks—you only get one chance. Either you make it or you don't."

"You'll make it," said Anne. "You always do."

"Except she wanted to be Columbine instead of Pierrot. And in the fifth grade she wanted the role of—" Beth caught Anne's glare and stopped.

Vita gathered her hair in front and began twisting it. "Grade school and high school plays are just for fun. This is different. I think what I'm really so afraid of . . ." She dropped her hands. "I'm afraid that I'm dreaming too big, that I want too much."

"No, Vita," Joey said. "You're right about dreaming big. Otherwise, it isn't much of a dream."

Anne and Beth turned to Joey, surprised at his words.

"Sounds like you've been listening to Vita." Beth put up her hands. "In a good way. Go for the things you want and all that. Don't give up."

Vita smiled at Joey. "You're right. I have to keep focused on the dream. Not my fears."

"So . . ." Joey looked at each of the sisters, deciding if he should speak. "I kind of have a dream. At least I think I do."

Beth punched him in the arm. "Tell us! No holding back."

He became self-conscious, with all three looking at him, waiting for him to reveal his dream.

"What is it, Joey?" Anne asked.

"Well, I'm still kind of working on it." He rolled the hem of his t-shirt. "And I'm not sure exactly how . . ." An impatient groan from Beth made him laugh. "Okay. Well, I guess being here reminds me of how much I wanted to be an explorer."

"You're always looking at the map," Anne said in encouragement.

Beth shook out her braids. "Like slashing through the Amazon jungle?"

"No." Joey grinned. "That's how I used to imagine it. More like being a traveler. Seeing as many places as possible. Maybe work while I'm traveling. Vita and I were talking about how I could do photography."

Beth sat up and took in an excited breath. "You could take pictures and sell them! Oh, this is perfect. It's a good thing you came this summer and are learning photography."

"That's kind of what I was thinking. I don't know if anybody would buy them. But it would be fun to do." Joey grew excited at the idea. "Maybe when I get good, I could show my pictures to someone and get hired for an expedition or something."

Anne opened her arms. "Or work for a travel magazine. You could do lots of things!"

"Yeah," Joey said, looking far off.

"Okay, Marco Polo," said Beth, "now that you have your dream in place, time for your secret."

"He doesn't have to, Beth." Anne put a protective arm around Joey. "He's new to the game." She turned to him. "You can just do the dream part for now."

He bit his lip and twisted his hands.

Vita saw his anxiety. "You don't have to Joey. Maybe the next time, if you feel like it."

"No—I want to. Now. I want to be a part of this."

Anne hugged him. "You already are."

"Come on," Beth urged. "Secrets are the best part." She waited for Joey to look up at her. "You game?"

"Only if you want to Joey," Vita said, giving Beth a warning look.

He took a breath and started to speak. They all leaned in as if it would help him.

"I think . . . I think . . . I think Mom and Dad might get a divorce. Because of me."

All three girls stared at Joey with wide eyes. He realized he shouldn't have said that. "Or, or maybe we'll move again. Sometimes that happens."

Vita leaned her head on one side. "Why do you think that, Joey?"

He tried to think how to tell them without sounding like a bad kid. And he didn't want his parents to seem bad. They weren't. And he loved them so much.

"I'm a hundred percent sure it's not your fault," Anne said.

"It was my fault I got lost. That was kind of the last straw, I guess. I shouldn't have wandered so far from home."

"Lost? What happened?" asked Beth.

Joey scrunched up his face. "I wasn't paying attention to where I was going—I just needed to walk." When his parents started arguing he couldn't stand it. The last time he had run. It had felt so good to just keep running, letting his feet make all the decisions for him. As long as he kept running, he felt good.

"I started to run. And ran and ran and ran, turning corners, crossing streets, dodging traffic. And I kept on running some more. Finally, I stopped. I bent over and tried to catch my breath. When I looked up, I had no idea where I was. And it was starting to get dark.

"I checked my pockets, but I didn't have any money. It wasn't a good neighborhood. A few people on their steps were staring at me like I didn't belong there."

"Oh my gosh," said Vita. "What did you do?"

"I started walking like I knew where I was going. After a couple of blocks, I spotted a parked police car and I asked them for directions. They shook their heads and told me to get in. So I did. I heard them say 'dumb kid,' and 'just asking for trouble.' I felt like a stupid little kid.

"They drove me home. Mom was so mad. And it was just another thing for them to fight about."

Beth looked from Anne to Vita, confused. "Who?"

"Mom and Dad. I mean, I think they were scared. I didn't mean to do it. I just started running and couldn't stop. It was like I was someone else."

Anne gave it some thought. "People don't get divorced over stuff like that. I'm sure they were just worried."

"Yeah," said Beth. "Running and getting lost isn't such a big deal."

Vita looked off in thought, and then sat up straight. "I think you did something bold and brave. And you learned from it. You got help when you needed it and arrived home safely. I would call that a successful adventure."

For the first time, Joey saw the disaster in a different light. "You would?"

"Yes. I would. Getting lost doesn't have to be bad, after all."

"Yeah," said Beth. "I bet the early explorers got lost all the time."

"Of course, they did," Anne said with authority. "That's how most of them found anything. Look at Columbus. He thought he was on the other side of the world. And that was so brave of you to tell us." She reached out her hand

and they layered their hands over hers. "You're really one of us, now, Joey."

"Whether you like it or not!" added Beth. "All for one and one for all!"

"All dreamers! And you . . . an adventurous explorer!" Vita jumped to her feet. The sun had long ago set, and the blue sky above was slowly darkening. "You have entered the Night Realm, D'Artagnan! You have magic and powers you didn't even know about."

"What would you grant us, wise magician?" asked Anne, standing, and pulling Joey up with her.

Joey remembered a line from a story his mom used to read to him. "The sun, the moon, and the stars!"

"I'll take the sun," said Beth, jumping to her feet. "What name will you give me?"

Joey looked around for inspiration. "Sunshine?"

"I want the sun," said Anne.

"Okay. I name you—Day Princess."

"I'll take that. Thank you, Joey," she made a sweeping bow.

"And me?" asked Vita. "I belong to the moon and the stars. What name will you give me?"

Joey looked up at the sky and then to Vita. "Night Queen."

Vita threw open her arms. "Perfect!" She raised her hand to the sky. "*The moon, methinks, looks with a wat'ry eye. And when she weeps, weeps every little flower, lamenting some enforced chastity.*"

"Whatever *that* means," said Beth. She made a swipe at the bottle and emptied the last splash of pinkness into her cup.

"Beth," protested Anne.

"As Sunshine the fairy, I'm entitled to the elixir of night!"

Joey watched the three magical sisters, slipping in and out of make-believe so effortlessly. All theater and drama and dreaming, a casual part of them. And now he was a part of it, too. Explorer. Name giver. Dreamer.

He focused the camera and took more pictures of the three sisters. Then he frowned up at the sky. "I don't think these will come out. It's too dark." He set the camera back down and shifted his attention to Anne as she raised the paper bag.

"Then it's time for these." She opened the bag. "I've saved the best for last."

"What?" cried Beth.

Vita looked on with interest. "What do you have?"

Anne let the suspense build for a few seconds, and then held out a box of sparklers. "Let the magic begin!" she announced dramatically. "Leftovers from the Fourth of July. I was saving them for you, Joey."

His eyes grew wide. "I love sparklers!"

Anne gave the box of matches to Vita and raised a sparkler. "A bit of fire, Night Queen."

Vita brought the flame to the tip of the sparkler, stepping back as it burst into life. "To dreams and magic and all things wondrous!" She handed it to Joey, while they lit another.

Joey whooped and waved it high above his head.

"Hurry!" Beth pointed to the lightning bugs beginning to glow above the grass. "The fairies are starting without us!"

One by one, they lit the sparklers. They made designs in trailing lights as they twirled. Joey made figures with his sparkler and ran across the yard holding it high. Beth attempted a cartwheel and when he tried one himself, colliding with her, they all burst into laughter.

He lit the next round of sparklers and handed them out to the beautiful fairy-like sisters. A step into wonder and magic, a wild romp in dreamland. Why not? At that moment, Joey believed that anything was possible.

And then, as if the door to dreamland had been flung open, Abby appeared on her bike, coasting into the back yard.

"Sparklers? I want one!"

"Abby!" Joey lit one for her, laughing as he handed it to her.

She and Beth and Joey made designs together, circles and figure eights and wide arcs. Anne and Vita twirled with theirs, their long hair and long skirts swirling about them.

They moved in a world of dancing lights, sparking a thousand possibilities to life. Bright points set against the night, mixing dreams and laughter with youth—the most magical of crucibles.

As the last sparklers slowly extinguished, they plopped down on the tablecloth.

"Come on," cried Abby, leaving fairyland. "Let's go to the Dairy Queen. I have money." Joey and Beth ran to get their bikes and soon joined her.

"Are you guys coming?" Joey asked Vita and Anne.

"Mark's going to stop by later."

"And I want to go over my lines one more time."

"Come with us!" urged Beth, tugging on Vita's skirt.

Vita shook her head and jumped up on the bench by the flower garden. She spread her arms out before her. *"Fairies, away, and be all ways away!"* She stepped off the bench. "Go on—we'll clean up here." She waved them away.

Joey turned back to look at her. She made a graceful fairy wave of dismissal, and the three of them left on their bikes.

She and Anne gathered up the cups and plates. Just as they were folding the tablecloth, Mark showed up.

Anne ran to him and he swung her around in his arms. She ran back to Vita.

"I don't want to leave you all alone. Why don't you come with us?"

Vita gave a short laugh and playfully pushed her. "Away! I have things to do."

Mark took Anne's hand, but she snatched it from him and ran, making him chase her. Their laughter followed them to the front yard, and soon Vita heard the car drive away.

She looked up at the night sky, at the stars just beginning to prick the darkness.

When she picked up the cups and empty box of sparklers, she found one last stick. She set the tablecloth and empty cups down and lit the sparkler. Sure that there was no one there to see her, she twirled alone. She held the sparkler high, and watched it glitter against the evening sky.

"Bring me luck, night realm! Bring me luck."

CHAPTER 12

Vita looked beautiful as she left for the audition in the afternoon. She wore a lavender peasant top patterned with dark blue leaves, Anne's long navy skirt, and simple lapis drop earrings. It hinted at woodland romance, without being too obvious. Beth had tried to convince her to add strands of beads to her hair—"like the college girls"—but Vita wanted it unadorned. It hung loose down her back, though she allowed Anne to rub in a hint of oil for a slight sheen.

Beth couldn't wait for Anne and Vita to leave the house so that she could start working on the cake she and Anne had planned. They wouldn't be back until late afternoon and the creation she envisioned would take several hours to make. A two-layered cake with the words *A Midsummer Night's Dream* written on the top and decorated with real flowers from the garden.

"Smells good," Millie said later, returning from the grocery store. She saw that the cake layers were set out to cool. "I thought I'd make baked chicken and scalloped potatoes for tonight."

"Uh huh." Beth stood hunched over the table, making small sounds of frustration.

Millie glanced over and hid her smile. Beth was practicing the letters for the words. Several globs of icing, various letters, and vines covered a sheet of wax paper.

Beth took a step back and frowned at the letters she had written in script. "Why couldn't it be *Hamlet*? This is going to take forever to write."

"You're getting the hang of it. Though I still think you should've waited until we know for sure."

"Anne insisted. Besides, it's too late now. Even if Vita doesn't get Titania, she'll get one of the H roles. So the cake will still be appropriate."

Beth set the first layer on the glass cake stand, spread buttercream frosting on it, and carefully placed the second layer on top. Then she began to cover the cake in frosting. "I'm going to use dark blue for the letters and green for the vines. And real flowers to surround the base—roses and cornflowers. Violets, if I can find any. Maybe a sprinkle of marigold petals."

"It's going to be beautiful." Millie took out several potatoes and washed them in the sink.

Beth assessed the cake, filled in a low spot with more icing, and turned the cake stand around. She smiled over at Millie. "There. That looks pretty good. Now for the fun part."

Millie kept glancing at the clock and making comments about the audition. "I wonder if Vita has already been called. She seemed a little nervous." She began to slice the potatoes. "I wonder if they'll have her read for more than one part . . . He does seem like a rather stern man, but that shouldn't matter. His wife is very nice. I spoke to her after the play."

Beth too thought out loud as she worked. "I'll do the vines and leaves first. Then I'll know how big to make the letters." She carefully squeezed the pastry bag with green icing, forming a vine to encircle the top and another at the base. She paused now and then to nod at her work or add another leaf or tendril. "I can't believe Joey has a job."

"He was so eager to get started. I didn't even have to wake him this morning. He was dressed and ready to go by 8:00. I packed him a lunch and he ran over to Abel's."

Beth washed her hands and took a deep breath. "Now for the words." She picked up the dark-blue icing bag and began to painstakingly write the letters, squeezing the tube gently.

"Darn! . . . Oh no! . . . Shoot. This is harder than it looks." After fretting over several uneven words, leaving out a letter and having to start over again, cursing the tubes and using extra icing to cover her mistakes, Beth had fitted *A Midsummer Night's Dream* onto the cake.

She stood back and admired her work. "Not bad." Then she went out to the garden and picked the flowers, washed them, and set them on a dish towel to dry.

Within an hour, the kitchen filled with the smells of dinner. Millie watched Beth carefully place the last of the flowers on the cake.

"Oh, Beth! I think that's the most beautiful cake I've ever seen."

"I think she'll like it. I can't wait to hear how it went. I'm sure Vita dazzled them."

"I'm sure she did."

Beth was making a fresh pitcher of iced tea when she heard Joey come home.

"Joey! The working man. So how was it?"

"Really good! Abel let me mow the wide areas. He did the narrow spaces and around the headstones. It's nice out there." He inhaled the aroma. "That smells so good. I'm starving! And thirsty. Any word yet?"

"They should be home soon." Millie poured him a glass of water that he downed immediately. She poured another and smiled at how dirty he was. Sweaty, with grass clippings stuck to his arms and clothes, the knees of his jeans stained green, and his face flushed with heat.

"I got pretty dirty," he said with a laugh. "I'll go shower before dinner."

"We're having a celebration meal," said Beth. "Hurry! We thought they'd be home by now." She eyed the clock. "They're probably talking about rehearsals."

After a few minutes, they heard Anne's car pull up. Millie and Beth ran to the door and held the screen door open. They looked around, seeing only Anne. By her expression, they knew it wasn't good news.

"Where's Vita?"

"She had me drop her off by the college. She wanted to walk for a bit."

Millie followed Anne into the kitchen. "Well?"

"Tell us! Did she get Titania?" asked Beth.

Anne shook her head.

"On no," said Millie. "What'd she get—Helena?"

"Hippolyta?" asked Beth. "I told her she'd make a good Hippolyta."

They watched Anne's face.

"Hermia?" Beth counted off the H characters on her fingers. "That's the only other female. Am I missing someone?"

Anne dropped onto a chair. "She didn't get anything."

"What do you mean?" asked Beth.

Anne opened her hands. "*Nothing.*"

Millie blinked in surprise. "No minor role? No understudy or anything?"

"No speaking part at all? Or nonspeaking?" Beth's eyes grew wide in disbelief as Anne shook her head to every question. "Not even a fairy?"

Millie sat down next to Anne. "Oh no. She must be crushed! She pinned all her hopes on that play. I always tell you girls not to count on things. What on earth happened?"

Anne searched around her memory for any clue. "I have no idea. Vita was silent all the way home. Stunned, baffled. I'm sure she's blaming herself. It's hard to know what they want. I saw most of the people trying out. Vita was by far the most beautiful. At least I thought so."

"Do you think she messed up the lines?" Beth asked. "Or tripped and fell, or had a coughing attack? What else could it possibly be?"

Anne raised and dropped her hands. "No. She knew her lines. Maybe—"

"What?"

"Maybe she was nervous or something. She didn't quite seem herself. I can't put my finger on it."

Millie took a deep breath. "Well, she'll tell us, when she's ready. And we'll let her know that we still think she's wonderful."

"We're not the ones casting," said Beth.

"You know what I mean." Millie went back to tossing the salad. "Don't pressure her with questions when she comes."

Anne put her keys on the counter and saw the cake. "Oh, Beth, it's beautiful. But—"

"Don't even think it. Do you know how long it took me to get those letters to fit?"

Joey came out of the shower, and they filled him in on the news.

His expression of initial surprise shifted to defiance. "The people in charge don't always know everything."

Beth slapped him on the back. "Well said!"

They heard Sal arrive. He came into the kitchen, his face filled with expectation. "Well? Where's the star?" He looked from one to the other. "Why all the long faces?"

"I'll go watch for her." Beth planted herself at the living room window, her eyes on the direction of the college.

"Well?" asked Sal again. When no one looked directly at him and no one answered, he turned to Anne. "Did she blow the audition?"

Millie let out a huff. "For heaven's sake, Sal, don't put it that way."

He raised his hands in defense and headed down the hallway. "I'll just go wash up."

"She's coming!" cried Beth, running back into the kitchen.

"The cake!" cried Anne.

Beth groaned and took out a knife. "This is going to kill me." She swirled the letters into a mash of blue. "That looks awful!" She picked up a rose and stuck it in the middle.

Anne also frowned at it. "Act nonchalant. Don't stare at her."

Millie met Vita at the door and wrapped her arms around her.

Vita raised her eyes. "Anne told you?"

Millie smoothed her hair. "Don't let it get you down. There will be many more auditions. You know you won't get all the roles you want."

"I know. I know that. I just—I just had such a good feeling about this part. I—I don't know what I did wrong. Mom, they didn't give me anything!" Tears filled her eyes.

"They obviously don't know what they're talking about," said Beth, pulling out a chair at the table for Vita.

"They *do* know." Vita sat down and stared at the floor.

Beth plopped down next to her. "Who cares what they think?"

"Everyone who auditioned. That's who."

Beth gave an "I tried" look to her mom.

Joey didn't know what to say. "You'll get other roles."

Vita stared out in disbelief. When Sal came back, her eyes filled with disappointment. "I didn't get anything, Dad."

"Can't win 'em all." He gave her a pat on the back and took his seat. "Come on. Let's eat. Nothing a good meal won't fix. At any rate, you're still the best witch in town!" He looked up when no one else laughed. "What I mean is . . . there will be other roles that you're suited for."

"Witches? With red hair?" said Vita.

Millie poured iced tea for everyone. "Did you get a chance to speak to them about it? The directors?"

"I didn't try."

"There wasn't time," said Anne. "Everyone waited and after the names were called out, they were swarmed. We went up just to make sure. Mrs. Radcliff was nice. She told Vita she was very good."

"Good doesn't count," said Vita. "I don't know what I did wrong. They had me read again and again. And the more I read, the more unsure I became. I felt like I wasn't giving them what they wanted."

Milly took her seat and scooted her chair in. "When things quiet down, I think you should speak to them. You'll never know otherwise. You might learn from . . . from . . . for the next time." She handed the salad bowl to Vita.

"I couldn't. I feel ashamed, somehow. I didn't get *anything*. It feels like a punishment."

"Don't see it like that. Many very talented people never—I mean, they just have to keep trying. That's the nature of the business. Help yourself to the chicken, Joey."

"It's really good, Mom," said Beth.

Sal had been quiet, enjoying the food. "There's always secretary school." Millie's sharp stare let him know that he had said the wrong thing. "Or college. You could be a teacher. You could teach this stuff. And not have to audition. Might be more enjoyable that way. Less pressure."

Vita stared at the food on her plate. "I'm not hungry. I'll eat later, if you don't mind."

Millie nodded. "Go ahead. I'll keep a plate for you."

Vita left the table and walked outside.

They saw her wander to the flower garden and sit on the bench.

"Maybe she was just 'off' today," suggested Anne.

"Maybe *they* were," said Beth.

Millie let out a sigh. "These things happen. The sooner she gets back on track the better. Joey, when is that photoshoot? That might cheer her up."

"Tomorrow."

"Or depress her." Beth saw that her mom looked pained. "She'll bounce back, Mom."

"She's right," said Anne. "Vita's strong. She'll just keep moving ahead with her dreams and plans and her portfolio and things." Her words fell flat.

Millie shifted the conversation and asked Joey to tell them about his first day working with Abel. Everyone was relieved when the celebration dinner was over.

They cleared the table and Anne placed the cake in the center of the table. "The sooner we cut this up, the better. Sorry, Beth."

Sal leaned forward and eyed the smeared cake. "What's this supposed to be? A lake?"

Anne cut the cake and passed slices around. In between talking about Joey's work with Abel, and Millie's next book club evening, and the backdrop Beth and Abby spray painted for the Titania shoot, other phrases popped up: "Best not say anything just yet. You know how she is."

"Don't bring it up for now."

"I can't image what happened. She was so sure."

And the thud of Sal's comment: "Now maybe she'll pick a more sensible career." He pushed his chair back. "Joey, let's go check on the tomatoes."

In the garden, Joey held out his shirt to hold the vegetables Sal picked.

"You can put these on the ledge to ripen. I'll bring the cucumbers and peppers in." Sal gestured over to Vita by the flower garden. "Maybe you can try to cheer her up."

Joey brought the tomatoes to the window ledges. They were already lined with tomatoes in varying shades of green and red. He walked over to the flower garden bench.

"Hey, Joey," Vita said softly.

Joey sat next to her. He was angry that the directors hadn't seen how perfect Vita was for the role.

"*I* would have given you the part."

Vita gave a hint of a smile. "Like Mom said, it's just one audition. Not the end of the world."

Joey didn't believe her easy acceptance. He knew that all her plans hinged on the audition. He wondered if he should ask about it, or change the subject, or not say anything.

"The worst of it is that now I feel so unsure of myself." Vita opened one hand. "Maybe I was overconfident." She opened the other. "Or not confident enough." Her hands dropped to her lap.

"I guess it's hard to know."

A wry smile twisted her mouth. "Or maybe I'm just a small-town girl with a dream too big. Mediocre, average in everything."

For a brief moment, Joey tried to see her like that. Just a regular girl, with all the magic dropped from her. But he couldn't.

"No, you're not."

She let out a deep sigh and reached for a dandelion puff. She raised it to her lips and blew sharply, releasing the tiny seedlings. She watched them float away into the air, and then tossed away the stem. "The truth is, Joey . . . I'm as ordinary as dirt."

"That's not true. Even if you were, your dreams make you different."

Vita laughed and Joey realized that his words hadn't come out the way he intended.

"I mean—when you talked about your dream, I felt excited, like I could see it and feel it, and it made me want my own dream. That's what's different about you. Not your hair or whatever."

Vita turned to Joey. "What about my hair? My witch's hair."

Joey looked at her coppery waves, catching the early evening rays. "Your hair's beautiful. Mom always says that. 'Vita has hair like gold.' Especially like now, with the sun on it. It's like you're part of the sunset." His words were all over the place. Maybe it was better if he didn't say anything.

"Don't worry, Joey. I might have fallen, but I haven't given up. I'll keep on my path even if I have to crawl an inch at a time. It's where I want to be."

"See? That makes you different."

Vita gave a breathy laugh. "It's just—I had everything so carefully planned. Now, I feel like I don't know anything. What to do next. And part of me can't help wondering— what if I'm no good?"

"Even if you're not, you can get good. If that's what you want. You said all that matters is that you try. And then you'll get closer and closer to the thing that you want."

"So you're telling me to take my own advice."

"I don't know. I guess so."

She rose to her feet. "Let's go inside. I'll let Mom know I'm okay. Taste the celebration cake and tell Beth how good it is."

Joey smiled to think that she had noticed the cake after all. "Are you coming to the fair with us? We're going out with Anne and Mark."

"I think I'll stay home with Mom. Tonight is Dad's bowling night."

They went inside just as Sal was leaving and Mark was pulling up. In the kitchen Anne and Beth made last-minute adjustments, Anne changing shoulder bags, and Beth telling her that's why she should wear jeans.

"If you have pockets, you don't need to carry a purse." She held up her free hands. "Less is always better."

Anne had Vita arrange a silver barrette in her hair. "It's the last night of the fair. Come with us."

"You're not going, Vita?" asked Millie. "It might help to take your mind off things."

"No. I think I'll stay home."

Milly put her arm around Vita. "It's been a long day. You can keep me company." She walked the others to the door, whispering to Anne. "Keep an eye on Beth."

Anne smiled. "I will. Bye, Mom!"

"Have fun, Joey." Millie waved from the door and returned to the kitchen. Vita sat at the table, staring out the window.

"The book club meets tomorrow and I'm making something new. Sweet and savory pastries. Want to help? I've made the fillings, but I need to make the shells. Then I'll fill them and sprinkle them with nuts."

"Sure, Mom." Vita knew her mom's remedy for being down was to keep busy, to make progress in another area.

"Here you go. You can chop the walnuts."

Vita brought the nuts, a chopping board and knife, and a bowl to the table. She sat quietly, chopping the nuts.

While Millie mixed the ingredients, she kept glancing over at Vita. "Joey sure seems happy. He's like a different boy from when he arrived, isn't he?"

Vita nodded. "He is."

"I think he has more fun with you girls than with the boys at the park. Going to the fair with Beth and Abby. And he's quite taken with the camera." Millie glanced at her recipe and preheated the oven.

"Especially with David teaching him," added Vita. "He's really excited about it."

"He seemed a little sad those first few days. Preoccupied."

"I think he's afraid his parents might get divorced."

Millie gave a surprised glance to Vita. "Oh, they would have done so by now. They've made it this far. Most couples struggle at one time or another."

Vita looked at the back of her mother. Her beautiful mother, always at the stove, always cooking and cleaning and doing things for everyone else. She cocked her head. "Did you and Dad?"

"Did we ever. We had a rough spot. I wasn't sure we were going to make it.

Vita stopped chopping and stared. "You're kidding. You and Dad?"

Millie let out a sigh. "You girls were not much more than babies. And I had a hard time. It was after Mom died. I missed her so much and felt so alone. Sal was working all the time, trying to make a go of the shop. Spending too much time after work at the tavern. I felt like I was on my own.

"For a time, I considered moving back to St. Louis, to be near Nellie. I could have found work. It would have been hard, but at the time it seemed a happier option."

"So what happened?"

"Sal said he couldn't live without me. Would change his ways. And for the most part, he was good to his word. You girls got older. I got older. I guess I learned how to deal with things better." Millie smiled at Vita and began to press the dough into the cupcake molds.

Vita observed her mom, as if seeing her anew. She tried to imagine her unhappy.

"I began to volunteer at the library a few days a month. Then we formed the book club. That helped. It gave me something else to think about besides changing diapers and mopping floors and cooking dinners. And then Sal expanded with the new shop, and I was needed there."

Vita had a pang of what Joey had described—feeling responsible for the unhappiness of her parents. "Gosh, Mom. I'm sorry."

Millie brushed aside the idea. "Nothing to be sorry about. That's life. You learn to make the best of things."

Vita slowly chopped a few more nuts. "Have you been happy since then?"

"I have. For the most part, I have. But that's why I want you to pursue your dreams. I want your life to be full. I want you to have as few regrets as possible. So we'll figure out a way for you to keep moving on your path. Then, it's up to you. There will be disappointments, but that's to be expected."

"I know." Vita felt that she hadn't handled the audition failure in a mature way.

"Don't let yourself get sidetracked. By boys or setbacks or doubts. Just keep on pushing ahead. If you're sure it's what you want."

"I am sure. At least I'm sure I love it. I'm less sure about how to make it happen."

Millie placed the shells in the oven and set the timer. "I think you should start by speaking with the directors. You might learn something that will help you with the next audition."

Vita winced at the idea. "I'll think about it. I will. Right now, I just need to get over it."

"Take all the time you need. But not a moment more." Millie rinsed the mixing bowl and utensils and set them in the dishwasher. "You don't want to waste any time moping when things go wrong. If you're sure about this path, you'll have to be strong."

"I am sure. It's the only thing I ever found that makes me feel so . . . I don't know how to explain it. Connected, to life."

Millie took off her apron, poured herself a small glass of wine, and sat at the table. She took a sip and sighed. "Feels good to sit. So, tell me. When did you first really feel that? I know you always enjoyed putting on skits and being in the school plays. But the last year or two, you've really had a fire under you. Was it the *Macbeth* play?"

Vita put her chin in her hand and looked out the window. "That was the beginning, in a way. But I think what really did it was the time I spent with Aunt Nellie last year.

That's when I knew I would do whatever it took to move to a big city and become an actress."

"I knew that would be a good idea. You've always loved cities. I thought a few nights in St. Louis with Nellie would be just the thing." Millie took another sip and smiled.

"You always know, Mom. You've always tried to give us whatever you think will help."

"We're lucky to have Nellie. I miss her being away."

"So do I. I had such a wonderful time with her." Vita's face shone with remembered happiness. "She showed me a book of paintings of beautiful women with red hair like us. The Pre-Raphaelites. And it made me feel special. I think it was the first time I began to like my hair."

"I never knew you felt that way. You and Nellie have such gorgeous hair."

"And we talked about so many interesting things. She told me about her travels and the university and the different people she knew. One day I waited for her while she taught a class. She showed me a little café near the campus, the Pierrot Café. I felt so grown up, Mom, being in a café in the city all by myself. There were posters all over the brick walls of Pierrot and the moon."

The timer sounded and Millie took out the first batch of pastry shells. She lifted them from the molds and set them on a tray.

"So, you had a special connection to Pierrot. Perhaps that's why you portrayed him so well." She put a second batch in the oven and set the timer again.

"I think I identified with him, longing for something beautiful and faraway. I felt like—this is how it could be for me. In a big city, where I could be a part of something, where I could become the person I want to be."

"You're making me quite envious. Sometimes I miss the city. Nellie lives such an exciting life. At least from the outside, as she likes to remind me. It wasn't easy for her. She worked hard to get where she is. You're very like her and I thought it would be good for you to get a taste of another way of living."

"It was like I fell in love with the way life could be."

Vita was silent for a bit, comparing that vision with the reality of the failed audition.

"Do you think I'm just a dreamer?"

"We're all dreamers." Millie took a sip from her glass. "Some people make them happen. Others give them up."

Millie gazed out at the yard and squinted in thought. "I think having dreams help. They give us something to hope for and infuse life with meaning and happiness. Most people would probably disagree with me, but. . . ." With her eyes still on the yard, a soft smile came to her lips. "A dream garden is better than no garden at all. At least your mind is filled with flowers and color and beauty. And I think, without even being aware of it, we slowly move towards what we hold in our minds."

"I hope that's how it works. What do you think about me and my dream?"

Millie leaned towards Vita. "I think you have a lot of potential. And I think once you overcome your fears and doubts, you'll be unstoppable." She tapped the table. "That's what I think."

"I had no confidence, Mom. At the audition. I didn't know it, until I saw the others there. I realized how empty I was, how afraid. And then I tried to cover it and I just made things worse. I was fake."

"So you learned something about yourself. Now you can take steps to improve. Talking to the directors will shed some light. If it doesn't, at least you tried. That's the main thing."

Vita nodded, taking it all in. She looked at her mom and thought how lucky she was. To have a mother who was on her side, who didn't judge, who encouraged her and believed in her.

"Are you happy, Mom?"

"Am *I* happy?" Millie looked at Vita, blinking. "Well, nothing gives me more joy than to see my children happy."

"But—are *you* happy?"

Again, Millie was thrown by the question and gave a light laugh. "Well, I married the man of my dreams. And have three wonderful daughters. If that's not happiness . . ." The timer rang, and she took the pastry shells out of the oven. "I'll let these cool."

Vita took the chopped nuts to the counter and washed her hands before sitting back down. "Was there anything you ever wanted to do—that you didn't do?"

Millie dismissed the idea with a wave of her hand. "Oh, Dorothy and I had big plans to travel when we were young. Then we both got married. Sal and I want to go to Italy one day, and travel through Europe. But there's still time for that." She sat back at the table.

"Anything else—just for you, that you always wanted?"

Millie gave a shy smile and twisted her glass around before taking the last sip. "There was one thing. I've never told anyone. I would have liked to go to school. To college."

"Really, Mom? I never knew that."

Millie tilted her head, twirling her empty wine glass. "Sometimes, when it's slow at the library, I wander around and look at different books, so many subjects. Geography. Science. Foreign literature. All those biographies of important people. There's just so much to know. The world is such a big place."

"Could you have gone?"

"Oh, it was different back then. After the war, all of us just wanted to get married and have babies. Especially once I met Sal. I was so in love."

Millie smiled at the memory. "Nellie was different. She was brilliant and nothing was going to get in her way. And look at her now, teaching at the university among mostly men. But she gave up having a family."

They sat quietly for a few moments, lost in their thoughts.

"I certainly don't regret my decision. I've loved being a mother to you girls. But sometimes, I think about it. I guess that's why I like the library."

"Maybe you could take a class out at the college?"

Millie laughed at the idea. "And sit there with all those young smart students? I could never." She shook her head. "But I hope that you girls will get an education. And follow your dreams. Nothing would make me happier."

"I will, Mom. I promise. I think we all will. We all want good jobs. Well, you never know what Beth will do. She could be a scientist or a Spanish professor or run an art gallery. Nothing would surprise me."

They both laughed, and Millie lovingly ran her hand over Vita's hair. She brought her glass to the sink. "Oh, look at that gorgeous sky, all lavender and pink, the air that shimmery gold."

She turned to Vita, her eyes lit up like a girl's. "Let's take a walk out to the college! How appropriate that would be. Stroll around the grounds on this beautiful summer evening."

Vita's smile and eyes mirrored her mother's. They slipped on their sandals and walked out into a sunset world that was half small town reality, half lovely dream.

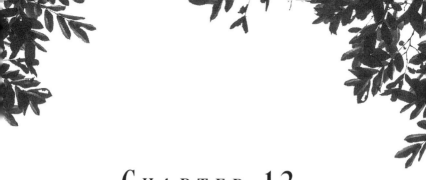

CHAPTER 13

Joey awoke to the hum of lawnmowers and birds chirping. The fun of the fair the night before was fresh in his mind and a faint smile formed on his lips. The window by his bed was raised, and he could smell the scent of cut grass. A shaft of light found its way through a crack in the curtains and lay across his bed. He moved his hand into it, catching the morning sun.

He whipped the blanket off. Boyland awaited. He pulled on his clothes, splashed water on his face in the bathroom, and went out into the kitchen.

Sal and Beth were about to leave for the shop.

"You're up!" said Beth, finishing her toast and jam. "Dad only needs me in the morning, so after lunch we'll go to Abby's and help with the Oberon and Puck shoot. David wants a certain kind of light for the Titania scene so that one will be later, around 6:30. You'll love their yard. It's huge and the back of it runs right into the woods."

"I want to see that." Joey poured himself a bowl of cereal and milk.

"It leads to a pond and there's a stream we can explore." She heard Sal start his truck and hurried to catch up with him. "Bye! Bye Mom!"

Millie waved as she sipped her coffee at the counter. "So, your first photoshoot."

Joey nodded. "David's going to teach me some more things. And he's going to show me the photos I took at the fair with his camera. I can't wait to see how they turned out."

"And I dropped off the roll of film from my camera to be developed. It takes about two weeks to get it back."

"Thanks." Joey was happy he had a job. He had spent most of the money from his parents on the fair and two more rolls of film. He didn't want to waste Millie's film on practice shots.

"What will you do this morning, Joey?"

"Abel's not working today so I thought I'd ride my bike around and take some pictures. Then see if the guys are at the park."

"I'll be at the library for a few hours in the morning if you need anything, and you can always go to Sal's shop. But I'll be home for lunch."

"Okay." Joey brought his bowl to the counter.

"I'll get that, Joey. You go on and have fun." She smiled to see him dash out of the house.

Joey hopped on his bike and zigzagged through the streets. Today he rode to the west, on the opposite side of town from the college.

He slowed a bit when he passed an old, dilapidated shed. He recognized it as the "Rufus shack." On his last visit, the boys had told him that was where Rufus Sharp lived. They used to dare each other to knock on the shed door and holler, "Hey, Rufus, you in there?" and then speed off on their bikes.

It had made sense to Joey when he was eight years old that Rufus might live there. The shed was long and narrow, Rufus was tall and thin. Now, he realized that it was just a regular old shed.

He passed a couple of houses with flowers and big vegetable gardens and turned onto the road that led to the country. He coasted down a small hill with a meadow on one side and green fields of soybeans on the other.

This stretch of road passed through a small dip in the land, and he found it more interesting with pastures and curves in the road. He pedaled up the other side, where the land flattened again.

There were a few white farmhouses with long drives set back from the road. Tall trees surrounded them—for shade, Joey guessed—and tractors and farm machinery sat parked near the barns.

Joey soon came to a fork in the road. One way connected to the highway, the other led out to the country. One of those endless pencil-straight roads Beth had described, with fields of corn on either side, stretching as far as you could see.

There was an abandoned trap shoot at the fork. The open wooden structure was full of tall weeds and buzzing insects. With the long straight road in the background, it had a lonely feel about it.

Joey took out his camera and tried different angles to take a few pictures. Some up close, some farther away. Satisfied, he headed back and coasted down the hill.

When he got to the bottom, he leaned his bike against an old fence that ran alongside the road. There was a wooden section with a gate that still showed old bits of white paint, but for the most part it looked forgotten.

The rest of the fence was made of wire. Wildflowers and clumps of weeds grew on both sides so that from a distance, it looked like a mound of tangled green hemmed in the meadow.

Joey climbed the wooden gate, sat on the top and gazed out. A small stream meandered through the grasses, winding around low bluffs formed by erosion. In the distance, a few cows grazed on the other side of the stream. They raised their heads when he sat on the fence, stared a moment, and then went back to munching on grass and swishing their tails. He focused the camera on them and took some shots.

Everything was lush and green. Even the air seemed tinged in green. Joey inhaled deeply. Summertime air—already thick with the humid heat of morning, smelling both sweet and pungent. A mix of scents coming from the grasses and trees and meadow flowers.

Joey ran his eyes over the landscape, part grassy meadow, part pasture. If he ever lived in this town, he would want a house right here. Close to town, but with a country feel. More animals. A big sky and wide green hills. More birds chirping. A real peaceful place that looked fun for exploring. Maybe even for having adventures.

He imagined D'Artagnan crouched by the stream, allowing his horse to drink. Or standing at the top of the gully with his gauntleted hand outstretched, waiting for his falcon to return. Did D'Artagnan even have a falcon? It didn't matter. He could imagine anything he wanted to in this place, and no one would ever know.

He was completely alone but didn't feel a bit lonely. Just the opposite. A robin landed on the fence next to him and cocked its head at Joey. He was afraid if he moved the bird would fly away so he sat perfectly still and watched it. After a few hops along the fence, the bird let out a chirp and flew away. Joey followed it with his eyes and saw it flit across the meadow to a tree.

Joey decided that this would be his spot. The place he could come to and just think about things and watch the cows and birds and clouds. When he had more time, he would go down to the stream and see if there were any frogs or minnows. He smiled, feeling that he had a most wonderful secret. He felt like singing. He opened his mouth but couldn't think of a song that would go with his meadow, and laughed at himself.

He looked up through the trees above him where sunlight sparkled through the leaves. He aimed the camera at the treetop but decided it wouldn't be a good shot. David had told him that some things couldn't really be captured on film.

The sun was getting much higher in the sky. He wanted to check out the park before lunch, so he said a silent good-bye to his meadow and climbed off the fence.

He walked his bike up the steep part of the hill, and at the top he mounted his bike—like D'Artagnan mounting his steed—and pedaled hard towards the park.

He was happy to see a few of the guys playing ball and felt even happier when Eddie and Matt called out to him. He dropped his bike and ran to play with them. He didn't have to worry about the time because the town whistle sounded every day at noon. He'd play until he heard it and could be home in two minutes.

Joey used up the last of the film on the ballpark and then heard the camera make a funny noise. He tried to take the film out but it jammed. He hopped on his bike and rode home.

"Aunt Millie!" he cried, running into the kitchen. "I think I broke your camera. I don't know what happened."

"Did that thing jam again? That's the third time that has happened." She was able to force the back open and take out the cartridge. "Thank goodness the film won't be ruined. I'd say it's time for a new camera. I'm afraid you'll be without one for a few days."

"I'll buy one for you since I broke it."

"You didn't break it, Joey." She laughed and ruffled his hair. "I needed a new one anyway. Maybe you can ask David what he would recommend."

"Sure. I'll ask him today at the shoot."

ॐ

Vita had been alone at work all morning with no customers. She watered the plants, plucked off brown leaves, and dusted the shelves. Time passed slowly.

When the little bells jangled, she looked up and was happy to see Laura. She wore a sleeveless blue dress with several strands of long beads and little round sunglasses. Her wavy dark hair was piled loosely on top of her head. She pushed her glasses up into her hair when she came inside.

"Hi, Laura!"

"Hello, Vita. How'd your audition go? I've been dying to hear."

"Not so good. I didn't get the part I wanted. Or any part."

"Ohhh. I know what that's like. Well . . . there will be others."

Vita gave a tired smile. "That's what everyone says."

"You just have to keep trying. It took me years before I made the orchestra in college. I finally made the cut in my last year. It was well worth the wait."

Laura walked among the potted flowers, turning them around. She finally decided on a thickly blooming pink geranium. She set it on the counter. "For my porch."

"The prettiest porch in town."

Laura took out her wallet and observed Vita as she rang up the sale. "Don't let it get you down. It can be good experience. It makes you try even harder."

Vita nodded. "That's my plan. To keep trying."

"Rejection can make you strong. It tests your resolve like nothing else. I should know," she added with a laugh. "Have you seen him?"

"Some. He bites my head off whenever I mention your name."

Laura smiled. "I'll take that as encouragement." She lifted the geranium and put her sunglasses on. "Stop by sometime. I'll play you some Chopin." She opened the door and turned around. "Or maybe some ragtime would be a better choice for now."

Vita laughed and waved goodbye.

A few customers came in over the next two hours, but Vita didn't sell anything other than some wind chimes and a gift card.

Mrs. Cole came in the afternoon. "Hello, Vita." She looked through the sales receipts and let out a long sigh. "Slow, slow, slow. And not a holiday in sight." She took out the ledger and studied it at the counter. "It's slower than last year, that's for sure."

Vita pulled off the dead leaves from the ferns. "Dad says the same thing. That business is down everywhere. He said the farmers are really hurting too." She tipped her head at the potted plants. "Maybe I can set a few of these outside the door. If people knew what was in here, I'm sure they'd come in. Your shop is so pretty."

"I suppose it can't hurt. Oh, how was the audition?"

"I didn't get a part." Vita looked at the plants, deciding which ones to place outside.

Mrs. Cole returned her attention to the ledger. "Well, it does seem a bit frivolous. Maybe it's not the right path for you."

Vita stood with a large red begonia in her hand. "It *is* the right path. I'm just not good enough yet. I don't know enough."

"But surely you know as much as the teenagers who got the parts."

Vita didn't have an answer. She hadn't thought of that, and yet it was true. She stared down at the plant.

"What I mean is that sometimes it's easier to keep your feet on the ground. Lower your expectations."

Vita gave the words some thought but didn't like the idea. Was that a way to happiness? She set the plant by the door and looked for another.

"Is that what you do, Mrs. Cole?" As soon as the words were out, Vita stiffened. They sounded like a reference to her husband's betrayals. "I mean—do you think that's what some people try to do?"

Mrs. Cole shut the ledger. "There's that boy, again! I told you, Vita. No visitors."

Vita looked out the window and saw Vic approaching the store. "I told him not to stop by. I'm sorry. I'll tell him again."

Vita walked out the door and confronted Vic. "Are you trying to get me fired? I told you not to come by here."

"I just want to talk to you. I've tried to call, and they always say you're not at home."

"It's over, Vic. Look, I don't want to drag this out. I wish the best for you, but we're over." She folded her arms.

He saw that she meant it. He looked down and shoved his hands in his pockets. Then he rested his eyes on her. "I'm sorry, Vita. I really am. I . . . I thought we had something."

"So did I." She watched him leave and felt bad. Bad about everything.

She arranged the flowering plants outside the door and went back inside to sweep. She heard Mrs. Cole greet a customer and glanced over at the counter . . . and was mortified to see Easton.

"Hey, Vita. So this is where you work." He strolled around the small shop, touching a few plants. He pinched a flower. "Is this real?"

"Of course, it's real." She spoke in a low voice as he inspected another plant. "I can't have visitors here."

"She won't mind me." He flashed a smile and went to Mrs. Cole. "Maybe you could recommend a nice plant or two for my mom."

"Of course. Something flowering or a green plant?" She suggested several different plants and the care they required. Easton looked at the price tags and chose the three most expensive ones. He paid and they each carried a plant out to his car.

"I'm sure Mom will be happy with these. Thank you." He gave Vita a wink, infuriating her.

"Please come back again," said Mrs. Cole, and returned to the shop.

Vita brushed her hands on her apron. She felt manipulated by Easton's behavior and regretted being nice to him at the fair.

"I have to go back inside."

"Hey," he said, grabbing her arm. "I saw Vic leaving. You still seeing him?"

"I'm not seeing anyone."

"Good." He ran his hand down her bare arm. "Then you can see me." He winked again and got in his car.

Vita hoped he wouldn't become a problem.

Mrs. Cole took the broom to sweep around the vacated spots. "Another one of your admirers?"

"I hardly know him. He—he's home from college."

"Where does he work?"

"He doesn't have a job."

"Lucky rich kid," Mrs. Cole muttered under her breath. "I guess it's easy to spend someone else's money. At any rate,

I thought I'd never get rid of that schefflera. It was taking up too much room. Let's put the fig tree in its place."

Vita and Mrs. Cole cleaned and reorganized the shop. It looked a bit more open and welcoming. While Mrs. Cole chatted with a few browsing customers, Vita worked outside, tending to the window box and potted flowers. She was glad Mrs. Cole's spirits had been lifted, but she was also glad when it was time to go home. She wanted to get this day over with. She was not looking forward to the Titania photoshoot.

~

As Vita set the dinner table, she saw Joey and Beth riding their bikes up the alleyway and turn into the yard. They laughed and talked as they ran into the house.

"Aunt Millie, you're not going to believe it!" cried Joey. "David's going to loan me one of his cameras! A Pentax!"

"Well, that is good news. And perfect timing."

He saw Vita and waited for her reaction.

"That's wonderful, Joey. You'll be a professional in no time."

Beth was nearly as excited as Joey. "David said he never saw anyone take to photography so quickly. He developed the photos Joey took at the fair and some of them are really good. Especially the latest ones."

Joey smiled. "He said I can use it for as long as I'm here. I took more shots this afternoon and we'll develop them later. They have their own darkroom. Abby knows how to develop film. She's going to teach me."

"So no waiting for the film to be sent away to be developed." Millie carried a hot dish to the table. "That will help you tremendously. You'll see your results much quicker."

Beth and Joey washed up and sat at the table, continuing to talk about how they staged the afternoon scene. They described how Dylan, Rob, and Ernie took turns posing as king of the fairies and had everybody howling every time they got into character.

Joey scooted in his chair, aware of how hungry he was. "That smells so good."

"Mom's tuna casserole is the best." Beth pushed the dish to Joey. "Anne's working the dinner shift?"

"And Sal will be late, so it's just us." Millie brought a bowl of sautéed green beans to the table.

Beth took a helping of casserole. "Too bad. I was hoping Anne could help with the costumes. I have to get right back to help Abby with some last-minute details."

"What details?" asked Vita.

"We now have *five* fairies," said Joey.

"And we only have wings for three. They're so cute. Becca's little sisters, and Darlene brought her niece—three years old. You should see them, Mom."

"I took a few shots with the Pentax. I'm starting to get the hang of it. I kind of know what to look for, how to get a different feel by doing little things, like shifting the angle and focus and stuff like that."

Milly took her seat and looked from Beth to Joey as they excitedly described the set up.

Vita smiled at Joey. "What do you think of their yard, Joey? Did you set up near the woods?"

"*In* the woods." Joey took a long swig of milk. "We finished shooting the Oberon scenes. Ernie ended up being the best for the part. He was the only one comfortable on the horse."

"Ernie as king of the fairies?" asked Vita.

"Using the same horse as . . . you know," Beth added. "At first, we tried to make his ears pointy with paper, but it didn't work, so we just gave him a cape. I think he was relieved."

"Their yard is so cool! They showed me the path down to the pond. David said in the winter they go skating there and have bonfires. And sometimes they pitch tents in the woods and sleep outside."

Beth turned to Vita. "David wants to try a Titania shot by some of the tall flowers when the sun goes down. The other shots will be in the woods. They wanted to run a string of lights from the trees, but the extension cords wouldn't reach. So they're hunting down lanterns and flashlights. David's going to use a filter so it looks like night. He's not sure if it's really going to work but he wants to try."

For the most part, Vita was quiet during the meal and let Beth and Joey do all the talking. Before the audition, she had been looking forward to the shoot and had spent hours on the Titania costume. She loved it, the best so far, and now it would be a reminder of the part she didn't get and the crashing of her summer plans.

Beth quickly finished. "I have to go help with the wings. You guys can come in an hour or so. Bring some flashlights if you can find any."

Joey described the yard with the overturned canoe, the fire pit with a circle of rocks around it, and the big tree that he climbed with Beth and Abby, all the way to the top.

Millie dished out another helping for Joey and when he was finished, she gave him a bowl of chocolate ice cream.

"I'll go get my costume," said Vita. For the shoots she always wore the bodice with cutoffs and slipped on the skirt at the last moment. It was the simplest solution.

She put on the bodice, tied a floral garland around her hair, and applied a little eye makeup and lipstick. She held up the skirt and looked in the mirror. It was a beautiful costume. Her eyes filled with sorrow, and she quickly folded up the skirt.

Millie was sorting through a few flashlights on the table. "I found three that work." She smiled on seeing Vita in the bodice. She gathered Vita's hair in her hand. "To me, you will always be Titania. Beautiful and magical. I can't wait to see the photographs."

"Thanks, Mom."

Vita set the flashlights on top of her skirt in the bicycle basket, and she and Joey rode off.

"If Hogie's out, let's stop by. I promised to tell him about the audition."

As they neared his house, they saw a woman leaving.

"That's Laura," Vita said, stopping her bike.

Laura stormed off, the screen door slamming behind her. She got into her car and drove away.

"I guess he chased her away again." Vita hesitated, knowing that Hogie would be in a bad mood. But so was she.

She walked her bike into his yard. "Come on. We'll make this quick."

She knocked on the door. And knocked again.

When there was no answer, she hollered through the screen door. "Hogie! It's Vita. And Joey. Can we come in?"

After a long pause, Hogie answered. "Door's open."

Vita frowned at the lukewarm response.

Hogie sat in his living room, sorting through the mail. Opened letters lay scattered around a table.

"Have to be a fuckin' Einstein to make sense of this insurance crap." He kept his eyes on the papers.

They looked around the room. It was messy, with books and papers and beer bottles everywhere.

Joey remained by the door. "Hi, Hogie."

"We won't stay long. I just wanted to let you know about the audition. I didn't get the part."

She sat on the chair by the door. "They kept asking me to read so at first I thought maybe I had it—but then . . . It was awful."

Hogie remained fixed on the mail.

"I didn't get *anything*, Hogie. Nothing!"

"So?" he asked, still not looking up.

Vita's anger flared. "So I just thought you might like to know."

Joey grew uneasy with the tension. He saw a guitar leaning against the back wall. "Do you still play the guitar? I remember one time you—"

"Don't got the time."

Vita watched Hogie, gauging his mood, and then tossed care to the wind.

"He used to play all the time and he and Laura would sing. You should have heard that. She has a beautiful voice."

"Enough, Vita." Hogie shot her a warning look.

"They would sit right there, or out under the tree. And Hogie would play—"

Hogie's head snapped up. "I said drop it!" He wheeled over to the kitchen and took out a cold beer.

Vita decided to leave that subject alone. She held out the shimmery sleeves of her bodice. "And now I have to wear the costume for the part I didn't get. For our shoot."

She waited for some response from Hogie, some sign that her words mattered. "Anyway—I just wanted to let you know I bombed at the audition. Made a mess of things and ruined my plans for summer."

Hogie popped off the cap and lifted his head back in a guzzle. "So what are you going to do about it, mope? Feel sorry for yourself?"

Vita shot to her feet. "Like you? No, I'm going to do something with *my* life."

"Then do it and stop complaining about every little thing that trips you up! You didn't get a part in the audition?" He scrunched up his face in mock sorrow. "Boo-hoo! Life can't get any worse for poor little Vita. I thought you were made of stronger stuff than that. You're full of shit, Vita. All talk."

She opened the door. "Let's go, Joey."

Joey pressed his lips into a smile. "Bye."

The screen door shut behind her with a bang.

"That was a mistake. He can be so awful sometimes." They got on their bikes and rode off.

"I think he got mad when I asked about the guitar."

"No. It was my fault for bringing up Laura. I knew he'd be mad. But I can't help it. I remember how happy they were. Laura got a degree in music and teaching. They were going to open a music store and give lessons. Sell guitars."

"Gosh. That's too bad. I mean, it sounds like a good idea."

"There's a lot of sadness in this town, Joey. A lót of sad people. You don't see it on the outside. But inside, they're hurting. If you close your eyes, you can feel it and it makes you want to cry."

They rode in silence for the rest of the way. They hopped off their bikes when they arrived at Abby's and walked around to the back of the house. Abby ran up to them and pulled Joey to the group in the back.

David handed Joey the Pentax and he slung it around his neck. "It's official. You're part of our photography club."

"Thanks!" Joey lifted the camera and showed it to Beth and Vita.

Carla walked up to Vita. "Sorry the audition didn't go your way. Mr. Radcliff has a reputation for being exacting. Listen. Darlene and I are going to a commercial audition in Foreston. Why don't you come with us? No preparation, no lines, you just read and ham it up."

"Thanks. I'll think about it." Vita pulled the skirt over her cutoffs.

"It's not Shakespeare, but it pays, if you get lucky. Wow! That is gorgeous. Too bad you didn't wear that to the audition."

The next few hours went by in a blur. Joey helped wherever he could, with the lighting, changing the scenery, and taking a few photographs. The shoots with the children took the longest because they kept running off and playing.

They finally sat spellbound around Vita when she began to tell them a story.

Joey was mesmerized by Vita and couldn't imagine a better fairy queen. He didn't really know what the play was about, but he knew that Vita was beautiful and mysterious. She belonged to the world of moonlight and starlight and changeling babies and magic. He wished her lines would have lasted longer and was glad when David said they would take more shots when the sunlight shifted.

Carla played Helena and they convinced Dylan to pose as the mischievous fairy Puck, which caused Abby and Beth to fall into hysterics.

The sun was beginning to lower in the sky, darkening the woods, and David got the lighting he wanted. Joey saw Vita standing off by herself, in between shots, and wanted to capture the expression in her face. He adjusted the zoom and took several shots, hoping to capture the mix in her. The magic and the doubt. The dream and the wistfulness. The fairy and the girl.

At the final click, Joey lowered the camera. He was sure he had a few good shots. Maybe even a great one.

When they began to wrap up, David and Darlene discussed the Ophelia scene in *Hamlet* with Vita.

"You know it will mean getting wet," David said.

Vita shrugged as if it didn't matter. "The pond?"

"The creek will work better. Got a long dress you don't mind getting dirty?"

"I'll find something."

On their way home, Beth and Joey laughed about Dylan's antics as Puck, and Joey told Vita that David and

Darlene were going to make a bonfire sometime soon since he had never sat around one.

"There's something magical about a campfire, Joey," said Beth. "David said we could do it after a shoot and roast hotdogs and make s'mores."

"What's that?"

"Don't tell me you've never had s'mores! Vita! Did you hear that?" Beth filled him in on what he'd been missing.

Vita rode behind them quietly. A few sequins and beads glittered on the moss-and-gold skirt in her basket, filling her with longing.

When they got home, Joey heard a sound that didn't go with the house. Angry voices. Anne was arguing with Sal, and Millie was trying to calm them both down. "Now, Sal…" "Listen to your father, Anne." And "There's no need to raise your voices." They both ignored her.

"Not again," said Beth, rolling her eyes as they walked into the kitchen.

"Mark's entitled to his own opinion and I agree with him! Most people agree with him. No one knows why we're fighting over there and—"

"That's the problem with these long-haired kids to-day," said Sal. "No backbone, running off to Canada! Shooting themselves in the foot! We didn't hesitate to do our duty when—"

"I wish he would go to Canada! I'd go with him."

"You'll do no such thing!" Sal grabbed his wallet and keys from the counter and shoved them in his pocket.

Joey knew that meant he was going uptown to the tavern.

Sal whipped around in the doorway, determined to have the final say. He pointed a finger at Anne and raised his voice. "And our government does *not* go around killing our own boys!"

"That's *exactly* what they did!" Anne hollered back, getting the last word before the door slammed.

Joey watched Anne with something akin to fascination. She was always so soft and sweet and gentle. Here she was, taking on Sal! Her eyes flashing and her voice louder than his, moving about like a storm in the kitchen.

She was dressed to go out, and looked beautiful in a long floral dress and her hair swinging about her shoulders. She slung her fringed purse over her shoulder and continued the argument alone. Now her anger was directed at Mark.

"I told Mark not to bring up Kent State or the war. And that's exactly what he did! What's wrong with him." She grabbed her keys, mirroring Sal's actions.

Beth jumped out of her way in an exaggerated manner.

"Don't wait up for me."

Joey noticed that Anne's angry tone was unfairly directed at Millie.

The door slammed a second time, and everyone breathed a sigh of relief. Joey realized he had a knot in his stomach. He hated arguments and hollering.

Beth and Vita must have been used to them. Vita put her arm around Millie's shoulder, and Beth let out a "Whew! Glad they're gone."

Millie gave a huff of exasperation. "Exactly alike, those two. And I get caught in the middle. Sorry, Joey. They shouldn't have fought in front of you. They both have tempers."

"That's okay. I'm—" He started to say he was used to it, but changed his mind.

"Never saw Anne like *that*, huh?" said Beth. "Let me tell you, she's the toughest of us all." She made her voice and gestures sugary sweet. "So delicate and feminine and dainty." She dropped the act. "Until you cross her. Then, watch out!"

Vita had to laugh. "And now it's Mark's turn. I hope she's not too hard on him."

Millie looked at the clock. "You kids up for a swim? The pool's open for another hour. How about a quick evening dip?"

"Yes, please!" cried Beth. "This is what I love about summer—swimming at night! I'll get my suit. Go get your trunks, Joey."

"A way to erase all that," Vita said, looking towards the door. "I love the pool at night."

"And we don't have to worry about getting sunburned," Millie added with a smile.

CHAPTER 14

Joey twisted the phone cord with his fingers, smiling widely as he updated his mom and dad on all the things he was doing every day. He had just got home from working with Abel and was still flushed from the heat of the day, grass clippings and smudges of dirt on his clothes. He had a hard time standing in one spot as he described his job, the fair, the photoshoots, the bike rides, and swimming at night.

Millie flushed with pride to see Joey so animated and happy. She noticed that the last few times his parents called, he was the one to do most of the talking, making small-town life sound like high adventure.

"It's kind of hard work but I like it. Abel said it's going to make me strong. He's teaching me how to mow and trim. And when we're driving, he tells me about when he was a kid. I told you about the Pentax, right? There's another shoot I'm going to help out with."

He fidgeted as he listened to his mom. "No, I'm not in the way. I'm helping them. And I do play with the boys at the park. Baseball. And I'm going to make some crafts. And Uncle Sal's going to take me fishing!" He listened and twisted the cord. "Oops, I'm getting grass all over the floor. I better go take my shower." He gave a laugh. "Don't worry, Mom. I will. Bye."

He took a big sniff of the air and went to the stove to see what smelled so good. "Fried chicken? My favorite!" He hurried to the shower.

Millie took out the last pieces of chicken from the frying pan. She smiled when she heard Joey singing in the shower and felt a mother's happiness.

The table was set, the potatoes were mashed, and the chicken was in the oven to keep warm. She glanced at the clock when Vita walked in. "You're home early."

Joey came into the kitchen, his wet hair slicked back. "Hi, Vita!"

Vita sat quietly at the table and leaned forward on her arms.

"Vita?" asked Millie. "What is it?"

"I lost my job."

"What do you mean? Mrs. Cole's always been so happy with you."

"Not anymore."

Joey stood next to the table. "What happened?"

Vita dropped her arms to her lap. "I did something stupid. You remember Mrs. Higgins? She came in to buy plant food and about ten minutes after she left, I saw her wallet on the counter. I knew how worried she'd be, so I ran after her. I should have locked the door and put a sign up."

"Did you find her?"

"It took me a while. She was at the square doing some shopping. When I returned to the shop Mrs. Cole was there. Furious that I had left the shop unattended." Vita winced in guilt. "There were three customers. I tried to explain what happened, but I could tell she was mad. When everybody left, she said that she didn't need me anymore, that she would work there herself from now on."

Vita left out the part about spending too much time on her audition lines and too many boys visiting her. She didn't want Joey to think her being fired had anything to do with him.

"Well," Millie said, trying to make light of it. "You said business was slow. I'm sure she's just trying to cut costs where she can. She'll hire you back in the fall, you'll see."

Joey pulled out a chair and sat next to Vita. "At least Mrs. Higgins got her wallet."

"That's right, Vita." Millie went back to the counter and drizzled vinegar and oil over a salad. "You did the right thing. That's what I would have done."

"Me too," said Joey.

Vita gave him a small smile. "So much for my grand summer plans. Now I don't even have a job. I'll have to start looking for something else."

"Summer's half over," said Millie. "Why don't you just relax and work on your reading and portfolio. That'll keep you busy. You can always help out at the shop."

"I'll get my license in a couple of months and I'm going to need gas money. Carla and Becca and I already talked about going to Foreston to see plays and stuff. They both have jobs. During the schoolyear, I can't work as many hours. I have to have a summer job." She was also saving up for classes. Somewhere, anywhere.

"Something will turn up," said Millie. "Don't give it any more thought for now. Can you pour the iced tea?"

"Why don't you try that audition Carla was telling you about?" Joey suggested.

"Maybe I will." In response to Millie's questioning look, she said, "In Foreston. A commercial audition."

Millie nodded in agreement. "I know in general that's not something you want to pursue, but I think it's a good idea. We're lucky Foreston is only an hour's drive. Otherwise, you'd have to go to St. Louis for such auditions. Hardly practical."

"Who knows, you might get lucky," said Joey. "And David said we can do the Ophelia shot whenever you want."

"Ophelia. How appropriate." Vita saw his worried look and gave a tired laugh. "Don't pay any attention to me."

"He said it will be a small shoot. A simple set."

"I'm not looking forward to floating in a river."

"It that what you have to do? You mean in a boat?"

"No boat. Just me and a bunch of flowers. Talk to David. Whatever he thinks."

"We'll get some good shots that you can add to your portfolio. You'll still be doing part of your plan."

❧

With the fair now over, Joey spent his evenings watching ballgames at the park or riding his bike around town taking pictures. Sometimes Millie took them all swimming and they stayed until the pool closed at 10:00 p.m. He learned how to play "Sharks and Minnows" and "Marco Polo," and he could now hold his breath under water for the entire length of the pool. Some evenings he sat with Abel on his swing, listening to stories, or songs on the harmonica. And sometimes Anne drove them up to the Dairy Queen for ice cream.

On Saturday, Sal took Joey fishing. Beth also went and they invited Abel to go along. That evening, Millie fried up their catch and they all ate outside on the picnic table, Abel recounting how Joey had caught two fish.

Joey worked most mornings with Abel, and the girls were often busy with their jobs. But a week had passed, and Vita was still searching for a new place to work. She tried the clothing stores, the restaurants, the grocery stores. No one was hiring mid-summer.

As she walked home from her latest search, she saw Easton parked on the square. He was leaning against his car talking to Carla and a few others. He called out to her and waved her over. "Hey, gorgeous!"

Vita hated to admit that his words made her feel better. She was beginning to think that no one wanted her and that she had grossly overestimated herself.

Carla, Becca, and Darlene were talking about how they were going to the audition in Foreston the following day. Once again, Carla tried to persuade Vita to join them.

"Come on, it will be fun. What have you got to lose? Becca made fifty dollars last time. It was a boring trade show, but it was better than detassling corn."

Vita laughed at the reference to the previous summer when a group of them signed up to detassel corn. Vita had gotten a terrible sunburn, Carla developed a rash, and Becca was stung by something that made her arm swell up.

"Even if we all bomb, we can still stop by The Golden Tiger and have Chinese food. So it won't be a total washout."

"I'd like to go. Thanks."

Easton's admiring eyes acted as balm, and Vita was glad he had called her over to them. She knew she had a tendency to isolate herself and it often worked against her.

᠕

Once again, Anne and Beth fussed over Vita as she dressed for the commercial audition.

Vita wore a long peacock-blue dress that hugged her slender form, and sandals. She wanted to keep things to a minimum, but Anne and Beth had other ideas.

"You have to stand out!"

"You can be a little bolder," said Anne. "Darlene says bigger is better at these auditions. You have to make them notice you. Let me put a touch of liner on your eyes."

"And I'm putting these beads in your hair, whether you want them or not," said Beth. "They'll look so pretty. Blue-green against the copper of your hair. They'll add a little magic."

"Do you know what you're reading for?" asked Anne.

"Soap, I think. It doesn't feel like acting at all."

"Whatever it takes," said Beth.

"Can't hurt," Anne added. "There. At least you'll look beautiful. And you can bring us home some fried rice."

"And egg rolls."

On the ride there the girls talked about everything but the audition. Boys, clothes, and the party at the lake that night and what they were going to wear.

"Remember," Carla told them when they arrived. "You have to really ham it up—exaggerate, overdo it—have fun with it."

Vita considered her words. Maybe it was good not to take everything so seriously. But at the same time, she felt far from her dreams. Instead of expressing interesting characters and beautiful lines, she would be trying to sell soap.

When she saw the crowd at the audition, she lost her nerve. There were so many girls, all made up, hair just so, giggling and whispering. Several of the older teens wore suits and had their head shots and acting resumes ready to submit. Vita was clearly out of her element, and she felt that it was a mistake to come.

After a whirlwind of filling out forms and trying to figure out the protocol, Vita's name was called.

A woman with a clipboard approached and looked her up and down. "What part are you reading for?"

"I . . . I don't know."

The woman gave an exaggerated eye roll. "Bitch boss or ditzy secretary?"

Vita's face betrayed bewilderment at the choices. She hesitated a moment too long.

Another eye roll. "Ditzy secretary." A script was shoved in her hand.

"Oh. Thank you." Vita glanced over the lines. A hurried procedure, a frenzied atmosphere, next, next. She went inside a room where a video camera was pointed at a tall stool. She sat down and made the mistake of looking directly at the spotlight. She tried to appear confident but sweat trickled down her back.

A group of people talked amongst themselves, busy with the camera and clipboards and lists. All at once, they faced her and one of them barked a command.

Vita blinked. Did they say "state?" What did they mean? She saw them growing impatient.

One woman looked up from her notes. "Miss Vitale?"

Vita swallowed. "I . . . I'm from Illinois. But hope to move to New York City to pursue acting."

A snicker from the women, and a huff of impatience from the cameraman. "Slate! Slate! Your name!"

Vita felt her face turn red. The spotlight blinded her, and its heat spread the flush to her neck and arms. "Vicky," she started to say, startling herself. Where did that come from? She felt like a little girl. She sat taller. "Vita Vitale." Where was her voice? It came out in a whisper. She had no heart for the lines. It was quickly over.

Vita sat on a bench in the hall and waited for the others to finish. They walked to the Chinese restaurant across the street and shared their experiences over lunch, talking excitedly.

"They had me read for both parts," said Carla, "and asked for my head shot."

"I don't think I got it, but it was fun," said Becca, clearly more interested in the menu.

When Vita related her experience, they roared with laughter. "I thought they were saying *state*. I didn't know *slate* meant to tell them my name. I was so embarrassed."

"Well, you'll be prepared the next time," said Darlene. "And don't let them intimidate you."

When they pulled into town, they went to the Dairy Queen for cold drinks. Easton saw them and made a U-turn. He got out of his car and walked up to Vita.

"Hey beautiful. You famous yet?"

Easy words, Vita knew, yet welcome to her bruised ego. "Hardly," she said with a laugh. "It didn't go so well."

"Their loss. You going to the party at the lake tonight?"

"I don't know."

"How about I pick you up at 7:30?"

Vita felt Carla's elbow in her side. "We're all going."

"Promise to have you home by 11:00."

Vita nodded. "Okay. Sounds good. Thanks."

Up, down, up, down. But she was tired of moping. Of failing and being disappointed. The party would be a distraction. Vita knew that, for the most part, *party* meant drinking, smoking pot, and loud music, everyone sitting outside somebody's cabin. Anne would be there with Mark, which gave Vita some comfort.

Anne and Vita stood before the mirror as they got ready. Anne positioned the snake bracelet on her upper arm. "I still think Easton's too old for you. He's cute, but so is Vic. And Vic is nicer."

"It's just a party, Anne. I'll see how it goes."

Vita looked in the mirror and dabbed on the amber oil. She knew Easton wasn't right for her, but she was tired of brooding at home.

Easton gave her a big smile when he came to pick her up and she enjoyed the ride to the lake with the convertible roof down. She liked it out to the lake. The woods were pretty in the setting sun, and she saw several of her friends there. Some people were inside the cabin listening to music, but most of them sat outside on folding chairs or the hoods of the cars.

At first, Easton was sweet and they talked about the summer and his plans for college and her plans after high school. But the more he drank, the more she felt like he was claiming her, pulling her by her hand when they walked, putting his arm around her when they were seated. As the hours passed, the bolder he became, putting his hands all over her, in front of everyone.

"I think I'd like to go home now," she said.

"What are you talking about? It's just getting started!" He was playing a drinking game that involved making animal sounds with three of his friends. They howled in drunken hilarity. One of them rushed to the woods to be sick.

"I'll go home with Anne." Vita walked over to her sister and Mark.

"Can I catch a ride home with you?"

Anne looked over at Easton and raised her eyebrows. She put a protective arm around Vita. "For being a college boy, he's not very mature, is he? Of course, you can ride with us."

CHAPTER 15

The next morning, Joey looked for Vita. She had gone out early to apply at a few more places. He saw that she was sitting in front of the flower garden. She hadn't been on the roof since the Shakespeare audition. He walked out and sat next to her on the bench.

"Hey, Joey. No work today?"

"Abel had to get a part for the lawnmower. He said we'll go out after lunch. How was the party?"

"It was okay."

"Still no luck finding a job?"

Vita shook her head. "Nothing. I'll just have to keep looking."

Joey wriggled uncomfortably, not sure if he was going to make things better or worse. "I was thinking . . . Well, I mean, you probably won't want to do it, but—"

Vita turned to him with curiosity.

"Abel can probably use you. He said he might have to hire another person to help out until Rusty Cooper gets back."

Vita gazed out at the garden. "Working in a cemetery?"

"It's not so bad. Mowing, trimming. There's a lot of hauling, but I can do that."

Vita nudged him and smiled. "So we'd be working together?"

Joey shrugged. "You could still look for another job."

"That's true."

"Who knows, you might even like it. It's nice to work outside." He glanced over his shoulder and saw Abel's truck in his driveway. "Looks like he's home. We could go ask him."

Joey was surprised when Vita stood. "Okay. Let's go ask."

They crossed over to Abel's and found him in his back yard, adding fresh water to the birdbath that nestled among the roses. He stood back, watching a little bird splashing.

When they greeted him, Abel chuckled and pointed to the bird. "Look at him. Couldn't be happier. The birdbath was Fran's idea. They sure love it."

"Abel," said Joey, "we have a question for you."

"As long as it's an easy one," Abel said with a grin.

Vita stood tall. "Joey said you might need another person temporarily, and I'm looking for work. How about using me?"

Abel scratched his chin. "Oh, I can use another person, all right. But it's not work for a girl. Me and Joey don't mind it, but you'll get your hands all dirty."

"I got them dirty at the plant shop, too. And when I work in the garden. I don't mind getting dirty." She saw his hesitation. "And I'm stronger than I look."

Abel took the bill of his gray cap and pushed it back. "Rusty comes back in a few weeks, so it won't be for long. That okay?"

"More than okay." Vita and Joey exchanged a smile.

"Most days we get an early start. Try to get the heavy mowing and hauling done 'fore it gets too hot. We're going out to the Calvary after lunch. Want to give it a try?"

"I do. Thanks, Abel. I won't let you down."

"All righty. Come on over at 1:00. Wear a hat. And bring a pair of work gloves. I got extras if you need."

When they went back home, Millie was just answering the doorbell. Anne stood next to her, excitedly looking out the window. "It's the florist!"

"Oh, how lovely!" Millie said, taking a large bouquet of flowers. "Thank you."

Joey and Vita looked on with curiosity.

Mark had sent Anne a bouquet for her birthday, and everyone assumed they were for her. She searched for the card. "Oh, they're gorgeous! Mark knows I love pink and blue mixed together. They smell heavenly, don't they?" She lifted the card and her face fell.

"They're for you, Vita."

"Me? I've never gotten flowers before. Are you sure?"

"I guess this is to make up for being an immature jerk last night." Anne handed her the card.

Vita broke out into a smile. "From Easton."

"What does it say?" asked Millie.

Vita blushed as she read: "One day you'll be getting lots of bouquets on stage. This is for practice. Dinner tonight?"

She buried her face in the flowers. "I guess he's not so bad after all."

"Let's put them in water," said Millie. "Anne, get the crystal vase out of the cupboard."

Anne pursed her lips in annoyance. "All right, all right. Don't let this fool you, Vita."

"Don't worry, I won't." She remembered Mrs. Cole's words: 'It's easy to spend someone else's money.' Still, he didn't have to do it. He could have spent the money on himself.

Vita took off the protective tissue paper around the flowers and admired the pretty colors. She couldn't help but feel cheered. Hopeful. And his note showed that he understood how important acting was to her.

Millie kissed Vita's cheek. "Perhaps your luck is starting to turn."

"It is!" cried Joey. "She just got a job."

When Millie and Anne turned in surprise, Vita laughed. "Working with Abel and Joey. Starting today."

Anne opened her mouth and stared. "At the cemeteries? Vita!"

"Just for a while. At least I'll be earning money. I can still look for something else."

"I agree," said Millie. "It's best to keep busy. Let's get lunch on the table before Sal and Beth get home."

Vita found that she actually enjoyed the work at the cemetery. The hard work felt good to her body and working with Joey and Abel was a nice change from Mrs. Cole's watchful eye.

The Calvary was the town's oldest cemetery and Vita often went there to stroll around the tombstones and paths. It was on the edge of town, part of it on a hillside, with lots of old trees that provided ample shade. The entrance was bordered by a fence that was heavy with sweet-smelling honeysuckle, forming a mound of white and yellow flowers.

"While I mow, I'll let Joey show you the ropes," Abel said. "We'll work on the hillside today."

The afternoon passed quickly, perhaps because Vita was excited about her date with Easton. She wondered where he would take her and what she should wear. She would keep the conversation on the interesting things about him.

Finally, she was back on track and the old excitement stirred in her once again. She had a job, a date, and her first bouquet of flowers related to acting.

She helped Joey and Abel unload the tools when they returned home. "Thanks for giving me a chance, Abel."

She ran home to take a shower and get ready for her dinner date.

❧

"Evening, Mrs. Vitale, Mr. Vitale." Easton showed up in a sports jacket and chatted with Sal and Millie as he waited for Vita.

Vita wore a pale-green shawl over her favorite sundress—a vintage piece she found at one of the antique stores. A swirl of soft pink and peach flowers with pale green leaves, the top crisscrossed over in pleats, and the waist cinched in. It gave her a more womanly shape and set off her coloring beautifully.

"Home by 10:00," said Sal.

Millie walked them to the door. "Have fun."

When they got in the car, Vita put on her sunglasses.

Easton stared at her. "Wow. You look like a movie star. I want everyone to see you. Let's drive around town before going to the restaurant."

"Or we could drive through the country," suggested Vita.

They drove around town. When Easton turned onto the square, he laid on his horn. "Watch out, freak!"

Vita had been tucking her purse next to her and looked up to see Rufus Sharp crossing in front of them.

"We have the stop sign. Let him pass." She watched Rufus as he mumbled and staggered past them, oblivious.

They drove with the top down, the breeze welcome in the summer heat. Every time they passed someone Easton knew, he tooted the horn.

Vita felt on display and was happy when they left town. She knotted her hair to keep it from blowing in her face and when Easton flashed her a smile, she smiled back. He looked handsome with his long hair blowing in the wind.

He took her to the Lakeview Restaurant, midway between Greenberry and Hawthorn. They were seated at a table overlooking the lake and the surrounding woods.

"This is nice, Easton. Thank you."

Easton reached across the table for her hand. "Thanks for coming. Sorry about last night. I guess I had a little too much to drink."

Vita gave him a sympathetic smile. Sometimes he seemed almost like a schoolboy. A little unsure of himself. Perhaps his bad behavior was just a cover.

After they placed their orders, Easton casually mentioned some of the vacations he had taken with his family. Vita asked him about his impressions of London and Paris, Venice and Rome. Although Easton answered her questions, she had the feeling that he hadn't enjoyed the trips very much.

"I would love to see those places," said Vita. "Where would you like to visit next?"

"Honestly? I'd rather stay here and go to the ballgames in St. Louis. Play darts. Party!" He slipped out a flask from inside his jacket and took a quick sip. "Vodka. No scent. Want some?"

Vita shook her head and glanced at the other diners, hoping no one saw him. They would be thrown out, or worse. Easton had a reputation as being a partier and a little reckless. Some people said he was just wasting his parents' money at school. And yet she believed that everyone should be given a chance. It was easy to get a bad reputation in a small town.

When their main course arrived, she shifted the conversation to asking him about college and which subjects he liked. He told her about some of his classes but was soon describing the toga party, the Halloween costume party, and the foosball championship where everyone got blasted.

"It was a riot! Most fun I ever had. And we came in second." He took another sip from his flask.

She told him about her plans to major in drama and to move to New York City.

"You have to be careful out there. I hear bad things about New York from some of the guys at school. They know what they're talking about. It might be better for you to stick around here."

"You sound like my dad," Vita said with a laugh.

They finished their meal, and when she came back from the ladies' room, she saw him draining the flask.

They drove around the countryside after dinner and parked on a bluff to watch the sunset. The sky was filled with hazy strands of deep orange and purple above the tree-filled bottoms. A few fluffy pink clouds were scalloped in gold. Vita filled with happiness to be part of such loveliness.

"This is just beautiful. Look at those clouds!"

"I knew you'd like it. Here." He handed her a glass. "I brought some wine."

She held up the small wine glass etched with grapevines. "How pretty! They look like antiques."

"Thought you'd like that touch."

Though she was concerned about him drinking more, she allowed him to fill their glasses. The idea of watching the sunset with a glass of wine seemed like a very fine thing to do. Like something she would do when she was older. Easton was soon on his third glass.

"These glasses don't hold much."

"No more for me, thanks. I guess we should be going."

"Aw, c'mon!" he said, filling their glasses. "I went to all the trouble of getting wine and bringing these glasses just for you. I would have preferred beer. Out of a can."

Vita was disappointed to find the evening a basic replay of the previous night. More than anything, she was disappointed that he didn't have anything interesting to say. They watched the sun sink into the trees and the rosiness slowly left the sky. Easton was soon sloppily kissing and hugging her, and he grew sulky when she pushed him away.

She finally convinced him to leave and head back to town. He drove without saying a word. When he circled the square, he pulled in next to a few of his friends. Some of them were old enough to buy alcohol. He soon had his flask filled and was emptying it again.

He pulled her next to him as if claiming her. She tried to enjoy herself, but the conversation had turned into the guys talking about cars and the girls sitting off by themselves, talking and smoking cigarettes. Vita asked him to take her home several times, but he ignored her and tightened his arm around her. When she asked a fourth time, she broke free.

"I'll walk home."

"Fine! Be that way," he hollered after her. "Thinks she's a fucking princess."

She heard several of the guys laugh and tease him. "Not getting what you want, huh? She too much for you?"

Vita felt humiliated and vowed not to see Easton again. When she was halfway home, he pulled up alongside her.

"Get in."

Vita ignored the command. He jumped out of his car and caught up with her. "Come on. I'm sorry. I—I promised your dad I'd get you home." He pushed her hair back and lifted her chin. He gave her a light kiss. "Come on."

Joey and Beth were outside shooting hoops by the light of the streetlights. Easton walked Vita to the door and said goodnight. Beth ran inside to hear about the date, while Joey made another shot.

When Easton passed Joey, he sneered. "Hey, kid. How come you're always playing with the girls? Loser."

Joey made a final shot and went inside. He could tell by Vita's short answers and her expression that she wasn't happy about the evening. Anne soon came home and also began to ask questions. Vita gave a few details and said it was fine, but that she was tired and wanted to go to bed.

"At least tell me what you had to eat," Beth called after her. "Did you have dessert?"

"I told her he was all wrong for her," said Anne.

"I think she's tired," said Millie. "And she and Joey have an early start tomorrow."

CHAPTER 16

The next morning Vita helped Joey and Abel load up the lawnmower, wheelbarrow, and landscaping tools into the back of the pickup truck.

Vita noticed that Abel had cut a red rose and set it gently next to him. She knew it was his habit to bring fresh roses for his wife's grave.

They spent the morning at the larger cemetery just outside of town, which had fewer trees. The work was harder in the direct sun, and even though Vita wore a hat, she still got sunburned.

They ate their lunch under a shade tree. There was a moment when Vita looked out at all the monuments, all the slabs of granite in the green grass, and had the gripping thought—I'm actually working in a cemetery. Land of the dead. What if this is my future? What if the other is all just a dream? That would be too sad. I couldn't bear it.

While Joey swept the cut grass off one of the cemetery roads, Abel went to tend his wife's grave. Vita watched him place the red rose near the headstone and bend his head. He had taken off his cap. He rested his hand on the stone and bent over to kiss it. He then made his way back to where Joey was sweeping.

Vita was glad when they went to the older part of the cemetery where the trees were larger and there was more shade. Some of the gravestones were over a hundred years old. She and Joey looked at the dates of several from the previous century.

They found a row of small markers. "Oh, Joey. This family lost all these children in a single year." She touched each one, softly reading the name aloud.

She continued to walk around and came to an ornate monument with an angel on top. "How beautiful." She made out the worn dates and the name. "It's for a little girl. Look! Someone has placed flowers here." She touched the wild bluebells and looked around for the giver.

Joey stood next to her as she bent over to make out the inscription. Her shoulders slumped as she read the words—*Never forgotten.* "Sometimes the world is just so sad, isn't it?"

Abel strolled over to them. "Another hour should do it. Just a little trimming over by the hedge."

"Abel, someone left flowers here. Did you see anyone?"

"Oh, people come and go. Joey, can you fetch the clippers in the truck?"

Once Joey was gone, Abel spoke in a low voice. "The human heart's a funny thing. He feels some kind of connection to that little girl."

Vita watched Joey hop into the truck bed to get the clippers. "Joey left the flowers?" She looked at the row of small markers. "I wonder why the little girl rather than all those?"

Abel pushed the bill of his cap back. "Guess he figures they got each other."

Once home, Vita took a shower and felt desperate to do something related to her acting plans, something that connected her to her dreams. She felt they were drifting farther and farther away. She took out her portfolio and discussed the next photoshoot with Joey and Beth.

Millie was getting ready to leave for her bridge party and Sal had gone uptown to an Elks meeting.

"I still think you should add the Pierrot scene," said Millie, glancing at the opened portfolio. "You have the costume. Well, I'm off."

Anne looked down at the photographs of Vita. "You're going to need a lot more pictures to fill up that album. I don't know why you're so against doing the Pierrot scene."

"I know why," said Beth, turning to Joey. "Vita's jealous because she didn't get the role of Columbine. Her friend Priscilla got it."

"I wasn't jealous. Priscilla deserved that role. She'd had ballet classes and could pirouette beautifully."

"Pierrot the sad clown was more interesting," said Anne. "Everyone said how believable you were, how your eyes glittered with tears. She was brilliant, Joey."

Without saying a word, Vita closed the portfolio and returned it to the living room cupboard.

Anne opened her arms in perplexity.

"We never understand her, but we're used to it by now," said Beth.

"The problem with Vita," said Anne, "is that she's too desperate."

"She dreams of being an actress, like that's going to solve all her problems."

"Maybe it will," Joey softly replied.

Anne stood up and stretched. "Let's go swimming. That will get her out of her funk."

"Good idea." Beth ran to get her swimming suit.

Two hours later, Anne and Vita were rinsing off the chlorine in the ladies' showers. They dropped off their wet things in Anne's car and looked around for Joey and Beth.

They heard hollering from the picnic area where there was a large swing set with gym bars.

"Over here!" Beth waved. She and Joey were both hanging upside down, Joey from the rings and Beth from the horizontal bar. Beth's long black hair reached the ground as she began to swing.

"Beth," cried Anne, "your hair is touching the sand! You'll get all dirty again."

"This damned hair," Beth said, knotting it while still upside down.

Anne and Vita sat on the swings, and Anne brushed out her wet hair. Vita began to swing, leaning back and pointing her feet to the evening sky.

When Vita slowed to a stop, Beth offered the bar. "Trade?" Vita shook her head but gave the swing to Beth and sat on top of the picnic table.

Anne sat next to her on the bench, and continued to brush her hair.

Joey dropped from the horizontal bar and stood before them, smiling. "So, I have something I've been waiting to tell you."

"It must be good news," said Anne. "You're happy about something."

"It is. My dad called today, and I told him all about the Pentax and the photography club and everything."

Vita gave Joey her full attention, happy that he wanted to talk about his plans. "Is this related to your dream path?"

"I guess so."

"Secrets and Dreams? Wait for me!" Beth jumped off the swing and landed with a tumble, causing them all to laugh. "I'm not playing unless we do secrets too. That's the fun part."

"Not that game again," said Vita. She wasn't in the mood to talk about her plans. They felt too fragile.

"Don't be so selfish," said Beth. "Joey has something to tell us."

Vita made room for Joey next to her. "Sorry, Joey. What's your news?"

"I've been telling Mom and Dad about the photoshoots and how David loaned me his Pentax and how I've been taking pictures. And that I'm even learning how to develop film."

They all waited, smiling. "Yes? And?"

Joey broke out into a smile. "Dad said if I'm still so interested in photography by my birthday, he'll buy me a camera. A new one!"

Beth sat next to him and gave him a high five. "Your own camera? That is so cool."

"Your thirteenth birthday!" exclaimed Anne.

"And it's in September so I don't have long to wait."

"That's really good news, Joey." Vita gave him their "pact" nod.

Joey nodded back. "Like you said, just keep trying for what you want, and things start to happen."

"Too bad Vita isn't following her own advice," said Beth.

"I am." Vita sat cross-legged, facing them. "It may look like I'm doing nothing, but believe me, that's all I'm thinking about. And I've made a decision."

"Dream related?" asked Anne.

"Completely. I've decided to speak to the directors. I'm going to ask them for information about what happened."

"Finally!" said Anne, throwing her head back. "That sounds more like you. I'll drive you there. Just say when."

"I want to go soon."

"So you don't change your mind?" asked Beth.

Vita raised and dropped one shoulder. "I guess. I just keep wondering—How could I go from 'she'd make a stunning Titania' one day, and the next day not get any part at all? I think if I don't find out, it'll make me crazy. Once I know, then I can move on."

"Good," said Beth. "Sometimes you're very logical and clear-sighted."

"Sometimes?"

"Most of the time you're way too dreamy. Believe it or not, Joey, Vita used to be the boldest of us all. The most daring." She faced Vita. "What happened?"

"So let's hear about *your* dream and how practical it is to make clay pots out in the dessert."

Beth laughed at Vita's sarcasm. "I might still do that. But I'm also thinking how cool it would be to buy a farm outside of town. A big farmhouse with a barn that I could convert into a studio. For making clay pots," she said to

Vita. "I could still work at Dad's shop. Maybe have some goats. Or keep beehives. I could make honey and sell it. Grow fields of clover and whatever flowers bees like."

Anne smiled at the vision. "I'd come out and visit you every day. We could have tea and put honey in it."

"Won't you be in New York with me?" Vita asked, skeptically.

Anne let out a breath of air. "I guess it's my turn. Mark and I have been talking about our future."

Vita waited. "And?"

"We've talked about getting married."

"Married! You're only seventeen!"

"I don't mean now. Like I said, we're just talking about things."

Silence followed.

"Secret?" asked Beth.

"Okay, but you can't get mad, Vita. I want to go to college here in town and get a degree for teaching."

Vita wasn't surprised. "What happened to costume design in New York City?"

"Oh, come on, Vita. You know my chances of making a career as a costume designer were never very good."

"So you're not coming with me to New York at all?"

"That's years away. It will depend on—what happens with the war. And where you end up going to school. I'll still visit you there, or wherever you are. But I have to make plans that work for me."

"You mean for Mark."

"He's part of my dream now. If I have a degree, I could teach school around here or wherever Mark finds work."

"I'm with Anne on this," said Beth. "If I go to college, I'll major in something that will definitely get me a job when I get out. A good job."

"So you can buy your farmhouse," said Joey.

"Exactly."

Vita threw her hands up in the air. "I can't believe you're both changing your minds so much."

"You might too, Vita," said Anne. "After all, acting isn't a very dependable career. You have to be practical."

Beth agreed. "I'd never put all that work into something that might not happen."

"I am going to *make* it happen." Vita looked from one to the other. "I have to."

"Desperate," muttered Beth.

Anne gestured to Joey. "Even photography has a practical side to it. Joey could always photograph weddings. And graduations."

Joey's head snapped up at the comment. That's not what he had in mind.

"Joey's going to be a travel photographer. He already decided." Vita gave Joey a look that said, 'stick to your vision.' "He's going to make a career of it."

"But maybe he'll shoot a wedding in his travels," said Beth. "To make it work for him."

"The same way you might have to do commercial work," Anne added. "It's not giving up on your dreams. Look what you're doing to make yours come true."

"Working in a cemetery!" Beth said, in disbelief.

Vita was becoming downcast again. "I know it won't always be easy."

Beth used her hands and arms to demonstrate the difficult path. "No, it will meander this way and that and there will be detours, maybe even roads washed out—"

"Okay, Beth. I get the idea."

"So let's be practical, Vita," said Anne. "Let's stage the Pierrot skit. You're taking Mom's advice about speaking to the directors. Why not take her advice about Pierrot?"

"Vita said there weren't many lines," said Joey.

They waited for her to respond. She looked down at the ground. "That's not why."

"She wanted to be Columbine," said Beth. "Priscilla got the best part because she knows how to dance. She moved from a big town and knows stuff like ballet. So the last thing Vita wants is to be reminded that she never had dance lessons."

"It's not that, either."

"Then what is it?" asked Anne. "Why do you always get so bent out of shape when we mention Pierrot?"

Vita took a deep breath. "This is a secret. Just between us."

Joey agreed, Anne crossed her heart, and Beth zipped her lips.

"On the day of the Pierrot play . . . We were in costume, going over our act. Priscilla danced so beautifully. I was offstage, watching her. I saw Vic watching her, too. With a look in his eyes that I thought belonged to me."

Anne waved her hand. "That doesn't mean anything. She was interesting to watch. Especially in that costume."

"She smiled at him. They thought I had gone to get one of the props. I was just about to leave, but then I saw them move closer and closer in their dance. He pulled her to him and kissed her. She looked surprised the first time. But not the second time. And there I was, watching. Dressed like a clown."

"A boy clown!" said Beth, "while she got to wear that pretty dress."

"A fool clown." Vita spoke softly to Anne. "So much for true love."

Anne jumped to her feet and stared at Vita. "The jerks! Did you tell them that you saw?"

"They must have figured it out. I couldn't look at them. I tried to 'act' like everything was the same during the skit. So you see, I'm a phony . . . I wasn't acting that night. Sometimes I see myself as just a loser clown, watching the world from the sidelines."

"Not a clown!" said Beth. "Pierrot! I love Pierrot!" She hugged Vita. "He's a beautiful dreamer."

Anne paced alongside the picnic table. "You should have told us, Vita. We're your sisters! To think I've been so nice to him all summer, feeling sorry for him. Thank goodness you dumped him. And her! She's nothing special."

"Not at all," said Beth. "That dress was the only reason anyone watched her at all."

Vita gave a sad smile. "It was me who convinced them to try out. I told them how much fun it would be. I thought she was my friend. And Vic . . . we were together for over a year!"

"And here I've been defending him all along as a nice guy."

"Yeah," said Beth. "We wouldn't have been so friendly to them."

"Did Vic say anything?"

"He kept asking what was wrong. I finally told him he was a good Harlequin, in pursuit of Columbine. He squirmed and said it didn't mean anything. That he didn't mean to do it."

"Yuck!" Beth threw her hands out like she was shaking off something disgusting. "He could at least own up to it."

Anne put her hands on Vita's shoulders. "You can do a hundred times better than him. Though I don't think Easton is right for you."

Vita groaned. "Not that again. Beth . . . your secret."

Everyone was relieved to move on to a different subject.

Beth didn't hesitate. "Dylan and I smoked pot."

Anne's mouth dropped open for a second time. "Beth! You're fourteen! Are you crazy?"

"You can't try everything that comes your way," Vita said.

Anne had her hands on her hips. "Mom and Dad would be furious if they knew. You'd be grounded for the rest of summer. I don't like being in charge of you. You're too unpredictable."

"You are *not* in charge of me! Anyway, I didn't even like it. It smelled! No wonder it's called skunkweed."

"That Dylan is leading you down the wrong path," said Anne. "Posing nude, doing drugs."

"I wasn't really nude. And pot isn't a drug. It's a . . . weed." She gave a laugh. "Anyway, it was just a puff or two."

"From now on I'm keeping a closer eye on you."

"My gosh," said Vita, "the way we're all going. My plans falling apart, Anne changing her mind, Beth doing God knows what . . ."

"It's my turn," said Joey.

They had almost forgotten about him, he was so quiet.

"You have a secret?" asked Beth.

Vita faced Joey. "You don't have to be a part of this crazy game."

"I . . . I want to. Besides, there's something I want you all to know. I've been wanting to tell you for a while. Something I haven't told anybody."

The tone of the game changed, and Anne's anger dissipated. They looked at him with concern.

Beth scooted closer to him. "Go ahead, Joey. What is it?"

His eyebrows pinched together, and he found it hard to get started. "Well . . ."

They nodded gently and waited for him to continue.

"You can tell us," Anne said.

Beth nodded. "Your secret's safe with us."

Vita was just about to say that he could tell them another time.

"I . . ." Joey looked at each one. "I . . . I had a sister."

Beth gave him a push. "You can't make things up!" she said with a laugh. "You're just trying to change the subject."

"I'm not! It's the truth."

"What do you mean, Joey?" Vita asked.

"I had a baby sister. But she died."

"Did your parents tell you that?" Anne looked to Vita and Beth. "We never heard about it. Are you sure, Joey?"

"I saw a picture. When I was nine. Sometimes Mom would go to a drawer and unlock a little box. She was always sad or mad afterwards. One day, the phone rang, and she left it open. Inside was a photo. It was of me when I was about two, and there was a baby on my lap. I was holding the baby's hand and Mom and I were smiling big.

"When my dad was driving me to baseball practice, I asked him who the baby was. He just kept driving but tears came to his eyes. He said it was Baby Leah. He said she died in her sleep one night. And that Mom never got over it.

"I asked him if it was my fault and if that was why they always fought. He pulled over. He said it was no one's fault. And that they still loved each other, but sometimes things get in the way. And not to ask Mom about it. Maybe someday, but not now." He blinked out at the memory.

They sat speechless, watching Joey trying to be strong. Anne sniffled. "That's so sad."

"Do you know what happened?" asked Beth.

"No. I didn't want to ask. But sometimes I wonder . . . Maybe it *was* my fault. Maybe she cried out or something and I didn't hear her. Maybe I could have saved her."

Vita gave him a hug. "Oh, Joey. I'm sure it wasn't your fault. You were practically a baby too."

They watched him in silence, unable to think of anything to say.

Joey's expression shifted to defiance. "I wish I could ask about her. I wish they would tell me more."

"They will, someday, Joey," said Vita. "Maybe it's just too sad for them." She remembered Joey's face when he looked up at the little angel in the cemetery. She remembered the bunch of bluebells.

They sat quietly, weighted by sadness.

Joey started to feel bad that he had told them. "Sorry. But I wanted you to know. I can't really tell anyone else."

Vita put her arm around him. "We're glad you told us. So you have four sisters."

"A baby angel and us," said Anne.

Beth twisted her hands. "Sorry I didn't believe you, Joey."

"That's okay. I just . . . I just wanted someone to know. It makes her more real."

ॐ

The next evening, while Beth was getting ready for bed and Joey was taking a shower, Vita sat in the living room, inspecting the long dress she had in mind for the Ophelia shoot. She had accidentally splattered it with bleach several months ago and couldn't wear it anymore. She became aware that Anne and Millie were speaking in low voices in the kitchen.

She put her dress down and walked closer to where she could hear them. She thought they were probably talking about her, worried about her. She would have to make more of an effort to hide her ongoing disappointment.

But then she heard Anne ask why Joey's parents never had more children.

"This is between us," said Millie. "They still haven't told Joey, which I don't agree with." Millie was quiet for a few moments, and then spoke almost in a whisper. "They had a baby girl. Who died when she was just two months old. It was a terrible time. Devastating for them."

Vita knew she shouldn't be listening, but now she was riveted.

"We felt so bad. You know it was Sal and I who introduced them. Walter was the younger brother of one of Sal's army buddies." Millie's voice filled with sorrow. "Those two were lovebirds. Meant for each other."

"What happened?" Anne asked.

"It was no one's fault. Sad things happen in life. Walter told Sal about it. Once. He said it was a night of romance. They had put the baby down. Joey was asleep. A few hours later, Dorothy woke up and went to check on the kids one last time. Walter said he still hears Dorothy's screams. For a long time, she couldn't bear to be touched by him."

"How terrible! How sad."

"It was a sad, sad time. She goes every year to visit the grave. They buried her in Dorothy's hometown, next to her parents. That was some consolation to her."

Vita heard her mom and Anne make soft sounds of sorrow and for a while they were silent.

"A few years later, she thought she was pregnant again. But was mistaken."

Millie's tone shifted slightly. "Sal's cousin Mary lost a baby the same way. Died in its crib while sleeping. They were devastated and blamed themselves, of course. That's what parents do. But they went on to have more children. And healed, as much as you can from a loss like that."

"Is it too late for them now—Joey's parents? To have more children?"

"I suppose it's still possible. She's a few years younger than I am. We all married so young back then." There was another pause and Vita heard a chair being scooted back. "Where are the kids? It's way too quiet."

Vita took a quick step back . . . and bumped into Joey. Her eyes widened in surprise. She grabbed him by the arm and pulled him to the front door. "Joey! How long were you there? We shouldn't have been listening."

"Long enough to know the truth."

She stepped outside with him, and they sat on the front steps.

"I'm so sorry, Joey."

He knotted his hands in front of him. "I'm glad I know."

"You see, it had nothing to do with you, Joey. It wasn't anybody's fault."

After a long silence, he raised his face to Vita. "Do you think there's anything I can do to help my parents?"

"Gosh, Joey. I don't know. Sometimes I don't understand the world at all."

"Me either."

They jumped when they heard the screen door open behind them.

"There you are!" cried Beth. "Come inside. Mom said there's some Neapolitan ice cream we can have if we want."

"That sounds good," Joey said, hiding all evidence of his sadness.

That night as he lay in bed, Joey knew that—at the right moment—he would show his mom the photo he took of the little angel tombstone. And he would ask about his sister. He wanted to claim her, make her a part of him. It might crack his mom in two, but it would also, eventually, unite them. She might get mad, but at least it would be out in the open. No more secrets. He was scared. But he knew he was going to do it.

CHAPTER 17

Anne tried to keep a light conversation going as she drove. "It's just to get more information that might be useful. But remember, they're not the only directors in the world."

"They're the best around here. They're all I have for the next two years. Maybe more, if I have to go to college in town." Vita let out a soft moan. "Oh Anne, I *have* to get away. I'm sure of it. I can't be *me* here."

"Don't be so desperate."

The closer they got to Hawthorn, the more agitated Vita became.

"I can still change my mind. That was the deal. We'll drive by the studio, and see if they're there. I might or might not talk to them."

"Right. But it's better to get it over with. And then move on."

"I didn't know I was so afraid. What can they say? The audition's over. There's nothing that can really happen now."

"Exactly. And it might help."

"I might learn something valuable." She kept her eyes fixed outside the window, and then placed her hands on her stomach. "Oh, I don't know, Anne. Maybe this isn't a good idea. Maybe they'll think I'm being pushy."

Anne pulled onto the frontage road alongside the highway and turned into the town.

"When did you become so unsure of yourself? Like Beth said, you used to be the boldest of us, the bravest by far."

"I've been thinking about that. When Beth said it, I knew it was true." Gazing out at the road, Vita narrowed her eyes in thought. "I think knowing that I want to be an actor makes me doubt myself. Makes me unsure, less bold. Because I want it so badly. It's more than wanting. You guys tease me about being desperate—but it's true. I caught a glimpse of something so beautiful, so right for me—and I know that I can't live without it."

Anne glanced over at her with concern. "That sounds too all or nothing. There's a darkness to your beautiful dream."

"It *is* all or nothing. It's both beautiful—and terrifying. Without it, I won't be me."

"There you go again. Don't talk to them in that desperate way or you'll frighten them off. Just gather information, be happy and cheerful. Remember, you can get up and leave anytime you want."

"Right." Vita closed her eyes while she took a deep breath. "Thanks for doing this, Anne."

"I'm your sister. Of course I'm going to help you. But I'll be mad if you chicken out. Or if you let their words get you down."

"Okay, okay, don't lecture me now, just when I'm trying to get my courage up."

Anne turned onto the street that led to the studio.

Vita drew in a sharp breath. "Oh my God, they're there. Keep driving! Don't slow down."

"I'm not slowing down. There's a car right behind me."

"Park over there. By the square. I'll . . . I'll walk to the studio."

Anne parked under a shade tree.

Vita looked over her shoulder at the studio and took another deep breath. "This could take a while. Or a minute."

"Take all the time you need. I'll look at the shops. If it gets too hot, I'll go into the soda fountain. How about we meet there?"

"Okay." Vita got out of the car and smoothed down her blouse. "I'll just ask a quick question. They'll say this or that. Then . . . I'll then move on with, with . . . whatever."

"Exactly." Anne walked away before Vita could change her mind.

Vita felt she was in a waking version of her nightmare about scaling the mountain—going up and up—only to be paralyzed by terror at the top.

Though she had tried to minimize their importance, the Radcliffs had a reputation for being masterful directors. Exacting, perfectionists, artists with a vision. They had carved out a little realm in their mid-sized town, competing with the bigger theaters in Foreston. They were well respected and in demand. They could mold words, actors, and sets into a transformative experience.

They both taught at the college in Hawthorn. They lived above the studio where they held classes and auditions.

It was also used for small performances, as well as for their fall workshop.

Vita looked up at the beautiful old building. Inlaid at the top was a decorative stone with the year 1882 carved into it. The front of the façade was made of brick, with long windows on two floors, shaded by tall leafy trees. Several boxed planters decorated the outside, filled with red and pink geraniums, small white phlox, and trailing ivy.

Mrs. Radcliff stood outside, eyeing the poster that her husband was taping to the window inside. Even in this simple act, he looked stern and judgmental with his pointy beard and bushy eyebrows.

Vita observed Mrs. Radcliff. She was beautiful in an unusual way. Like one of the paintings in her Aunt Nellie's old masters books. She had a strong curved nose, and a long, graceful neck. A gossamer floral dress fluttered about her legs. She wore her hair in a chignon and in one hand she held a fan, lightly fanning her face and neck. Vita had heard that the couple had met in a college production, years ago. She crossed the street and walked up to the studio.

The notice announced a theatrical production for their children's class. Next to it was a poster for the performance of *A Midsummer Night's Dream* in the fall. Vita almost lost her courage and was ready to retreat when Mrs. Radcliff saw her reflection in the window and spun around.

"Why, hello, Vita! What are you doing here?"

"Oh, hi, Mrs. Radcliff. Anne wanted to do some shopping, so I thought I'd see if you were here. If you had a minute for me. To talk about the audition."

"Of course." She led Vita inside the open door to the studio. "Harold, look who's here. Vita would like a word with us."

"Ah, Vita. Good afternoon." He glanced at his watch. "I have a committee meeting at 2:00. Let's go upstairs. We can chat while I gather my things." He locked the studio door, gave a glance at the posters, and opened the outside door that led upstairs to their apartment above.

Vita cringed. She should have made an appointment. How foolish of her. Of course they were busy. "I don't want to take your time—"

He moved briskly and was halfway up the stairs. At the top he turned to her, before opening the apartment door. "You're here now. Let's talk." His bushy eyebrows and penetrating eyes made her wish she hadn't come.

Mrs. Radcliff followed from behind. "You came at a good time, Vita. We had a morning class, but we have some time now. We'd be happy to talk with you."

Mr. Radcliff opened the door, switched on the ceiling fan, and waved Vita to a seat.

Vita mumbled "thanks" and pressed her mouth into a smile. She sat at the edge of a chair.

Mrs. Radcliff walked to the kitchen, her airy dress floating behind her. "How about a glass of lemonade? Or some iced tea?"

"No, thank you. I won't stay long."

"Well, I'm going to have a nice tall glass of lemonade. Harold?"

"Not for me." He sat in a chair and fixed his eyes on Vita. "Now."

Vita swallowed. "Well, it's about the audition."

"Let me guess, you expected a role."

Vita opened her mouth to speak but he cut her off.

"I thought as much."

"I . . . I was just wondering if you could tell me, did I . . . do something wrong? I think I did, but I'm not sure what. I thought it might help me to know."

He leaned back and tented his fingers, furrowing his brows. His wife sat down opposite Vita.

"I brought you a glass, anyway. It's such a warm day."

"The audition," Mr. Radcliff said. "I'll admit . . . I was disappointed. Surprised, even. I've seen you on stage. You know how to inhabit it, how to own a character. That's why I kept at it, having you read again and again."

Vita listened, preparing for the blow.

"The long and short of it is . . . you gave me nothing to work with." He opened his hands. "No highs or lows. No heights. No depths. Too high, and I can rein it in. Too low, and I can shape that depth. But I must have solid material to work with. I saw only a façade."

Vita blushed deeply because he was right. She had listened to Carla about being dramatic. She had used external tricks to hide behind. Because she was so afraid.

"For example, that hair toss—though it was quite memorable—did nothing for your delivery. What were you thinking? You must rid yourself of such gimmicks."

Vita filled with shame. It was as if he had told her she was shallow.

"Fine for farce or melodrama or musical theater. Inappropriate for serious acting."

"I know. I know what you mean." It had felt false. She knew it was all empty without that inner connection.

"You do realize I gave you more chances than the others. Any thoughts?"

Vita looked from him to his wife and then out at the floor. "I became nervous for some reason. And I . . . I thought maybe you had me in mind for the role, so I . . ."

"Had you in mind? Before the audition? Because we praised your school performance? I'm afraid it doesn't work that way."

"I know it was stupid of me. It was that comment you made. At the café." Vita wished she had never brought it up.

He cocked his head and turned towards his wife. "What comment was that?"

Vita gave a light laugh as she repeated the words. "'She would make a stunning Titania.' And you agreed. I thought maybe it meant—"

It took a moment to register. "Oh that! Yes. We were watching Anne, saying how fairylike she was."

Vita's stomach dropped. Her face blazed with heat. How presumptuous of her! She sat frozen in disbelief at her mistake.

"No, our decision was based solely on what we saw at the audition." He leaned back and sighed. "You simply weren't there. You were mediocre at best."

Vita sank deeper into the chair, wanting to disappear.

"Auditions are unforgiving." He held up an iron finger. "One chance . . . and one chance only to knock their socks off."

The phone rang and his wife rose to answer it. She spoke a few words, and indicated that it was for him.

"Remember that." He fixed her with another stare, and then shifted moods as he took the phone. As he spoke, he was no longer the steely director, but a frazzled professor and committee member. "Yes, yes. Indeed. Good point, good point. We'll be sure to discuss that as well. Fine. I'll be there momentarily." He hung up the phone.

"And on that note . . ." He kissed his wife on the cheek and grabbed his satchel, saying a few final words to Vita. "Remember, Miss Vitale, no one is born a great actor. It takes work. Work!" He swung his fist for emphasis.

He opened the door, paused a moment, and addressed Vita. "The best actors use setbacks as the most valuable of tools, lessons to be learned from. Nothing is more boring than easy success. Goodbye."

His wife followed him to the door, smiling.

Vita stood, ready to leave.

"Stay a moment, Vita," said Mrs. Radcliff. "I would like to give you my take on it. After all these years, I know how to read between his lines. Please." She gestured for Vita to be seated.

"I'd be grateful." Vita took several gulps of lemonade, aware of how thirsty she was. "It's good. Thank you."

"Let me fill our glasses." Mrs. Radcliff came back with a slender pitcher of lemonade with mint leaves and slices of lemons. She refilled their glasses and returned the pitcher to the refrigerator.

For the first time, Vita relaxed and let out a deep breath of pent-up tension. Only then did she take in the apartment. High ceilings, one wall of exposed brick, a Persian rug over polished hardwood floors. There was a fireplace with a few logs left over from colder weather, and an antique carved mirror over the mantel. Against one wall, stood tall wooden bookcases filled with books and small objects—boxes and ceramics, framed photographs, a few glittering rocks.

There were several comfortable deep chairs in rich velvets and paisleys in all the colors she loved—moss and hunter greens, plum, old gold. Near the window sat a wine-colored Victorian chaise lounge, velvet, with fringe along the bottom.

She knew that Mrs. Radcliff taught both theater and art classes at the college and saw signs of her influence in the watercolors and sketches that covered the walls. Vita's lips softened into a smile. She felt at home here. All these things spoke to her. Sparks to the mind, sensuality for the eyes, delight in the knowledge of a larger world out there.

Vita decided that the visit was worth it, if only to see this place—to know that these artists had created their own rich world right here amid the cornfields and small towns. She leaned forward to see more of the alcove off the living room. An easel was set up, and she saw shelves with books and art supplies. That must be Mrs. Radcliff's space.

The living room appeared to be Mr. Radcliff's office. Textbooks and several notebooks were piled on a table next to an old roll-top desk. Above it hung two maps of Shakespeare's London, and a rendering of the Globe Theatre. And a plaque—painted by Mrs. Radcliff no doubt—with a moon and stars and the words:

> *We are such stuff*
> *As dreams are made on, and our little life*
> *Is rounded with a sleep.*

Mrs. Radcliff returned to the couch. She set a small plate of cookies on the coffee table.

"Thank you, Mrs. Radcliff."

"Please. Call me Daphne."

Vita smiled at the invitation to familiarity and raised her eyes to take in all the images on the walls.

"Your apartment is just beautiful. Did you paint that quote?"

"I did. My favorite line from Shakespeare."

"*The Tempest* is my favorite Shakespeare play. I mean, I haven't seen very many, but I really love that one." Vita observed the graceful way Daphne moved. She had a gaze—not unlike her husband's—that bore deeply into you to see what was there. But her gaze was tempered by a lovely smile. She was utterly, exquisitely feminine—but with an element that disturbed. As if she had a secret power that she kept to herself.

Mrs. Radcliff took a sip from her glass and tucked her legs beneath her. "Lemonade is so refreshing on a hot summer day, isn't it?"

"It is. Thank you." Vita took another sip and relaxed in the chair. For the first time, she detected a slight accent. Something European? Or perhaps—

"Now. Let me tell you something about my husband. He hates to be wrong. He was so sure of you. I could see him getting frustrated, just as I saw you getting frustrated the more you read." She gave a sympathetic smile.

"When students come to ask why they didn't get a role—as happens with every audition—he usually tells them they need to work on their delivery, or projecting their voice, things that will come with experience. Not so, with you. He was hard on you, just now."

Vita almost nodded. So it wasn't just her imagination.

"We've seen two of your performances directed by Mrs. Simon. You were exceptional as Viola. You brought something new and fresh to the role. Harold knows what you're capable of. He was expecting that. And you didn't deliver. It was a different Vita at the audition."

Vita looked down at her hands.

Mrs. Radcliff's lips curled in amusement. "I have a little test of my own. You see, the real test is with the audience. When we see plays, Harold studies the performers, while I . . . I study the audience. You had them, in both plays. You captivated, controlled. You became the characters, understood how to shape the lines. You just need to be bolder and bring out that inner . . ."—she waved her hand around as she searched for the right word—"*stuff.*"

Vita raised her eyes to the quote again. "The dream stuff?"

"Yes. The illusion. The beauty. The connection." Her piercing gaze landed on Vita. "Without which, life would be unbearable."

A deep, dark door flung open inside Vita. Her murky feelings and nebulous thoughts about dreams and quests and beauty lay spread before her in startling, troubling clarity. To her conscious mind, for the first time, rose the awareness that on the other side of the dream, was the unbearable.

Vita felt exposed, her dark desperation laid bare. Mercifully, Daphne didn't linger in such depths, but smoothed her floral dress, tucked a stray strand of hair behind her ear, and offered a tender smile. They were back on the surface, safe, manageable. Where the tangible resided. The things Vita could get her hands into.

"You have beauty, magnetism, voice, stage presence. But those are common things possessed by many. The real question, and what really sets the artist apart, is: How badly do you want it? How hard are you willing to work? The path is not an easy one. You have to be strong."

Vita took in all her words, thinking that Daphne sounded very much like her mom and aunt. And Hogie.

"Learn to embrace your fears, your failures, as Harold said. They're part of the artist's path—part of life. They make us stronger." She looked up at the words from *The Tempest*. "A dream is only as good as its connection to others. That's what it's all about, really, the stage—collaboration. A group effort to express a dream. Not everyone can do that. I believe you can. With work, experience, maturity."

"I know that I really don't know very much," said Vita. "I just know that I love it. I'm sorry I disappointed you both."

"It's not about us. And don't be hard on yourself. You're young. Like Harold said, much of acting is just plain old hard work, like anything else. You will grow with experience." She took a sip of lemonade and studied Vita. "You feel things more when you are alone. Am I correct?"

Vita swallowed. "I do. I always have." Was she really so obvious?

"And yet you seek out a collaborative art form. Why is that? It forces you out of yourself—and yet allows you to be alone. That's not a judgment. I'm very like that myself." Daphne let her gaze fall outside the window.

Vita had always worried that at heart she was a loner, and that it was something to be overcome. But to hear Daphne speak of it made her reconsider how she viewed herself.

"I think you're holding yourself back, out of some fear or insecurity. Don't worry, that's true for all of us. But we must come to terms with our weaknesses, and not be ruled by them. Good actors convince the audience—great actors convince themselves. You're not quite there. You haven't yet convinced yourself."

"I know. I know that's true." At the bottom of everything, she was ruled by her fears.

Daphne gave an airy laugh. "It's part of the process. Allow for growth and discovery. Read. Study. Observe. See as many plays as possible—note what works, what doesn't work, what moves you, what gets in the way. Learn to unravel the mystery and magic of the stage."

Vita nodded at her words, expressing her willingness to do whatever it took.

"You have the externals. You could meet with some success by your looks alone, but that would be a loss. There's more to you. The heights . . . and depths. *That* is what the audience is hungry for. A plain woman who can connect her soul to powerful, stirring words will bring the house down, every single time. We are all hungry for soul stuff."

Daphne took another sip of lemonade and when she set her glass down, she smiled wistfully. "We dream. That's who we are. We work, play, study, fall in love, fight wars, have families . . . But behind it all is the dream. That is what propels us through life. What gets us through. Give them *that*, Vita—and you will succeed."

Vita wanted to hear more, wanted to take every word with her, and make it a part of her. She understood that Mr. Radcliff was the Prospero, the technician, the craftsman. He was his books and learning, his experience and authority. But it was his wife—the beautiful, unsettling Daphne—who was the quiet force, the dreamer, the Ariel of their partnership. She had wings—he was earthbound. And it was that combination that made them a formidable couple.

Daphne smiled, as if alighting back to earth. "Well. I am glad you stopped by."

"Thank you so much for talking with me. I . . . I think I understand a little better now." Vita rose to her feet, fearing that she had already taken too much of her time.

Daphne also stood and smoothed back her hair. "The journey is a long one—but wondrous."

Vita almost laughed out loud at her choice of word. She hid her smile as she walked to the door.

"I see a path ahead for you, Vita. One filled with a lot of work, as well as joy. Best of luck."

Vita thanked her again and was surprised when Daphne gave her a hug.

Vita smiled at the kindness and went down the stairs.

She walked slowly to the square, wanting to let the words sink in. She felt almost overwhelmed by Daphne's perceptions.

And the combined advice from her and her husband? Was it overall good? Or would the mistaken assumption about a "stunning Titania" haunt her? Vita felt foolish—and hopeful. Most of all, she felt that someone had understood her.

When she walked into the soda shop, Anne was seated at a booth with two friends from school. "There you are! How about a phosphate? They're really good."

Vita shook her head. "No thanks."

One of the girls smiled. "Anne told us about the audition. I know the feeling. That happened to me once."

"Better luck next time," said the other girl.

"Thanks," Vita said.

On the drive home, Anne recounted news of her friends and waited for Vita to talk about the visit.

Vita was still enveloped in the experience and impressions of the Radcliffs. She went over their words, deciding on which advice she would follow immediately, and which she would tuck away for future reference.

Anne finally grew impatient. "Well?"

Vita turned to Anne and laughed. "Sorry, Anne. I was just trying to remember everything. I'm so glad I went. They gave me really good advice. A lot to think about. And it helped to put things in perspective."

"What did they say about the audition?"

Vita let out a sigh. "That I wasn't there. I didn't give them anything to work with. And that I have a lot of work ahead of me. But that's okay. That's what I want."

Anne darted a smile at Vita. "That sounds more like you."

"Mrs. Radcliff—Daphne—was especially kind and encouraging. I liked her so much. She said such interesting things about dreams and connection and collaboration. She talked about things I had felt but never put into words. And their home!"

The rest of the ride back to Greenberry, to Anne's delight, was filled with details of their apartment and workspaces—Mr. Radcliff's old London maps and roll-top desk, Daphne's easel and paintings, the velvet paisleys on the chairs in colors of plum and moss, the long windows with lace in them. And the wine-colored chaise lounge with fringe, positioned for gazing out at the treetops, or perhaps the moon and stars.

CHAPTER 18

J oey spent the morning with Abel, cleaning tools and
helping him tend his yard. In the afternoon he rode
his bike around town and stopped by the Jack and Jill
Park. He got a soda at the concession stand and watched a
Little League ballgame for a while. Then he walked over
to where he saw a few of his friends in the playground area.

Matt and Felix were at the crafts table making pencil holders out of Popsicle sticks. He saw Greg and Wiley
nearby at a picnic table.

Wiley cocked his head to Joey. "Hey, city boy. Matt and
Mutt are doing girly stuff." He tossed a few rocks at the back
of them and snickered. "Bull's eye."

Matt spun around. "I said cut it out!"

"Hi, Joey." Greg had his bike upside down and was
attaching playing cards to the spokes using wooden
clothes pins.

Joey watched Greg choose several new cards from his
pocket. "I used to do that to my bike. In Chicago."

"Ooooh," said Wiley. "In the big city? We're so impressed."

Greg spun the front wheel and smiled at the sharp fluttering sound of the cards.

Wiley threw a rock at the sliding board where it made a loud ping.

Greg looked up from his bike. "Watch what you're doing! There are kids playing there." He flipped his bike over and rode off, shaking his head. "See ya, Joey."

Wiley spotted Rufus Sharp walking along the street, took aim, and raised his arm.

Joey grabbed Wiley's hand and twisted it until he dropped the rock. "You're nothing but a bully, Wiley, a stinking coward! Good thing you're not in Chicago. You'd be beaten to a pulp." Joey got on his bike and began to ride off.

"Loser!" Wiley called after him. "You're just here because nobody else wants you! Your parents don't even want you! You're just like Rufus—a loser!"

Joey ignored the taunt, but a tiny place inside of him wondered if it was true. He biked around town for a while, and then rode past Hogie's. He was in the garage lifting weights, so Joey coasted up the driveway.

"Hey, Hogie." His mood seemed okay. Joey used the kickstand and bent down to pet Hogie's yellow-striped cat.

"Where you been? How're you spending your time?" He let out a grunt with each lift, his muscles straining and bulging. Sweat trickled down his face.

"I was at the park. But there's a kid there I can't stand. He picks on little kids, and he always makes fun of Rufus Sharp. And says really dumb things."

"Can't fix stupid." Hogie let out another grunt as he lifted the barbell.

"No, you sure can't." Joey sat on the chair at the side of the worktable. He watched Hogie pick up a set of free weights and extend his elbows behind him in lifts.

"What do you think happened to him?"

"Who?"

"Rufus Sharp. I've heard so many different stories about him and why he's that way. What do you think happened?"

"Who knows."

Hogie did a few more reps and set the weights down. He downed a bottle of water and picked up a towel to wipe his face.

"Do you think he was hurt in the war?"

A shadow of a smile came to Hogie's mouth. "Maybe that's it. I guess he's just walking around in his own battle-field. Like the rest of us."

The cat jumped up on Hogie's lap. "Isn't that right, Tigress?" He stroked the cat and smiled at her purring. "What a name. I never saw such a sissy cat. Do me a favor and pour some milk for her. It's in the fridge. Grab a bowl or something."

"Sure." Joey went inside and poured the milk into a cereal bowl. He glanced at the mail sitting on the counter. "Huh."

He placed the bowl at Hogie's feet, and the cat was soon lapping it up.

"There's a letter on your counter for Patrick J. Hogan. Who's that?"

Hogie jerked his head back. "Who the hell do you think it is?"

Joey's perplexity shifted to an embarrassed laugh. "Oh! I didn't know—I thought . . ." He let his words drift off.

Hogie smiled at him. "And what do you think that 'J' stands for?"

Joey's face lit up. "Joseph?"

"Yep. You and I have a lot in common."

Joey felt like he had just earned a little badge and smiled widely.

"Including our friend. Where is she?"

"She and Anne drove over to Hawthorn. She wants to ask the directors why she didn't get the part."

"Good for her. That's how I taught her to be. Not all mopey and feeling sorry for herself." He took the towel and rubbed his neck with it. "The other two—Anne and Beth—they'll be all right. They'll be happy in life." He wheeled to the little fridge and took out a bottle of cold water. "Vita? She wants more, expects more, from herself and the world. That's dangerous—but to my mind, it's the only way to be." He took several gulps of water.

"Then why did you give up?" Joey looked startled. He didn't mean it to come out that way.

Hogie stopped drinking and lowered the bottle. "I didn't. Not yet, anyway. Sometimes I feel like it—but some part keeps kicking me forward. I know what Vita feels. If she listens to that part, she'll be okay."

"It's part of her dream path, so she will. She's helping me to figure out mine. She says it's easier if you have one." Joey leaned down and stroked Tigress, then looked up at Hogie. "So you think she'll be happy?"

Hogie wheeled to the shelves and lifted a can full of miscellaneous nails, screws, bolts, and nuts and set it on his worktable. He had made a box with different small compartments, and he began organizing the nails and screws into it by size.

"Happy? I don't know about that. I think she'll always be questing—her word—but I guess that brings a satisfaction of its own. Maybe getting closer to a point in the distance is as good as it gets." Hogie sorted through the parts. "I'm not the answer man, Joey. All I have are a bunch of questions."

They sat in silence for a few minutes. Joey brought the bowl into the kitchen, washed it, and set it in the rack. He looked around at the sparse apartment. He wondered if Hogie was lonely. When he came back, he saw Tigress was on Hogie's lap, with her paws on his chest. Hogie had his face close to hers and was talking to her.

Joey put up his hands and made a frame around the image.

Hogie looked up and raised his eyebrows.

"It'd make a good picture. Would you ever let me photograph you?"

"Doubt it."

"Just for practice?"

The sound of a car pulling up ended their conversation. It was a guy named Roger.

Joey was getting to know Hogie's friends who stopped by, fellow vets for the most part. Sometimes they went fishing or target shooting.

Roger came in and pretended to attack Joey, giving his head a knuckle rub. "Young Joseph! Staying out of trouble?" He went to the garage fridge, took out a cold beer, and leaned against a sawhorse. "Hoge—I need your help with something."

Joey knew that was code for something they couldn't talk about in front of him. He was in the way. "Well, I gotta go. Bye Hogie. See ya, Roger."

Joey went home and grabbed the Pentax. It still had several shots left on the roll of film. He took a spare roll, just in case, and looped the camera around his neck. He would take some pictures. He had several hours before dinner.

Millie was on the phone. "Just a moment." She covered the receiver when she saw Joey. "I thought you were with the boys at the park."

"I was. But I want to take some pictures."

Millie smiled. "You're becoming a real photographer."

"Nah. Just a learner. Would you pose for me sometime?"

Millie sat up. "Why, I'd love that! I've been wanting a picture of me and Sal, but I can't get him to go to the studio uptown. I think he'd be fine with a casual one outside. Could you do that?"

Joey nodded and let Millie get back to her conversation.

He bicycled out to his spot at the edge of town to the west. He wanted to take pictures of the meadow. He rode down the hill and leaned his bike against the old fence. The meandering stream sparkled in the afternoon sunlight.

There was an area just behind the stream that was flat and grassy. He had been thinking lately that it might be good to have a tower of his own. Kind of like Vita's water tower, but nothing to be afraid of. Just a place that could hold all his dreams. If he ever built such a tower, the grassy clearing in the meadow is where he would choose.

He looked around and relished the freedom of being all alone. *Couldn't do this in Chicago*, he thought. He could be anything in this spot. D'Artagnan on a quest, or a famous explorer. He leaned against the fence and lifted the camera. The lighting was a little flat, as David would say, and he didn't want to waste any film. He would wait.

Joey glanced around him, and up and down the hilly road. Not a soul in sight. He had the whole place to himself.

He looked at the grassy spot behind the stream and tilted his head. A stone tower. With steps running all around it, up to the very top where he could see far away. He stepped on the first rung of the fence. With a voice Vita had coached him on, he called out.

"I, D'Artagnan—" What did he want to say? He wanted to claim his tower. He climbed to the second rung and spoke in a deeper voice with more authority.

"I, D'Artagnan, of—of the four sisters, and the four winds, and the sun, the moon, and the stars—sole creator and owner of this, this Tower of Dreams. I hereby declare that . . ." Again he was stuck. What did he want?

"That from the top of my tower, I can make anything come true! I can see into the future and—and see the paths that will take me on my quests."

He jumped down from the fence and opened his imaginary cape. "From the top, I can see into other lands, and other times!" He spun around, imagining the cape was making a circle around him. "I—"

He whipped his head up, aware that someone was standing close by, watching him.

Rufus Sharp!

Where did he come from? Had he been there all along, watching him?

Joey froze, his eyes wide with fear. He took a step back, ready to run, but tripped on a tree root and fell to the ground.

What if Rufus really did have a knife strapped to his leg? What if he really did have superhuman strength? What if . . . this was it?

Rufus stared at him, holding the rag in his hand. He leaned his head and looked at Joey, then out at the meadow, and back at Joey.

For a brief moment, they switched roles. Joey was the crazy one, muttering in his own world, and Rufus was calmly observing him. But not judging him.

Joey slowly pushed to his feet. He watched Rufus squint into the distance, his face transformed. Was he seeing the tower?

Something bigger than fear overtook Joey. He would later wonder at his boldness.

"Rufus."

When Rufus turned, Joey held up his camera and pointed to him. He mimed the question: Can I take your picture?

Rufus looked back out at the meadow.

Joey slowly lifted the camera. Click. Click.

The noise made Rufus turn to Joey.

He focused the camera again—eye to eye now, click, and click. Rufus was staring directly at him; Joey was being granted a rare glimpse inside the man. He knew the moment wouldn't last long and he kept clicking away. One more, one more—and then Rufus began to move.

Joey lowered the camera. Did he imagine the smile, or the softening in Rufus's face? Why was Joey filled with such a flood of joy? He felt that he had connected to something utterly important. And beautiful.

Rufus shoved the rag back into his mouth and staggered off, firing that hand downward, his body jerking.

"Wait!" Joey cried after him. But the moment was already gone. The door that had momentarily allowed him entrance, had closed.

Joey continued to take photos of Rufus receding, trudging up the hill, and disappearing where the road turned at the top. He cursed when he came to the end of the roll and understood why photographers had several cameras around their necks. The miraculous was fleeting.

Joey leaned against the fence, blinking at what had happened. He looked back up the hill, but Rufus was long gone. Then he dropped to the grass, rewound the film, pocketed it, and loaded a new roll.

He took a few more photos of the empty road where Rufus had just been. Then he climbed the fence and took several of the meadow. Several of where the tower had stood. He wanted to anchor this moment, this experience, to concrete images.

He wanted to document the day, the place, where he had stepped into his own world, claimed it, and connected to it and to another human being. He had never felt so powerful as in that moment.

Joey was one hundred percent sure that he would follow this path of discovery and connection—that was all that mattered. He now knew exactly how Vita felt and how she had no choice but to follow her path.

He understood now what she meant about the magic of other realities, other realms. His camera would be his magic wand, opening worlds and capturing their existence.

CHAPTER 19

Vita wanted an excuse to see Hogie. She was upset by the distance that had grown between them. When Joey mentioned that Hogie had asked about her, she decided to stop by. She and Anne had baked a batch of brownies earlier in the morning, so she set a few on a paper plate and walked them over to him.

Hogie was seated at his worktable, sorting through a metal box of receipts. A cup of coffee sat next to him.

"Good," Vita said, setting the plate down. "These wouldn't taste good with beer."

"Hey, Vita." Hogie bit into a brownie and washed it down with coffee. "Not bad. Been too busy to visit your old friend?"

Vita almost took the bait, almost fired back that he was the one always angry at her. Instead, she bent down and petted his cat.

"So what kind of soda does Joey like?"

Vita looked up, surprised by his question. "Root beer. And orange." She walked around his garage, inspecting the items he had been working on. "A chest of drawers?"

"A change from birdhouses. I need to get busy with that. So, the cemetery?"

Vita faced him. "I haven't changed any of my plans. I just needed a job and—"

Hogie held up his hands. "You won't get any criticism from me. I believe in hard work, you know that."

She waited to see if he was going to tease her, but he appeared to be serious. "It's not as bad as I thought it would be. Other than the heat, it's kind of nice."

Vita ran her hand over a bench he had recently completed. "Nice color." She looked at the label on the paint can. "Sage green."

"I need to give it another coat today."

Vita reached for the paint brush next to the bench. "Can I?"

"Help yourself."

Vita pried open the can and dipped in the brush. "This feels like old times." She sat on the piece of cardboard that was placed under the bench to catch drips. "I like painting. It's relaxing. Joey said you let him help sometimes."

"He's a good kid. And a good worker. Though all his talk about dream paths has me worried. He's starting to sound like you."

Vita raised her eyes to Hogie. "You know a lot of that thinking came from you."

"Yeah, well, you've taken it to a whole new level."

They worked in silence for a few minutes, as was their old habit. "I ran into Laura uptown. I don't see her much now that I'm not working at the plant shop. She asked about you."

"It that why you're here now? So you can report back to her that I'm still an angry old bastard and to keep away?"

"She already knows that. I'm here because I like it here." Vita checked her work and smoothed out a drip. "And it's nice to be around someone who understands me."

"That's giving me a lot of credit."

"Well, someone who won't pity me."

"That's more on the mark."

Vita dipped in the brush and painted another slat. "I know my problems are nothing compared to yours, and probably most adults. But it still feels bad to fail."

"I told you, don't see it as failure," he said impatiently. He smoothed out a few crumpled receipts and entered their amounts into his notebook. "You're learning. It's experience. Just keep pushing ahead."

Vita kept her eye on her work, careful to avoid streaks. "You know, Hogie, sometimes I start to feel sorry for myself—and then all of a sudden, you're right there!" Vita put her hand in front of her face. "In my head."

"That must scare the shit out of you."

"And I hear you saying, 'Stop moping and do something!' or 'what'd I teach you about perseverance?' or 'stand tall and don't take crap from anyone.'" Vita smiled. "Even when I don't want to listen to you, I still do. Because I know you're right."

"Nice to know someone thinks so."

"Laura does, too."

Hogie set the receipt down. "Here we are, having a nice time, and you want to go and ruin it. Why can't you leave it alone?"

"Because I know how she feels. And it bugs me that you get to make her decisions."

"What the hell are you talkin' about? You know that Laura does what she wants. She doesn't take shit from anyone."

"She makes an exception for you. How come you get to determine her life? Cause you got injured? Because you're a man? Older?" Vita knew she was treading on dangerous ground, but she said it gently, wanting to know what he thought.

"Get real, Vita. She deserves a hell of a lot better." Hogie unfolded a few more receipts and circled the amounts at the bottom.

"Would you desert her if she got injured? Never. You'd stick by her even closer. Wounded, hurt, disappointed. We still all need each other."

"Pearls of wisdom."

Vita checked her work and then dabbed at the edges of the slats. "Laura says you're a true person, and that's a hard quality to find, and she's not giving up."

Hogie shut the lid to the box with a bang. "That's it. We're through with this conversation. If you have a problem with that, you can leave."

"All right, all right. I've just been thinking about things lately. I mean besides you and Laura."

"If you mean that spoiled punk you've been seeing—"

"Not him. Anne and Mark. And Easton's not as bad as everyone thinks." Vita still had doubts about Easton, but after he had called her a few times, she'd decided to give him another chance. "He's taking me to a movie tonight. He's got a nice side."

"Don't we all." Hogie began to enter more numbers on the page.

"Anne and Mark are getting pretty serious. Like marriage-one-day serious. Even though they argue a lot now. About the war. Mark's decided to go if he gets a letter. It could be as early as January."

That caught Hogie's attention. "Shit!" He leaned back and stared off.

"I know. Anne's pretty upset. She spends all her spare time with him. He gave her *The Lord of the Rings*. They've been reading it together. They want to finish it before—"

Hogie snapped, suddenly angry. "You tell him to toughen up! Don't let him go to 'Nam with his head full of love and fairy stories. It's crazy over there! Dark and cruel and hopeless."

Vita raised her head to look at Hogie. "Maybe those stories and the memory of reading them with Anne will help him through the hard times."

"The *hard times*? You make it sound like he might have a bad day over there! When are you going to learn? It's hell! Life is hell. It's hard and full of disappointments and makes no sense."

Vita stood and brushed at her jeans. "That's part of it. If the world was as awful as you say, no one would want to live in it."

"You're learning." He wheeled over to the small re-frigerator and reached for a bottle of beer. "Time for my afternoon tea."

"It's still morning." Vita crossed her arms. "You drink too much. It messes up your thinking. Life is also full of goodness and kindness and beauty."

"I'm going to need something stronger if you keep this up." He made a low grunt at the absurdity of her words and took a long guzzle.

"It is! Think of all the books and plays and paintings and music that prove it. You think all those people are wrong?"

"I think they're delusional."

"What about those songs you used to sing—about love and hope. Playing music was such a big part of your life. Don't you believe in it anymore?" She waited for him to agree with her, but he remained silent.

"Music was everything to you. Music and Laura. Hogie?"

"Whatever you say, Vita." He looked over at her. "Sometimes I forget you're just a kid. I talk to you like. . . . You're right. I'm messed up. And I drink too much." He finished the beer and threw the empty bottle like he was shooting a basket. It landed in the trash on top of the others. "Best to ignore me."

"I could never do that. Any more than I could ignore my sisters. Or Joey."

"Where is he? Working?"

"He's developing his film. Abby's teaching him how. He's really taken to photography."

"Don't I know. He's trying to get me to pose. That'll be the day."

Vita laughed at the thought. "We're doing the Ophelia shot this afternoon—you know, the woman who loved Hamlet and was rejected by him. I have to float in the pond or stream. Joey's going to take some of the photos." She circled the bench, checking for any drips, and then put the paint brush in a container of water.

Vita looked around the garage. "It's almost lunch time. What are you going to eat?"

Hogie fixed her with a stare. "Peanut butter and jelly sandwiches, with a glass of chocolate milk." He cursed under his breath and returned the metal box to the shelves.

"All right, I'm going. Beth's probably waiting for me. I worry about her. She's growing up too fast."

"Worry about yourself. Beth's a wild one. But sometimes those are the quickest to settle down."

Vita turned to leave. "I don't see that happening anytime soon."

"Tell Joey I could use his help," Hogie called after her. "Need to make a trip to the hardware store."

At home Vita walked into the heat of an argument between Anne and Sal. Beth watched them from the table.

Sal waved his arms as he made his points. "And when you turned seventeen, you wanted a car. I wanted to wait, but you complained and pestered me until I gave in. How many other seventeen-year-olds have a car—not many!"

"This isn't about money!"

"And this one!" Sal said, pointing his finger at Vita. "Going to New York City for school? You can go to college in town. I'm not paying for this hare-brained acting scheme of yours."

"But Dad," said Beth. "It's been her dream for a long time."

"A long time? She's only fifteen! What are you talking about? And dreams don't pay the bills! Dreams don't pay the mortgage!"

Millie tried to motion to the girls not to talk back. She gave a little shake of her head—all to no avail.

Sal turned to Anne again. "It's final! No road trip with that boy. He's too old for you, for one thing." He pointed his thumb at Vita. "Now you've got this one doing the same thing."

"And you!" He spun around to Beth, causing her eyebrows to jump in surprise. "Out at all hours. All of you! I'm going to put an end to that."

Anne wasn't backing down. "Mark might get his letter any day!"

"You know as well as I do that it won't be before January. The war could be over by then."

"This could be our last summer together for a long time! It could be years before we have another chance."

"The answer's NO!"

Vita went to the bedroom and took out the old print dress with bleach spots. Would it be years before she could get to New York? How would she ever save enough money for all the things she wanted to do?

She knew that her dad's business was unusually slow and that it was worrying her parents. She couldn't ask her dad to pay for acting classes. Anne's voice was getting louder.

Last week Anne had argued with Mark, saying "You wouldn't be helping anyone by going!" They had stopped seeing each other for several days and Anne was miserable. Now she was putting all the blame on their father. Vita cringed at Anne's words.

"I hope you're happy, Dad! He's going because of people like you, telling him to go. If he doesn't come back, I'll never forgive you!"

Millie jumped in on that. "Anne! Don't you dare blame your father for a decision that is Mark's. What's wrong with you?"

Anne stormed out of the kitchen and into the bedroom, slamming the door. She sat on the bed with her arms crossed.

Vita gave a deep sigh. "Sorry, Anne. I know you're upset. But Mom's right. You can't pin this on Dad. And Mark needs your support. Not your criticism."

Anne's lip started to tremble. "I can't help it. I just keep thinking—what if he doesn't come back? Or comes back injured? And I could have prevented it?"

"Oh my gosh." Vita sat next to her. "Honestly, I don't know what I would do. Sometimes there's just not an answer for everything."

Beth poked her head around the door. "You shouldn't talk to Dad that way, Anne. You made him feel bad."

Anne put her head in her hands, and then dropped her hands to her lap. "He knows I don't mean it. I'm just—I don't even know who I'm so mad at. The world."

Beth spoke to Vita. "I'm going to Abby's. They should be setting up by now. You coming?"

"I'll be there soon. You go ahead." Vita slipped on the dress over her t-shirt and cutoffs and checked it in the mirror.

Anne noticed Vita's blank expression. "The Ophelia shoot? You're not looking forward to it? That's not like you."

Vita adjusted the dress in the mirror. "I'm starting to doubt everything. Maybe it is a hare-brained idea."

"Don't you dare say that! You've worked too hard, and I know you can do it." She stood next to Vita and tugged the dress down in the back.

"Because I've convinced you I could. What if I'm wrong?"

"The only way you can be wrong is to give up." Anne gave Vita playful push. "That's what *you* would say, anyway."

Vita took off the dress and folded it. "Want to hear something funny?"

Anne tipped her head, wondering at Vita's expression. "I could use a laugh."

"You know when we were at the café and we heard the directors say, 'She'd make a stunning Titania.' And Mr. Radcliff replied, 'Indeed she would.' Remember?"

"Yes. What was all that about? How could they say that and then not give you anything?"

Vita turned to Anne. "Because they weren't talking about me. They were talking about *you*. You're the beautiful fairy queen. Not me."

"*Me*! But I'm not remotely interested in acting." She looked out at the room and gave a laugh. "That's ridiculous! Oh, Vita. I'm so sorry. That must have made you feel terrible."

"Foolish. I let those words give me too much hope. Maybe I should stick to witches."

"A stupid misunderstanding that means nothing." Anne put both hands on Vita's shoulders. "Come on. You know what Mom would say. What Hogie would say. What *you* would say!"

Vita blew out a deep breath. "I know. I'm trying to put it behind me and move forward. But I feel different. I feel like I'm just a ball of fears and doubts, trying to fool everyone."

"No." Anne walked with her to the door. "Just keep doing what you're doing. You'll get to where you want to go. Today, you'll be Ophelia. You'll add the pictures to your portfolio. And tonight, you're going out. You'll dress up and enjoy your date with Easton." She nudged Vita. "He *is* cute."

Vita smiled. "I know. Sometimes I find myself really liking him."

"Go on. They're waiting for you."

Vita gave her a hug. "Thanks, Anne."

In David's darkroom, built in their basement, David, Darlene, and Abby were teaching Joey how to develop film. They were seeing the results from Joey's roll of film: photos of Abby and Beth, various streets and houses around town, and the meadow.

David and Darlene found them interesting, and pointed out composition, contrasts, and vantage points. David stared at the ones of Rufus that were just beginning to emerge.

"Whoa! Joey! Look at these." They all crowded around the images.

Abby leaned in closer. "Wow, Joey."

Joey smiled, studying the results. "I had a feeling some of them might be good."

"Good? These are great! Trying to outdo your teacher, huh?"

Joey laughed at the idea. "Not even close."

"I think we have some serious competition here, David."
Darlene winked at Joey.

"We sure do. At this rate, you're going to have one heck
of a collection by the end of summer. Promise me you'll
find a photography club to join when you get back home.
Take some classes."

Joey kept his eyes on the photographs of Rufus Sharp.
"I promise."

"Becca and Rob and the others are at the creek setting
up," Darlene said. "And Vita and Beth should be here soon."

"Right. Finish up here," said David. "We'll meet you
guys at the creek. I want to do the Ophelia shot before Vita
changes her mind. Her mood has decidedly changed, and I
want to complete my Shakespeare section."

After David left, Abby looked at the photos hanging
to dry. "They're so good, Joey. I bet no one has ever seen
Rufus looking like this." She leaned over and kissed Joey
on the cheek.

Joey was so surprised that he didn't say anything. It was
the first time he had ever been kissed. That kind of kiss.
He didn't know if he was supposed to do anything. So he
just smiled.

Abby didn't seem to think it was a big deal and simply laughed at his response. "Come on. Let's go down to
the creek."

❧

Two hours later, almost home, Vita was asking herself why
her luck was so bad. Why hadn't she expressed her opinion
about the creek instead of passively going along with it? The

water was low and muddy. Nothing like the paintings she had seen depicting the tragic Ophelia scene.

Millie and Anne watched her come through the door in her cutoffs and t-shirt, muddy, with mascara running down her cheeks, her hair dripping.

Beth soon followed, also muddy, but was laughing. "Vita, don't be so upset! Where's your sense of humor?"

Vita went into the bathroom, and they heard her turn on the shower.

"What happened?" Anne asked.

"Leeches and a snake!" said Beth, starting to laugh again. "We all ran when we saw the snake. We all looked ridiculous, not just Vita."

"Where's Joey?" Millie asked.

"He's rinsing his shoes off with the hose. What a disaster! But we couldn't help from laughing. She kept sinking! And after she saw the leech—she went screaming! And David kept taking pictures! She was furious!"

"Well, stop laughing now," said Millie." She's had one bad thing after another happen to her."

"You'd be laughing too, Mom. At first it was working. They had rigged up a submerged plank she could lie on. Kind of flimsy but it was working. We had flowers floating next to her and in her hands, her hair was fanned out."

Beth heard Joey come in and turned to him. "Did you guys get any photos before she sank?"

"I think David got a few," said Joey. "It all happened so fast, I'm not really sure."

"Oh no," said Anne. "Poor Vita. She was filthy."

"I was in that water too. Look! I lost a shoe!" Beth began laughing again. "I was fanning her hair out and I saw a slithering black snake and screamed and tried to get out of the water, but my feet got stuck in the mud. Then Darlene saw a leech on Vita's arm and screamed 'leeches!' And Vita forgot all about being Ophelia. You never saw her scramble so quickly. Becca and Rob had been wading nearby, holding the diffuser umbrella, and in their rush to get out of the water, they kept slipping on the bank and falling. And then Dylan!" Beth's laughter grew until she was holding her side.

"I tried to help," said Joey. "I put the camera down and grabbed Vita's hand and pulled—"

"And then they both fell in! By then we were almost wetting our pants we were all laughing so hard."

"Except Vita," Joey pointed out. "We thought she was going to their back yard to rinse off, but she just kept walking. She was a mess!"

"We hollered after her to wait. We hosed off most of the mud on us and got on our bikes to catch up with her." Beth had finally stopped laughing. "The worst of it? Guess who drove by and saw her like that?"

"Oh no," said Anne. "Not Easton!"

"And his friends. He was driving around with them, and they all started to laugh. Then I felt bad for her. He's such a jerk."

"He didn't even try to help," said Joey.

Millie was listening with her hand on her hip.

Beth spoke defensively. "Vita was laughing too, Mom, until she saw that leech, and then—" Beth lost it and mimed Vita's actions, causing everyone to laugh.

Millie shook her head. "The things you girls get into. Anne, help me set the table. Is she still going out with Easton?"

"He thinks so," said Beth. "He hollered after her—'I'll pick you up at 6:30!'"

Joey didn't tell them what Easton said to him after Beth rode off. "Still hanging around girls? You a sissy?" Joey was humiliated in front of all those older boys.

"Anne, bring these things to the table. Beth, stop laughing. And go take a shower!"

Beth sniffed at herself and made a face. "Oh Joey, we stink!"

"I'll shower in the basement," said Joey.

When Sal came home for dinner, Millie filled him in on a brief version of what happened. He simply shook his head. He and Millie and Anne began to eat. There was a lingering coolness between Anne and Sal.

Joey and Beth soon joined them, and Vita finally came out and began to eat in silence. Once or twice, Beth started to laugh and bit her lip.

"Oh, go ahead and laugh," said Vita. "I know it was funny. I don't know why I was so afraid of that leech. I was afraid they would get all over me." She shuddered at the memory.

Beth let out a pent-up laugh. "It was the snake that sent me scrambling. Even David started to run when it slithered over his shoe. Did you see him? Darlene was laughing her head off."

The phone rang and Anne jumped up to get it. She covered the mouthpiece. "Vita."

Vita levelled her eyes at Anne and mouthed the word *No!*

Anne waited a moment. "She says she can't go out tonight. Okay. I'll tell her."

Millie kept a worried eye on Sal and Vita throughout the meal. She dished out a little more pasta onto Joey and Beth's plates. "Eat up, kids. How about more penne, Sal?"

"No. Just right. A good meal." He pushed his chair back. "I'll be out in the garden."

Anne glanced at Vita. "Not going out tonight?"

"Not with him."

Millie let out a sigh and began to bring the dishes to the sink. She looked out the window and watched Sal. He had positioned the hose by the tomatoes and was pulling a few weeds.

Joey brought his dishes to the sink. "Can I go help him?"

Millie nodded and smiled. "He'd like that."

Joey walked out to the garden and stood next to Sal.

"Hey, Joey."

"I can water, if you like."

Sal picked up the hose and handed it to him. "The beans and cucumbers."

Joey swatted at a few mosquitoes on his legs and held the hose high. The sunlight slanted through the water, making a prism.

Sal looked up and smiled. He turned a tomato in his hand, checking its ripeness. "Sometimes this is the only place I can find that makes sense."

He was quiet for a few moments, lost in thought. "My old man used to say we all need something that offsets the woe of the world. That's how he put it—the woe of the world." Sal plucked a red tomato and eyed its perfection. "Work is good—but there has to be something else, that brings pleasure, and connects us. For him, it was gardening."

Sal bent over to pick a few cucumbers. "And for me. It runs deep with me. Something I can get my hands into."

Joey nodded and moved the hose over to the beans. He reached his hand through the rainbow mist.

"Nowadays, with the war and the things the girls want to do, it's hard to know what's right. I'm beginning to feel like old Abel—at odds with the present. More connected to the past."

"Dad feels the same. I asked him what he thought about the Vietnam War. He said, 'the world is too much for me. Got my hopes in you now.' I don't know what he meant. But I hope I don't let him down."

Sal ruffled Joey's hair. "You could never do that. I'm sure you're what keeps him rooted. The girls—though I don't always understand them—make us happy." A weary look crossed his face. "I shouldn't have argued with them. Got a temper sometimes. Let's go see if they're all up for some ice cream. I think Millie bought some pistachio for me."

"And I saw some chocolate."

They walked up to the patio, turned off the water, and went into the kitchen. Vita and Anne had brought a few photo albums to the table. They looked at Sal, trying to judge his mood.

"Joey and I were just saying we could do with a bowl of ice cream." Sal winked at Joey.

"Good idea," said Beth. "I'll get the bowls."

Millie smiled at Sal and took out the ice cream.

Anne was dressed to go out. She wore a long light blue skirt and matching midriff. "We wanted to show Joey old pictures from his visits here. Oh, look! Do you remember this, Joey?"

They gathered round and laughed at the images. Millie dished out the ice cream and Beth and Vita passed the bowls around.

Anne rested her hand on Sal's shoulder. "We were all so little. Look at you, Dad. Carrying Joey on your back. You were only four or so, Joey."

When Mark drove up, Sal looked at Anne. "Go ask him if he'd like some ice cream before you go out."

Anne kissed his cheek and ran out to get Mark. He was soon seated at the table with a bowl of pistachio ice cream before him. Millie stood next to Sal, flipping through the albums and making comments.

After Anne and Mark left, Vita followed Beth and Joey outside. She sat on the front steps and watched them climb the box elder. She frowned when Easton drove up and got out of his car.

"Hey gorgeous! Got all the mud off?"

"No thanks to you."

Easton sat next to her. "I would have helped you with that in a heartbeat." He nuzzled her neck.

"After you finished laughing?"

"I couldn't help it. You were a sight. But look at you now." He stroked her hair and lifted her chin. "My beauty."

"Flatterer." Vita hated that his words made her feel better.

"So no movie tonight, huh?"

She shrugged. "I'm not up to it."

"I guess I can understand that. Though I don't like being turned down. So how about tomorrow?" He leaned into her. "Dinner and a movie?"

She looked at him and weighed what to do. She felt like she wasn't thinking clearly, that everything was as muddy as the creek had been.

He gave another nudge.

"All right." She would give it one more chance.

"Unless you'd rather see a play?" he teased. He pulled out two tickets from his shirt pocket and handed them to her. "I was going to surprise you."

She read them and gasped. "Chekhov! For tomorrow?"

"At the playhouse in Foreston. I know a nice little Italian restaurant. They know me there. Then we'll see *The Seagull*, whatever that's about. And you'll forget all about being Juliet or whoever you were supposed to be today."

Vita had to laugh.

"I knew I could make you smile. Brad and Dean said it was all over, but I told them no way. *I* know what to do." He thumped his chest with his thumb.

Vita almost changed her mind. He always ruined it. No matter what, it always ended up being about him. And she kept falling for it.

He left and called back to her. "I'll pick you up at 5:30. Wear something nice!"

It sounded like an order. Much as she tried to like him, he kept getting in the way. She waved goodbye and went inside.

Joey and Beth dropped from the tree just as Easton walked by. They both gave him a look of disapproval.

"Spies everywhere," he muttered. He hopped into his convertible and put on his sunglasses. After checking his reflection in the mirror, he turned on the radio, and sped off.

Beth made a gesture as if she might gag.

CHAPTER 20

Millie and Anne were tackling the large pile of zucchinis from the garden and turning some of them into zucchini bread. Millie smiled to see Vita in a more hopeful frame of mind. Over breakfast she had talked of nothing but seeing the play that evening.

"I've never seen a Chekhov play before. Don't you think it was thoughtful of Easton?"

Anne gave a side glance to Vita and selected several more zucchinis to wash and grate.

"He's angling for something, that's for sure," said Beth.

"Don't be so negative. He's doing it because he knows it matters to me." Vita kept telling herself that although Easton wasn't perfect, at least he took her acting plans seriously. With so much going wrong lately, she was, reluctantly, grateful to him.

Beth let out a snort of disbelief. "Face it, he's a creep. You saw how he laughed at you."

"Beth!" chided Millie. "Don't put a damper on her plans. Now, the first batch of these will be ready soon. How about you girls take a couple of loaves to Mrs. Higgins? I think she misses you, Vita. She always asks about you at the library. She says her visits to the plant shop are not the same."

"Let's go, Vi," said Beth.

"I've been wanting to visit her. Joey, since we're not working with Abel today, how about you come with us? She'd love to show you her garden."

"Sure. I told her I'd come by to see it."

"I hate to miss out on her beautiful garden," said Anne, "but I have to run a few errands before my lunch shift. Tell her hello from me."

Millie eyed the pile of zucchinis that Sal had picked before going to work. "I always tell Sal not to plant so much."

"Especially since he's the only one who likes them," added Beth. "There's only so much you can make with zucchinis."

"Joey, why don't you put together a bag of garden vegetables for Mrs. Higgins. She'll like that."

An hour later, Vita, Beth, and Joey rode their bikes to the other side of town.

Joey brought his camera and two rolls of film. After the encounter with Rufus, he was eager to take more pictures of people. He had taken a few of Abel and some of Millie but he hadn't developed the film yet. He hoped Mrs. Higgins would allow him to photograph her. She had a special quality about her that he wanted to try to capture. And she looked different from other people, as if she was from an older time. Would all those things come through on film?

"I love this area of town," said Vita. "You might get some good pictures here, Joey."

He noticed that the homes were older, all with front porches. Tall trees and brick sidewalks lined the street and all the yards had flowers. "Can we walk? Maybe I'll take a few shots."

They hopped off their bikes and Joey snapped his camera. Many of the yards were crowded with purple and blue hydrangea bushes, bright pink roses, and flower beds of all colors.

"And here's Mrs. Higgins's house," said Beth. "With the blue door." She left her bike near the porch, ran up the steps, and began knocking.

Joey and Vita followed her with the bags of vegetables and zucchini bread.

Beth knocked again. "I hope she's home."

The screen door opened. "Hello! I thought I heard someone knocking. I was out in the garden and just came in to make my morning tea. Can you join me?"

"We'd love to," said Vita. "We wanted Joey to see your garden."

Joey noticed that she was once again dressed in a long floral dress reaching her calves and wore the black-tie shoes. He opened the paper bag to show her the vegetables. "We picked these for you."

Mrs. Higgins's eyes widened. "Just look at those beautiful vegetables! Still warm from the sun. Ah, zucchini. Such a versatile vegetable."

Beth's eyebrows shot up. "There's plenty more if you want. And Mom just baked zucchini bread. It's still warm, too."

Mrs. Higgins clapped her hands together. "How delightful. Tea in the garden. I do so want Joey to see it. Come in, come in."

"Wow," said Joey, looking at the fern on her front porch. "I didn't know they could get so big."

"That's one of my oldest plants," Mrs. Higgins said, lightly touching it. "It's been with me a long time." She showed them inside.

Joey didn't know where to look. The room was full of blooming flowers and green plants, and chairs and sofas with lace and doilies. It looked like a storybook cottage that a nice old granny would live in. Cozy. That was the word.

He noticed an old, framed photograph of a young man in uniform next to a potted plant and bent over to take a closer look at him.

"Ah, that's my double African violet. Isn't it exquisite?"

Beth stood next to Joey and whispered, "Her husband." She admired the plant's deep purple blooms. "Gosh, it's beautiful. We have a pale purple one in our family room, but it hasn't gotten any bigger since we bought it. You have a real green thumb."

"African violets can be temperamental. It can take them years to settle in." She smiled to see that Joey had moved to the back door, trying to see the garden. "Joey, why don't you explore the garden while Victoria and Beth and I prepare the tea. Make sure you see the birdbath next to the redbud trees. A pity you missed them in bloom."

"Would it be all right if I took a few pictures?"

"I'd be delighted. You'll find some treasures out there," she said, with a twinkle in her eyes. "Rocks, shells, a few small statues."

Joey opened the screen door and stepped into the garden. He had never seen such a private garden. It was hugged in by brick walls on two sides and a dense row of hedges in the back. A few tall trees kept much of it in shade, but the front area, where a small table was set up, was bathed in late morning sunlight.

He wandered around the paved paths, taking pictures. He noticed several areas thick with flowers and small benches next to them. Several rocks rested among the plants, and smaller stones ringed some of the flowers.

A statue of a little boy reading sat among a bunch of tall pink and blue flowers. When Joey looked closer, he found other figures tucked among the leaves and flowers—rabbits and birds, small cottages, a few fairies.

He had to stop and admire the birdbath in the back of the garden. It was surrounded by a cloud of dark blue flowers and three birdhouses of the same color hung from the tree above it. He framed the image and took several pictures.

A few metal chairs painted in sunny colors sat under the trees. Joey imagined Mrs. Higgins sitting in them, enjoying different views of her garden.

He sat in a bright-orange one to see how it felt. There were yellow and orange flowers planted near it. Begonias, he thought they were called. They matched the chair. He knew she had done that on purpose. Lingering notes from wind chimes softly filled the air, and birdsong came from all the trees. Two birds flitted onto the rim of the birdbath and began to splash. He raised his camera and tried to capture them in action. He smiled out at the garden. It felt good just to be sitting there.

He followed the winding walk back to the front and focused the camera on the potting table where it looked like she had been working. Green-handled tools and an old pair of gardening gloves lay next to containers of red and pink flowers. The trellis along one brick wall was covered with climbing pale-purple flowers. The other side had bright-pink flowers. Wherever he looked, he found something interesting.

He heard a clink and saw that Vita was setting the small table with teacups and plates. Beth held the door open for Mrs. Higgins who carried a round blue teapot. He went to join them.

"It's like being in a fairytale," Joey said, as they sat down.

"A fairytale! I'm so glad you think so." Mrs. Higgins began to pour the tea. "Victoria, I was so sorry to hear that you had left the plant shop. I hope it had nothing to do with me. Sometimes I'm so forgetful." She looked up at Beth and Joey. "There I was at the dime store, ready to purchase some twine. I began searching my purse, quite in a panic, when Victoria came into the store with my wallet. I was so relieved." She made sure they all had a slice of zucchini bread.

"I was happy I found you," said Vita. "Business was slow at the shop. It should pick up in the fall." Vita told her how she and Joey were temporarily working with Abel out at the cemeteries and how they enjoyed it.

Joey took a sip of the hot tea and his mouth puckered. Beth shoved the sugar bowl to him and spooned in two heaping teaspoons. He took another sip. Much better.

"Is that a new flower box?" Vita asked.

"My nephew Owen made that for me. Raised, so I don't have to bend over as much. Wasn't that thoughtful of him?"

Mrs. Higgins took a bite of the bread and placed her hand on her heart. "My, but that's delicious."

"Just look at those flowers!" Vita delighted in the profusion of bright blooms. Multi-colored Sweet Williams in the front. Begonias and zinnias of all colors, tall clusters of larkspur and lythrum growing in the back.

"I just love it here," said Beth, leaning back in her chair. "It always smells so good. Like flowers and damp earth and sunshine. Someday I want a private little garden like this."

"So do I," said Vita.

Mrs. Higgins asked after Millie and Anne. "And the rest of you. How are you all filling your summer?" She listened with interest, and exclaimed over Joey's learning about photography, the photoshoots, and all their stories about the fair, their jobs, and their plans.

"You young people live such fascinating lives. Climbing trees and painting stage sets and swimming at night. Studying Shakespeare and learning photography. And all of you with jobs. I do love hearing about it all." Mrs. Higgins finished her tea and smiled over at Joey.

"When I saw this young man at the train station, I knew our paths were going to cross. And here we are, having tea in my garden. It just goes to show you."

"I'm glad I got to see it. My mom would love it here." Joey glanced around the garden and back at Mrs. Higgins. "Can I take a picture of you in your garden?"

"Me?" Mrs. Higgins pressed her hand to her chest.

"Joey's been taking pictures of the town and some of its people," said Beth. "He has pictures of us and Abel. You would make a nice addition."

"Well, I don't know about that, but you're certainly welcome. Shall I wear my sun bonnet?" She reached for the straw hat hanging from her chair.

Vita and Beth suggested a few pretty settings, with Mrs. Higgins perched on one of the little benches, another of her tapping the wind chimes. She moved about the plants, gently talking to some of them, cupping a lily to inhale its fragrance, and caressing a bunch of pale-pink carnations. All the while Joey clicked his camera.

"These carnations." She sniffed the air, tilted her head. "I always think they smell like cinnamon. A delicate, rather exotic scent. Don't you think?" He hoped he captured that searching expression.

Joey knew he had some good shots. He got a few of her talking to Vita and Beth as well. The town was rich with characters and interesting settings. When he took pictures, he felt like he was uncovering a story. He wondered if every place was like that.

"Let me take a few of you with Mrs. Higgins, Joey." Vita focused the camera. "Ready?"

While Mrs. Higgins made sure Joey saw the purple clematis, Vita and Beth brought the dishes in and washed them.

"Oh, you girls, you're my guests. You shouldn't be doing the dishes."

"We wanted to," said Beth. She and Vita gave Mrs. Higgins a hug goodbye.

"I'm so happy you stopped by. Oh! Before you go. I must show you . . ." She walked over to the little cottage planter on a deep window ledge in her living room. "Victoria was kind enough to arrange this little planter for me and it has positively thrived in this spot. It seems to prefer the morning sun."

Joey took a last look around her home and once again felt like he was inside a storybook cottage. He thanked her for the tea and for showing him her garden, and for allowing him to take pictures.

"The pleasure's all mine, Joey."

Mrs. Higgins walked out with them to the porch. "Be sure to tell your mother hello from me and thank her for the delicious zucchini bread and the vegetables. I go to the library on Wednesdays when I know she'll be there. She always suggests the perfect books for me." She patted Joey's arm. "She knows I like a good mystery." She stood near her fern and waved goodbye to them all.

"We'll stop by again," Vita called back to her. "Soon!"

Joey glanced back at the little house with the blue door.

"Wasn't that a cool garden?" Beth asked. "Lucky for us we have the flower garden at home. Dad made it after we described Mrs. Higgins's hidden garden. We asked him if we could have one."

"We were all surprised when he made it," said Vita. "He even added the brick sidewalk around it. Mom's favorite place to read is under the ash tree, facing the garden."

On their way home, they passed a yard sale and stopped to browse. Beth found a box of old games and checked out a bag of marbles, while Vita looked at a few dishes.

Joey's eye was caught by some pink items. Remembering that Abby liked the color, he took a few pictures. A music box with a ballerina inside, and a pink-and-white vase with flowers on it.

They opened boxes, lifted items of clothing, and sorted through old jewelry and pieces of lace.

Vita saw Joey rummaging through a box of old wooden frames, carefully looking at some of them. "See something interesting?"

He held up a frame with painted vines running around it. "If the photos of the garden turn out good, I could put one of them in here and give it to Mrs. Higgins."

"She would love that, Joey."

He had wanted to make gifts of his photographs to Millie and Sal and the girls. Now he began to think how much nicer they would look framed. He reached in his pocket to count his money. "I'll go ask how much these are." The more he thought about it, the more he wanted the frames.

Beth walked over with the bag of marbles. "I just bought this whole bag for fifty cents. Look at these." She spilled a few marbles into her palm and held a large blue one up to the sun.

Joey walked back, smiling. "Four dollars for the whole box. I didn't want them all, but he said he was selling the box as one item."

Vita lifted out a few frames. Some were loose or broken. "You should ask Hogie to help. He can repair anything."

❧

After lunch, Joey took the box of frames to show Hogie.

"I can help you with these. Some of them are in pretty good shape. I'd say these two are Victorian. This one is later, 1920s—that'll clean up good."

"How do you know that stuff?"

"Laura. She was always on the lookout for antiques. Got a few minutes? How about you come to the hardware store with me. I could use an extra hand."

"Sure."

This was Joey's second trip to the hardware store with Hogie. The first time they went for supplies, today they delivered two benches, two small garden stools, and several birdhouses.

The owner said one customer asked if Hogie could make a custom worktable, and another person wanted some bookshelves. He gave Hogie their phone numbers.

As with the first time, Joey was fascinated by Hogie's truck. It was converted for him to drive without having to use his legs. And the back had a tailgate that went up and down and made it easy to unload the furniture and fill it with lumber.

Joey was growing more comfortable with Hogie as the weeks went by. The first time he ever saw Hogie drive was when he went out shooting with Al, just outside of town. Joey had asked to go along, and Hogie agreed. He wanted to shoot but Hogie wouldn't let him.

"Don't think your parents would appreciate it."

Joey didn't really care. It was just fun being outside with Hogie and Al. They never treated him like a kid.

While Al was setting up the targets, Hogie casually turned to Joey. "Why don't you go take a hike."

Joey's mouth dropped open and he wondered what he had done wrong. He figured he was in the way and began walking back towards town.

"Joey! Where the hell you goin'?" Hogie called after him.

Joey came back. "You told me to take a hike."

Hogie let out a deep laugh. "Don't be so literal. I just meant for you to turn away. I had to take a pee."

Joey's face remained blank.

"Empty my bag. Thought you might be squeamish."

Joey tilted his head, and then understood. "Oh."

Since then, they had been out a few times, delivering items. Twice Hogie took him out into the country so that Joey could take photographs. Hogie always brought cold sodas to drink as they drove around. Sometimes he would pull over, empty his bag, and continue on. Joey got used to it and it became normal. Just the way Hogie was. Sometimes it was Joey who had to stop and take a leak, sometimes Hogie.

Hogie knew where all the interesting spots were, things that would be good to photograph. A covered bridge out on a lone country road, an old farmhouse that looked ready to cave in, the remnants of a small town that was now deserted—it still had two old gas pumps next to a rundown station.

Once, out at the lake, Hogie parked on a grassy point. He gazed over at a dock across the lake.

"Right there was where I proposed to Laura. Six months before I left for basic training. She packed a picnic and we parked right here and rowed across the lake. There was a little clearing in the woods we had been to before. Our spot. We'd swim in the lake, then lie naked with the sun warm on our bodies.

"That day we spread a blanket and when she unpacked the picnic basket, she found a little ring box I had tucked inside. She froze for a second and then jumped on me and said YES. Before she even opened the box." He laughed at the memory. "I think it could have been empty and she still would have said yes."

Joey waited for him to continue.

But Hogie just kept staring across the lake. On the way back home, they were mostly silent.

Joey bit his lip in indecision. "Hogie, I hope you don't get mad at me for something I did."

Hogie looked at him in surprise. "Don't think that would be possible. What'd you do? Kidnap my cat? Sneak a beer?"

Joey fidgeted in his seat. "You know I'm taking pictures of the town and all, making a collection."

Hogie nodded. "That's why I take you around."

"Well, I've been taking photographs of people, too. Millie and Sal and the girls. Rufus Sharp. Abel. Mrs. Higgins."

Hogie turned to him and waited.

"I took some of Laura."

Hogie stared back out at the road.

"Vita and I were riding bikes and we passed Laura's house. She was on the front porch, so we stopped by. It's a neat old house. I asked if I could take some pictures and she said sure. Then I asked if I could take some of her."

"That's your business," said Hogie.

"They came out pretty good. Some of them are really good, like the ones where she's playing the piano. And on the porch with her dog jumping on her." Joey watched Hogie's stony face. "Hope you're not mad."

"Like I say, that's your business. You don't have to report to me."

Now they were returned from the hardware store, had unloaded the supplies, and were working in comfortable silence.

While Hogie measured and cut pieces of wood, Joey picked up scrap pieces and put them in the empty five-gallon paint bucket and swept up wood shavings. He then made room on one of the shelves and stacked his frames.

"Shit," Hogie said, as if to himself. "He won't make it over there."

Joey turned around. "Who? Won't make what?"

Hogie lowered his eyes and made a pencil mark on a piece of wood.

Joey saw that Anne and Mark were strolling by hand in hand. They both waved. Joey waved back at them.

When Joey looked over at Hogie, he wouldn't meet his eyes.

"Fetch me a beer, will you?"

Joey took a beer from the small refrigerator and set it on the table. Hogie was eyeing a round piece of wood.

"Want me to sand that?"

Hogie handed it to him along with a fresh square of sandpaper. "For a three-legged stool. The kind Miss Muffet sat on. Special request from Mom's neighbor. Going to paint a butterfly or some crap on it." He took a long swallow of beer.

Joey folded the sandpaper into quarters as Hogie had showed him, and lightly sanded the wood, occasionally blowing or brushing off the dust.

"How's Vita doing?" Hogie asked. "I think that audition got to her more than she's letting on."

"I thought you didn't care."

"Course I care. She's the one I worry about."

"What do you mean?"

"I've known those girls since they were babies. All charmers. Anne," he pointed his head in the direction she and Mark walked in and gave a laugh. "That one, she always gets what she wants. Soft and sweet. And made of iron. A little powerhouse. Always has been.

"Beth? More unpredictable but bounces back fairly easily. Always surrounded by people who want to be her friends. Miss popularity.

"Vita? She's going to have a harder time. She doesn't quite fit in. She's going to have to go out and find her place." Hogie glanced at Joey. "I expect the same might be true for you. I think you're alike in that way. The quest, as she calls it. Both thrilling and scary."

Joey looked up and smiled. Hogie described it exactly.

"I try to teach her to be tough, but she's vulnerable. Feels everything tenfold. And expects too much of the world."

"I think Vita could do whatever she wants to do."

Hogie grinned. "I do too, Joey. That's why I keep after her. If she succeeds, then part of me does too. If she's happy, then part of me is too. Sometimes I think—"

Joey looked up. "What? What do you think?"

"Nah. Just . . . I used to think if Laura and I could have had a daughter—just saying—that she would have been like Vita. Determined, stubborn, proud—sweet and tender and vulnerable. Laura has all those qualities. She makes things happen." He took a swig of beer.

"Vita makes things happen. They don't always work out, but she keeps trying." Joey smoothed his hand over the round piece, blew on it, and lightly sanded a rough spot on the edge. He handed it to Hogie to check.

Hogie ran his hand over it, gave an approving nod, and set it in front of him. "Vita and I are alike. That's the truth of it. That's why we argue sometimes. We both know exactly where our weak spots are. And we're self-righteous enough to tell each other off from time to time," he added with a chuckle.

"Want me to sand these?" Joey took the three pieces for the stool's legs and began to rub the sandpaper over them. "She's going to a play tonight. She seems happy about it. About anything related to acting."

Hogie looked up. "Who's she going with?"

"Easton."

Hogie made a low sound of disgust. "I can't stand that kid."

"Me either."

"Full of himself. Arrogant. What the hell is Vita thinking?"

"I'm not sure she really likes him. They were arguing one time when he brought her home. It looked like he was pulling her arm."

Hogie's face darkened.

"So I came out and stared at him. He didn't like it. After she left, he called me a loser."

"I'd like to shove my fist down his scrawny throat." Hogie took a gulp of beer. "Damn, these warm up quickly in this heat." He set the bottle down.

Joey handed the legs to Hogie and went to the shelf to look over the frames. "I think I'll start with this one, for

Mrs. Higgins." When Joey lifted the frame, one side of it came loose in his hand.

"An easy fix," said Hogie. "Come back after supper if you want. We'll sort through those and see what they need."

Joey saw the time and ran home for dinner. "That'd be great. Thanks, Hogie!"

With Vita excited about seeing the play, and Anne and Sal on good terms once again, there was the feeling that things were back to normal. Millie and Sal were in high spirits, setting up for the poker night they were hosting. Anne arranged a snack platter and set it on the kitchen table, next to the black plastic carousel that held red, white, and blue poker chips. Beth unfolded extra chairs and placed them around the table. Vita had gathered a large bouquet of flowers for the kitchen counter.

Millie smiled and told Joey that the card game was just an excuse for them all to get together to talk and laugh and eat.

Millie set out a light meal for whoever wanted it, and there was the usual bustle as the girls got ready. Anne was going to the drive-in with Mark, and Beth was attending a birthday party with Abby and Becca. She invited Joey but he knew he would be the only boy there. He said he was going to help Hogie with some projects.

Joey was used to the girls' routines by now, but he still found them intriguing. They all chatted while they fixed their hair and decided on clothing and jewelry and perfume.

Joey stood in the doorway. He asked if he could take their picture, without them posing.

Anne laughed. "Of course, you can. It's like being backstage before a production, isn't it Vita?"

He clicked away and listened to the fragments of where Vita was going for dinner, the present Beth had picked out for her friend, how Mark's family still wanted Anne to join them on their vacation and how Sal had finally given in.

Once again, as he looked at them, he saw them as three beautiful witches or fairies. Completely unaware of the magic they possessed.

"Anne!" Millie's voice came from the kitchen. "Mark's here."

One by one they left. Anne-Galadriel-Day Princess dressed in flowing white and pale blue and silver. Beth-Indian Maiden-Sunshine wore a bright pink-and-orange mini dress, her shiny black hair almost reaching the hem. And Vita-Titania-Night Queen, was dressed in her gauzy purple dress with Millie's gold shawl about her shoulders, her hair in loose waves down her back. All embarking on a night adventure.

When Millie announced that Becca and Abby had arrived, Joey ran out with Beth to see if he could take their pictures. They were more than happy to accommodate him, striking poses and laughing. He had never been around so many girls before. To him, they were all like stories and he always wondered what was coming next.

Still, he was looking forward to being with Hogie for the evening. Guy stuff. Sometimes no talking or anything. There was something easy and comforting about it. Like how he felt with his dad.

And he knew Hogie felt the same. He had told Joey that talking to him was kind of like talking to his cat, Tigress. He could say anything, or nothing, and there would be no judgment or demanding questions or raised eyebrows. Just companionable silence. An unspoken agreement that they were glad the other was there.

Joey waited until evening before walking over to Hogie's. Millie and Sal wanted to introduce him to their friends as they arrived, and Millie put together a snack tray for him and Hogie: a cheese roll and crackers, garden vegetables and dip, and a sampling from Sal's famous antipasto platter.

Joey eyed the tray as he carried it down the street. He was already full from the sandwiches Millie had made, and then Sal insisted that he try everything on the platters and waited for a nod of approval after every bite. Joey hoped Hogie was hungry.

When he walked into Hogie's garage, he saw that Al and Roger—both smelling like skunkweed—had stopped by. It turned out that they were exceptionally hungry and ate every morsel from the tray and then ordered two extra-large pizzas. After drinking a couple of beers, they went into the living room to listen to music and dozed off. By the time they left, it was dark and Hogie and Joey were just getting started on the frames.

Hogie sorted them by the condition they were in, deciding which ones simply needed a fresh coat of varnish, and which ones would be fine with a few repairs. Joey already had an idea of which frame he wanted to use for which photograph.

There were two or three that were almost beyond repair. They would work on those last. Joey was setting those
on the bottom shelf when they heard voices from the street.
One of them sounded like Vita's.

He walked to the front of the garage and looked down
the street. Underneath a streetlight, he saw Easton's car
parked with the doors open on both sides. Vita was walking away from him, angry. As she neared the house, Hogie
wheeled out onto the driveway.

They saw Easton catch up with Vita and pull her around
to face him. His finger was in her face. "It's over when *I*
say it's over."

Vita yanked her arm back. "You don't own me. I keep
hoping you'll improve but the more I get to know you the
worse you are!"

Easton scrunched his face into a sneer. "You're nobody.
Just a small-town girl with stars in her eyes. And you think
you're too good for *me*?"

She turned her back on him, her face full of loathing,
and continued to walk away from him.

He followed her, raising his voice. "Everyone knows
why you want to be an actress. Because you're *nothing*. So
you pretend you're other people. You're the pathetic one!"

Joey and Hogie had moved to the end of the driveway.
Vita groaned when she saw them. Just then Easton grabbed
her bare arm and twisted her around. "You don't walk away
from me when I'm talking!"

"Hey!" Hogie wheeled up to them. "Get your hands off
her, you worthless piece of shit."

Joey ran up to them. "Leave her alone."

"If it isn't the little sissy. Always spying because he has nothing better to do."

Joey could smell the alcohol on his breath.

"Don't get involved," Vita said. "We were just saying goodnight."

"That's not what it sounded like." Hogie wheeled closer.

They saw that Rufus Sharp was walking along the street, lost in his own world. He stopped on seeing Vita and held the rag in his hand.

Easton let out a buffoonish laugh and looked from Rufus to Hogie to Joey. "What is this? The Vita Vitale fan club? A freak, a cripple, and a loser kid!"

Joey had only been in a few scuffles, but the taunting words unleashed a fury inside him. Without thinking he lurched at Easton, taking him by surprise and landing him half onto Hogie's lap.

In a flash, Hogie's muscular arm twisted Easton's scrawny one behind his back. He leaned over Easton and spoke in his ear. "Don't you *ever* come near her again. You understand?"

Easton squirmed and yelled, "You crazy damned vet!"

"That's right." Hogie spoke calmly. "I might snap. Think I'm back in 'Nam." He tightened his grip and Easton let out a howl. "Might accidentally twist your fuckin' head off."

"Hogie, stop it!" Vita's eyes flashed with anger.

Hogie ignored her. "You tell us all, nice and clear, that you're not going to come near her."

"All right! I won't come near her."

Hogie released his grip and Easton fell to the ground. He rubbed his arm and took a step back. "Because she's not worth it!" He faced Vita and spit on the ground. When he was at a safe distance, he pointed to Hogie. "You're crazy."

"You come around her again and I'll show you crazy."

Easton stumbled off, rubbing his shoulder.

Vita watched him leave. When Easton got to his car, he peeled out, making a loud screech. Vita closed her eyes in disgust.

Rufus stuffed the rag back in his mouth, gave a final look at Joey, then at Vita, and staggered off. Joey felt like Rufus was the sanest of them all at that moment.

Vita whipped around to Hogie. "I don't need you to protect me!" She faced Joey, her eyes ablaze. "Or you. I can fight my own battles!"

"Didn't look that way," said Hogie. "You going out into the big bad world you need to be a better judge of people. If anyone brings you down, in any way, you walk away from them."

"Well, that would include you!" Vita jabbed her finger in the air at Hogie. "You talk big, but your best friend is the bottle. Exactly like him!" she said, pointing to where Easton had been. "And the way you treat Laura? You hurt her more than that asshole could ever hurt me! But you can't see that, can you? The high and mighty Hogie!"

She clutched her shawl in one hand and walked away.

"Get her home, Joey."

She spun around and yelled at Joey. "Stop following me!"

Joey stopped in his tracks. He looked at Hogie, unsure what to do. Hogie motioned for him to go ahead.

Joey followed her at a distance.

"Just leave me alone!" She threw her arms down at her side.

Joey slowed his pace. Couldn't she see that they were on her side? He couldn't let anyone hurt her. Why had she yelled at him?

Vita went into the house by the front door, avoiding the merry crowd around the kitchen table.

Beth had arrived home shortly before and saw that something was amiss. When Vita told her to mind her own business and locked herself in the bathroom, Beth went to Joey, out on the front steps.

He gave a quick recap of what happened but left out the part about Vita yelling at him.

"Good! Maybe now she knows what a complete loser he is."

Joey let Beth go on about the birthday party and the food and some of the games they had played. He laughed and pretended to enjoy it but inside he felt miserable.

CHAPTER 21

Anne drove Vita around town so that she could apply to a few more places. Rusty Cooper had returned early, reducing Abel's workload. He still needed Joey a few days a week, and he told Vita he could use her help, but she knew he was just being kind. She was back to job hunting.

Anne parked outside the small cluster of stores down from the square. Vita was in and out of the first three stores in a matter of minutes, but the drug store was taking longer. Vita finally came out.

"They can use me three days a week for a month, maybe two. Brenda Jenson went into labor early, so she'll be out for a while."

"I heard she had twins." Anne glanced at Vita as she pulled away. "You're not happy about it?"

Vita remained silent.

"You don't want to work there?"

"It's all so quiet and neat and orderly. And there's a smell—like pills and antiseptics."

Anne gave a laugh. "You can keep looking. School starts in a month, anyway. There will be jobs opening up, with people going back to college."

Anne drove around town for a bit, down the streets with the pretty houses that she knew Vita loved. "Let's drive out to the college before going home."

They were soon parked and strolling around the campus.

"I always feel better out here," said Vita.

"That's why we came. You seem kind of lost, Vi. You need to focus on what you want. Forget about everything else."

"I keep trying. I had everything so carefully planned. Except for Joey being here, the summer has been a disaster."

"No, it hasn't. You're just letting boyfriend stuff get you down."

They crossed the little wooden bridge and sat at the top of the steps that led to the art department. Vita looked around and gave a sigh.

"I wanted to get into the fall workshop more than anything. Even more than getting the role of Titania."

"You'll get in next year. And in the meantime, you can study on your own. And see plays."

"Only if you and Beth or Mom comes with me. Hogie was right about being more careful with who I spend my time with. Maybe I'm not a good judge of character. I've messed up twice, after all. Vic and now Easton."

"It's hard to know what people are like until you really get to know them. Don't be so hard on yourself." Anne leaned back to gaze out over the campus. "It is pretty out here."

Vita looked at the old brick buildings with their arched windows, and the shade trees over the network of sidewalks with benches scattered about.

"This is the one place in town that gives me a glimpse of the outside world. Can you imagine living in a big city with beautiful old architecture and museums and so much to do? I could take classes and see a different play every week, if I could afford it. Study in coffee houses, meet friends in cafes. I would just love it. I would love to be a part of all that."

"It'll happen. You just have to be patient." Anne rested her hands on her lap. "Do you want to talk about what happened with the play, and get it out of your system? Did Easton get drunk?"

Vita stared out at the shadows on the grass.

"It was all going wonderfully, in the beginning. We had a nice dinner and talked about different things. It always starts out like that. Then he ruins it. He always brings a flask. I think he's afraid of being sober. He sipped on it through dinner, and again once we got to our seats at the theater. They were good seats, and I was so looking forward to seeing *The Seagull*. It's about actresses and writers."

Vita drew her knees up and linked her arms around them. "The play had barely begun, and I was so excited. I was leaning forward, taking it all in—the stage set, the lighting, the costumes. But Easton kept talking. People were telling him to be quiet. I was so embarrassed. Then just a few rows ahead of us to the right, guess who was there?"

Anne shrugged. "The Radcliffs?"

"Vic and Priscilla."

"Are you kidding!"

"He had his arm around her. I was hoping so badly Easton wouldn't notice them. No such luck." Vita imitated Easton's manner. "Well, well, well. Vic got over you pretty quickly."

"What a jerk!" said Anne.

"I told him to be quiet. He kept at it, and I told him to shut up. That just made it worse. He spoke in an even louder voice: 'Course Priscilla *is* really hot. I might have a go at her myself.'"

Anne gave a huff of indignation. "What a creep."

"They must have heard him. They both looked around. And then an usher came and told us to be quiet. Easton started to argue with him, saying he paid good money for the seats." Vita buried her face in her hands. "I was so ashamed. I got up and left. I didn't know where I was going or how I was going to get home. I thought I could find a phone booth and call you to come get me."

"Mark and I would have come. But we were out at the drive-in."

"I knew you wouldn't be home. And I couldn't call Mom and Dad. He came out to the lobby, and I told him I wanted to go home. 'Good!' he said. 'What a stupid, boring play.' All the way home, he honked at cars and drove too fast. And complained about me, the play, and what a waste of time it was."

"Oh, Vita. What a disaster."

"It gets worse. When I didn't want to go up to the square, we started arguing. I told him I didn't want to see him again. That set him off. He pulled over and said no one walks out on him. I got out and started walking home.

"As luck would have it, Hogie and Joey were outside Hogie's garage—I think they heard everything. And poor Rufus Sharp walked by. He looked at us and I think he was worried for me. Easton called him a freak. He called all of us names. I was never so ashamed in my life."

Anne put her arm around Vita's shoulder. "It's always worse when someone else sees. That explains why Joey seemed different this morning."

"Then Hogie and Joey got involved. And I snapped at them. I know I shouldn't have, but I was just so humiliated and hated that they saw me at my worst. Then I yelled at Beth when I got home."

"So, you yelled at all the people who are on your side."

"Poor Joey. I hope I didn't hurt his feelings." She stood. "We should go. Mom will have lunch ready. I know she's worried about me. I'll act like I'm happy about the job. I can keep looking."

They walked back to Anne's car and drove out of the college. When they approached the square, Vita sat up and put her hand on the dashboard. "Anne, pull over. Quick."

"Why? What—" As she pulled to the side, she saw Easton sitting in his car up ahead, talking and laughing with two girls. By their giggles and body language, they were clearly enjoying his attentions.

"I don't want him to see me."

"Ugh. He doesn't even look cute anymore."

Vita gave a breathy sound of disgust as she watched him. "*Methought I was enamour'd of an ass. How mine eyes do loathe his visage now.*"

Anne turned onto a side street. "Well said, Titania."

333

❧

Joey brought his envelope of photographs to show Hogie along with the ones he had framed. One of the finds in the box was a three-part standing frame which gave Joey an idea. He fitted in some photos that he had taken of Millie and Sal. On the right was a picture of Sal by his vegetable garden, and on the left a photo of Millie reading by the flower garden. In the center he put the best one of them together. Sal was seated on a chair under the oak tree, and he had impulsively pulled Millie onto his lap. They were both laughing.

There were several pictures of Abel: sitting on the porch swing playing his harmonica, one where he was pointing to Fran's roses. He was smiling in that photo. Another one of him out at the cemetery.

"These are good, Joey."

There were a few of him and Abel standing together by the wheelbarrow, one of them loading the tools into the truck, and another of them with their arms around each other, smiling.

"Vita took those."

Hogie studied the picture Vita took of him standing by the gravestone of the baby girl. "You look kind of sad in this one."

Hogie lifted the photo of Mark and Anne reading Tolkien. They had raised their heads at the same time, with a faraway look still in their eyes. Anne, as beautiful as Galadriel.

There were several of the three sisters—individual ones as well as all of them together—getting ready for a night out, some with their friends, a bunch of Abby and Beth, and several of the photography club as they worked on various shoots. The photos of Mrs. Higgins and her garden had turned out well. Joey's favorite was of her tapping the wind chimes.

Hogie raised his eyes to Joey, as if seeing him anew.

"These last two are my best," said Joey. One was of Rufus Sharp, looking directly into the camera with a question in his eye. The other was of Vita as Titania.

"I'm still working on Vita's. But I'm not sure if I'll give it to her. I think she's still mad at me."

"She's angry at herself, Joey. I know her. She's had a bad run and is blaming herself. Has nothing to do with you."

"I hope not." Joey studied the photograph of Vita. "I want to find just the right background. Kind of like what I did with this."

He handed Hogie the final picture. It was a full-figure photo of Rufus in profile, layered over a photograph of a bombed-out battlefield with muddy ditches and barbed wire. Rufus, staggering alone in his own war.

"How'd you do this?"

"I found some of Uncle Sal's old *Yank* magazines. That's what gave me the idea. And what you said about Rufus being in his own battlefield.

Hogie was silent, studying the image. Joey waited for him to say something.

"W-What do you think? Do you like any of them?"

Hogie sifted through the photographs again. "You're a real artist, Joey."

"An artist! I think of myself as an explorer. Discovering things."

"Maybe it's one and the same." Hogie handed the photographs back to Joey and looked up at him. "Maybe I'll let you take my photograph after all."

"Really?" Joey's face blossomed into happiness.

"Yeah. Something for Mom to remember me by. Maybe you could add some old photographs of me as a kid for the background. And some blue sky and puffy white clouds, something happy."

"Sure! That's a great idea."

"Think you could add in the scent of freshly mowed grass?"

Joey grinned. "I can sure try." He could hardly wait to see what the camera would bring out in Hogie.

Vita was in a deep sleep, dreaming that Easton and Vic were directing her in a play, but they kept giving her the wrong lines. *Vita! Vita!* She slowly became aware that Anne was whispering her name and gently shaking her.

"Vita, wake up!"

"What?" Vita pushed herself up and looked around at the dark room and at Beth's empty bed. "Where's Beth?"

"She's spending the night with Abby, remember? Get dressed. Hurry."

Vita threw off the blanket. "Why?" She could tell by Anne's tone that it was adventure calling, not trouble. A glance at the clock told her that it was only 11:00 pm. She must have fallen right to sleep.

Anne went to the open window between their beds and whispered through the screen. "Give us five minutes!"

"Where are we going?" Vita asked, pulling on her jeans.

"There's a meteor shower! Mark said there's a bunch of people at the Lone Tower already. Falling stars! Hurry." Anne already had one leg out the window.

Vita grabbed her arm. "Let me get Joey."

"Well, be quiet. If Dad finds out he won't let me go on vacation with Mark. But I can't miss this."

Vita went into Joey's room, roused him, and told him about the falling stars. He dressed quickly and met Vita in her room. They climbed out the window and followed Anne, cutting across the neighbor's yard to the street. Mark had his car parked around the block.

Anne ran into his arms.

"You have to see this," he said. "It's amazing! David said it will last several hours."

"David's there?" Joey's heart was racing at the unexpected adventure. He had never done anything like this before. He felt bold and daring and wished he had his Pentax. But he couldn't go back, and he was sure that David would bring his camera.

They drove to the Lone Tower and parked behind a few other cars. Vita recognized David's car and they soon found him and Darlene with several others from the photography club, setting up their tripods. Joey was thrilled.

A few girls were swinging, leaning back to see the sky. Their laughter and voices mixed with the rhythmic creaking of the swings. Several groups of people were gathered on blankets, exclaiming at the stars. It was like the Fourth of July.

"Did you see that?"

"Look! There's another one!"

"Oh my gosh!"

"Where? Where?"

"Let's find a good spot," Mark said. There were a few streetlights at the edge of the park, but further inside was dark. They moved away from the others and found a place not too far from the water tower. Vita helped Anne to spread a blanket near a patch of wildflowers.

The warm summer night held the faint scents of grass and flowers. Vita inhaled deeply and filled her eyes with the inky sky aglitter with stars.

"What do you think, Joey?" Anne asked.

A look of wonder filled his face as he scanned the sky. "Wow! I think I saw one!"

"Me too!" cried Vita. "It's the night realm, Joey. Magical and beautiful."

He turned to Vita, happy that she wasn't still mad at him. "Thanks for bringing me."

"I didn't want you to miss it. Too bad Beth isn't here to see it."

Vita was just about to sit down when she heard, "Hey, guys!" Beth flopped down on the blanket.

Anne raised her eyebrows to Vita. "When will we ever learn?"

"I knew you would be here. Isn't this fantastic? Wondrous even?" Beth said, putting her face close to Vita's.

Abby soon ran up. "Come on, Joey. We have a blanket over there. With Dylan and Rob and the gang. David's going to try to take pictures of the falling stars."

Joey turned to Vita and Anne, his eyes filled with hope.

"Of course, you can go," said Anne. "Just stay where we can see you." The three of them laughed as they ran away to join the others.

"I'm so glad you woke me, Anne." Vita felt a wash of happiness flow over her. "This is just the kind of thing I love. And Joey couldn't be happier."

She looked over to where the photo club was set up. There was David, aiming his camera at the sky and showing the view to Joey and Darlene.

Beth and Abby were racing to the boards at the base of the water tower. When they got there, Abby shook a can of spray paint. Vita was close enough to make out that she wrote *A+J* and sprayed a big heart around it. Then Beth did the same, spraying *B+D* inside a heart.

Dylan! thought Vita. So they were more than friends. She watched them tuck the can behind a slat of wood and run off, laughing at their daring. They flopped onto the blankets next to the tripods. Vita was glad when they had settled in with David and Darlene. She wanted to give all her attention to the night sky.

The party atmosphere soon gave way to a quieter tone as the streaks of light became more numerous. Soft *ahhs* and *ohhs* came from the scattered blankets. The uneven squeak of the swings finally stopped, and a hush fell over the park.

David was still pointing his camera to the stars, but Joey was now lying next to Abby. Vita saw that their heads were touching, and now and then they would point to the stars. Dylan and Beth were sitting up talking, gesturing to the sky.

Vita noticed a few couples stroll off into the darkness. Including Anne and Mark.

Vita was alone. But didn't feel at all lonely. This is what has been missing, she told herself. An infusion of beauty. And here it was. Right overhead. A fragrant summer night filled with shooting stars.

Vita lay back and filled her eyes with the starscape. Each time she saw a falling star, she made a soft sound of amazement. Certain stars drew her attention, by their twinkling or by subtle differences in color—gold, blue, silver. She imagined the sound of the glittering stars to be like thousands of tiny glass wind chimes. When she closed her eyes, she could almost hear them.

This is the counter to sadness, she thought. Beauty. Wonderment. The door that sometimes opens and reveals how marvelous the world is. It *was* wondrous. There was no other word to describe it. She felt a profound sense of connection, and a reconnection to her dreams. It all came from the same deep place of beauty and love and yearning.

She lowered her gaze to the water tower, the receptacle of her fears. And dreams. A dual giant that dominated the town for her. Whether staring it down from up on the roof or catching glimpses of it as she rode her bike through town, it was always there. Reminding her of the high points of life she so desperately sought. And the literal heights that so terrified her.

Yet tonight, for the first time, it was all dream tower. Perhaps it was the backdrop of shooting stars that changed her perception. From this angle, her old nemesis appeared to be up there with the stars. Mythological in the night—a ladder to the night realm. Not her enemy at all, but part of the dream stuff.

A sense of peace came over her, along with the acceptance that her fears and dreams were bound together. And the realization that her dreams were far stronger than her fears. It didn't matter how long it would take, or how much she would struggle. She would be true to her dream path.

Vita filled her eyes with the gleaming tower set amongst the stars, and smiled at the thought that formed in her mind. *I may not always believe in me, but I will always believe in the dream.*

CHAPTER 22

Walking home after one of her days working at the drug store, Vita passed Easton with another girl in his car. It reminded her of how quickly Vic had paired up with Priscilla. She wanted to get away. She would finish high school and then leave, go to a university with a good drama department.

But what if she didn't get accepted? What if she couldn't afford it?

When she began to despair, she would remember the water tower against the shooting stars and the feeling of connection and belief in her dreams. She would glance through her portfolio to be reminded of her meager successes and look at her list of plays she had seen and read. She would stroll through the campus and envision the kind of life she wanted. She would remember the directors' apartment and her aunt's apartment in St. Louis. Maybe she could start in St. Louis if she couldn't get to New York. Maybe her aunt could help her find a job.

All the maybes made her exhausted. It was so much easier to have a solid plan.

Millie and Sal went to their friends' house for a cookout and a game of bocce ball, so Anne and Vita put together a light meal of leftovers and a garden salad. While they sat at the table, Joey told them how he had developed a roll of film all on his own in David's darkroom, and Anne talked about the upcoming vacation with Mark and his family.

Beth kept trying to get Anne's attention, but Anne avoided her, and finally said, "Later!"

Vita had been half-listening, but now turned to Anne, and then Beth. "Later what?"

"There's a Western on TV tonight," said Anne, smiling at Joey. "I told Joey we'd make popcorn."

"But it doesn't start for almost an hour," said Beth, again fixing Anne with a stare. "So . . ."

"What?" asked Vita. Anne was definitely hiding something. "Tell me."

Anne began to clear the table. "Beth thinks we should have another round of Secrets and Dreams."

"I don't feel like it." Vita brought the rest of the dishes to the sink, while Anne loaded the dishwasher.

Beth hopped up on the table and faced them. "Oh, come on, Vi. It'll be fun."

"I don't feel like talking about my dreams right now. And I don't have any more secrets."

"Joey wants to, don't you?" Beth winked at him without Vita seeing.

"Yeah. Sure. Do I have time to take a shower? I'm kind of dirty from mowing."

"Go ahead," said Anne. "We'll start the popcorn. Beth, get out the pan and the oil."

The corn was soon popping, and Beth began to melt the butter. Anne listened for the last few kernels to pop, shook the pan, and emptied the popcorn into a large bowl.

"Just a quick round before the movie starts," said Beth. "How about it?"

"Why are you so insistent? I really don't have anything to say." Vita got out several smaller bowls while Anne drizzled butter over the popcorn and added salt.

"Well, I do," said Beth. She carried the bowl of popcorn to the table. "And I want to tell my secret before Joey gets here. It's kind of private." She poured the popcorn into the smaller bowls.

Anne and Vita exchanged a worried glance.

"Oh no," said Vita. "This better not involve Dylan."

Anne put a hand on her hip. "Don't even mention his name."

"Okay." Beth looked up at the ceiling. "So. I did you know what with you know who. And let me tell you, it's not all it's cracked up to be." She took a handful of popcorn and nodded. "Pretty good."

"Beth!" cried Anne, coming to the table. "You better not have. You are way too young!"

"*You're* doing it," argued Beth. "What's the big deal?"

Anne huffed and whispered. "That's different."

"You're out of control, Beth," Vita said.

Beth scoffed. "And we know *you* have—Miss Wondrous Universe."

Anne paced around the kitchen. "Beth, what were you thinking? You don't just do it to be doing it. It has to be out of true deep feelings or it means nothing."

"Was that the problem?" Beth reached for more popcorn.

"Be serious, Beth." Anne sat next to her at the table. "Do you . . . do you love him?" she asked gently.

Beth jerked her head back. "Who, Dylan?"

Vita shook her head. "You do things for the wrong reason, Beth. I can't believe you're so careless. If you get pregnant, you'll be stuck here forever."

"Trust me, I was *not* careless. Curious, yes. Stupid, no."

Anne sat up, offended. "You make getting pregnant and wanting to stay here sound like a crime."

"Don't tell me that's *your* plan," said Vita.

Anne averted her eyes. "Maybe."

Beth slammed her hand on the table, laughing. "Are you pregnant?"

"Shh!" Anne looked around. "Not yet. But I want to marry Mark. Soon."

Vita jumped to her feet. "What is wrong with you two! What about all your dreams of moving to New York, of going to the Southwest? What about all the things you said you wanted to do before settling down?"

"Nothing's getting in my way," said Beth, taking a handful of popcorn.

"Those are *your* dreams, Vita. You can't push them on everyone else. I'm in love with Mark. Just because things didn't work out for you and Vic—"

"That has nothing to do with it. I couldn't care less about him!"

"Well maybe that's your problem. You care more about your crazy dreams than people! He must have felt that."

Beth sat up. "Girls, girls! No need to get testy. And here's Joey." She pushed a bowl of popcorn to the empty seat across from her.

Anne and Vita looked away, both furious.

"Did you start without me?" Joey sat down and ate some popcorn.

"Not really. Vita doesn't want to play. But Anne and I have a secret that we have to share with her."

"I've heard all I want."

"Actually, you might want to hear this."

"What are you talking about?" Vita asked.

Beth gestured to Anne and ate more popcorn. "Go ahead, Anne."

"Me?"

"You started it all. Go ahead."

Anne got up and brought four cold sodas to the table. "Well, I was at work yesterday. And Mr. Beaton came into the café. As he often does. You know how he loves the chicken pot pie."

Vita folded her hands impatiently.

"You know he organizes the performances at the carnival, which is coming up." Anne sat back at the table.

"And?"

"Well, while he was finishing his dessert—he chose the lemon meringue pie—I asked how the carnival was coming along. And we chatted a bit about the lineup. A few skits and some singing. And then I asked him if there might be room for a short performance at the end of the carnival."

Vita's eyes darted from Anne to Beth.

"Long story short," said Beth, "he's adding a twenty-minute slot for you. And he needs to know the title of the piece soon, for printing."

"What!" Vita scooted her chair back. She stared open-mouthed at Beth, then Anne. "And you didn't even ask me?"

"And that's not all. Tell her about today, Anne."

Anne took a sip of soda. "Well, Beth and I were uptown on the square and we happened to see the Radcliffs there."

Vita's eyes widened in fear.

"And well, we thought that, we kind of told them . . . We said that maybe you—"

Beth jumped in. "We told them you were doing the grand finale piece at the carnival. Solo. And would they come to see it."

Vita jumped to her feet. "You said *what*!"

Anne ate some popcorn and looked away.

Beth nodded. "Yep. A one-man show. One-woman. And Mrs. Radcliff said of course they would be there. They wouldn't miss it."

"Anne! Did you?"

"It just kind of happened. First, I was just seeing if it was even a possibility. And the next thing I knew it was a done deal. Beth said the part about it being a solo piece."

Vita dropped back into her chair. "I can't believe you guys would do that."

"All summer," Beth began, "No—all *year*, we have heard nothing but how you have to make things happen, go for it, don't let anything get in your way, blah, blah, blah. And we all believed you. Now, one little audition goes the wrong way, and you get all bent out of shape!"

"This will be good for you, Vi," Anne said softly. "A chance to get back on track."

Beth took a handful of popcorn. "You have two whole weeks to put something together."

Vita put her hand to her forehead. "I don't believe this."

"We'll help you," said Anne. "I can make a costume."

"Abby and I can help with the set."

"I'll help," added Joey. "I can take pictures. You can add them to your portfolio."

Vita threw open her hands and looked at them all in exasperation. "A costume and set and pictures of *what*? What is this piece you're all talking about?"

Anne and Beth and Joey all traded questioning glances.

Beth raised her glass. "That's for you to decide. You're the actress."

Vita leaned back in her chair. "Two weeks!"

"More like twelve days, actually," said Beth. "You can't back out now. The directors are really looking forward to your performance."

"And I'm supposed to find and rehearse a twenty-minute one-woman piece in twelve days?"

"You can do it, Vita," said Joey. "We could go to the library and check out some plays."

Anne looked at Beth. "You better tell her the rest."

Vita's head snapped over to Beth, fearing the new information.

"Well, the Radcliffs asked the name of the piece. And of course, I was making it up as I went along, so I told them you were writing your own play. Something Shakespearean."

"Beth!" Vita whispered in disbelief.

Beth grinned. "You could tell they were impressed."

"I don't even know what to say." Vita sat stunned, staring out ahead of her.

"Don't stop to think and worry about it," said Anne. "Just do it. It will be fun!"

Beth raised her eyebrows to Vita. "So, do you have a secret or dream you want to share?"

"No! I don't have anything I want to share with you!"

They sat in silence, no one daring to say anything. Now that it was out in the open, it did sound like a reckless idea.

Beth shrugged and turned to Joey. "Joey?" She gave a little nod for him to say something.

"Well. I've taken a lot of photographs and some of them are not so bad. I think I'm getting better."

Anne gave a wide smile, relieved for the subject to have changed. "That's wonderful, Joey! Anything else?"

He searched for something he could safely talk about. Then his eyes lit up. "Hogie agreed to pose for me! I've already taken a few pictures. And he's helping me with those frames I bought."

Vita's attention shifted. "Hogie agreed to pose? That doesn't sound like him."

"Yeah! I was showing him a picture I made of Rufus Sharp, and he liked it. He said he wants a photo for his mom to remember him by. So we took some out in his back yard by—"

Vita stiffened. "*What* did he say? For his mom to remember him by?"

"Yeah. I'm going to use some of his old pictures and—" Joey stopped talking when he saw Vita's troubled face. He looked to Anne and then to Beth but they were watching Vita.

"It doesn't mean anything, Vita," said Anne. "You know how he talks."

Beth kept eating the popcorn. "So what if he wants a picture for his mom. I think it's nice of him. She'll be happy."

Vita covered her mouth and sat quietly for a few moments, staring out the window, her eyes darting around in thought. Then she rose to her feet and went outside.

"Vita?"

They heard the screen door close behind her.

Joey looked from Anne to Beth. "I thought that would make her happy."

Anne spoke softly. "She worries about Hogie. That's all. It's nothing new."

"I feel like I keep saying or doing things to make her mad."

"You? Look how mad she is at us," said Beth. "It's just Vita being Vita. She overreacts all the time."

"She's not mad at you, Joey," Anne said.

They watched Vita walk down the sidewalk barefoot and turn down the alleyway.

Hogie's garage door was down. The shades were all pulled. The house was unusually quiet and dark. Vita stood outside and began to knock on his door. She tried to open it. It was locked. She used both hands to bang on the door.

"Hogie! Open up. Hogie!" The knot in her stomach tightened. It was too quiet. "Hogie!" she cried desperately, her heart pounding.

She heard the door opening.

"Jesus Christ! Why the hell are you pounding on my door?"

She almost burst into tears on seeing him. She stepped inside and leaned against the wall while he wheeled back into the living room. There were several empty beer bottles on the coffee table. A lone lamp cast a dim light.

"Well? What is it now? You come to lecture me about something? Because I thought you said more than enough the other night."

Vita could see that he had been drinking heavily. His words came out slightly slurred and his eyes were red. But she had to speak. "Joey told me."

"Told you what?"

"That he took pictures of you. That's not like you, Hogie."

"It made the kid happy."

Hogie stacked a few beer caps on the coffee table, not looking at her.

"He said—" Vita heard her voice quiver and she realized she was shaking. She couldn't get the words out. "It was for your mom—to remember you by."

His eyes froze on the beer caps. "Get the hell out of here, Vita."

"Hogie," she said, in a pleading tone.

"I'm tired of you butting in. You're a fifteen-year-old girl who doesn't know shit! Go on home." He wheeled to the kitchen and took out a cold beer. He popped the top, took a mouthful, and wheeled back to the coffee table.

She knew what his words meant. And she couldn't bear the thought of it. She was aware of her body trembling.

"Hogie." Her voice came out weak. "You're like my brother. You can't—don't ever . . . You're my hero, Hogie."

He raised his head, bloodshot eyes afire. "Don't put that shit on me!"

"You are. To a lot of people."

"A hero. What do you think I did? Rushed into enemy fire waving the flag? Carried wounded men back to camp?"

"I don't know. I only know that—"

"Come on, Vita. Where's your famous honesty? You've heard the stories. There were no heroics." He gave a bitter laugh. "My buddy shot me, cleaning his goddam gun. Just a dumbass kid I was always looking out for."

He started to take another drink from the bottle, then hurled it in fury at the wall. It shattered onto the floor.

Vita jolted to attention, afraid to move.

"He ruined two lives! Last I heard he's shooting up, got no life. So don't give me that hero shit." He thumped his chest. "I'm Hogie the birdhouse maker! The bench maker. That's all I can handle for now. So get away from me with your talk of heroes and love and shit."

Vita moved to clean up the glass, but he turned on her.

"Leave it!" He started to wheel towards her.

She spun around and they stared each other down.

"You were my hero *before* the war. We—I need you. I need to know that—"

"You don't! You got yourself. That's all any of us get."

"I need to know that our old Hogie is safe—somewhere inside there—and might be happy one day."

"Happy!" Hogie gave a sneering chuckle. "Damn, you're exhausting!"

Vita remained rooted to the floor, afraid of setting him off again. She watched him wheel back to the coffee table. He lifted a few bottles and realized they were all empty.

His shoulders slumped and he hung his head. "Go on, Vita. Go on home. I know you're trying to—" He looked up at her. "You can't fix me. You can't fix what happened in here." He tapped his head.

Vita waited a long time before answering. Her voice came out small and soft. "I can try."

Hogie began to laugh. "You don't give up, do you?" He let out a deep moan. "That's enough, now. Go on. Go read your Shakespeare, or memorize some lines, or dress up like Juliet. Go put your dreams up there with the stars . . . Do it for those of us who can't lift our heads to see that high."

It was the first time Vita ever heard his voice shake. She took a step towards him but the fierceness in his eyes stopped her.

"Go on! Go!" He jerked his head towards the door.

She hesitated, afraid to leave him.

"Go!"

She put her hand on the door, but still couldn't leave.

"Go," he said in a whisper.

She pushed open the door and stepped out into the night.

She stood outside his door for a few moments. Then she walked up and down the streets until the shakiness left her. She walked until the sickness in her stomach lessened and the trembling disappeared. She found herself out at the college and sat on a bench until the street-lights came on.

When she went home, she minimized what had happened and told Anne that everything was fine. Vita was glad that Joey was on the phone with his parents, and that Beth was glued to the TV show, cheering on the Indians. She was glad that Mark had stopped by and that Anne was cuddled up next to him. She was glad that her parents soon arrived home and filled the house with laughter and stories from their evening.

After she took a bath, after everyone had gone to bed, she lay staring at the ceiling. Hogie was always difficult, ever since he came back. All darkness underneath. There were rare glimmers of hope but they were overlaid with anger and despair.

Vita tried to remember the old Hogie. He had been his happiest when he was with Laura, before the war.

A thought slipped into her mind.

She went into Joey's room. "Joey!" she whispered.

He rubbed his eyes and sat up.

"Where are your pictures? I need a photo of Laura."

He turned on the desk lamp and reached for the envelope. He lifted out the pictures of Laura.

There was one photo of her looking directly into the camera with a slight smile on her lips.

"Can I take this?"

"Yeah. I can make another one."

"Thanks, Joey."

"Want me to go with you?"

She smiled to know that Joey understood why she wanted the photo.

"No. I'll be right back."

He heard her leave and return in a few minutes. Only then could he lie back down.

Vita had set the photograph between Hogie's screen door and door. She hoped it wasn't a mistake. But she had to try.

Her worst fear was that one night she would hear a single gunshot, and her heart would shatter forever. To know that something beautiful had left the world because she couldn't convince it to stay.

Or was that giving herself too much importance and power. She knew what Hogie would say to that.

CHAPTER 23

Millie observed the tension among the kids the next day. She saw Beth and Anne whispering, and Vita looking distracted. Vita had gone out before breakfast and when she returned, she told Anne that she had seen Hogie working in his garage. Her spirits had improved somewhat, but it was clear that she was still upset at Anne and Beth for arranging the performance piece.

"I don't agree with the way it was handled," said Millie, "but I do think it's a good idea. You're usually up for a good challenge."

Vita sat slumped at the table. "I guess so."

"You know they were just trying to help you."

"I know."

"Go look through your books. Maybe something will inspire you."

Vita went into the living room, took out a few books, and set them on the library table. "Shakespeare?" She buried her face in her hands.

When Beth and Joey went outside, Millie took Anne aside. "Everyone seems dispirited today. Why don't you all take Joey on a picnic for lunch? Whatever's going on between you girls is affecting him. I thought he looked worried at breakfast."

"Good idea, Mom. Can you come with us?"

"I have a meeting at the library. But I can pack a lunch for you."

Anne threw her arms around her. "I'll help you. Vita! Beth!"

Vita came into the kitchen, carrying her book of Shakespeare plays.

"Go tell Joey and Beth we're going on a picnic."

"They rode over to Mrs. Higgins to deliver her photograph. Joey framed it."

"They'll be back in a few minutes," said Millie. "Let's get started on the sandwiches. It'll be lunchtime soon."

By the time Beth and Joey returned, they had packed the wicker hamper with sandwiches, bags of chips, drinks, and a bunch of grapes. Millie added the blue-and-white checkered picnic cloth.

"Let me get my camera," said Joey, running to his room. "I'll take pictures."

"In that case . . ." Anne pulled Beth and Vita into their bedroom. They came out wearing the peasant tops they had embroidered.

Joey smiled to see them dressed alike—bell bottoms and the gauzy tops in pale summer colors.

"I'm not finished with the sleeves yet," said Beth, "but Anne insisted."

"You girls look lovely," said Millie. "What a good idea. I can't wait to see the pictures."

Anne drove them to the small park at the far end of town and they spread the cloth under a shade tree.

Joey spoke to Vita as they unpacked the hamper. "We rode our bikes past Hogie's. He was busy in the garage but didn't seem mad or anything."

"I'm glad. Thanks for letting me use the photograph. I don't know if will help or not."

The blue picnic cloth looked so pretty against the green grass and the day was so mild and lovely that Vita smiled over at Anne and Beth. Her relief over Hogie put her problems in perspective. What was a twenty-minute play if Hogie was all right?

"This is what I love about summer," said Beth, lifting out the drinks. "There's nothing better than a picnic under a shade tree."

They were soon discussing ideas for the performance.

"We got you into this mess," said Beth, "and we'll help get you out."

Anne arranged the plate of grapes next to the sandwiches and chips. "Will you do a monologue? That seems the simplest choice."

Beth scrunched up her mouth. "It's the final performance. She has to give them more than that." She looked through the sandwiches. "Tuna or chicken salad?" She passed them around and bit into a chicken salad sandwich. "What's your favorite Shakespeare play?"

"*The Tempest*," Anne answered for Vita. "Right?"

"I suppose so. But I'm not sure what I could do with just one character."

"What are some of the main scenes and characters?" asked Beth. "Maybe you could do a couple."

Vita described the play in a nutshell and looked discouraged.

"So why don't you do different roles?" suggested Beth. "That would show your range. And it would be fun! You could be Prospero the magician, then his daughter Miranda, then that wild man Caliban!"

Vita appeared doubtful. "I don't think it would make any sense to most people. If they don't know the play already."

"The Radcliffs will know," said Anne.

"And they'll be the harshest judges." Vita remained skeptical.

"What can they expect?" asked Beth. "It's only twenty minutes."

After they finished lunch, Joey began taking photographs of the three sisters stretched out on the cloth. He peered at the street on the far side of the park. "What train tracks are those? They look different from the ones I came into town on."

Anne packed up the hamper. "That's a freight train track."

Beth jumped up. "Let's go show Joey the train trestle. It's not far."

"It would make a good photograph," said Vita. "Let's go."

Joey took pictures of the sisters walking ahead of him on the tracks, their long hair hanging loose down their backs. Three in a row. Pale yellow, pale blue, pale green. He knew it was a good composition.

The tracks dipped and curved through the woods, and he stopped now and then to capture the scenery. Up ahead he saw the wooden trestle high above a deep ravine. A grassy area served as a good vantage point to view the trestle.

"Wow!" He positioned his camera and took a few shots of the structure. Strong lines, and a good contrast with the trees. He tried different angles and zoomed in on parts of it. The sky behind it had feathery white clouds and added interest to the images.

"Come on!" cried Beth, starting to cross the trestle. "The view's great from the middle."

Vita hesitated but was determined not to be afraid. She concentrated as she placed one foot after another on the wooden ties. When they all stopped in the middle, she kept her eyes level on the trees over the ravine.

They crossed from one side of the trestle to the other, taking in the views. A mild breeze blew the girls' hair as they lined up on one side. Joey clicked away, knowing that he had some good shots.

Beth inhaled deeply. "I love that smell. Tar and old wood. Want to go to the end of the trestle?"

"No. Let's turn back," said Anne. "I don't want to get stuck on the other side if a train comes. I have to be at work in a few hours."

They began to walk back when Beth stopped. She squatted down and placed her hand on the rail. Her eyes lit up. "A train's coming. Run!" She took off sprinting and soon reached the grassy opening where she flopped down laughing, closely followed by Anne.

Joey reached them and turned around, expecting Vita to be right behind him. He saw her frozen in the middle of the trestle.

"Vita!"

"Run!" cried Anne and Beth.

Joey saw that there was nowhere for her to move aside when the train came. He ran back and grabbed her hand.

Vita was staring down at the ground. "I can't move."

"Don't look down! Vita!"

They heard the train whistle blow as it neared the trestle.

Joey pulled on her hand. "Just follow me. One step at a time. Come on, you can do it."

She moved one foot, then the other. She followed him slowly. When the train rounded the curve and came into view, Anne screamed out.

"Vita! Run!"

They were nearing the end where the ground sloped up, filling with shrubs instead of empty space. They picked up their pace just as the train began to cross the trestle. They ran the last bit and jumped off to the side where Anne and Beth were.

Anne was in tears. "Vita! Why did you do that!" She wrapped her arms around her.

"Just trying to scare us," said Beth. "She wasn't in any danger."

The train chugged across the trestle and passed them, sounding its whistle as it headed into town. They watched it disappear around a curve in the tracks.

"Oh my gosh, that was so exciting!" Beth burst out laughing. "Bet you've never done *that* before, Joey!"

Anne was furious at her lightheartedness. "You and your crazy ideas!"

"We had plenty of time," said Beth. "Those freight trains move like slugs."

Joey tried to laugh, relieved to have gotten Vita off the tracks. For a few moments he had been terrified.

"What happened?" cried Anne. "Why did you stop?"

Vita stood bewildered. "I—I don't know. I was fine. Then—I looked down. I didn't mean to. I was focusing on the ties, and all of a sudden, I saw the ground down below. And it made me dizzy. And I—I couldn't move! I'm fine. I'm fine now."

Beth gave Anne a light push. "Come on, admit it, Anne. That was exhilarating!"

"It was until I saw that Vita was still out on the trestle."

Vita smiled and made light of it. "Just a moment of panic. Come on. Let's go back home."

Anne raised her finger to Beth. "Not a word to Mom and Dad. If they knew half of what we did they'd never let us out of the house."

Joey worried about Vita after dinner when he and Beth rode to Abby's to develop the film. And later when they rode their bikes up to the Dairy Queen. He worried about her when he came home and couldn't find her. He went outside and was surprised to find her up on the roof.

He shinnied up the antenna pole, walked over to her, and sat down.

"Hey, Joey." She gave him a quick smile and returned her eyes to the distance.

Joey followed her gaze. The water tower appeared rosy in the setting sun.

"I didn't know I was still so afraid. I thought I had conquered my fears. But I haven't." She stared out at the tower. "I'll never be anything more than I am right now."

It bothered him that she didn't know how wonderful she was. Courageous and beautiful and magical. Her faraway eyes matched the green of her blouse, and the slanting sun turned her hair a shimmery coppery gold.

"You're a lot right now. I thought you'd be too scared to come up here. Every time something scares you, you come up here and fight your fears. You're one of the bravest people I know."

"I'm a coward, Joey. My fears will always control me. If it hadn't been for you . . ."

"Nah, Beth was right. You would have run."

She did her best to sound playful. "You rescued me, Joey. All for one…"

He gave a big smile. "So I'm still your D'Artagnan?"

She rested gentle eyes on him. "Always."

"I thought . . . I thought I wasn't. I thought I let you down somehow."

"How could you think that? You're the only good thing that has happened to me all summer."

Joey blinked in surprise. "I am?"

Vita laughed at his expression. "You've cheered me up and helped me, and when my dreams seem far away, you remind me to keep going. You believe in me."

Her words made him smile. Joey looked out at the treetops, the water tower in the distance, the soft summer sky. "This has been the best summer of my whole life."

"Has it, Joey?" A surge of delight filled her face. "That makes me so happy."

"It's been great. Because of you, and Anne and Beth. And Aunt Millie and Uncle Sal. The fair, swimming and fishing. Riding my bike out into the country. Working with Abel. Being friends with Hogie. And I . . . I found something that I want to do forever. My dream path."

Vita's lips pressed into a soft smile.

"It's because of you, Vita. You convinced me."

"It's because of David and Abby and Beth. And you're a natural, Joey. The credit goes to you."

"But you got me thinking. I saw how important acting was to you. And it made me want something of my own. You made me believe I could make it happen."

Vita looked back out at the water tower. "I'm not sure anymore. I mean . . . I know it will work for you . . ."

"You can't change your mind now. I will, if you will, right? That's what you said."

Vita gave an unconvincing nod. "I will, if you will." They sat in silence looking out at the sky turning magenta and gold in the west. Then Vita stood. "Let's go."

They walked to the pole and slid down.

Vita turned to Joey. "Will you help me with something?"

"Sure.

"I want to climb the fire escape."

"Now?"

"I have to do it now. On my own."

"Okay."

They walked to the schoolyard and Joey waited at the bottom of the fire escape while Vita climbed it. Twice.

"Believe it or not, this helps. I don't feel so afraid." She climbed a third time and stood alone on the third floor platform. She made herself look through the slats, down at the ground. Then she gazed out at the sun setting over the treetops and smiled.

Joey followed and stood next to her. "I knew you could do it. You just got stuck in your head. That's all." He gave her their quick nod of alliance.

Vita returned the gesture and laughed. "You're right. Absolutely right."

They left the school yard and started to walk home.

"Let's go down Oak Street." Vita wanted to check on Hogie. Not to bother him, not to intrude, but to see if he was working in his garage. To see if everything looked normal.

Her face filled with worry when she saw that his garage was dark.

Then she came to a halt and stared at Joey wide-eyed. She grabbed his arm.

"What?" He looked around.

"Listen." She cocked her head. "Do you hear that?"

A smile slowly spread across Joey's face. "His guitar!" he whispered.

Vita's eyes grew bright as she heard a strum, and then another. And then a melody being picked out on the strings. A low voice followed and a song took shape. Sweet and sad and hopeful.

Vita was engulfed by one powerful feeling. *Maybe*, she thought. Maybe. She realized how desperately she needed there to be a maybe for Hogie.

CHAPTER 24

Vita worked tirelessly on her performance. Having a focus to put her energies into helped, though she remained skeptical about the piece itself. She was running out of time and the best she could cobble together in a week's time was a few monologues, a few lines, strung together from *The Tempest*. She would give it her best, and then let it go and move on.

Anne, Beth, and Joey helped her with ideas for the stage and a costume that would allow her to transform from Prospero to Ariel to Caliban to Miranda—with the help of a two-sided cape. They worked on the stage set at Abby's. Vita took some comfort in the fact that David and Darlene were acting as joint director and stage manager. That would help to hold the whole thing together and at least it would look good.

Joey continued to add to his collection. He had made several gifts of the framed photographs and was waiting to find the right time to give his favorite one to Vita. It had turned out the best.

He was also working on a special gift for Abby. He was saving the largest of the frames for a collage. Knowing that her favorite color was pink, he had taken pictures of Abel's pink roses, a soft-pink dress hanging on a neighbor's clothesline, a pink bicycle, and a close-up of a bright pink hydrangea bush. He had photos from the yard sale of the pink music box and little vase and a few others he might be able to use. He wanted to add a pink sunset and maybe a picture of Abby the next time she wore pink. He had his camera ready.

When the carnival was just two nights away, Anne drove them up to the square in the evening so that Vita could see the stage that had been erected. One of the side streets was already roped off. Various booths and rides for children were being set up. Strings of lights crisscrossed the street.

Vita stood on the stage, anxious and uneasy. The performance was no longer just an idea that Anne and Beth had cooked up. She would be standing alone on the stage delivering lines that at best were only loosely connected. She wished she had more time to prepare.

She moved about the space, getting a feel of the distances and imagining where the audience would be seated.

"Yours is the last piece," said Anne. She also wore a worried expression. "So there's no knowing how many people will stick around for it. People with kids will probably leave early. And if the beer tent is full . . ."

"I know."

"Don't be disappointed if it's just a handful of people."

Vita looked out at an imaginary audience. "All the better."

"It's still experience for the ole resume," said Beth, "and Joey will be sure to take some great photos."

Vita nodded and tried to envision the stage set. She had never performed outdoors and knew there would be many distractions. Again she thought, *All the better.*

They drove to the Dairy Queen for ice cream sundaes and were just leaving when they saw Abby in the little park next to the parking lot. She was seated on her bike, next to a boy on his bike. They were leaning close together, sharing an ice cream cone and laughing. Joey tilted his head to look at them.

"That's Troy," said Beth. "He was at his cousin's for most of the summer."

Abby leaned over and kissed him on the cheek and the boy put his hand on her hair. He said something that made Abby laugh.

Anne and Vita glanced at Joey. His eyebrows were pinched in confusion.

"Let's go." Anne started the engine and quickly drove away.

"Abby's such a flirt," said Beth. "It doesn't mean anything, Joey. They were hanging around together before he left. That's all."

The girls kept the conversation on the carnival and the different booths that were usually set up, but they saw that Joey was upset. He stared out the window and remained silent, his ice cream melting.

When they got to the house, Millie was on the phone. "Joey, it's your parents!" She turned back to the phone.

"You'll hardly recognize him. He's filled out and gotten tan. And his hair is longer. No, no. Of course not, I understand. Just let me know. Here he is."

Joey listened to his mom, then to his dad. His expression grew stony and stayed that way.

Millie whispered to the girls. "They want him to come home immediately. Tomorrow, if possible. Walter accepted a promotion, but it means moving. To Denver!"

"Oh, no." Vita covered her mouth. She knew that the summer would eventually come to an end and that Joey would leave, but she hadn't wanted to think about it.

Joey listened with an angry set face. "I'm not leaving before the carnival," was all he said, and handed the phone back to Millie.

He went to his room, took all the pink photographs and ripped them into small pieces. He walked outside and sat on top of the picnic table.

All three girls went out and stood next to him.

"I wasn't ready for that," said Beth. "You're just going to have to come back soon, Joey."

"I can't stand the thought of it," said Anne.

Vita sat next to him. "Gosh, Joey. I'm sorry."

"This is what I hate about summer," said Beth. "There's always something you have to say goodbye to."

When Joey's mouth began to quiver, Anne motioned for Beth to leave with her.

"Nothing ever works out for me." He swiped at the tears on his cheeks.

Vita placed her hand on his shoulder. "Don't say that, Joey. Stick to your plans. Dream big, dream hard. Make it so real that you can see it, and then go after it—promise me."

Joey jerked his head up, his eyes full of anger. "Do you know what it's like to always be the new kid? I hate it! New school, new neighborhood, where I don't know anyone! Dreams are just a waste of time. Sooner or later they fall apart. Always."

"No they don't, Joey. They're the one thing in *your* control. You own them. Wherever you go."

"Yeah, right. I want to go tell Hogie." He jumped off the table and cut down the alleyway.

⤸

A gloom settled over the house. No one was prepared for Joey to leave so soon. There were still so many things they had planned—more fishing, camping out at Abby's with a bonfire, a barbeque cookout with the neighbors, a picnic to the state park just outside of town, more night swimming at the pool . . .

Millie let out a sigh and thought that at least they would all be kept busy so they wouldn't have time to brood. With the play the following night, there were a thousand things to do. Yet every time she looked at Joey her heart ached. He wore the same sad, lost expression as when he arrived—though with more anger and defiance, as if the summer had turned him into an older boy.

Joey went over to Abel's in the morning to tell him that he had to return home. He sat with him on his swing and they stared out at the yard without speaking.

Joey looked at the rose bushes and remembered his first night there with Abel and the peach ice cream. He thought about their days out at the cemetery, his first real job. He

371

thought about all the conversations they had riding out to the cemeteries, or cleaning and oiling the tools, or just sitting on the swing, like now. He was happy that Vita had taken some pictures of them together.

Abel patted Joey's arm and pulled out his harmonica. He brought it to his mouth and played a sorrowful tune, full of longing and loss. And yet it was beautiful. Joey saw tears on the old man's cheeks, and his own eyes filled up.

When the song was over, Joey stood.

"Thanks, Abel. I'm going to miss you. Guess I'll see you at the carnival."

He crossed Abel's yard and turned around to wave. With the permanence of a photograph, Joey knew that image would forever stay in his mind. Old Abel sitting on the swing meant for two, his weathered face creased in a smile that made Joey want to cry.

Joey got on his bike and rode out to his meadow. He sat on the fence and stared at the grassy clearing where he had built his tower. Had it helped him? Did he need a tower? Would he bring that spot with him wherever he went?

Dreams were tricky. Without them, life was blah. Yet they could crush your heart when they went wrong. He tried not to think of Abby kissing that boy. He tried not to think of Denver and of never seeing his friends. He tried not to think of being so far away from the Vitales. From Vita.

He had seen her stumble again and again on her dream path and pick herself back up. But that happy spark she had—before the audition—was gone, and it made him sad. She would fight to the end, whatever happened. But could he? He was not D'Artagnan now. He was just a twelve-year-old boy who didn't know anything. Was it worth having a dream if it was just going to hurt you? He felt like Hogie. I'm not the answer man.

Joey let his eyes settle on the grassy spot and his tower slowly emerged—gray stone against blue sky, turreted at the top. His heart swelled. It was wonderful, strong, and connected to a thousand things. How could he love something that was only imaginary?

In his mind, he walked over to the tower, and began to climb the stone steps that spiraled around. He imagined standing on the top, with his cape fluttering in the wind, seeing far off into the future. He saw himself in Africa and China, paddling along rivers with a camera held up to his eye. He saw himself riding in a jeep with an expedition, several cameras jangling around his neck. He saw his photographs spread out before him, images of old people and little children in a foreign land, and girls like Anne and Beth and Vita looking into the camera.

He felt such a grip in his heart that he knew he would never give up his dream. He would take it with him, wherever he went.

He jumped off the fence and gave a final look at the little river meandering through the grass, the cows grazing in the distance, the clumps of trees. Then he said a soft "goodbye" to his meadow.

He walked his bike up the hill, and rode through the town. He went to the park and said goodbye to his friends. He rode through the college and around the square. And he rode alongside the Lone Tower Park, where he said another goodbye to Vita's tower.

A chaotic afternoon followed, everyone busy with last-minute tasks. Millie helped Joey to gather his belongings, did a last load of laundry of his clothes, and packed his suitcase.

Beth drove over to Foreston with Darlene to get supplies for the stage set. At the last minute, David had decided on a second small backdrop, which required a second pulley that they didn't have. So while Abby and Becca spray painted a stormy ocean scene, Beth and Darlene picked up the supplies and ran a few errands.

Anne and Vita spent the afternoon making small changes to the costume and the two-sided cape she would use for Prospero and Caliban. They went to the dime store and chose a few rolls of trim and some glittery blue-green fabric to suggest Ariel.

They talked excitedly as they walked to Anne's car, holding up the different trimmings and deciding how to arrange them on the costume. Up ahead of them, they noticed two girls walking and laughing.

"That girl looks just like Beth from the back," said Anne.

Vita glanced up. "Except for the hair." She stuffed the materials back in the bag. "Let's get these sewn on as quickly as possible so—"

Anne abruptly stopped and yanked Vita's arm. She gave a loud gasp and covered her mouth.

"What?" Vita looked all around. "What?"

"It *is* Beth!"

Just then Beth whipped around—without the swing of long black hair—and burst out laughing when she saw their expressions. Her hair was cropped in a short, chic style.

She ran up to them and twirled around for them to see it. "Well, what do you think?"

"Beth!" Anne's eyes filled with tears. "All your beautiful long hair! Gone!"

"Oh, Anne. You're so old-fashioned." Beth ran her hands through her hair. "This feels so good, I can't even explain it. I love it! It feels so light and—free!"

"When—"

"Just now, in Foreston. Darlene got a quick trim and I asked the hair dresser if she could cut mine. Off." Beth leaned her head back in sheer pleasure. "I should have done this years ago."

She heard Darlene tooting the horn. "I have to go. David's waiting for this stuff." She waved goodbye, looking several years older. Mature, stylish, vibrant.

Vita faced Anne, her mouth still open in surprise. "I can't believe it."

"I can't either. Are we old-fashioned, Vi?"

"I didn't think so. But maybe we are."

Anne ran her hand down her long blonde tresses. "I'd feel naked without my hair."

"Maybe that's what she likes about it."

Sal wanted to take everyone out to dinner at the nicest restaurant in town. He wore a sports jacket and had slicked back his hair. Once again, Joey thought how he looked like a movie star, and Millie was glamorous in her aquamarine dress. Vita wore her floral vintage dress, Anne her blue and white sundress, and Beth her coral mini.

"My three beautiful sisters," Joey said, causing them to smother him with hugs.

They took turns taking pictures with Joey, passing the camera around, until Sal told them to pile into the car.

Beth ran her fingers through her hair. "I know you were shocked, Joey, but you didn't tell me what you think. Dad says I look like a boy. Mom says I look like a young Audrey Hepburn."

He leaned sideways to get a fuller view. "At first, I was just surprised. But it kind of goes with you somehow."

"See? Joey gets it."

Joey did his best to put on a good face through dinner, and thanked them all for giving him the best summer of his life.

When they returned home, they took a few more shots by the flower garden in the setting sun. Joey took several family pictures and promised to send the best ones.

"Enough of that," said Sal. "I'm going to get out of these clothes and give the garden a good soaking. Want to help, Joey?"

After he was finished in the garden, Joey went to his room to get Vita's gift. He found her seated in the living room with her costume spread before her.

"I can't get used to the thought of you leaving, Joey."

He couldn't talk about that. "Are you ready for tomorrow?"

"I guess as ready as I'll ever be." She tipped her head to the side when she saw that he was holding something behind his back.

"I have something for you. I've been saving it for just the right time, but since I'm leaving after tomorrow . . ." He handed her the framed picture.

She took in a long slow breath. "Joey!"

It was a photograph of her dressed as Titania. He had captured her looking up at the trees, the sky, something far away—proud, beautiful, otherworldly. He had super-imposed it over a fairytale background of a tower with a crescent moon and glittering stars.

Beneath it, he had written *Night Queen*. Touches of silver and gold paint enlivened the tower and the stars, her bodice and skirt. Subtle dots of silver shone on her tiara, her hair had flecks of gold.

"David helped me with the superimposing. Beth and Abby helped me with the paints. I showed it to Hogie yesterday. He repaired the frame for me and varnished it."

She smiled. "What did Hogie think?"

"He said I had made something true. Do you think so?"

Vita filled her eyes with the beautiful, magical image.

"I think you made a dream, Joey. But I will do everything I can to make it come true." She wrapped her arms around him.

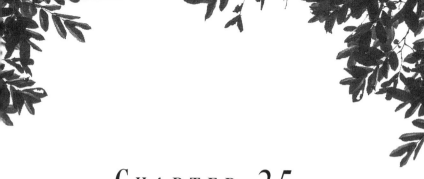

Chapter 25

The day of the carnival went by in a blur. There was a last-minute change that made Vita uncomfortable. Originally, she had planned to begin her piece with no introduction other than the rolling down of the ocean backdrop. However, Mr. Beaton now felt that the piece should follow the format of the others with a brief introduction. He himself would say a few words about Vita and her performance. She had wanted to be the one to set the tone.

Joey and Beth rode their bikes over to Abby's house to help David organize the stage set materials. David gave him advice about taking evening shots. Joey would use up his final roll of film and return the camera to David after the performance.

He and Beth helped roll up the canvas backdrops, practicing the unfurling to make sure everything worked smoothly. David and the photography club would be in charge of setting up the stage.

Joey was more distanced with Abby though she was as friendly as ever. Beth teased her about kissing Troy but Abby just laughed like it was nothing. Joey thought that she probably kissed a lot of boys.

When they arrived home, Millie and Anne were putting together a light supper for everyone, and Vita was pacing the kitchen.

They all turned, relieved to find that Joey was smiling.

"You two look happy about something," Millie said.

"Tell them," said Beth.

"David and the whole photo club are going to have a party for me, after the play!"

"A party?" asked Anne. "I'm going."

"They're going to build a fire for Joey and make s'mores since he's never done that before. It might get a little late."

"Well, we can't rush Joey's first campfire," said Millie. "Anne can drive you all home."

"What a perfect ending to your visit, Joey," Vita said. She had been worrying about him all day.

Millie put her arm around his shoulder. "Remember, we have an early start tomorrow, to get to the station by 8:00. But I guess you can always sleep on the train."

"Come on, Vi. Let's get started on your hair and makeup," said Anne. "I know, I know. A light touch."

"I'm going to take a shower before dinner," Beth hollered, running down the hall.

Joey leaned in to whisper something to Millie that made her laugh, just as Sal came home from work.

Sal appeared more agitated than Vita. "Where is she? Is she ready? Does she feel prepared?"

"Of course, she's prepared. Anne's helping her get ready. Don't go making her all nervous."

He went to check on Vita. "This is a big deal. I was talking to Mr. Simon at the shop and he said they've never had a play at the carnival and might make it a regular part. The grand finale, every year. See what you started?" He grinned broadly at Vita.

Beth soon joined them, towel-drying her hair. "Almost dry! I'll never need a hair dryer again."

Sal stood before his daughters. "My three girls. Couldn't be more proud of you all. Though this is going to take some getting used to." He rubbed the top of Beth's hair. "So we're all set, are we? You don't need anything?"

"No, Dad," laughed Anne. "Vita's ready."

"Waiting is the hardest part," said Vita. "But I'm determined to enjoy the carnival with Joey. I'll meet David and the others at 9:00 to set up. That gives us half an hour. Darlene's in charge of my costume."

"Right. Well, I'll go and get dressed."

The girls exchanged smiles at his nervousness.

They were soon all in the kitchen helping Millie bring things to the table, everyone talking at once about the performance and the party for Joey afterwards. Sal told Millie that he wanted to make sure to get to the stage early enough to get a front row seat.

"It's not every day your daughter's the star of the show. I told Abel I'd save him a seat and bring him home with us. He's going up there early with Rusty Cooper."

Sal sat down and the others followed. "Well, let's eat. Save room for the funnel cake at the carnival, Joey. Best you ever had."

Beth told Joey how delicious it was and began describing all the things he had to try at the different booths. She brought the breadbasket to the table and was just taking her seat when she let out a scream and her arms went flying all around her. In a flash, she realized that Joey had given her the broken chair. She burst into a peal of laughter with the others.

"You got me!" she cried, and gave Joey a punch on the arm. "I should have been on my toes. Oh, that was good, Joey!" She replayed her "fall" in an exaggerated manner, causing the laughter to grow.

"I wish I had my camera for that," Joey said, laughing harder than anyone.

✧

Mark picked Anne up, and Sal drove the others and parked off the square. Vita walked around the carnival with Joey and Beth and had him try the funnel cake. Beth was soon flocked by all her friends, exclaiming over her hair.

As the day began to fade, the strings of little lights came on and gave the carnival a festive air. The lines for the funnel cake grew in length and the bingo tables were packed to capacity. The small town square became more and more crowded and it was as if someone had turned up the volume on everything.

Joey saw Millie and Sal standing at a crowded booth. Beth explained that it was the cake-and-pie wheel and they went to join them.

"Look what Sal just won! Lemon." Millie held up a cake with white icing.

Joey saw Mrs. Higgins standing with her nephew, the man who had picked her up at the train station. Sal leaned into Joey. "Go ahead, Joey. Pick a number."

After a few spins on the wheel, Joey's number won. He asked Millie and Sal if he could give the prize to Mrs. Higgins.

"Of course, you can," said Millie. "I happen to know she loves angel food cake." She pointed to the array of cakes and pies. "We'll take that cake with the sprinkles."

Joey presented the cake to Mrs. Higgins and told her that he was leaving in the morning.

"For me? Why, thank you, Joey! I'm sorry that you can't stop by for a piece of this, like old times. You'll just have to come back next summer to visit me."

When it got close to 9:00, Anne helped Vita change into her costume, and Beth and Joey helped David set up the backdrop.

Vita peered around the edge of the curtain and saw several high school teachers and students. She felt the first flutter of nerves in her stomach. Then she spotted the Radcliffs talking with Mrs. Simon and flashed on the words of Daphne—how theater was an act of collaboration.

Vita felt sick to her stomach. A one-woman show might appear egotistical, the opposite of collaboration. Why had she agreed to it? She saw Vic and Priscilla seated in the second row. And there was Easton with some girl on his arm. Why had he come?

Vita realized she was becoming distracted and losing her concentration. She knew better than to look out at the crowd before a performance. She closed her eyes and breathed deeply and tried to remain calm.

But now she became aware that there was a problem with the canvas. It wasn't rolling down on one side. And it was so hot! Even though the sun had set, she was sweating in her costume. She patted at the perspiration on her upper lip and forehead.

She saw Mr. Radcliff looking at the program. Was she imagining it, or was he already frowning?

What was I thinking? Rewriting Shakespeare? I can't do it. I'll make a fool of myself!

The crowd was settling down, fanning themselves with the folded programs, when Mr. Beaton walked onto the stage and greeted everyone. He tapped the microphone and when he said "testing" a screech of feedback rang out. He backed up and gave a surprised chuckle.

"Thank you all so much for coming. We will close tonight's events with a little Shakespeare, performed by our own Vita Vitale." He smiled and waited for the applause to lessen. He cleared his throat and read from his notes.

"Vita is an old pro."

Vita closed her eyes backstage and groaned.

"She has performed in numerous productions to date." He listed her high school performances, including the Pierrot skit. "And she was a most convincing witch in Shakespeare's *Macbeth*." In a moment of inspiration, he threw his arm out and spoke dramatically: "*To be or not to be!*"

"That's *Hamlet*!" someone shouted from the audience.

He shrugged, took a moment to enjoy the laughter from the crowd, and raised his notes again.

"And tonight—tonight, ladies and gentlemen, Vita will once again delight us with some Shakespeare! A condensed version of one of his plays."

He took off his glasses, pocketed them, and wobbled his head in thought. "A sort of reworking of *The Tempest*, but in a nutshell." His held up his finger. "A Tempest in a teacup!" he said, chuckling heartily at his wit.

Vita put her hands over her face. This was all such a bad idea.

"And now, without further ado, I give you Miss Vita Vitale and *The Tempest*!" He tripped over the cord and gave a final chuckle as he made an exaggerated exit, bowing with a sweep of his arm.

Joey had positioned himself at the side of the stage to get a few opening shots. He waited for Vita to step out. When she didn't, he stepped behind the curtain.

"Vita," he whispered. "Vita!"

She lowered her hands. "I can't do it. I'll fail miserably."

"Only if you don't try. Go out there! Be wondrous!"

She locked her eyes on his, and he gave her their quick nod. She swallowed and did the same. She shut her eyes, took a deep breath, and opened them. Then she raised her chin and stepped through the curtains.

She took center stage, spread her arms and began to speak, but no sound came out. In Mr. Beaton's trip, the microphone had become unplugged. David ran onto the stage and replugged it.

There was a little laughter, along with coughs and fanning and chatter. Sounds of an audience growing bored.

A soft evening breeze blew over the stage and rustled the leaves in the trees. Vita used it. Standing in front of the stormy ocean, she raised the shimmery blue-green fabric in her hands, letting it flutter while she spoke.

"Full fathom five thy father lies . . ." Vita's voice wrapped around the audience and pulled them into her story.

The audience became silent. For the next twenty minutes, Vita became Prospero, Ariel, Miranda, and at one point a horrible crouching Caliban. She ended with Prospero. The lights went down. She tucked one leg behind the other and made a low sweep.

The crowd applauded. A few people scratched their heads and wore expressions of confusion, not quite sure what it was all about, but clapped out of politeness. Some trickled off and made their way to the beer tent.

Vita gave another brief bow for those who remained and kept clapping. She was gracious in her thanks, but her mind raced with what she would say to the Radcliffs, how she was going to explain her decision. She exited through the curtains and dropped the cape.

She made her way to the front and was hugged by her parents and sisters. Abel gave her a nod of approval and Joey smiled widely. Suddenly Mrs. Simon and the Radcliffs were before her.

Mrs. Simon squeezed her. "You were marvelous, Vita!"

"That was quite a performance," Mr. Radcliff said.

Vita wasn't sure of his meaning. Was he criticizing her?

"I only had twenty minutes and I probably should have just done a monologue, but—"

Daphne put her hand on Vita's arm. "That took courage, up there all by yourself."

Vita looked at Mr. Radcliff's furrowed eyebrows and stumbled out an excuse. "I think I know what you're going to say. I thought it was a good idea at first, but then I realized that the lines were never meant to be apart from the others, but by then it was too late and—"

"That's not what I was going to say. But you're correct. That's where years of hard work come into play."

"As a matter of fact," said Daphne, "we were just saying . . ." She looked to her husband.

He gave a cough and linked his hands behind his back. "We had a cancellation for the fall workshop. We'd like to have you. You never know what part might open up, but at the very least you will enjoy the classes and learn a thing or two."

Vita wanted to jump up and down. "Really? I would love that! Thank you." She felt Beth's finger in her back and heard her say, "This was all my idea, you know."

He handed Vita his card. "Classes start next month." Daphne smiled goodbye and Vita watched them walk away.

Millie embraced Vita.

"Did you hear that, Mom? I can't believe it!"

Other teachers, neighbors, and friends made their way to greet her, including Vic and Priscilla. Easton made a show of kissing his new girlfriend. The photography club surrounded her and told her it went well, and to hurry to the party.

Sal soon became her stage manager, telling everyone of her previous performances and how he helped her to get her witch's cackle just right.

Mrs. Higgins came up with her nephew, and took Vita's hands. "You were splendid, Victoria. What a treat it was to watch you perform!" She pointed to the cake Owen was holding and smiled at Joey. "We're going home to sample some of this. Thank you, again, Joey." She gave a goodbye kiss to him, linked her arm with Owen's, and waved good-bye to them all.

The photography club soon had the stage set broken down and the canvases rolled up. Darlene added the cape and a few supplies to the props bag.

Anne hugged Vita. "I'm so relieved it's over. I don't know how you can handle the pressure. I was a nervous wreck."

Vita walked over to Joey. "Well?"

"You were wondrous. You really were. And look who's here."

Vita looked behind him and her mouth dropped open. There was Hogie—and Laura! With her hand resting on his shoulder.

"You came!" Hogie had shaved and combed his hair. He looked so handsome, but Vita knew better than to mention it.

"She made me," Hogie said, pointing his head to Laura. "And I wanted to see you in action."

Laura laughed. "You were wonderful, Vita."

"Thanks, Laura. You saw it?" she asked Hogie.

"The whole damned thing. Whatever it was."

"And? What did you think?"

"You were great. Though I still think you're full of it." Hogie jerked his head to the stage. "So was Shakespeare."

Vita laughed and impulsively hugged him. He backed away from the sentimentality and began to wheel away. "We'll see you at the station, Joey. We have to get to the beer tent before it closes."

Laura gave Vita a quick embrace, and when Hogie raised his face to Laura, Vita caught a glimpse of the old Hogie.

Maybe, thought Vita. *Maybe*.

Beth ran up and grabbed Joey's arm. "Come on! We have to hurry if we're going to make that campfire. We'll ride with David. Hurry, Vita!"

Joey said goodnight to Abel and let Beth pull him away. Millie and Sal called out to Joey to have a good time at the party.

Millie put her arms around Vita. "I'm so proud of you!"

Vita leaned into her embrace. "Thanks, Mom. I was so nervous." She stepped out of her skirt, and now stood dressed in cutoffs and her bodice. "Can you take this home for me?"

Sal patted her back. "We should get Abel home. Go enjoy the party. I'd say you deserve it."

Vita walked with Anne and Mark to his car. By the time they arrived at David's, the fire was brightly burning and a table for s'mores was set up. Joey was laughing and talking with everyone. He took out the roll of film from the camera, pocketed it, and handed the camera to David.

"Thanks for letting me use it. And thanks for teaching me so much."

"You taught me a few things, too," said David. "I'm going to try superimposing a few images like you did. Great effect."

Darlene gave Joey a hug and told him to send his work to them from time to time, and they would do the same. David was soon taking photographs of everyone, causing Darlene to roll her eyes and laugh.

Vita visited a few people who wanted to talk about the performance. At one point, she caught Joey's eye and smiled at him across the campfire. This was the perfect way to end his trip, and she was grateful to the photography club for all they had done for him. And her. *Collaboration*, she thought with a wistful air.

Anne and Mark sat on a log, roasting marshmallows, and Beth and Abby put together a s'more for Joey. They made sure David had the camera focused on Joey, and a cheer went round when Joey bit into the melting, messy treat.

Joey was soon posing with all the members of the club and laughing as they recounted their antics of the summer.

At the height of the party, Vita leaned over to Anne. "I need to air out my thoughts. I think I'll slip away."

"Are you sure? We'll be leaving in an hour or so."

"I just need to sort through things a bit. Take it all in."

Much as Vita enjoyed the party, she was happy to be alone, to untangle her jumble of thoughts. As she walked, she tried to decipher how she felt about the performance.

She was relieved that she had pulled it off and was happy it was over. And she was thrilled that she would be attending the fall workshop. It made her feel that she had salvaged her master plan for the summer. She was back on track.

Yet there was an anticlimactic feeling she couldn't put her finger on. She felt that she could convince other people of her ability. But she hadn't convinced herself. And until she did, there would always be something lacking in her performances. That spark of truth that made good actors great.

When she passed the Lone Tower Park, she walked inside. She wanted to be alone with her tower, as Joey called it.

Thankfully, the park was empty. She went to the spot where she had watched the shooting stars. She had come close that night to making a connection, to understanding her fears and doubts.

But all that had vanished on the trestle. Underneath everything, she was still dominated by her fears.

She dropped to her knees and let out a sigh. How would she ever cross over to that other way of being? Or would she always try to fool people and cover her lack? She didn't want that.

She lay back on the soft grass and looked up at the sky. The stars were bright and clear. Tonight the tower loomed over her in the dark. It stood before her like a taunt, telling her that she would never succeed until she faced her fears and accepted them as a part of who she was.

There was her dual tower: ordinary structure that served the town, and mythical dream tower. Symbol of her paralyzing fears, and silvery ladder to the stars.

An unexpected surge of energy shot through her, and a shiver of pinpricks flooded her body—terrifying and exhilarating. She felt her breath quicken.

She rose to her feet and locked her eyes on the tower high above. It was speaking to her. Inviting her to be a part of something grand and wonderful, up there in the night sky.

A faint smile came to her lips, and she swallowed hard, knowing what she was going to do. Never had she felt so capable and sure of herself. There was no fear, only a sweet welcoming. She could feel herself stepping from her old life into the new, crossing over the threshold into her future.

She took off her sandals, and walked barefoot through the grass to the base of the boarded-up water tower. There were enough two-by-fours mounted to the plywood that she could use to hold onto. She was a good climber.

She reached for the stashed can of spray paint, hoping it was still there. She shook it. Nearly full. She tucked it into her bodice.

Then, she took a deep breath. Through the obstacles of crisscrossed boards and planks, her hands and feet found places to anchor and pull herself up. She reached the beginning of the ladder running up the side of the tower.

Vita crossed over and stood on the silver steps. They were hard and cool to her bare feet. She looked below her and, for a dizzying moment, her knees weakened. Then she gazed up at the gleaming silver tower set among the stars—and began to climb.

CHAPTER 26

The morning was a whirlwind of a hurried breakfast and last-minute packing. Millie phoned Dorothy to assure her that Joey would be on the train. Joey briefly told his parents about the carnival and Vita's performance and the campfire celebration with s'mores. Millie heard him say softly, "I love you, too."

As Joey ate a piece of toast, he related what his dad had said. "Dad said we can have campfires in Colorado. He said we'll move to a house, not an apartment, and that he'll help me build a darkroom."

Beth was soon recounting the highlights of the party.

"It took a while for everyone to get there. People kept showing up. It was so much fun, wasn't it, Joey?"

"I loved it. Everyone was there. They gave me a really nice leather photo album, and I must have eaten four s'mores."

Anne's face fell as she presented their gift, a leather photo album. "Now you'll have two!"

Joey laughed, thanked them, and went to add it to his suitcase.

Sal gave Joey some money. "For film and camera supplies when you get home. Come on, you and I will ride in the truck." He grabbed Joey's suitcase.

"Me too!" cried Beth, following them. She talked non-stop all the way to the station, telling Joey to call when he got to Chicago, and to let them know his new address in Denver.

When Joey got out of Sal's truck and stepped onto the platform, he saw Rufus Sharp staggering by. Joey took a step towards him and waited, hoping for a look of recognition. A sign of their connection. But Rufus simply walked by, firing off his finger, with the rag shoved in his mouth.

Millie soon pulled up beside the truck and they all gathered together as they waited for the train. They could hear its whistle in the distance.

Now that they were at the station, Joey was afraid he might cry. Millie gave him a sack lunch she had made for him, and she and the girls kept kissing his cheek and saying things to boost his spirit.

"You'll have to come back next summer," said Millie. She gave him a long embrace, and Sal did the same, sniffling. "Come back and visit us."

"Or maybe we'll come out there," said Beth." Maybe I'll move to Colorado instead of the Southwest. We could go skiing!"

Anne gave him a tight embrace. "Will you write to us? Let us know how you like Colorado."

He heard a horn toot and saw Hogie and Laura pull up. Joey ran over and said a final goodbye to Hogie. Laura reached over and took Joey's hand. "Thanks for everything, Joey. We're going to miss you." She looped her arm around Hogie's shoulder.

Joey looked up at Hogie.

Hogie stared ahead of him. "Just wanted to see you off." It took him a few moments before he could face Joey. "I'm not good at goodbyes. You take care."

Joey nodded and gave one last look at Hogie. "Thanks, Hogie. Bye." His eyes filled with tears as Hogie drove away.

"Joey!" Abby jumped off her bike and ran up to Joey. "I was afraid I'd miss you. Here!" She handed him a paper bag. "I made some more s'mores after you left. For the train ride. They're kind of gooey but they still taste good." She kissed him on the cheek.

Joey grinned and took the bag. "Thanks."

Vita stood before him, smiling serenely. He filled with a sense of panic. And loss. He didn't want to leave her.

He let himself be hugged by her. When the train whistle sounded its approach into town, he hugged her tight and looked up at her.

"I'll be on my own now," he said in a shaky voice. "You won't be there to help me."

"You don't need me. You know what to do."

Her words made him feel older and stronger. He wiped at his eyes and stood tall. "I will, if you will."

Vita placed both hands on his shoulders, looked him in the eye, and smiled. "Then, you will."

Her eyes had never been brighter, she had never been more beautiful, more mysterious. He tilted his head in wonder at her. What did she mean? He wanted to say more, ask more, but the train had screeched to a stop and

Sal and Millie came to walk him to the steps the porter was putting out.

A few people got off the train, and a few more boarded. Joey looked at the Vitales. He wanted to thank them all for everything but he couldn't speak. Millie and the girls kissed and hugged him and Sal gave him parting advice.

Vita gave him a final kiss goodbye. "Joey, do something for me."

"Anything."

"Face us. Face the town."

"I will." Again, he was puzzled by the change in her. Of course he would face the town. He would fill his eyes with it until it was just a speck.

They heard the "ALL ABOARD!" and handed Joey his suitcase and sack lunch. He climbed the steps and waved goodbye.

He looked at Vita and she gave him their nod. Brisk, sure, full of promise.

He smiled and nodded back. *I promise.*

There were plenty of open seats. Joey took a window seat and put his suitcase next to him. He placed his hand on the window in farewell.

The train began to move slowly, and the whistle sounded.

He heard their muffled voices and saw their hands and arms waving, and Beth and Abby running alongside the train. He saw them all get smaller, Sal and Millie, their arms around each other. Anne. Vita.

The town began to recede. There was the courthouse dome, the grain elevator, the steeples. Then, just as the train rounded the curve, the water tower came into full view—and Joey saw that words had been spray painted on the tower.

He jumped to his feet and leaned closer to get a full view. As the train rounded the curve the message made itself visible.

He gasped and a shiver of joy shot through him. There, in bold, brave letters was Vita's message to him:

DREAM ON, D'ARTAGNAN!! NQ

"Night Queen," he whispered. Then louder, "She did it. She did it!" He pressed his palms on his eyes to block the tears, but he was smiling. Her message to him—if I can do it, you can do it.

All her dreams, and his, were boldly emblazoned on the future. There was no undoing them now. Joey fixed his eyes on the tower until he could no longer see it, smiling and laughing in triumph. Their triumph. The world of possibilities was thrown wide open. He could hardly wait to begin.

The town shrunk to miniature and disappeared into green treetops, and then changed into wide fields and even wider skies. The whistle sounded, hopeful and promising, as the train chugged forward.

His smile deepened, for all the wondrous things that lay ahead of him, for his dreams that were already set in motion. He knew he would take Vita's words on all the journeys he would take through life.

Joey took his suitcase and crossed to a seat facing the direction of travel. Facing home, facing his future.

Made in the USA
Middletown, DE
17 March 2022